11 J

To my

with an good wishes.

Harold

THE ADMIRAL

The. Admiral

Harold Jacobs

The Book Guild Ltd.

Sussex, England

The Book Guild Ltd
25 High Street,
Lewes, Sussex

First published 1992
© Harold Jacobs 1992
Set in Baskerville
Typesetting by Kudos Graphics
Slinfold, West Sussex
Printed in Great Britain by
Antony Rowe Ltd.
Chippenham, Wiltshire

A catalogue record for this book is
available from the British Library

ISBN 0 86332 758 3

FOR SUSAN

1

It was a spring day in the desert town of Kalkfontein, South
West Africa. The sky was blue and clear, devoid of the usual
gathering storm clouds of the forenoon. On the ground lay
a fine dew that in a few minutes would be vaporized to
supply moisture for the coming clouds. The town was
ringed, in the far distance, by sugar loaf, dark grey
mountains. The full debilitating heat of summer was
months away. Ben Brookhouse, aged six, was playing on the
verandah of the family home with a friend of similar age,
Ampies, a black boy, the grandson of his aiya, a woman of
the Herero tribe. Their games were interrupted by the
arrival of another friend, a white boy, Petrus Oberholzer.
Petrus and Ben had been life long familiars. Older by three
years, Petrus was unpredictably moody. He declared
toleration of the younger boys, but in reality was inordinately jealous of the closeness between the white and the
black boy. His Afrikaaner background placed him in an
awkward position, and he dealt with his confused attitude
by submitting them to a variety of diabolical pranks, most
of which misfired. Having no close friends of his own, he
hung around them when it suited him, and sometimes,
superciliously, joined their games.

'When Dad and Sebastian get back,' Ben announced to
the small multiracial gathering, 'he'll take us to one of his
farms. If you behave and stop bugging us, Petrus, I might
let you come along and . . . who knows . . . shoot a gun, ride
a horse, or something.'

The statement was greeted with silence.

'He doesn't know his father's dead and his brother's gone
away,' mouthed an astonished Petrus in a hoarse, stage

whisper in Ampies's ear. Ampies looked down at his feet. Petrus squinted at the sky, scuffed his shoes, squirmed, and hurled a stone at a pigeon perched in a nearby pepper tree.

'What's that? What are you talking about?' demanded Ben, 'Dad's away on business. He goes away often for days, weeks, sometimes. He takes me or Sebastian along. This time it was Seb's turn, his treat. I didn't mind.'

The boys remained stoically silent.

'I'll ask my mother about this. Wait here.' Ben stalked off in search of his parent.

Ben found his mother in the sitting room. He had noticed that she had been quiet and withdrawn of late but, busy with his own interests, he had paid little attention. His grandparents, his most accessible confidants, were nowhere to be seen.

'Mummy,' he burst out, 'when are Dad and Sebastian coming home?' His mother responded by lowering her head until her hair covered her eyes. Her shoulders shook. When she looked up, Ben was shocked to see that she was crying. He knew then that his friends had been telling the truth.

'Why didn't you tell me?' he asked, coldly. His mother tossed her head wordlessly and rushed from the room. Ben crumpled into the nearest chair, shaken.

The bleak reality of the news failed to register in his young mind. He knew little about death, except as an abstraction. The concept of death or separation as applied to his parents, was incomprehensible. Until this day they had been forever conjoined. How could his father have simply left? And his twin, Sebastian . . . was he never coming back too?

He went off in search of his grandmother and found her in the garden, leaning back in a deckchair, gazing into the distance, a book on her lap.

'Grandma,' he began, without preamble, 'is it true that Dad and Sebastian have gone . . . forever?'

'Come here Ben dear,' she said gently, 'come and sit by me.' Ben walked up to her and was rewarded with a long, warm embrace.

'Yes, darling, they are gone. Forever.' Her sad brown eyes looked steadily down into his face. She kissed him on the forehead, and hugged him against her ample breast.

'But why? Was it my fault? Why didn't anyone tell me?'

'I suppose your mother was too upset . . . and didn't want to make you unhappy too.'

Ben's eyes searched his grandmother's face. He tried to read her thoughts.

'Do you remember when your mother went to visit your Aunt Jenny in Rhodesia?'

'Sort of,' said Ben doubtfully.

'It was that year.'

'A whole year ago?'

'Do you remember your dad?'

'Of course I do,' replied Ben, stoutly, but was having difficulty visualizing his father's face at that moment, 'of course I do. I remember EVERYTHING about him. I remember he spanked me for sucking that stupid shilling. I remember walking with him to see the new powerhouse.'

'We'll always remember your father. He was a lovely man. One day you'll grow up to be just like him.'

'But why did he go . . . and with Seb? Did they hate me? He didn't say anything to me. I never knew anything.' Suddenly Ben began to weep uncontrollably. His grandmother continued to hold him close, rocking his small sobbing body.

'Why didn't you tell me?' he repeated.

'I'm not sure I should have told you this much, but I suppose we've all been waiting for you to ask. Your mother and your father . . . well they had some differences. One day you'll understand. He was very cross about something silly, and your mother was very upset. He said he wanted time to think things over. So, he and his friend, Sergeant Brenner of the police, went off on horseback to do some prospecting. He felt he had to work it out. We all thought that it was for the best, a good idea. We were all sure it would be all right in the end. His taking Sergeant Brenner along seemed good. We were sure he would return. But it was not to be. He had a bad cold when they started off. It turned into pneumonia.'

'And?' Ben began to fear the worst. He had only the vaguest idea about pneumonia. It was something doctors dealt with in their solemn way. Lots of thermometers and pulse taking. They could cure anything.

'He became terribly sick while they were camping in the cold desert, just where it dips down into Port Nolloth. It

9

freezes there at night. Sergeant Brenner brought him, dying, on his horse to Port Nolloth. There was no hospital or doctor, only a hotel. And that was full. They took pity on your dad and put up a camp stretcher in one of their draughty corridors. Sergeant Brenner sent a telegram to your mother. We didn't tell you then, we thought he'd pull through. He was such a strong man.'

·'But he didn't, did he?'

'No. When your mother got there he was delirious. She sent a telegram to your Uncle Jack, a doctor, in Cape Town.'

'Did he go?'

'Yes. It took him several days. There were no proper roads and the cars he hired kept breaking down. He got there too late. But there wasn't much he could have done anyway.'

'What became of Uncle Jack?'

'He stayed on with us for two years and then went back to England. He went with your father's old friend, Sergeant Brenner.'

'Sergeant Brenner?' Ben frowned.

'Yes, we all thought it strange. At first we thought he'd simply left his wife and children. But they went too. He was close to your dad. Said he was off to England. Something to do with new police work.'

'Wasn't he a German?'

'He was an Afrikaaner. Descended from German and Huguenots ancestors, like many of our friends. After your Dad died we saw little of him. I often wonder what became of him. His wife and children left ages ago. We don't know where they are.' A thought struck Ben.

'If Dad's dead, then he must be buried somewhere? Why haven't we seen his grave?'

'It's too far,' she said, turning her face away, 'in Namaqualand. It's hundreds of miles from here.'

The thought of his father lying in a lonely grave in the desert set off a fresh wave of sobs, and this time he was joined by his grandmother.

'Have you seen his grave, Grandma?'

'Yes.'

This knowledge seemed to comfort the little boy. He sat

up, squirmed onto the bench beside his grandmother. After a while he began to swing his heels back and forth, lost in thought.

'What about Sebastian? What happened to him?' Before his grandmother could reply he cut her short.

'I think I'll go and find Mum.' Ben set off, stopping on his way at the verandah, but his friends had left. He retraced his steps to the sitting room, but she was not there. He turned and walked to her bedroom where he found her lying on her bed, curtains drawn, her eyes closed.

'Mummy, are you awake?'

'Yes, I am.'

'I'm sorry I made you cry. I didn't mean it,' said Ben jumping onto the bed, 'but I had to find out.'

'Ben dearest, I understand. I should have told you, but you were so small when Daddy died, and I . . . I . . . just got into the habit of not mentioning it. It's taken me a long time to come back to life. Too long. I'm afraid I neglected you. But that's over now.'

'I understand,' said Ben, his small face serious, 'I wish he hadn't died. My friends told me, you know. But what about Sebastian? Is he dead too?'

'Oh my God, Ben, I don't know. That's the awful part.'

'What do you think happened to Seb?'

His mother wiped her eyes and sat up. 'When your Dad was so ill, his older brother, Randolf, the one none of us could stand, arrived from Johannesburg. I was much too upset to notice anything. On the day your Dad died, Randolf and Sebastian,' her voice faltered, 'vanished. He must have taken Sebastian with him. Sergeant Brenner alerted the police all over the country. But they were gone. I was beside myself with worry. I didn't think I could live through it. I think I nearly went mad.' She paused to look down at her young son's face, etched with concern and bewilderment. 'I was afraid this would happen. I really didn't want to upset you. I didn't know how to tell you. I left it too late.' She rolled over and held him tightly. He had not had so much attention in ages, but neither had he had such bad news. All in one short day. He rose from the bed feeling slightly relieved.

'What about Sergeant Brenner?'

11

'He was your Dad's closest friend in these parts.'

'What happened to him? Everybody . . . just went?'

'Sergeant Brenner was a good man. He fought with your Dad in the same army against the Germans. After the war, he became interested in the British. He was a good, kind man, and a good friend. But now he's gone. And none of us know where.'

'What's for supper, Mummy? Can we have Ampies and Petrus over?'

For primary education Ben, along with his friends, except Ampies, attended a village school. Ampies, as a 'native' had no prospect of schooling. There were no black schools. As the years went by, the white and black boys became estranged. Their paths seldom crossed. Gradually their friendship faded, to be replaced by a cursory acknowledgement of each other's existence. Social customs inhibited further contact. They were to be forever separated. For a while Ben was saddened. But soon he forgot. In later years recollection of his enforced attitude towards his black friend induced shudders of shame. There was no doubt in his mind that his treatment of Ampies was nothing short of shabby.

When he turned nine Ben's mother determined that it was time to enrol her son in a more formal and structured school. An opportunity arose when she attended her younger sister's wedding in Bulawayo, Southern Rhodesia.

The wedding over, Ben's mother decided on a prolonged holiday in Bulawayo and registered him in a Rhodesian boarding school. Holidays were spent at home in South West Africa. In time Ben completed his studies and left Bulawayo for university in the Cape. It was there that he re-established contact with Petrus Oberholzer. The latter had registered in the Faculty of Economics and had embraced the Afrikaaner philosophy of racial superiority. He had become an extremist nationalist and had joined one of the more outspoken anit-British political sets on campus. Ben and Petrus observed some casual contact, but the two old friends were never again close. It was to be years before they were to meet again.

☆   ☆   ☆

'It's imperative,' said the Admiral, enunciating his words
slowly and clearly, 'that we investigate all possibilities,
without declaring our hand.' Squinting at the ceiling, he
leaned so far back in his swivel chair that he was in
imminent danger of tipping over. But it was an old trick and
he knew the limits of his balancing act. 'The problem, my
friend, is how to proceed, shall we say, with dispatch and
discretion?'

Before him sat an earnest, slightly built man, with blue
jowls and pinched features. He was dressed in standard
uniform – a well cut, three piece grey suit. He was
ensconced in a matching, but smaller chair.

'Well,' ventured Grey Suit, trying to place the speaker's
faint accent, 'Admiral, I've been doing some research. May
I tell you?'

'Of course.' The Admiral scrabbled a fingernail ineffec-
tually over some of the more blatant food stains on his
jacket. He leaned forward. The executive chair settled into
a normal position. 'Smoke?' He opened the lid of a box of
Havana cigars.

'No thanks. Don't smoke. Especially those.'

'Carry on. Do you mind if I . . . ?'

The man from the CIA shook his neat head, reached for a
briefcase, placed it on his lap, extracted a file, and adjusted
his spectacles.

'We've managed to trace most,' he began, eyeing his host
squarely, 'if not all, the nuclear material as coming from a
source somewhere east of Suez. Somewhere along the east
coast of Africa. We received an unsolicited tip from the
Russians. The stuff's manufactured in a hidden plant, deep
in the interior of one of those independent principalities left
over from your colonial days. Probably Madagascar.'

'We knew that.'

'Okay. We want your help in locating the exact source –
you wouldn't happen to know where?' The man from the
CIA paused. His host grimaced but made no response.
'Anyway, it shouldn't be too difficult. We place an agent or

13

two, over there, take a quick look inside, and get him, or her, out.'

'That's my position, entirely. The question remains, though,' the Admiral pursed his lips, 'whom to send and, more difficult, how to go about it . . . to get him inside? Why have you come to us at this late stage? You must have plenty of resources . . . er, agents?'

'I wouldn't be here if I didn't need your help. Besides, you owe us. It's time to call in. Anyway, you were on the same track.'

Leaning back in the larger chair, the Admiral, exhaling a cloud of blue smoke, smiled suddenly. He sat up and pressed a button on a communications panel. 'Maeve, bring me the file on Ben Brookhouse.'

The man from the CIA snapped shut his briefcase, and placed his file on the desk before him. He betrayed no sign of the faint surge of surprise he experienced at the display of British efficiency and cooperation. His face remained politely devoid of expression. Both men sat quietly contemplative, awaiting the documents. The CIA man's countenance loosened. He smiled apreciatively as his eyes wandered around the room. The office was imposing. The desk and cabinets were finished in grey oak; the chairs, burgundy leather; the walls covered in unobtrusively textured, rose coloured material. Enormous, floor to ceiling windows opened on a grand vista of Green Park.

The Admiral, he noted, provided a comical contrast to the surrounding elegant environment. His quite remarkably scruffy clothes were twenty years out of date, and totally mismatched. He seemed completely unconcerned and oblivious of this select surroundings.

'Yes, it's nice,' agreed the Admiral, divining the CIA man's thoughts, 'Nothing like a dash of luxury to liven up our trade, ey?'

'Very soothing,' agreed Grey Suit, 'I've nothing like it.'

'I've no idea who's responsible. It's a bit of a fudge,' added the Admiral waving a deprecating pudgy hand, 'It IS restful though. Arranged by some designing female. Cost a packet.'

His comments were cut short by a tap on the opaque glass inset of the door. A bespectacled, young woman with

14

blond, streaked hair entered swiftly. Her arrival and the preceding knock had been separated by a split second. The CIA man glanced up. The woman was striking. She moved with quick, flowing movements. She wore a tailored suit of light blue wool. A single strand of pearls surrounded her neck. Her cheekbones were set high in an oval face with lucent, intelligent, deep brown eyes. Full, bow curved lips were parted in a humorous smile. Her expression was open, guileless. Fine, laughter lines radiated from the outer corners of her eyes.

Grey Suit noted that in repose her expression was alert and, at the same time, serene. She exuded self-confidence.

She's got presence, concluded the man from the CIA to himself, I'll bet anything she has a history too. He dropped his gaze to her hands. She wore a ring on the middle finger of her left hand. She smiled at him in a neutrally friendly manner and handed the Admiral a folder. Despite himself, the man from the CIA became lost in an erotic fantasy.

'Here you are, Admiral,' said Maeve, 'I believe this is what you want.'

'Thank you,' murmured the Admiral, dismissing her. Maeve turned, and with fluent, coordinated movements, left the room. The CIA man's interest was not lost on the Admiral.

'Very intelligent, that Maeve. Independent . . . efficient . . . don't know what I'd do without her.'

'So I see,' said the CIA man with a small, prim smile. 'By the way,' he said, changing the subject, 'I hope you don't mind my asking, I know very little about you. Er, for instance, you are . . . an admiral? Not that it matters much,' he smiled, 'but I like to get my allies, and my facts, right.'

The Admiral responded with a prepared chuckle, 'You've no doubt heard of the late, unlamented head of German Intelligence . . . Admiral Canaris? Well, he was a naval person, and who knows who he really worked for?'

The CIA man was not amused, 'Which is, or was, your navy? Your accent's not quite Brit, is it?'

'Let's say, for the present, that it's an honorary title. From my native South Africa.'

'South Africa? Is there a connection that I should know about, with Brookhouse, or the business in Madagascar?'

'Perhaps,' said the Admiral, raising an eyebrow, 'call it a matter of conscience.'

'I'm not sure I get your drift.'

'Patience, my friend. It will, I assure you, become clear, eventually.'

'I hope so. A lot depends on this . . . on you.'

'Yes, indeed,' sighed the Admiral, 'a lot depends on me. The fact is I've been in the UK a long, long time. I left South Africa in the thirties. You know, when the Nazis took over in Germany and began to spread their tentacles. I made my way over here with a good friend. The rest's on file. It's available. I won't bore you.'

The Admiral inhaled a final lungful of smoke and stubbed out his cigar. 'I'm trained to be circumspect . . . but the long and the short of it is, I enrolled in Intelligence. But enough, we're not concerned with my position. Here, let's look at the file. I KNOW we've found our man. Yes here we are, Ben Brookhouse, born in South West Africa. Coincidence, ey? Bilingual. Cambridge graduate, age thirty five. The file's a trifle detailed. You'll have to read it in the library. Maeve'll show you where it is. When you've done we'll get together. We want someone completely unknown to the other side.'

The CIA inclined his head, accepted the dossier, and rose. The Admiral buzzed his secretary.

'Maeve, show Mister, er, my guest, to the library. He can take this file. When he's finished return it to it's proper place. See that he has everything he needs.'

Ten minutes later the CIA man, ensconced on a deep armchair, was busy reviewing Ben Brookhouse's file in a secluded, quiet corner of the library.

The cover of the file read:

SECRET: FOR YOUR EYES ONLY

[Narrative report on background of candidate Brookhouse]

'Jesus,' complained the CIA agent softly, as he began to page through the file, 'what's happened to summaries? Where's the bottom line?'

The document was in several parts. He skipped the part

16

about official secrets. A veteran speed reader he paused only when something caught his eye.

(General background)

Subject Ben Brookhouse. One of twins. (Twin brother disappeared aged 6 or 7 years. Whereabouts unknown.) Born 3 September 1930, in territory of South West Africa, now Namibia. Said to be intelligent. Brookhouse family once locally regarded as rich landowners.

Bullshit detail, grumbled the CIA man to himself, scanning the pages. But he read on.

Nearly all remaining members of family, generally accepted as decent and trustworthy.

'Wonderful,' muttered the CIA man.

Details of Subject

(Curriculum Vitae)

EDUCATION:
School: Milton School. Bulawayo, Southern Rhodesia.
University: Cape Town, South Africa.
Cambridge, England. Majored in Engineering.
Extra curricular activities: Secretary, Union Society. Half Blues for shooting and rowing.

That's better. The CIA man was more comfortable with objective reporting. But when he turned to the next page his spirits sank.
'Oh, shit,' he moaned, recognizing the unknown reporter's narrative style.

At Cambridge, subject demonstrated considerable social skills. Performance in engineering sound.

Several paragraphs later, the CIA man learned that Ben

had maintained a normal heterosexual, if not entirely angelic, behaviour: College staff interviewed commented on his being approachable, likeable, and generous.

No evidence to indicate unusual political opinions. According to our sources had a penchant for practical jokes. As a result was not regarded as sensible by older Dons at College. Character difficult to define. Impressed teachers and Tutor at Magdalene as logical. No known contacts with unfriendly agents, except possibly a certain South African Nationalist. Final opinion of Brookhouse is favourable. Worth investigating.

Personal details.
Married Marie Johnson, 1948. Divorced, 1951. No children.

Present occupation.
President, United Electronics. Assets estimated 2 million sterling. Shares held in majority by subject.

Interests.
Tennis, classical music. Reasonably accomplished pianist.

Present address.
Ground floor flat, 14 Queensway, Bayswater Road, London. Telephone unlisted. (438–6612).

END OF REPORT

The CIA man shut the file. What he he learned? Eyes dry and irritated, he sat back, and yawned. Finally, stretching an aching back, he rose from the chair. Ben Brookhouse was a potential candidate. He'd have to learn more, much more.

18

'So that's your idea of someone who might fit the bill?' asked the man from the CIA 'I can't quite see why. Perhaps you'd better bring him in for an interview?'

'We will, take my word for it, he'll do. I know.'

The CIA agent shrugged. 'It seems a gamble. Is there more to this than you're letting on?'

'Ah, yes. We had an agent look him over in Cambridge,' explained the Admiral leaning forward, elbows on desk, 'I took the trouble, personally,' he paused, 'to investigate his background and family in South West Africa. On that I have classified information, unique information. You have to accept a few gaps in his, er, background. To an outsider it might sound remarkably coincidental, but then, life's full of coincidences, isn't it?'

'What?'

'Coincidences.'

'I see,' said the CIA man frowning, uncertain, waiting. 'Something unexpected?'

'He'll need persuading,' mused the Admiral, ignoring his visitor, 'I know just the right person for that.' He swung round to his visitor, 'I'll fill you in over lunch. It'll take some time.' The Admiral purred happily. He liked tidy solutions. 'Well . . . ' he glanced at his pocket watch. It was late. He leaned over and prodded his secretary's intercom, 'Maeve, we're off to lunch. And, I need a favour. Come in and see me when I get back.'

It was drizzling when Ben Brookhouse eased the glistening, silver 300 ZX into his garage at the rear of his flat in Queensway. The bumper came to rest at a wooden barrier. Opening the car's hatchback, he extracted a briefcase and made his way, somewhat wearily, past the car to the flat's entrance. The garage door slid shut behind him.

Briefcase and raincoat were dumped as he collapsed into the nearest chair. After a few seconds he rose, gathered his mail, and reached for the TV remote control. The evening news was in progress.

'Reports from Bonn, Paris, and the Hague,' announced the precise female news reader, 'continue to indicate

19

concern amongst Western governments about large amounts of fissionable material being delivered to certain Middle Eastern states. The United States government has assured Israel that there was no immediate cause for alarm. Sources in Jerusalem suggest increasing determination by the Israeli government to take pre-emptive measures to block the use, by unfriendly states, of dangerous material.'

Ben switched off, and turned his attention to the post. The usual assortment of junk mail was discarded. The last item was a plain white envelope addressed to him in flowing script. He was about to toss it aside when he noticed the Cambridge postmark. He withdrew a small, plainly printed card.

Notice to members matriculating, 1947 to 1949
The Master and Fellows of Magdalene College request the pleasure of your company for dinner in Hall, Saturday, 16th October, 1987. Black tie. RSVP the Bursar's Office. The fee for dinner and one night in college is 25 pounds.

Hmmm, thought Ben, might be amusing. I should get away. Haven't been up to Cambridge for ages. Ben smiled as he enclosed his cheque and a brief note of acceptance in the envelope which he would mail the next day.

2

Much to his mother's gratification, Ben applied himself and graduated in engineering at Cambridge. Satisfied that Ben was about to be launched into independence, his mother, now living in Cape Town, set him up in a flat in Queensway, off Hyde Park in central London. After four years of study Ben allowed himself a break. But he was constantly aware that, sooner or later, he would have to begin a search for a suitable position. Inasmuch as his was a degree in electronics he felt reasonably confident about his future: the world was on the brink of an expansion into high technology.

However, a suitable post did not immediately materialize. There appeared to be a glut of experts in electronics; mostly brilliant, competitive, Chinese expatriates from Hong Kong and Taiwan. Temporarily discouraged, Ben chose to look up old college acquaintances now scattered in various parts of the United Kingdom. He had discovered that a sizeable number of his confrères were established in industry (usually in family businesses), farming, or in the arts. At any rate they had become more interesting.

There followed a series of encounters, often in country estates, with Magdalene contacts, some of whom, but by no means all, came from landed families. At Cambridge he had mingled with a few of the rich and famous. Generally Ben had distanced himself from the 'smart crowd', mostly because he regarded them as a supercilious, smug and, at the same time, boring group. He managed to overcome his feeling of hypocrisy and decided to enjoy, vicariously, the fancies of the really rich. It was at a typical weekend party on an estate that Ben met Marie Johnson. She was a vivacious, well endowed, black haired young woman who wore her hair swept back and tied in a bun. She had impressively glinting eyes that flashed boldly in Ben's direction. He soon discovered that Marie was also quite well endowed, by contemporary standards, with a sense of the ridiculous. She seemed to be warm, funny, and not overly intellectual. Ben, feeling himself attracted, treated her at first, with remote courtesy, a ploy that had been effective with other women.

Marie, on the other hand, was more direct, and spent much of her time occupying his attention. Despite himself Ben, whose main purpose at that time was to set himself up with a career, by identifying useful 'connections', began to respond. Marie seemed to be at almost every bacchanal he attended. But constantly in his mind was the knowledge that she belonged to a set that he neither aspired to, nor admired, and that he had to find a job.

Late on a Friday afternoon Ben, comfortably seated in his study, was disturbed when the front door bell rang. He rose lazily and ambled to answer the summons. Marie stood on the threshold. For some reason – it was mid-July – she wore a gleaming mink coat.

'Aren't you going to ask me in?'

Six months later they were engaged. Their nuptials took place five months later in order to put to rest rumours of a pregnancy. The wedding, somewhat to Ben's embarrassment, was billed as one of the social events of the year. Most of his friends attended. Some missed the reception, having lost their way to Marie's family mansion in Surrey (Marie's father's cronies had polished off all food, drink, and cigars).

The honeymoon took them to France where Ben was introduced to Marie's mother and her latest, sixth husband. They met in a restaurant on the South Bank. Ben had an impression of a tall, vague woman incongruously dressed in a flowery dress with a hat of bright yellow daisies. Adele, Marie's mother, towered over her latest spouse, a mouse-like man with a droopy moustache. Their first night in Paris was spent in a flat belonging to Adele, who vacated the master bedroom but insisted on using the bidet. Ben, slightly amused, made no complaint.

From Paris they flew to Venice to visit a famous aunt, Adele's addled sister. The latter greeted them by the back-door to her palazzo on the Grand Canal.

'You must be Adele's daughter?' The old woman, searching the remains of her memory, looked puzzled, 'Yes, of course, I remember you. And who's this? Your brother? You must,' she added, without waiting for a reply and turning on her heel, 'come and have lunch with me some day.' And she shut the gate to her palace on the Grand Canal.

'She has a magnificent collection of art,' explained Marie, grinning, 'but I think she's annoyed with my mother.'

Ben, standing by the high wall of the villa in Venice, three thousand miles from home, was not amused. The snub would surely have made the *Guinness Book of Records*?

'Look,' said Ben, 'I've some equally nauseating relatives. Let me prove it. How about a quick visit to South Africa?'

From Venice they flew to Johannesburg. Much to Ben's surprise his widowed, erratic aunts behaved impeccably. Marie, familiar with elderly dodderers, got on well with the old ladies. She was used to repetitious conversations.

When they returned to England, Marie's father offered Ben a post in a family ceramics company. Ben declined and set up, with the aid of a bank loan, a consulting firm specializing in designing hardware for computers. His speciality was dedicated electronic circuits for larger manufacturers. Soon, because of his ingenuity and expert-ise, his reputation spread. The small firm became a larger firm. Eventually work was subcontracted to distant Asian companies. The business thrived and Ben rose rapidly in the expanding industry.

Ben's frequent absences on business to Taiwan and Korea caused Marie to wax restless. Her moods became unpredictable. The last thing she had bargained for was a life without at least two parties a week. Ben, in turn, became disenchanted with the continual round of visits to and from shallow, brainless friends. He seemed to have nothing in common with Marie's chums. Becoming more and more exasperated with Marie and her life-style, he buried himself totally in his work. In retrospect Ben realized that he had acted against his better judgement in marrying before he was established, and worse, to someone from a social class that he had viewed with disdain. The relationship cooled inexorably. They began to bicker, usually about trivial matters. Neither attempted to please the other. Irritable, minor exchanges developed into endless quarrels of increasing ferocity, until inevitably hurtful words were traded.

In all the marriage lasted three years.

Their divorce was discrete, amicable, and done in the best of taste with the finest and most expensive of legal opinion. Once more Ben found himself alone. But now he had assumed the role of an eligible, rich bachelor. He was dismayed when he realized that he had also collected some of the trappings of wealth and, ironically, had joined the ranks of the beautiful people.

The prospect of a journey to Magdalene College in Cambridge for a reunion dinner with old friends managed, in the midst of his depression after his divorce, to evoke in Ben a thrill of anticipation.

While up at Magdalene Ben had journeyed by car to and from London on occasions too numerous to tally. Those excursions had to be clandestine because keeping a car in Cambridge while an undergraduate was, in the view of the university proctors, illegal. After graduation he had driven the same route with no sense of adventure. And then only for visits to the Science Park outside Cambridge.

On the appointed day Ben set out in a happier mood than he had experienced for months. He regretted the lack of female company. A nostalgic pang intruded when he thought of his former, relatively carefree life and the pleasures of showing girlfriends around his personal stamping ground. Recall of leisurely walks along the exquisite backs of the river Cam was, sadly, all that remained.

☆   ☆   ☆

Ben made slow progress through the crowded streets of north London. Traffic had deteriorated, as had tempers. Twice he had been misdirected by practically nonexistent signposting. His mood sagged.

What I need is a renaissance of happier days, he thought; maybe if . . . Ben braked sharply in order to avoid a young woman scurrying across the road. If only I could replay my life for a few years. I didn't know how lucky I was. I've made so many mistakes . . . and now all this ridiculous pain . . . I really should've done better.

Ben acelerated past the young woman walking on, unaware of her brief flirtation with disaster.

Ahead lay a roundabout before the motorway to the North. In preparation for the least interesting portion of the journey, Ben reached with his left hand to turn on the radio in the silver 300ZX. At that moment an aggressively driven, scarlet Alfa Romeo Spyder pulled out and overtook him with blinding ease. Ben had a glimpse of a sardonic face twisted into a grin. It's familiar, he thought. The face in the Alfa sped on.

Ben geared down and accelerated hard, thrusting himself back into the seat. The hum of the 300ZX rose to a tingling growl as he began to overtake the Italian. A flutter in his chest signalled increasing excitement. The adrenalin's flowing, he thought, derisively, what am I doing?

At over ninety miles an hour, with resurrected skill, Ben drifted the car through a curve onto the motorway. The Alfa kept pace and followed him through the roundabout. Swapping places, the cars hurtled along the road until they reached a turn off for Royston. With a cheery wave the driver of the Alfa peeled off, and disappeared into an exit. Although he had had only a few momentary glimpses of the driver, Ben waved back. He knew that face. The race over, he drove on more sedately, until the outskirts of Cambridge came into sight.

Exhaust tinkling as it cooled, the 300ZX rolled along King's Parade, and headed into Magdalene Street. Ben angle-parked it facing the river. He leaned back and stretched appreciatively. Ahead lay his familiar old college. Nothing had changed on the outside. Swinging his legs over the sill he stood up, stretched once more, and moved off with his suitcase and entered the college porch.

The head porter identified him.

'Ah,Mr Brookhouse, here for the reunion? Room's ready, Pepys Building, your old staircase.'

The atmosphere in the vacant room in the shabbily elegant Pepys Building was at once familiar, reeking of stale tobacco and mouldy, dusty tomes. The perpetually rank odour of the lavatory leading off the wooden staircase had not improved. The smell of Jeyes fluid and urine combined, as always, to offend and then to deaden his olfactory sense.

Nothing HAS changed, thought Ben. He unpacked, shaved, showered, and dressed in a dinner suit, and then wandered over to the Fellows' garden behind the Pepys building. By the Fellows' gate he noticed a group of dinnersuited men surrounding a senior don.

'Ben . . . '

The voice was unmistakable. The speaker, a tall man in his late thirties, gesticulated vigorously. Ben recognized the uneven features of Petrus Oberholzer, one of his oldest friends. Petrus's expression oscillated somewhere between a smile and a scowl.

It appeared to Ben that their lives had been inextricably, intermittently, intertwined. Initially as boyhood chums in Namibia, and later at Cape Town University they had remained in contact. By an extraordinary coincidence, both had won scholarships to Cambridge, but to different colleges. The rough, tough Afrikaaner of his boyhood had been astonishingly transformed into a suave, sophisticated professional. Petrus had become more British than the British, except for a trace of an Afrikaans accent.

'How's business, my old friend?' Ben gripped the dry, strong hand. 'How's it that you're not celebrating independence back in Namibia? What's happened to your nationalist principles? I've often wondered how you and your family would take to a black government? It was you on the motorway.'

Before Petrus could produce a rejoinder, a grating voice

26

intruded distinctly above the background murmur of conversation.

'It's that Brookhouse with his slimy good looks and his flashy friends, bloody South Africans, taking our jobs over here.' The speaker a short, plain, bandy-legged man, with a large, offset proboscis, turned his back ostentatiously.

'Some people don't change,' said Ben, shrugging, 'same old randy Sam, walking genitals, and nowhere for them to go.'

Petrus nodded, pleased to avoid political explanations. He stared at Sam. 'How could the British have won the Boer War? By the way, it was me. Thought I'd give you a run for your money. Nice car you've got. I had to give up. Took a short cut through Royston to look up an old friend.'

'Seriously, Petrus . . . this is a lovely surprise. I had half hoped you'd be here, but I thought you'd be at the celebrations in South Africa House. I'm glad you wangled an invitation. You must have, but the price for being here is that we may have to put up with Sam. Talking of Namibia, how's that brother of yours? I remember, when he came over on a visit from South West, he snitched Sam's Danish dish, the one Sam had imported for a May ball? It all comes back. One could almost feel sorry for Sam. Spent half the night puking in the toilets. Tell me about Christiaan.'

'Christiaan? He's a commercial pilot, somewhere. Flies with a small cargo outfit. I think he flies to Madagascar. I'm never sure where he is, no doubt skating on thin ice as usual. He told me he was in business ferrying waste material. I suppose I should worry about him, but I don't. He's old enough to look after himself.'

Petrus reached for a sherry. He had just managed to swallow the drink when the Master and Fellows moved off to lead the way into the dining hall.

'Talk to you later, Ben. I'm seated at the other end of the high table.' Petrus Oberholzer disappeared into the crowd.

The dining hall, illuminated with its flickering candles, with its stained glass windows, black coated waiters, dusty portraits of bygone worthies, its silver candelabra, all combined to consolidate Ben's pleasure in the occasion.

To Ben's right sat his tutor of old, a man now in his eighties. The elegant, handsome don could have passed for

27

twenty years younger. A sheltered university subsistence clearly had advantages. Opposite Ben sat an equally ageless don distinguished by a lack of any hairy adornment. The total bald egg effect was enhanced by an absence of pinnae. Rumour had it that this don, a pilot in the first World War, had been burned in an aerial dog-fight. Declining plastic surgery, he made do with a pair of ear muffs which occasionally, when drunk, he discarded. He was presently gazing benevolently at the gathering around him. The don nodded a vague, genial greeting in Ben's direction. At this point the Master rose to say grace. When all had settled, Ben became conscious of a seated figure to his left whom, at first, he did not recognize.

Occupied with decoding conversation emanating from his tutor, Ben paid the body on his left little heed. As dinner progressed he became more aware of the presence beside him. He glanced curiously in its direction. Suddenly memory cleared. He was sitting by an acquaintance, someone who had shared the same staircase, someone relaxed and seemingly oblivious of his surroundings. The face was that of a student with whom he had been moderately friendly. Unfortunately his name did not sur face. Ben, always bad with names, was at a disadvantage, but decided to make a go of it. Wine and the cordial atmosphere amplified his feelings of bonhomie.

'I say,' said Ben, smiling, 'it must be ages . . . since C staircase, how have you been?'

'Very well indeed, thank you,' replied the face, 'and what are you up to?'

'Oh, not much,' answered Ben, cautiously. What WAS his name? 'It's been a long time . . . let's see . . . twelve years?'

The face relented. 'You don't remember me. I'm George Stocking. I read commerce and economics. I shared C staircase and the set below you in Benson. I'm a prof in the Faculty of Economics, in the Western Province, East London and Dean of the faculty.'

'Ah,' exclaimed Ben, with exaggerated warmth, 'of course . . . you had a piano in your rooms.' Ben raised a glass in salutation to his recovered memory. He recalled George's persistent, dysrhythmic hammering on the piano which had disturbed many a study session.

'You used to play the piano, a lot.'

'Sorry about that,' chuckled George, 'but it didn't stop me grabbing the Chair in Economics at the University of East London. Musical ability was not a requirement. But I also have another job. It's always best to have more than one string to one's bow.'

Ben smiled and then frowned. 'George, I remember you as brilliant. At least that's what I was told. By the way,' a memory interposed itself, 'whatever became of your friend, the gorgeous Edgarda, the girl from Italy?'

It seemed to Ben that milestones in his life were flagged by one girl or another. I should have a calendar named after girls, he thought.

'Edgarda? She went off with an army type, but I don't think anything came of it. I lost out there,' replied George wistfully, 'you knew, of course, that she had the hots for you?'

'I didn't.' Ben was pleased. He had not dismissed fantasies of Edgarda's extravagant attractions. A third, and soon a fourth, glass of wine induced a forgiving glow. Ben began to regard his fellow diners with more and more tolerance. Not a bad lot. Not their fault that Marie ruined his life.

Fifteen years had passed since Ben's matriculation. Some of his contemporaries had changed not at all. Others were barely recognizable under bald pates or layers of prosperous fat. At the far end of the table the obnoxiously close set eyes of Sam Black glowered him. Ben waved a cheery greeting. A cold glare from Sam replied. Ben, undeterred, smiled with sincere enthusiasm at Samuel Black. Poor old Sammy, he thought sadly, unable to mellow, poor sod. A feeling of general well-being suffused his mind. He hoped it would not be temporary.

'By the way,' said George Stocking, breaking into Ben's thoughts, 'I'd very much like to have a word with you in private. Perhaps in my rooms after dinner?'

'Of course,'replied Ben expansively, 'any time. At your service.' Samuel Black continued to goggle contemptuously in Ben's direction.

'Shall we say, eleven thirty?' George raised his eyebrows

and without waiting for a reply, turned his attention to the fearless, earless don.

☆   ☆   ☆

At a quarter to twelve Ben and George crossed Magdalene Street, passing through the porter's lodge on their way to 'C' staircase in Benson Court. The carved oak balustrade was at once friendly and familiar.

'Have a seat,' invited George, shutting the oak outer door, 'long time since I sported my oak. Cognac?' Ben sat in the scuffed leather chair and sipped the golden liquid. It was good. He took another, larger, swig.

'I'll come right to the point,' said George, settling in the sofa. 'I have good information that you've been extremely successful in business. I understand, also, from sources I can't disclose at the moment, that you're divorced and bored?'

Ben scowled, his affable mood waning, despite the soothing effects of the cognac.

'What about it?'

'Let's assume I have impeccable sources of information, and let's, for the sake of discussion, accept my statements at face value. What I have to say to you is highly confidential. I must have your word that nothing that transpires here tonight must get out, no matter what happens? Do I have your word?'

'Of course,' agreed Ben shrugging, his irritation subsiding and now superseded by curiosity, 'I give you my word of honour.'

'I spoke to you earlier about my having more than one string to a bow. I wasn't rambling. I have two jobs,' said George, 'I wear two hats. One clandestine and the other above board. I am a professor of economics at my university, but I also keep in touch with government circles ... the fact is, as things stand today in South Africa I have connections with ... certain branches of Intelligence in this country.'

'Really. Intelligence? You mean your're a spy? A spook? Who for?' Ben wondered if the booze had unbalanced George.

'Not to worry, I'm on the right side. I know about your views. I represent a group of watchdogs, for want of a better term, who monitor distribution of thermonuclear materials, anything that could be converted into bombs ... d'you understand?'

'I think I do,' replied Ben doubtfully. Events were taking an unexpected direction. He was intrigued and not a little sceptical.

'I can guess what you're thinking, but I assure you, I'm on the level and quite serious. People you don't know, and some you might not remember, have selected you as a potential agent.'

'Me, an agent? Someone I might not remember?'

'If you accepted,' continued George the Dean, 'it'd mean adventure and, of course, danger. With your attributes you could do very well. It could be a most exciting life, or it could be rather dull. Depends. In your position, un-attached, no responsibilities, it could be just what you're searching for.'

'I don't expect an immediate answer, but I want you to think it over. When you're ready, you'll come for an interview. Don't worry, you'll not be bound by anything that happens at the interview. If you decline we won't come after you. It's not the Middle East. It will all become clear when next we meet, if we do.'

Ben was silent.

'I'm flattered,' he said softly. 'Can you tell me who these people are whom you refer to as 'we', and especially those 'who I might not remember'?'

'Sorry, no. I'm not at liberty to disclose much more, for obvious reasons, you must see that? If it works out you'll find out.'

'All right. I'll think it over. What about the interview? When is it to be, and where?'

George walked to a bureau and wrote an address on a visiting card. 'Take this and wait to be contacted. We'll be in touch.'

Sunday morning a month later the flat in Queensway was

chilly. The sky drearily overcast – typical London weather. The street outside was deserted when Ben, clad in raincoat over pyjamas, walked to the corner stationers to choose his selection of newspapers. He paid scant heed to the slim woman with blond, streaked hair, plaited at the back, pushing a pram. He stood absent-mindedly aside to allow her free passage while scanning the newspaper headlines.

'Good morning sir,' she said quietly as she drew abreast, 'how was the college dinner?'

'What?' Ben looked up, but the woman had already passed by and was fading into the grey distance.

3

A month later the Magdalene reunion dinner had faded into a distant event. In the intervening period Ben almost succeeded in obliterating recollection of Marie with the society of a variety of charming women of different configurations and intellects. None seemed to possess the vital combination he longed for. More often than not he wandered aimlessly in London parks, convinced his life was insignificant. Anything at all reminiscent of married life rekindled tedious soul searching. Well-meaning friends, largely in self-defence, convinced him he needed a change. In the end he became thoroughly sick of himself and decided to take action.

Late that autumn he suspended speculating about his dismal future. Something at the back of his mind challenged his memory. What was it? The card . . . George the Dean's card. Where was it? In line with his usual habits he rifled through his suits and discovered the card in a pocket of his dinner suit. It was scrunched but legible. Printed on the obverse side was a telephone number. Ben smoothed the card and placed it by the telephone. Still he hesitated. It was too fantastical. In order to gain time and come to a decision he puttered around completing postponed, minor chores. At length he seated himself and dialled the number on the card.

'Whitehall 5701,' drawled a superior voice. A long, confidence pause followed. Ben knew 'they' were waiting and was tempted to hang up. He could hear breathing, faintly. Whoever had answered was in no hurry and was patiently awaiting a response.

'Brookhouse,' began Ben, 'contacting, as instructed. I

refer . . . uh . . . to a reunion dinner, at Magdalene.'

'Oh yes?' replied the bored voice with no hint of encouragement.

'I'm ready to consider the interview.'

'Right,' the voice became perceptibly brisker, 'we'll be in touch.'

Deflated, Ben replaced the receiver. I hate disembodied voices, he thought, what am I doing? He walked to a window and gazed with envy at the carefree strollers in Hyde Park. What was in store? Anything was better than his present undirected existence.

At noon the telephone rang. If it's them they're pretty keen, he said to himself. Had they been expecting him to call? Ben forced himself to walk casually to the bedroom, and lifted the receiver.

'Good afternoon,' said a deep, confident, baritone voice, 'Mr Brookhouse?'

'Yes.'

'Message received. We'll be expecting you at 3 pm, Wednesday next. If for any reason you can't make it, please call the number on the card. The address is the same.'

The line went dead. For seconds Ben remained frozen. He was surprised by his boldness, but also by his unrestricted access to what appeared to be a clandestine organization. Obviously, he thought, they've been in touch with George the Dean, or whatever he was.

Ben began to develop second thoughts. It had been too easy. Had they been keeping tabs on him? Probably. Ah, yes . . . the woman with the pram in the street. She was one of them.

☆　　☆　　☆

Optimism was tinged with apprehension when Ben left the flat in Queensway and drove to Whitehall in search of a new (hopefully better) life. The streets looked less forbidding in the – for once – brilliant London sunlight. He left his car in an underground park, walked out into the dazzle of Trafalgar Square, and thence to the address on the card.

Inside a uniformed porter greeted him, requested identification, and checked a list in a book. The porter nodded toward the ceiling. Ben looked up and spotted an ubiquitous surveillance camera.

'The lift's over to your left, sir. Press button three. When you exit, turn left and go to the blue door on the right. I think you'll find that satisfactory, sir.' The porter tipped his cap and resumed his post by the door.

Although he had been uneasy about the interview, Ben found the actual reception somewhat of an anticlimax. Facing him at the far end of a conference table in the plainly furnished board room were two genial, middle-aged men. A third person, incredibly untidy, and distinguished by a large fleshy nose surrounded by plump, florid cheeks, sat nearby. His head, like his body, was spherical and adorned with a crown of wild, salt and pepper coloured hair. Situated below the rubicund features was an untidy goatee beard, resulting in a passable impression of Colonel Saunders of fried chicken fame. The expression was that of a pleasantly interested, absent-minded professor. His outfit consisted of a shapeless tweed jacket, faded baggy trousers of an indeterminate hue, and a pink checked shirt which clashed cheerfully with a purple bow tie peeping out over a blood red pullover. The range of colours was startling.

One of the tidier men at the table smiled in an encouraging fashion and motioned Ben to be seated. Ben was acutely conscious that despite their friendly, almost casual attitude they must be astute observers, assessing him with care. He had expected a probing scrutiny and had dressed accordingly.

Before them sat a young, slimly built man in his early thirties. He was dressed formally in a well pressed, double breasted, light grey suit. His shirt was white with narrow red stripes. His tie was a maroon paisley pattern. He was of upper medium height, with neat, well formed hands protruding from double cuffs. The fingers were strong, slightly flexed, and still. He appeared composed but alert. When he moved it was with fluid, precise motion.

Full, rather long, wavy, dark brown hair was brushed back. A few stray wisps hung down over a high forehead. His eyebrows were crowded and set over dark brown eyes. The face was somewhat longer than was regarded as fashionable, with a full lipped mouth set above a firm, slightly bluish, chin. A strong face, thought the second of the genial men.

Ben, in turn, took note of what he presumed were either old school, or regimental ties, and the flawless cut of their dark, worsted wool suits. Their contrast with the colourful wreckage near him was arresting.

'I will ask the Admiral to open the interview,' said one of the men. He gestured elegantly toward the Shambles.

'No doubt, Mr Brookhouse, you're aware we're familiar with your general background,' began the untidy Admiral, glancing up from the dossier open before him. 'A mutual friend recommended you, most highly. But before we proceed, we have to know how committed you would be to the idea of working for us under dangerous conditions?' He paused, carefully opposing his fingertips. 'I should explain that our type of work, if mostly routine, can occasionally be . . . perilous.'

Ben struggled for an appropriate reply. He had not expected such a direct approach. It was now or never. The interviewer obviously knew about the substance of his chat with the Dean.

'Well,' began Ben, 'I can't possibly predict how committed I'd be until I have a few details. I don't know much, do I? I have to hear more . . . much more.'

'Begin by telling us something about yourself.' suggested the Shambles, ignoring Ben's request, 'and something about your future intentions and er, motives.'

Ben took a deep, slow breath.

'All right, it's like this. My life's in a rut. I'm successful and have independent means. I've been through a traumatic domestic upheaval and I'm at a loose end. I want a change in direction. I'd like to do something . . . better. I want to refashion my life . . . I know it sounds pretentious, but I need a challenge.

'On the positive side, I have no responsibilities. I have no immediate dependants. I'd like to try something different, preferably useful as well as adventurous.' Ben hoped he didn't sound too self-righteous. 'As you are no doubt aware, I speak several langugages. I know a good deal about electronics. I could be useful . . . somewhere . . . in some way.' He paused.

36

The interviewers looked on with polite interest.

'I'm not completely in the dark as to what you want of me. I'm guessing it's something to do with Intelligence?'

'You must tell us a little more about your motives,' repeated the second of the distinguished looking men, again ignoring his query. 'Why, for instance, did you leave South Africa? Do you have political ambitions? Affiliations? Do you have relatives . . . friends, over there?'

'I see,' said Ben, convinced that they were genuinely interested, 'it's a long story.'

'We've plenty of time.'

'The plain fact is that I couldn't stand the all-white government. I had grown up under that system and had taken everything around me for granted. Then, as I grew up, I began to notice certain events. It became obvious what sort of privileged, cruel, and limited society I was part of. I had had to give up friends for no other reason than the colour of their skin. But, at the same time, I realized I couldn't take on a government by myself. So I left. Some of my friends thought I was a rat leaving a sinking ship. Perhaps I was.' Ben paused. 'May I have some water?'

The untidy man passed a decanter and a glass. With careful ceremony Ben filled the glass. He had to organize his thoughts.

'When I lived there I became more and more frustrated . . . and to be frank, more frustrated with my useless role in the affairs of the country. At the same time I knew that anything I might do, which could be construed as 'liberal', would attract 'official' attention. The police in South Africa are quite efficient. They don't tolerate those who oppose government policies. I was sure they had a dossier on me, so I avoided anything overtly concerned with black organizations. I did not support the blacks, at least, not openly. In behaving like that I became ashamed of myself.

'I contributed some money for the legal defence of political prisoners. But it was a drop in the bucket and too late, and not enough to attract official attention.'

'You were, in a sense politically motivated when you gave that money.'

'I suppose so. It wasn't much. You don't know what it's like to live under a repressive regime,' said Ben defensively.

'Students, as a matter of principle, oppose authoritarian governments. Clashes were inevitable. In South Africa we had a solid cause. Almost all students disapproved of apartheid. I, I'm sorry to say, was not particularly er, enterprizing. I regret that. The fact is that some of those on the right, anti-apartheid, side were a pain . . . opportunists, espousing the cause because it was fashionable to be a 'liberal'. I detested them almost as much as the Nats, the Nationalists. On the other hand, some of my Nationalist friends were decent people, if misguided. It's a very complex state. In the end, I could see no future or solutions. So I left.

'At one stage I thought of returning. But I had no great desire to become a dead hero. Anyway, here I am. Not too brave a specimen, but willing to try to do something useful.'

'Please, continue,' said the untidy one.

'A year after I arrived in England, with the help of family friends, I was accepted into Cambridge.

'After graduation I met the woman I married, and went into business . . . electronics . . . you know that part.' Ben stopped speaking.

'Continue,' ordered the crumpled Admiral, inclining his tousled head at Ben, 'what happened after you got into Cambridge? What about your South African friends? What about the Oberholzers?'

'The Oberholzers?' What were they getting at?

'I keep in touch, occasionally, with Petrus. I haven't seen Christiaan for years. I think he's a pilot. Shall I go on?' Ben looked around.

'Please do,' said one of the urbane men at the far end.

'After I got my degree, I fooled around a bit. During that time I met my future wife. After we married I started a small consulting electronics firm, designing electronic hardware. My wife's father was in ceramics in a big way. Government contracts and all that. I avoided joining his group I wanted to make it on my own. I succeeded, you must know that? My marriage was a failure. I don't like to talk about it.' Ben paused, then restarted. 'In the end I was well off, had no wife, and became depressed. I questioned my role as a citizen of any country. A question we should all ask ourselves. Nothing very profound in that. That's my story.'

☆   ☆   ☆

38

A week later Ben received a plain, brown envelope marked 'OHMS'. Inside was a brief note informing him that he would be accepted into 'The Service'.

Then followed several months of sequestered training in establishments in various parts of the country. Ben attended lectures, demonstrations, and classes in a large variety of topics. It seemed to him that he was surrounded day and night by a bewildering variety of instructors and fellow candidates. He was transported from one establishment to another, often at dead of night. He was aware of constant, close scrutiny.

At the same time he applied himself enthusiastically and worked harder, in a more concentrated manner, than he had ever done. He spent the final six weeks of intensive indoctrination training in the use of arms, explosives, and communications. Last but not least, he was groomed in lethal methods of 'self-defence'. His instructors, male and female, decided he was good material; a quick learner, intelligent, and as far as they could judge, reliable.

When it was all over Ben was granted a week's leave to set his affairs in order, and told to return to his flat and to await instructions.

At the end of his leave he was recalled to the office in Whitehall for a final briefing. On this occasion it was only the Admiral who interviewed him.

'Well,' said the Admiral, 'you've made excellent progress. I expected that. So far the Dean's, and my, judgements have been sound. Now, let me tell you about your mission. By the way, you will be accompanied on this er, exercise, by other persons, including one of your instructors, a female.'

'Oh,' asked Ben casually, 'which one?'

'You'll see soon enough. The assigned woman will act as your secretary. It's not a very original cover. You must appear to be in charge, but not too familiar. Do I make myself clear?'

'Understood. When does this caper get off the ground?'

'Caper?' The Admiral frowned, 'This is not a game. It's a serious and potentially dangerous mission. Forget those clever spy stories you've read. Mostly your work will be routine, although, as I said, it could turn nasty unexpectedly. You may never know what'd hit you. And, I hold you responsible for the others.'

Somewhat chastened, Ben assumed a respectful silence. For all his shaggy, disorganized appearance and his quiet demeanour, the Admiral exuded a considerable presence. He was, today, grimly serious. A few weeks ago he had been almost too casual and cheerful. Ben wondered which was the real Admiral?

'You will want to know what is your mission? Listen carefully . . . Your objective will be to locate and infiltrate a factory of sorts in Madagascar. We know that certain people are manufacturing nuclear material there. We have a good idea who they are, but not who, or which government is supporting them. It could very well be the South Africans, or a Middle Eastern state with money to burn, Iraq maybe. But we can't have nuclear material rolling about,' he searched for a metaphor, 'like a loose cannon on a deck. Needless to say you'll have to be circumspect.

'We have given you plausible credentials. We have made arrangements for you to appear to be a manufacturer looking for contracts in electronic industry. Arrangements for you to contact additional agents have been set up.

'Once you get there, you won't know who they are until they contact you. As a stranger on the island you will be under surveillance from the other side from an early stage. You'll not, at first, know who's on our side. I'm afraid,' the Admiral smiled for the first time, 'that it's going to tax you. But that's what you wanted, isn't it?'

'How'll I be able to contact you, or to report to you? What arrangements have been made?'

'You'll find all the answers in documents I've prepared. When you've read the first one, destroy it. Then go on to the next, and the next. It will become clear as you go along. However, remember this, and this is the most important message of all; we chose you because we believe you to be loyal, bright, and resourceful. At the same time we cannot accept responsibility for you. You will have to improvize should you run into trouble.'

'I'm not sure I like what I'm hearing. You flatter me with your trust and at the same time you tell me that you could

. . . sacrifice me?'

'What did you expect? This is no child's game.'

'Is there anything you've left out?'

For a while the Admiral did not answer.

'All right, I'll tell you. The CIA tipped us off . . . Someone's been making enquiries about you, someone, via a Middle Eastern country.'

'What do you mean? About me . . . why?'

'Well, that's the puzzle. I have my theories. I heard that word had got out that you, personally, were . . . in demand. I can't say more. But that's one of the principal reasons I am sending you. It's you they're interested in and you are our agent. They may know this, but it doesn't matter. We want you to contact them. After that you will have to improvize.'

'I hope I will, I sincerely hope so. It seems I've already blown my cover. What's the point? Am I a scapegoat . . . a bait? Is that it?'

'If we thought you were a disposable nincompoop, there'd be nothing to be gained by sending you off to the er, slaughter. No, the point is, if they want you, then you are our way in. Provided, of course, that you keep your wits about you. You'll recall we have agents stashed along the way. They'll be keeping an eye on you too. You're going to be a special sort of double agent. Not the first in history.'

'You never told me it would be quite so complicated. I hope they'll take the bait but not swallow it.'

'I'm sorry, Ben, for the present I can't disclose all my cards.'

Ben was not quite as indignant as he appeared. There had to be a catch, and he'd been expecting it.

'It's not too late to change your mind.'

'No,' he said, firmly, 'I agreed. I'll keep to my word. I'll go ahead.'

'I must stress once more, should you make a hash of it, and in so doing embarrass our government, we'll have to deny any connection with you.'

'There you go again. One minute you're reassuring me, and the next you tell me that I'm out on a limb.'

'That's how it is,' the Admiral smiled, 'tomorrow you get going. Everything is arranged. You are going to Madagascar.'

4

Heathrow was, as usual, tumultuously overcrowded. Ben, with passport, sealed instructions, and an airline ticket in his pockets, found his way to the VIP lounge. He looked casually around for a familiar face but saw none. Having nothing better to do, he scanned the other occupants of the lounge. Across the room he noted a bespectacled young woman with medium length blonde-streaked hair, sitting quiely by a set of expensive dark grey luggage, the type that at first glance resembled army issue. She wore a fitted, dark blue overcoat, and seemed to be immersed in a paperback novel. Her forehead was high and smooth. Her hair was drawn back from a widow's peak, and tied at the back with a red barette. A neat, tiptilted nose perched above full lips curved in a hint of a smile. Ben noted that her expression in repose was pleasing. He decided she was interesting. After a few more covert glances he fixed her image permanently in his memory. He did not see her again until they were installed in the cabin of the Concord supersonic aircraft. She was seated across the aisle, one row back.

One hour out of Heathrow Ben rose and made his way to the toilets at the rear of the aircraft. A black man in a window seat on the port side glanced up as he want by. Outside the sun shone brilliantly, outlining in stark relief the minutest features of the wing structures. Inside there was absolutely no sensation of movement. A thick white blanket of clouds below shut off any view of earth. Returning to his seat, Ben's gaze was drawn briefly to the blonde woman still absorbed in her book. Quite a stunner, he thought; those big specs don't do much for her. I wonder if she's as intelligent as she looks? He struggled into his seat and began to doze.

The black man reached into his jacket for a pen and scribbled a note on a scrap of paper. Scrambling out of the confining seat, he strolled up the aisle in the direction of the toilets. As he passed Ben's seat he managed, quite unobtrusively, to drop the small square of paper onto the open tray. Ben stirred, opened his eyes, and discovered the scrap of paper. He drew it towards him. Ben was surprised to see his initials on the folded note. His immediate reaction was to search for its source, but he saw only rows of disinterested faces. He opened the note.

☆ ☆ ☆

The Concord landed smoothly at Antananarivo International Airport. The professionaly jolly cabin crew bade deplaning passengers farewell. All disembarked without incident. Customs and Immigration treated Ben courteously and sent him on his way. Outside the terminal he hailed a taxi. The note, signed 'Admiral', had instructed him to go to the Imperial Hotel and to remain in the foyer.

'Good day.' A black man approached Ben seated in a deep couch in the crowded lobby, 'I delivered that note,' he said, without preamble. 'The Admiral and my boss,' he glanced nonchalantly around and lowered his voice, 'arranged for us to meet here.'

Ben nodded cursorily, noting the American accent, the Ethiopian black features illuminated by a friendly smile, and the tight muscles almost concealed by the well cut business suit. The face was disarmingly cheerful. Ben struggled upright from the couch amidst a pile of luggage, and reached out to accept the proffered hand.

'I was on the Concord. We work for the same er, interests.'

'Uhhm,' said Ben, 'do we? It's all a bit dark, for me.'

'I hope that's not a joke.'

'Look here,' said Ben, mildly amused, and allowing remnants of camouflage to dissipate, 'how do I know we're on the same side?'

'Allow me to introduce myself,' said the black man, hoisting Ben's luggage, and simultaneously propelling him

43

by the elbow, 'my name is Oliver O'Leary, at your service. Friends call me Sambo. You may call me Sambo. It's easier.' He guided Ben toward the swing doors.

'All right,' said Ben, recovering equilibrium, 'perhaps you'll be good enough to let me know where we're headed?'

'I'll tell you soon enough. We have to leave right away.' He peered through the rotating doors. 'Come along, move yourself, we have to contact your secretary. She's gone ahead. The next chapter's about to begin.'

Before Ben could protest, Sambo bundled him, baggage and all, into an elderly taxi and ordered the driver to head west.

'I suppose you've orders . . . you know what you're doing?'

'Leave it to me.'

'What about identifiction?' Ben, recovering from the whirlwind departure, began to assert himself. 'The Admiral didn't describe you. And, if you don't mind my saying so, he'd have had no trouble in giving me an accurate description.'

'He had no idea who I'd be. Anyway, man, I'm from the CIA. I got on the plane at Heathrow. Our seats had been booked ages back. I watched you get on the plane. You were picked out by one of the Admiral's agents, a woman. I know who YOU are . . . so relax. This part of the trip'll take a couple of hours. Our driver knows the route.'

As soon as they reached the city limits the driver of the taxi turned the car south, and drove steadily on until daylight faded. As they approached a fork in the tracks, the yellow headlights of the cab revealed a Range Rover in camouflage paint. Sambo removed their luggage, paid the driver, and sent him on his way home.

As the headlights of the taxi faded into the distance, the Range Rover was barely visible in the glimmering light cast by millions of stars scattered in the dome of the black sky. Ben and Sambo approached the parked vehicle. A familiar – to Ben – profile, outlined by softly glowing dashlights, took shape. The woman driver did not acknowledge their presence even as they loaded their possessions. Clearly she had been expecting them. As soon as they were seated, she released the clutch, and the Range Rover moved off. It was all smoothly efficient. Ben was sure he had seen her somewhere . . . of course, in the lounge and on the plane. As if divining his thoughts the woman said, in a clear, precisely modulated voice, keeping her eyes on the road,

'My name's Maeve Verster. You probably won't recognize me. I was one of your coaches. I taught Morse code, tracking, and so on. I wore standard overalls and a wig. You probably didn't notice your instructors.' Ben stared hard. 'I don't believe it, I would not have forgotten your face.' But he knew she was speaking the truth. He had been too preoccupied in training to pay attention to the many faces around him.

'Not to worry, the Admiral told me to take good care of you. It seems your sort are in short supply.' She smiled broadly, and drove on.

Ben, somewhat abashed, sat in the passenger seat by Maeve. Sambo, in lordly isolation, occupied the back. Ahead, clearly lit for several hundred feet by the vehicle's headlights, a winding, corrugated gravel road stretched off into the distance. Ben gazed as if hypnotized at the road. Maeve paid him no heed. After a while he became drowsy. Sambo opened a brief case, withdrew a package, and handed his somnolent companion a sealed envelope. It can wait, decided Ben. He was too weary to concentrate and dropped it into a pocket. It had been a long, surprising day. In few seconds he was asleep.

Four hours later, passengers slumped in their seats, the Range Rover drew up before a compound encircled by a high stone wall. Maeve released the steering wheel, hunched her shoulders to ease her aching back, and killed the engine. The sudden silence roused them. Ben dismounted, groggy with sleep, and inspected their surroundings. They were in a most extraordinary place. Around them was a menacing, shrill jungle, and before them, encircled by blazing lights, was an oasis of concrete and stone.

Set at regular intervals around the perimeter of the compound were white-washed sentry boxes, each lit by halogen floodlights. In the distance they could make out the murmur of voices, dogs barking, and faint music. An engine throbbed far off. The air was humid and heavy with the scent of bougainvillaea. Distant diesel engines occasionally missed a beat causing the lights in the compound to flicker.

'We're here,' announced Sambo redundantly, 'we've passed over the Isalo mountains. Drive through that gate. I'll speak to the sentry. We're expected.' The armed sentry left his box to open the heavy gate. The Range Rover moved in and parked before an imposing, whitewashed building.

'Okay, this is it. Here's where we meet an ally.'

Ben, still befuddled by sleep, suppressed a yawn. A group of white clad servants led by a black man in a red fez appeared and removed their luggage.

'This way please.' Red Fez motioned to the guests and strode ahead. They passed through a large portico into an atrium crowded with variously hued men, women, and children. Most were in some form of traditional garb. A few wore western apparel.

Ben squeezed Maeve's arm and swung her gently round to face him. Here at least was someone he felt he could identify with, a link with reality.

'I know you, you were on the plane. You're the one wearing glasses. So, you were one of my teachers? How could I not notice you? How do you fit into all this?' Maeve smiled through tight lips, shrugged, and turned away.

'Wait here, please,' said Sambo quietly, 'I'll locate our host.' And made off, melting into the crowd. A few moments later, a tall, grey haired black man approached. He was dressed from head to foot in a colourful garment. His dignified demeanour signalled authority.

'Good evening,' he said, pleasantly, 'so you've arrived . . . and safe and sound. I am so pleased.' He spoke fluent English with only the slighest trace of an African accent. 'I cannot express to you how delighted I am that you've come. You must be Ben? And this is your driver?' He paused, adding by way of introduction, 'I am the Chief, the Potentate, of this region. We are about fifty miles from Toliary on the west coast. In case you're wondering, I spent several years at university in England where I learned your language. Welcome to my domain.' He rearranged his robe over a shoulder. Maeve bowed her head respectfully.

'I take it you were expecting us?' said Ben. 'We have one more, a man called Sambo, he's out there, looking for you, I believe. May I ask . . . how do you fit in? Ben decided to make enquiries of his own. Lack of information placed him at a disadvantage.

'I was expecting you. Let me clarify my position,' explained the Potentate. 'While in England I became an associate of your admirable Admiral. We had mutual interests. As far as you are concerned I received instructions about making you welcome; providing nurture, and shelter. And, I was forewarned about Sambo.' The Potentate gestured towards his dwelling. 'Enough for the moment, we can't stand chatting out here. Let's go to my private study,' and he led off.

'I'm sorry my daughter's not here,' said the Potentate when they had settled. His expression had become drawn. 'May I offer you refreshments?' He pressed a button on the wall. 'From here on you will be in unfriendly territory. You will be travelling south east, deeper into jungle. I will do my best to help ... but ... ' he shrugged, 'we have our limitations.'

'How do you mean?' Ben spoke slowly and distinctly, 'What are your limitations, and how could you help?'

'I know the country, I know the people. I have trained men and equipment available. But I cannot go stumbling about in all directions. They'll see me miles away. If I am to help, I will have to be quick. It'll have to be a surprise. So, I need you to scout for me, to be pathfinders. When the time comes, and when you get back with the information I need, then I'll take action. Until then we have to temporize. I presume you know what I'm talking about?'

'The plain fact is,' explained Ben, slightly embarrassed, 'that none of us are completely briefed. I haven't read my instructions, yet. I was told little. Perhaps this is standard procedure? A ploy of the Admiral? There may be explicit orders in my documents. Anyway, as far as you are concerned ... you aren't prepared to escort us?'

The Potentate shrugged. 'No, I cannot. It's not that simple. But you are ... will be ... our pathfinders. I have to rely on you. I hope you'll succeed.'

'So do I,' replied Ben. He was not getting much from this source, 'I wonder what's happened to Sambo?'

'He's over there, I saw him make off. I thought I'd introduce myself directly to you.' The Potentate indicated

47

the crowded room outside the study, 'Not to worry. What I have heard about him is good. My connections with the CIA are as strong as my connections with the Admiral. We're happy to have him, and you. As I said, we have a mutual interest about what's happening on this island.

'Now it's time to eat. You must be famished after that long drive. I want to introduce you to my staff.' The Potentate led the way into an adjoining room filled with diners seated around an extended table, and motioned to his guests to sit by him.

There were many introductions, none of which meant much to Maeve or Ben. Finally Sambo, slightly irritated, arrived.

'I've been looking everywhere for you. I take it you found the chief.' Sambo found a seat. His annoyance faded when the Potentate expressed his regret. 'Please accept my apologies, Sambo. I believe we need no introductions. You must eat.'

Sambo reached for a plate and without another word began to eat. He was famished. Ben, taking food absent-mindedly, proceeded to engage in desultory conversation with various exotically clad dignitaries. He had not the faintest idea who they were. The cuisine, on the other hand was, for him, extraordinary. He managed to down what the Potentate described as peacock kebab, plus a tangy salad. He tried a glutinous stew but decided not to enquire as to its make-up. Sambo and Maeve enjoyed all the dishes, especially the fresh fruit. Ben finished with an excellent vintage port and Turkish coffee.

'Now my friends,' said the Potentate, breaking into the hubbub of conversation, 'you should retire. You will need an early start. You may stay on and enjoy the evening's entertainment if you wish.'

'Maeve and Sambo may,' said Ben, 'but I'm done in. I must have an early night. I've a bit of reading to do.'

'By all means. Read your instructions. You must be fresh for tomorrow. In the meantime,' said the Potentate, 'I will do my level best to organize my team. I stress again, a lot depends on your being our eyes and ears. I have to stay in the background. We don't want to forewarn the enemy.'

Enemy? Ben was more mystified than ever. Large pieces

of the jigsaw puzzle were missing. All he had was a sprinkling of hints and unfinished phrases. What was it that lay in store?

☆ ☆ ☆

Sambo awoke in the morning to find the residence stirring. Ben had already risen and had been helping their driver to cram the Range Rover with fresh provisions, field equipment, and extra fuel. A large crowd had gathered. The Potentate and his retinue were waiting patiently to see them on their way.

The heavily laden Range Rover started and moved off. Within minutes the establishment of the Potentate vanished from view. The trio, Ben, Sambo, and Maeve, found themselves heading once again along a narrow, winding, gravel road.

Having read his set of instructions, Ben tore them up, and tossed them out of a window. Maeve reached into the glove compartment, withdrew a sealed package, and handed him an envelope marked, 'Final'.

'When you see this,' he read, 'you should be in the company of a female driver, Maeve Verster, and an agent of the CIA, *but no one else*. I chose Maeve, not the CIA agent. I know her to be entirely trusworthy and capable. She will take orders from you. (The CIA agent with you is not directly known to me. I have to trust the judgement of my colleagues in the CIA.) At any rate you should have first-class assistance.

'You will already have met my contact on the island, an intelligent, resourceful man, a chief of a black tribe, (originally displaced from Namibia), now settled in southern Madagascar. I know his people. The Chief, or Potentate, will have introduced himself. You, and he, have a common target, but for reasons which will become obvious, he cannot be of much help at this stage. You must follow the coordinates on the map I have given you with this note. You will eventually come across an organization which will be expecting you. I do not know how they will contact you. You simply have to be visible. *You must not have escorts*, which is one reason why the Potentate cannot accompany you.'

49

Ben finished and looked at Maeve.

'Did you know what was in this note?'

She did not reply.

'I guess it tells you about us?' ventured Sambo.

'More or less,' said Ben, 'the only problem is that we do not have exact instructions. We have a map, and we are to travel south and locate an 'organization'. We are told we may be expected. But only we three. And here's the map.'

The Land Rover was by now struggling in the lowest gear of its four-wheel drive. It rolled and pitched alarmingly as it ground along a practically impassable track. Finally Maeve gave up and halted.

'It's no use. We can't go on in this. I'm going ahead to reconnoitre,' she said, 'I'll see if there's a track. We may have to walk. Wait here.'

'What,' asked Ben, with excessive politeness, 'do we do with all the gear so carefuly stowed aboard?'

'We may have to leave it.' Maeve moved off into the dense underbrush.

Ben and Sambo sat silently, waiting.

'Try the radio,' said Ben after a while, 'see if we've a link with civilization.' Sambo fiddled with the dial. The radio refused to cooperate. Loud static issued from the loud-speakers.

'Marvellous,' said Ben, 'no connection, nothing. Where's Maeve?'

Startling, crashing noises from the underbrush shattered the stillness.

'Sounds like a herd of elephants . . . ' Ben's remarks were cut short by the breakneck reappearance of Maeve, followed closely by a frazzled band of white, brown, and black men in army fatigues. What was really alarming was that the nozzles of their automatic rifles were wavering from Maeve's back to their general direction, and back again.

A tall, white man in officer's uniform of some sort, caught up with Maeve and brusquely shoved her aside. He approached. 'Out of the truck,' he ordered, 'out . . . right now . . . or we shoot.'

Ben and Sambo gaped in astonishment.

'Here, hold on, who the hell are you?'

'Get out,' bellowed the officer and let off a short burst of gunfire over their heads. Ben and Sambo scrambled from the Range Rover.

'From this point on you walk. No more questions, just follow.' The officer motioned to them to fall in line. He stationed soldiers on each flank, and strode ahead. The new prisoners were herded along in single file with Ben in the lead.

Three kilometres on and the undergrowth had thickened palpably. Foot passage had become slow and laboured as dense bush choked their path.

'Look here.' Ben appealed to their taciturn guide. 'What about a drink of water, and a rest?' The officer, relenting, allowed the almost spent companions a brief respite. They moved off the trail to sprawl in the shade of the undergrowth. Luke warm, brackish water in tin containers was passed around. The soldiers sat themselves a short distance away and munched their rations.

Ben lay stretched out, utterly drained. Maeve and Sambo squatted on their haunches and inspected the soldiers warily. Escape was impossible.

'I don't think this was in the general plan,' muttered Ben rolling onto his back, and shutting his eyes, 'it's not quite the reception I was expecting.'

A sudden commotion disrupted his somnolent state. He opened his eyes and was astonished to find a young, jet-black woman had materialized, literally out of nowhere. She had dropped, seemingly, from the sky, landing in a cloud of dusty leaves before their astonished gaze. Ben spotted a broken branch in an overhanging tree. Apparently unhurt by her spectacular fall, the black woman recovered before anyone could move.

With a single fluid bound, ignoring the escort of soldiers, she flung herself onto Sambo just as he was rising to his feet. Her sudden weight caused him to stagger. Hot, steamy, breath wafted up his distended nostrils. His rapid change in posture, plus the appearance of the dazzling apparition was too much for Sambo. He felt hot, sweaty, and light-headed. Everything went dark. When he regained consciousness, he was acutely discomfited to find a circle of inquisitive faces gazing down at him. The black girl was crouched by his side, her face close to his.

'I've been waiting,' she whispered, 'but I didn't plan to meet you quite in this manner.' She paused and glanced around at the staring faces, 'I must join your expedition.' She looked imploringly at the officer who was approaching. If he was at all surprised he gave no sign. He walked calmly over to inspect the new arrival and proceeded to search her thoroughly.

'I'm from this part of the world,' she said to him in an unfamiliar language, 'I'm not one of them. I'm lost. Can I come along?'

After a few hesitant seconds the officer shrugged and signalled to her to lift her belongings and to fall in line.

Sambo, slightly dizzy, regained his feet and joined the others. 'Any more surprises in store?' he asked, wryly. 'Did you know about her?' Ben pursed his lips and shook his head.

'No, of course not,' he replied, 'we're not supposed to have anyone else with us.'

'Come on, all of you, get going,' snapped the officer, 'we haven't all day. It gets dark pretty damn quick.'

Ben helped Maeve to her feet. Both men turned to look at their new companion. She walked on ahead looking neither left or right, seemingly unconcerned by the consternation she had caused. She had with her some incongruous pieces of equipment; a designer carry-all bag, a camera case, and a pair of powerful binoculars which she carried slung over a shoulder. Ben accelerated to match her stride.

'Who are you?' he asked quietly, keeping an eye on the officer walking ahead. 'Who were you waiting for . . . and why?' Nothing about her had been mentioned in his briefings.

'When it's time, and when we're out of earshot of this posse, I'll explain.' The black woman looked over her shoulder and dropped her voice. 'I know you're on a special assignment. I knew you'd be along this trail. I've been waiting hours. We have a common goal.' She waved a hand and brushed Ben aside. He shrugged and dropped behind to rejoin Maeve and Sambo.

'What did she say?'

'Not much. Said she'd tell us more later. It seems a lot of people here have a 'common goal'.'

'Getting a bit of our own medicine?'

'Looks like it.'

'Do you think she's one of them?' asked Maeve.

'Anything's possible,' replied Ben with a shrug.

Ben turned to their original female traveller, Maeve.

'My instructions were to behave discretely, but things have changed. This is silly. We have to trust each other entirely. Besides,' Ben managed a grin, 'you look ... so dependable.'

Maeve returned his gaze and beamed. Again Ben noticed her distinctive bow-shaped lips and her open smile.

'I heard,' said Maeve, 'your trust is reciprocated. It's the black girl I'm not sure about. Anyway, there's no need to say more.'

Five hundred yards on the impenetrable passage suddenly expanded. Their mysterious, final destination came into full view. What they saw was astonishing and not inviting. Before them rose a forbidding, concrete fabrication, surrounded by a high, steel fence. It seemed to Ben that fatigue had separated his brain from his body. He wondered if it was a mirage that rose ahead.

☆ ☆ ☆

As they drew nearer details of the ominous complex came into focus. Dominating lesser structures within the confines of the fence was a large featureless building, designed as a stockade, or a fortress. Few windows or doors were visible. The complete enclave was encircled by a wide paved belt, like a moat of black tarmac, which connected with a large quadrangular courtyard to one side. Beyond the furthest side of the barricade they could make out a wide, slow moving, murky, green river.

The courtyard literally teemed with an assortment of warlike equipment. A veritable army depot it seemed, packed with camouflaged trucks, Bren gun carriers, radar areas, and discarded ammunition boxes. To the left of the quadrangle, away from the fortress, was a large domed building with wide, tall doors. Ben recognized the outlines of an aircraft hangar.

Had they come upon a clandestine military camp deep in

the southern jungle of Madagascar . . . the headquarters of a rebel army?

A few men in muddy, green uniforms stood about cleaning and adjusting gear. Some looked up, mildly curious, at the approaching band of captives. For all the interest their arrival aroused they might have been a daily occurrence. Clearly the newcomers posed no threat.

Among the motley group of soldiers, one stood out, remarkable for his height and girth. His uniform was rumpled and slovenly. His team, for he appeared to be in charge of a group of men, complemented his general style and demeanour with equally dishevelled clothes. A steady stream of curses issued from his mouth.

'Who're these people?' Ben addressed the unhelpful officer in a matter-of-fact voice. 'Where are we?'

'Don't bother to ask, you'll find out,' interjected the black woman. 'I know this place,' she whispered, 'I've been here before.'

'Have you now?' asked Sambo with sudden interest, his suspicions alerted. 'We've a lot to learn about you, haven't we?'

'Look, I'm not one of them. I am a native of Madagascar. You can't expect me to tell you everything out here in the open. But this much I will. I was in this place, some time ago. It's miles away from the nearest town. The plain fact is you are the first foreigners to view this fortress. It's run by a white man. I think he's an Englishman. At least he speaks English . . . '

'Englishman?' exclaimed both men and Maeve, more or less in unison.

'Very odd goings on here,' said the black woman, adding to their general unease. 'If only you knew.' She glanced at the soldiers lined up by the fortress, but they were out of earshot and busily occupied exchanging information with the posse. The officer stalked off to the main entrance.

'This man,' said the black woman quietly, 'the Englishman, or whatever he is, and others, arrived here eight years ago. They bought a parcel of land from my clan and built this place. The man who runs it all goes around with another, older, man in an electric chair. Take my word for it, they're a bad lot. Real trouble.' She pulled a face, 'I, and

54

others, once overflew this place in a helicopter, but those soldiers there, those mercenaries, let off a SAM. Luckily we saw it in time. We had to give up.'

While they were speaking the officer who had brought them there halted at the entrance, rang a bell, and spoke into a microphone. He turned to face his captives. The black woman's voice faded.

'What now?' muttered Ben, 'How did we get into so much trouble so quickly?'

'Listen,' admonished the black beauty, 'there's no point in getting excited . . . yet. You may find the next few days far from dull.' Ben noticed that somehow or other, despite her lack of substantial luggage, she had contrived to change her appearance. Her hair was groomed, and the denim outfit, which partially disguised her figure, was clean and presentable.

'Come,' proclaimed the officer, 'you're invited inside. Soon you'll get all the rest you need.'

Somewhat reluctantly, all four, at the behest of the officer, approached the main building. Maeve's wide brown eyes fixed inquiringly on Ben and she moved closer until her arm touched his side.

'This is going to be interesting,' said Ben, with every appearance of nonchalance. He was, in fact, too tired to care. He had given up trying to make sense of their situation. He sought, not too successfully, for a common denominator. A link of sorts, but events were moving rapidly and nothing was clear. There had to be a master-planner. So far the instructions he had read were falling into place. One fact seemed clear, all this had been prearranged. It could not be happening by chance.

'In you go,' commanded the officer, pointing with a swagger stick to the vaulted entrance flanked by sentry boxes, 'I hand you over to your hosts. I bid you au revoir.'

One of the sentries stepped forward, signalled them to halt, and carried out a perfunctory search. Shortly thereafter another, smartly uniformed, red tabbed officer emerged from the fortress. The guards at the door came to attention. The officer approached the waiting group briskly, saluted, and smiled in a congenial manner. With a cordial gesture he invited them to enter.

☆   ☆   ☆

The interior of the building was astounding, not only because it was extravagantly luxurious, but because of the contrast with the filth and foetid heat of the jungle.

A cool, softly lit foyer, furnished in beige leather, with rich brown carpeting and pale, rose wallpaper, surrounded them. Clearly this was the work of someone who knew about good living. This was no commonplace military establishment.

'Amazing,' observed Ben to no one in particular, 'a stronghold in the middle of a jungle, with a super sophisticated interior. It's more like a ... castle ... a mansion. Who lives here?' The officer, overhearing, turned and nodded agreeably.

'Please, to follow me.'

Despite misgivings, Ben was intrigued. An extraordinary journey had brought them into an incredible setting. If this was a fortress, what was it's purpose? Why was it barricaded?

The whole group were led into another, larger, room. Deep, pile carpet of soft sage green covered the floor. The walls were covered with an astonishing collection of paintings, mostly of animals, horses, dogs, and various hunt scenes. Ben was amazed to recognize a series of prints entitled *The Quorn Hunt*. He began, once more, to wonder if his mind was playing tricks. Was he hallucinating? A powerful sensation of déjà vu passed through him. He began to recall an identical set of prints hung in a house somewhere ... where ... was it in England? Cambridge?

The quartet followed the officer into yet another room. Here they were confronted by an even more phenomenal collection of paintings. Ben noted a number of what appeared to be Dutch masters, French impressionists, abstract works, and full length portraits of vaguely familiar, pink visaged, portly men dating from a bygone era. Genial faces gazed upon the people below. A powerful impression of having been there before continued to permeat his mind. Ben shivered.

Across the room was some sort of reception area with a group of servants looking on expectantly. The soldiers, or guards, whatever they were, had disappeared, except for the lone escorting officer.

'Welcome to the residence of your family,' he said, facing them and bowing stiffly.

'Family? What family?'

The officer beamed.

'Mr Brookhouse you are about to find out,' he said, clearly amused. 'I ask you to make yourselves at home. Your host will be here shortly.' And with that he turned smartly and began to walk away, only to pause by the door. 'You're in for a surprise.' He left, grinning from ear to ear.

'Why was he sniggering?' asked Ben, his memory stirring uneasily. Those pictures and portraits, he'd seen them somewhere, and not too long ago.

'How did he know my name?' he added.

'It's clear they were expecting you,' said Maeve, 'the Admiral indicated as much. It said so in your instructions. Ben, you look done in. Let me take your bags. Sit here by me, while we wait,' whispered Maeve looking into his face, and holding his forearm in firm grip, 'remember, we're here to support you.'

'I don't think I'm fooling anybody. I'm out of my depth. I like to know what I'm up against. But thanks, thanks.' Ben nodded gratefully. He had again become acutely aware of her cool, calm beauty. It was most agreeable to have such lovely support. Preoccupation with his predicament had not blinkered him.

Maeve gathered the remains of their accoutrements and found them seats by a wall. With neat movements she sat and gestured to him to do likewise. Ben obeyed and sat by her. But a premonition of unpleasant events about to enfold occupied his mind.

5

Out of the gloom, into the softly illuminated room, stepped someone whom Ben, at first, failed to recognize. Yet there was something immediately and ominously familiar about the shape. Ben noticed his astonished companions staring first at the newcomer, and then at him. A split second later his memory came into sharp focus and he recognized the form. There was no mistaking that elegant shape. The features that confronted him were none other than those of himself. He was looking, for all intents and purposes, into a mirror.

'Sebastian,' breathed Ben, stunned. 'My God . . . where have you been?' A peculiarly dreamy sensation coursed through Ben's body. A strange, unearthly phenomenon, not unlike a vivid, lucid dream. The hair on the nape of his neck tingled. He felt he was awakening from a nightmore only to find he was into a continuation of the dream.

'Sebastian . . . I had an uncanny feeling it would be you. How the hell did YOU, of all people, manage this?' Ben gazed, eyes wide, at the suave reincarnation of a dead sibling.

Sebastian was impeccably attired in silk. His urbane image contrasted vividly with Ben's dishevelled appearance. Sebastian's suit was of the finest grey silk; his tie of soft, blue shot-silk; his gleaming white shirt was silk; a blue silk handkerchief protruded discretely from his breast pocket. His feet were encased in casual, expensive, black Italian loafers. He wore no jewellery except for a wafer thin gold watch. Not a single hair was out of place. But the features were indisputably those of Ben.

'Hmmm,' whispered Maeve, nudging Ben, 'he is pretty.

But I prefer you . . . any day.' She gave him a little smile.

Sebastian, dismissing Ben's consternation, continued calmly.

'Ah, yes, dear brother, this is an EVENT, for both of us. It must be thirty years . . . I've lost count.' He grinned and folded elegant arms across his silk jacket.

'We, all the family, thought you were dead,' murmured Ben, 'and here . . . ' he struggled for words, 'here you are. It's incredible. Where have you been?' A thousand misgivings flooded his mind. It was not possible that a dead brother could be resurrected.

'It's a long, long story,' said Sebastian, still grinning.

Ben began to feel acutely disorientated. He began to sweat. He was tremendously thirsty. His tongue seemed stuck to his palate; his heart pounded in his chest.

'But first, let me welcome you to our little place in the country,' continued Sebastian, sardonically. He was patently unaffected by the sensational reunion with his twin.

Then, suddenly, in a lightening flash, Ben recalled where he'd seen the paintings. Some, perhaps not all, were from the halls of the country mansion of his former father-in-law.

'I've been expecting you, but especially Ben,' said Sebastian, addressing the group.

'You knew we were coming? You knew I was alive? You knew I was . . . ? Sebastian, why did you not tell me . . . contact me?'

'I had very good reasons.'

'But, you're my brother . . . '

'No matter. Here we are,' said Sebastian, indicating he was not prepared to continue explanations, and changed the topic.

'I'm afraid, Ben, I know your game . . . what you're up to. I know all about that stuff . . . the secret service.' Sebastian's manner exuded confidence, 'I, we, knew everything about you and your friends. I'll leave explanations for later. For the moment I'm your host, as well as your long lost brother. Like it or not, you and your friends are my guests.'

Sambo, sitting to one side, viewed the interchange with mounting disbelief.

'Ben's brother?' he whispered to the black woman in the adjoining chair. 'His long lost brother? Did you know about this? What's going on? Are we idiots?'

She shook her head but made no reply.

'Now, would you all follow me.' Sebastian spun on his heel and led the way into a truly grandiose hall. Three heavy crystal chandeliers hung from the high, moulded ceiling. The paintings on the panelled walls were more impressive than those in the last room. The furniture here was distinctly different, antique, elegantly arranged with alternating wine and Prussian blue coloured furniture pieces.

'Find a seat. There are enough.' Sebastian waved a manicured hand at a row of Chippendale chairs. The guests sank, exhausted, into the seats.

Ben struggled to recover from his disorientation.

'Sebastian, what IS this all about?' Anger growing from astonishment took over. 'Some sort of joke, is it? If it is, it's the cruellest, stupidist, joke one could imagine.' The phrase 'weird and incredible' reverberated in his mind.

Sebastian ignored his outburst.

'I am sure you're all curious about what's in store. Perhaps I might give you some idea of what I am doing here.' Sebastian, crossing his legs, was about to proceed, when a thought intruded.

'You must be thirsty.' He motioned and waiters appeared to offer each of the tired and dusty travellers a selection of coloured liquids in tall glasses filled with tinkling ice.

The black woman sat back in her chair and sipped her drink, ostensibly at ease. She glanced without curiosity at her surroundings.

Ben attempted to clear his mind. He had not yet entirely recovered from the shock of discovering his twin brother alive and well and, apparently, their captor. And, in such a weirdly, magnificently appointed citadel-fortress. Why was Sebastian behaving so mysteriously? Was he Sebastian? Ben convinced himself that absolutely nothing more at this time could surprise him. He had known that extreme fatigue could induce hallucinations . . . But Sebastian was real . . . and those around him, they were real enough. Maeve was real.

Having dispensed drinks the waiters departed. Fugitives from a London club? wondered Ben. He blinked his eyes but nothing changed. Sebastian held his glass up to the light and studied the swirling liquid. It was clear he was enjoying every second of his performance. He had all the time in the world.

Ben's utterly disconsolate expression attracted Maeve's attention. She saw a series of conflicting emotions flitting over his face. Amazement . . . hope . . . bewilderment . . . and more ominously, mounting rage. Maeve was attracted in a way she had never experienced.

In the ensuing silence the black woman sat forward and, leaning toward Sambo's ear, announced,

'My name's Amelia.'

'I wondered when you'd let on.'

A short cough from Sebastian drew their attention. He set his glass down and re-crossed legs encased in immaculately creased trousers.

'I don't suppose any of you, including my brother, have a clear appreciation of your situation. In a sense you have all become part of historic events. Events about to enfold. I speak to all of you.

'A little background. We go back to my childhood in South West Africa, now independent Namibia. You may find this hard to believe,' Sebastian's voice hardened, 'but Ben, when I was very young, was impossibly and insensibly cruel to me. He ignored me, treated me as if I did not exist. He did the same to a favourite uncle. He managed, God knows how or why, to influence the rest of our family and stole my rightful inheritance.'

'Sebastian paused to allow his audience to absorb his words. His eyes were coldly dispassionate.

Ben was astonished.

'No, no.' Sebastian raised his voice as Ben opened his mouth to protest. 'Let me,' he said, grimly, 'continue. YOU believe the reverse. But let me finish. You swindled me out of my share. You lied about me.'

Ben was utterly baffled. He stared in dismay at Sebastian and held onto Maeve's firm, warm hand, his only link with sanity.

'You, Ben, were Father's favourite. I don't know why. But nothing I could do pleased him. You, on the other hand, could do no wrong. I bloody hated you. And, to make it

61

worse, you, you lied to him, and everyone, about me.'

Ben managed to find his voice,

'Lied? What about? What are you ranting about? We were kids, for God's sake. All kids exaggerate. You did.'

'Perhaps I WAS abnormally sensitive. But it was made clear to me that no one loved me. In my awful loneliness I started writing to someone who would understand and listen, so I wrote to Randolf. He became my only friend. He understood.' Sebastian, seething with indignation, lost his composure and sputtered, 'He listened and he comforted me.' Then, breathing hard, he gradually recovered his composure and continued.

'Then one day, (we had it planned), Randolf came for me. We went off, together . . . at about the time Dad died. No one notined. Certainly not you.' Sebastian took a breath,

'And there's something else. Something that came up later. Had you any idea that Randolf adored Mother? Did you know that Dad had whipped her away from him? I know he was our father, but he was a swine. Randolf never got over it.'

'Now look here Sebastian, what absolute crap. How can you say such things? Your own father. Are you mad?' Ben could not believe his ears. 'What rubbish! You've made it up. As for Randolf . . . he must be as balmy as you. I don't really remember him but I heard he was a bit of a slimy character. What right had he to take you off?'

'I'd watch my language if I were you,' replied Sebastian icily. 'You're in a precarious position. I am giving you facts. Don't argue. It's time to listen.'

At this stage Ben had become too angry to be intimidated. But he was staggered by the intensity of his twin's twisted hatred. He was sure Sebastian was unbalanced . . . paranoid, distorting evidence.

'No matter, let me continue the story.' Sebastian, in full flood, went on. 'A day came when, after years eking out a living, Randolf and I hit on an idea. A brilliant idea it was. We bought govenment surplus trucks and began collecting tailings from uranium mines in South Africa under the guise of garbage disposal. We started with one truck. As we grew we bought more and larger trucks. In the end we had a fleet. But there is more to it.' Sebastian, now recovered and calm again, went on.

'The master stroke was to extract radioactive materials in amounts too minute for large users to be concerned about. Randolf hired defecting East German scientists to build a factory. We did it secretly by setting up in southern Madagascar, far from prying eyes.

'Now we have airfields, and a hidden port, on the Mozambique channel. The advantage is that we are near our sources. In a sense, we're still in the garbage business.' Sebastian chuckled, mirthlessly.

'If it's all so secret why are you telling us?' asked Ben.

'Think about it. What have I just told you? I know that each of you was sent here to spy. The joke is that I let it be known, via Iraqi contacts, that we needed you for your electronics expertise. When British intelligence thought they had found out about us, they thought they would be smart and cooperate with us. But we were one step ahead. I always will be. That's my genius. I outguess the opposition. All you've succeeded in doing is to play right into my hands.'

'Then why, if everything was running so smoothly, are we here? Is it me you want, or is there more to it?'

'Have you heard of power?'

'What,' asked Ben, 'about it? Why are we here? What's really behind this? What do you mean by 'power'? Are you planning on taking on the world?'

'Ben, you've no idea about power. It's within my grasp. I have all the money necessary. You cannot stop me. No longer will I be a loner, treated as an outcast, rejected.' Sebastian wagged a reproving, manicured finger at Ben. 'I told you I have a role to play. I will be famous, I am destined to be great.'

'Sebastian, you're a megalomaniac. It's wrong. You're heading for disaster. In the first place we had no intention to, nor did we, treat you as 'an outcast'. It's all in your mind. And secondly, you can't be serious about your 'destiny' . . . .' Ben paused to swallow his drink; his mouth had gone dry.

'It's dreadful not to be wanted,' persisted Sebastian, disregarding his brother's protest, 'to have to go about cap in hand, bowing and scraping, watching your step . . .

kowtowing, always.'

'I can't imagine where you got those ideas. Mother was devastated when you disappeared, on top of Father's death. It's a wonder she survived. That bastard, Randolf, how could he . . . ?'

'It's no use. I'm going to repay you, and make my mark in the world.'

'You've got hold of several themes, and you sound like an old-fashioned, crazy nut, a dictator.'

'How little you know! There are great things in store for me,' intoned Sebastian.

Ben could see that further protest was useless. His brother was mad. He could not argue with a lunatic, a paranoid lunatic.

'Furthermore,' said Sebastian, almost as an afterthought, 'Randolf's near the end of his life. We decided, Randolf and I, that before he shuffled off this mortal coil, we'd have one last fling at revenge. But, with a difference. We're going to see justice done, once and for all. It's not simply revenge, it's setting the record straight.'

'We're not on the same wavelength,' said Ben wearily. 'There's no logic behind this. Spare us further details and arrange for a bite to eat, there's a good chap.'

Sebastian was about to refuse, then raised hands in supplication and apology.

'Forgive me, I had been looking forward to this moment for too long. I got carried away.'

'Not far enough,' murmured Maeve, sotto voce.

'I'll see to it that you are supplied with clothes, hot baths, and rooms. We'll meet for dinner in, say, two hours?'

No one replied.

'Then it's arranged.' Sebastian nodded an elegant head, his air of self-possession completely reinstated. 'The invitation's open to one and all.'

Whereupon he swung around, dismissed his audience, and departed.

☆　　☆　　☆

Unobtrusive servants escorted them along hushed corridors, and ushered them into their comfortable quarters.

Hardly a sound penetrated. All was still, save for the faint hum of distant air conditioners. The fact that they had been through a raging, mad, tirade, and were prisoners, was temporarily forgotten.

☆   ☆   ☆

'Jesus, I'm exhausted,' muttered Sambo, alone in his quarters, 'where are you, Control? I need help. We have to get away, and quickly.'

The idea of a hot bath and a change of clothes seemed wildly incongruous. What good was that? His eye settled on a bedside telephone. Absent-mindedly raising the receiver, he was surprised to hear a dialling tone. Not expecting much, he listened perfunctorily. He tried dialling a long distance code. After a brief pause, some clicks, buzzes, hissing noises, he heard a familiar beep . . . and then to his astonishment, a ringing tone.

'Hello,' said a female voice.

'Hello . . . who's that?'

'Marilyn . . . is it you . . . Sambo?' The voice rose to an excited shriek. 'Where are you?' Sambo was too stunned to reply. The line went dead. His mother had answered.

☆   ☆   ☆

Amelia walked into the bathroom of the suite adjacent to that occupied by Maeve. She was intrigued by the dainty furnishings, the bathrobes, the hair dryer neatly resting on spotless white towels, and the single red rose in a vase before the mirror. She began to unbutton her jacket, dawdling with each button. Her mind was far off. Sambo was a great deal more attractive than she had anticipated. She parted the tunic to her waist. Strong tapered fingers reached for the belt buckle. With precise movements she released the buckle and drew her trousers down over the rim of her hips. She yawned, stretched and let the trousers slide down to the ground.

Amelia took a deep breath and scrunched her shoulders to ease her aching muscles. She unpinned and let her hair cascade over her shoulders. 'Not too bad,' she mused, as she leaned closer to the mirror, 'but what's going to happen to me?'

☆   ☆   ☆

As soon as she arrived in the adjoining suite, Maeve walked over the telephone by the bed and dialled the operator.

'Put me through to Sebastian's quarters.'

'Yes ma'am, he's expecting your call. I'm to connect you right away.'

The phone rang twice.

'Hello.' Maeve recognized the ingratiating voice.

'Hello, Sebastian dearie,' she said and smiled, knowing he would be irritated, 'surprised to see me?'

'Don't be insolent, Maeve. The past's past. Things are quite, quite different.'

'Oh really?' Maeve pulled a face at the receiver. 'You're not at all like your brother.'

'I'm quite serious,' growled Sebastian, the smooth tone slipping noticeably, 'come and report.'

☆   ☆   ☆

Fat lot of good the Admiral and the secret service has been so far, thought Ben sourly. We walked right into this bloody trap. He designed it that way. But did he know what we were in for? Why was I given no hint or news about Sebastian? It's not right. He must've known. Bloody hell. Ben shook his head, what he'd heard had been the ravings of a lunatic. He was convinced that his brother was mad, crazy. He was disgusted by his impotence, and the knowledge that, were it not for him, his companions would not be in the same trap. Ben flung himself supine onto the bed.

'Shit,' he said to the ceiling, 'utter, bloody, shit, this is. What's this?' Ben found a card of instructions by the bedside, and read,

'You will find suitable clothes in the cupboard. Please dress appropriately. A servant will escort you.'

An hour later, clad in dinner suits, both men were collected by servants dressed in white robes and delivered to a reception area. Here they were shown a well stocked bar.

'Where're the women?' asked Ben, and reached for a bottle of Scotch. 'What'll you have?'

'Whiskey, water, ice … that's just right.' Sambo accepted the drink.

Two drinks later the door at the far end of the room began to open and two exquisitely gowned women entered.

They've started again … my hallucinations, thought Ben. The quartet eyed each other. The women were first to giggle. Anxiety faded as they looked around. The events of the day seemed remote and unreal.

Amelia wore a semi-transparent, superbly fitted, red dress of crêpe-de-Chine.

'I like that,' said Ben, 'quite a change.'

Maeve was even more striking. She wore a green taffeta dress cut low in front. Long slits down the side of her dress revealed her legs. Ben was reminded of old Charlie Chan movies. Her blonde-streaked hair was swept back and braided at the rear. From neat, lobless ears dangled silver earrings, shaped like lizards. Once more Ben was struck by her large, frank, brown eyes.

'Hullo, Ben,' she said in a soft, clear voice.

'You're both lovely, stunning … how on earth have you managed it?'

'It's always nice to get a compliment.'

'You know what I mean … it's so unexpected.'

'Yes, we know what you mean, ever so gallant.'

'How about a drink?' asked Sambo, cheerily interrupting.

'While we're waiting for our host I'd like to tell you a little tale, especially for you, Maeve.' Ben, trying to bury his lapse of gallantry, started to speak. 'Have I told you about my adventure, as a student, in Austria?'

'Do we,' murmured Sambo, 'have a choice?'

'Have a seat and I'll tell you.'

They found window seats overlooking the empty court-yard. Only a single guard was stationed by the fence.

'To this day I'm not sure whether I dreamed it all. I happened, at that time, to be living in a small town in West Germany. I had rented a small stone cottage, very old, and very comfortably modernized. At any rate, one evening, I was in my study pouring over some German text and finding it heavy going. I became more and more drowsy from the heat of the coal fire. At some point I must have drifted off. (I found myself in the same seat the next morning.)'

Ben's audience displayed mild interest.

'It seemed to me, while I had been reading, that I had heard a faint, far off, haunting little melody. It seemed to be a flute, or a recorder. I couldn't for the life of me recognize the tune, but it was beautiful and beguiling. After a while I was mesmerized. The music seemed to fill the room. I had an extraordinary desire to get up and open the front door. My heart was thumping in my chest and I strove with all my might to resist. I just knew I had to fight back. The door HAD to remain shut.

'I stuffed my fingers in my ears and the music diminished. But as soon as I relaxed it took hold of me again. I was drenched in sweat. And so I sat there until dawn. It took me some time to realize that the music had finally stopped. I rose from the chair and walked over to the front window. I saw only a faint dew sprinkled over the garden. The flowers seemed especially beautiful, with tiny beads of transparent crystal on their petals.

'I decided I had been dreaming. I ate breakfast and went for a walk into the town. It took me a few moments to realize that something was wrong, different. The place was deserted. A few elderly people were wandering in a dejected fashion. Some were weeping. What was going on? Then it dawned on me.

'There were no children anywhere in the streets of Hamelin Town.'

Ben's audience let out a collective groan. Maeve stared speculatively at him. 'Very good. You kept us distracted.'

☆　　☆　　☆

A servant entered. 'Excuse me,' he said, 'follow me. The master awaits you.'

Sambo came forward, gallantly offering Maeve and Amelia an arm, and trailed after the servant. Ben lagged, lost in thought.

As the quintet approached the doorway they were greeted by a scene from the romantic past. The décor of the room was blatantly grandiose. Everything in the room glittered or gleamed. The centre piece of the chamber was an elongated, silver laden table with enormous crystal candelabra complete with lighted candles. Floor to ceiling mirrors were set at intervals around the perimeter of the room. At regular stages around the dining table were men and women, all in formal attire. The combined effect was to provide a setting that would have been hard to equal in any large city.

The door at the far end swung inward. Sebastian, resplendent in white tie and tails, preceded by a footman, entered. He exuded charm and expensive after shave. He strolled around the table to greet warmly each of the new arrivals.

'Allow me to introduce you to my other guests,' he said, smiling broadly.

6

Sebastian came forward, relieved Sambo of his escorts, and ushered the two women to their seats. He then beckoned to Ben to accompany him on a trip around the enormous, scintillating table.

'I'm about to introduce you to the rest of my guests; but before I do . . . I advise you to take a moment to prepare yourself, Ben, for a surprise or two.'

Exasperated by Sebastian's patronizing, overbearing manner, Ben replied sarcastically, 'Nothing but surprises, is this a party?'

'Bear with me,' answered Sebastian, with more than a trace of superciliousness. 'You're about to come face to face with your past. It'll be interesting to see how you deal with it. We'll pass around the table that way,' he said, indicating counterclockwise.

Ben had a fleeting glimpse of expectant faces reflected in the tall mirrors. His view was partially obscured by Sebastian's shoulders and he accelerated in order to draw abreast. In so doing he came face to face with the first of the seated diners, and stopped dead in his tracks. He was, in spite of himself, staggered to find himself confronted by his erstwhile chief.

Not for the first time Ben wondered whether he was dreaming. The man seated before him might have been a character straight from a German operetta. His full, naval dress uniform had been enhanced by an array of medals and sashes. But the fleshy beak, the twinkling eyes set in a rotund, ruddy, humorous face, signalled, unmistakeably, the features of the Admiral.

'Dear boy,' oozed the Admiral, with a barely perceptible

70

wink, 'how delightful to see you, and safe and sound. Trust you had a good trip? What do you think of your brother, our host?'

'The trip had its moments,' Ben, recovering, spoke quietly, 'did you know about Sebastian?' There was no point in referring to his briefing, or lack of it, in London. A flash of relief passed over the Admiral's rubicund face. He gestured airily and, catching a glimpse of Sebastian's suspicius stare, expounded,

'Ben and I are friends. We knew each other in London. I found him a reliable professional engineer. Good firm, sound electronics. I advised him about the need to explore cheap labour here.' Without waiting for a response, the Admiral sank back into the brocade chair, apparently satisfied with his brief, if cryptic, explanation. Sebastian frowned and walked on.

By now Ben had become aware that all eyes were focused on him. Sambo moved forward to offer support. Sebastian interposed himself gently but firmly, and prodded Sambo back into line.

'You see now, Ben, that what you believed to be your boss, works for me. I do have considerable influence.'

The evidence seemed incontestable. They approached the next seated guest.

'Oh,' muttered Ben, automatically, his voice sinking in dismay. His gaze came to rest on a well-known shape seated before him, leaning forward, elbows resting on the table.

For the third time since their arrival in the fortress Ben experienced a shattering, nerve wrenching, shock. Sitting before him, twisting sideways to view him was Marie, his ex-wife. Apart from a slight coarsening of her features and a thickening of her waist, she had not changed much. There was no mistaking those regular, oval features. Her hair was worn piled high in tight, black curls, like an Astrakhan hat. Long, elaborate, ruby set, earrings dangled from her protruding ears. Deepset, green eyes glistened mis-chievously at him. She wore an extremely low cut, pale green, dress of sheer chiffon. Her cleavage was, if anything, more impressive than he remembered.

Despite heroic efforts to remain unruffled Ben found himself unexpectedly embarrassed. He need not have been

71

concerned. The woman before him behaved impeccably with a cool, friendly manner. Marie, looking directly at Ben, nodded graciously. A small smile hovered on her pouting lips.

'Let me introduce you to Marie,' beamed Sebastian, his manner, if anything, more unctuous, 'I believe you know each other.'

'Hello Ben,' said Marie, pleasantly. She might have been greeting an old acquaintance.

'Hello,' replied Ben, 'how are you?'

'Wonderful,' replied Marie.

'Am I living up to my promise about surprises?' interjected Sebastian. 'Incidentally Ben, Marie and I are engaged.' He gave her cheek an affectionate pat, as if rewarding a faithful hound.

'As a matter of fact we've been living together. You may not be aware of this, but we met a few months before you parted company.'

'I . . . don't quite know, what to say,' finished Ben, clearing his throat. He was surprised to experience a curious mixture of indignation at the news and simultaneous relief that she was doing well. He was bewildered to find himself so disquieted.

His parting from Marie had been bitter. The constant bickering in the final months of their marriage had been pointless and infantile. It was long afterwards that he realized he had been chronically annoyed with her. Marie's personality had been a façade. She had become a different woman after their marriage, and had been incapable of giving him support in his endeavours.

He had had, for a brief, early interlude, shared moments of happiness with her. But that was all past. The pangs which accompanied her memory had long since eased. But here and now she had been resurrected, and by none other than his revived twin.

'I'm pleased for you, Marie,' said Ben finally, with dignity, and looked ahead to the next guest. Sebastian, enjoying Ben's discomfiture, moved on.

'Hurry up, dear boy,' warbled Marie to Sebastian, in an excessively loud voice, 'we're all famished.'

Ben noticed that Marie had acquired a distinctly fruity,

upper-class British accent which, for reasons which he could not fully comprehend, disturbed him. He had an impression that his dream-state was becoming a continuous nightmare. This is my private Christmas carol, he thought, as he came upon the next seated guest.

George the Dean, his contact at the Cambridge reunion, leapt to his feet with alarming speed and, bobbing his head vigorously, extended a hand. 'What a surprise!'

Ben could not immediately reply. The comment was such a masterful understatement. What to make of George? Despite his slight build, the Dean had an enormously powerful grip. Ben winced as his hand was crushed. Releasing his paralyzing grip, George the Dean said, 'Ben Brookhouse? It's good to see you. How are you my boy?' George emphasized each syllable with a rhythmical bob of his distinguished head. 'Let's see . . . when was it we last met?'

The Dean's behaviour was so much out of character that Ben, had he not been in such a predicament, would have taken it as condescending and insulting. But this was not the man who had approached him at the Magdalene dinner. What was he then? Everyone present appeared to be string puppets manipulated by Sebastian. Ben was baffled. What was his role? In the end he nodded to the Dean, smiled, and made to move on.

Ben had the distinct impression that he was a male Alice in Wonderland. Nothing made sense.

Having circumnavigated the table Ben and company found themselves opposite the seats where their journey of introduction had begun.

Sebastian regained his chair at the head of the table and signalled to the waiters. Silver trays laden with an assortment of delicacies appeared.

'Ladies and gentlemen,' announced Sebastian, 'now that introductions are over, we shall begin to feast upon a meal prepared by my excellent chef. When we've finished I'll announce the final surprise. Bon appétit.'

'Bon appétit,' echoed Marie.

The Admiral, gazing speculatively at the two new beauties, conveyed the impression that his mind was a seething scenario from the Arabian Nights. Maeve directed a brief enquiring glance at him to which he replied with an imperceptible nod.

There remained only two diners who had not been formally introduced. One was a sullen, muscular woman sporting a bulging neck and a pair of biceps to match. She wore circular, silver framed spectacles, the side pieces of which were held in place by a length of scarlet thread. From time to time she paused in order to scowl at all and sundry. She was clearly in a disagreeable frame of mind and sneered uncharitably in turn at each of her fellow guests. Occasionally, for variety, she glowered at the unfortunate woman seated opposite.

The second unintroduced guest was a thin, twitchy woman, dressed in a loose, curtain-like dress. Unaware of the angry attention directed at her by her muscular companion, she sat in haughty silence, fiddling aimlessly with her cutlery. Her hair hung straight down, hiding most of her face, allowing only her nose to protrude. She reminded Ben of an English sheep dog. After a while she ceased fiddling with her cutlery, and began instead to concentrate on the wine glass before her.

The muscular woman, sneering visibly, reached for a bun and chewed it angrily. Clearly she regarded her dining companions as beneath contempt.

The meal proceeded for a while without incident. A wide variety of hors d'oeuvres were set before them. Conversation ceased as caviar and foie gras was consumed. Efficient servants discretely vacuumed the few scattered crumbs that had collected on the tablecloth.

'I wonder if Ben has any idea what the Admiral's up to?' Sambo paused and put down his knife and fork. 'Who could have contrived such a scenario? I don't like this.'

'I have utmost confidence in Ben,' replied Maeve, bringing to bear her dazzling eyes. 'He'll work it out.'

Some secretary, thought Sambo, lucky old Ben.

'Sambo,' said Maeve, quietly, 'Ben could not have got where he is without gumption and brains. He's okay, and so's the Admiral. You'll see. I know what I'm talking about.'

'I hope you do. It's very complicated. But Ben's the leader, so I was instructed. But I can't help being worried, and so should you be. This . . . seems out of control, and if

Ben's in trouble, so are we.'

'Sambo', she said, 'give him a break. He's had some stagger-ing surprises. It's a wonder he's still upright.' Maeve turned away exposing as she did so, her striking profile with its tip-tilted nose. Sambo looked imploringly upwards for guidance. His attention was diverted by the two unintroduced women who had been sitting tight-lipped, glaring at each other.

'Can't you say anything?' demanded the thin one angrily, 'anything at all? It's just a pain for me to sit here, watching you chewing the cud. You must think I'm a bloody mind reader. Have you heard of the art of conversation?'

'Watch your tongue,' snarled the muscular woman. 'Too much talk at meals is for peasants.'

'I suppose, so is being polite?'

Sebastian, brushing aside the acrimonious interchange at the table, rose to his feet. He paused irascibly, while the Admiral completed an inspection of his molars. Alerted by the silence around him, that worthy looked up, caught Sebastian's eye, and ceased his activities.

Ben studied his brother as he prepared to speak. How, he thought, how could I have been so dreadfully mistaken? All those years in Kalkfontein when we mourned his loss. How could we have known he was crazy?

'Ladies and gentlemen, your attention.' Sebastian tapped a crystal glass with a spoon. 'Now,' he announced, benignly, 'I must let you in on the final surprise.'

He raised a languid hand, exposing an inch of white cuff. Almost instantaneously servants cleared the place settings.

Marie, luxuriating in her role as hostess, smiled in cheerful anticipation. With unaffected solicitude she looked around the table, pausing to nod friendly encouragement to the muscle-bound woman beside Sebastian. She was confi-dent that the fine food and drink had established her premier position amongst the guests.

The muscular woman, misinterpreting Marie's affable smile as condescension, scowled and muttered a curse under her breath. Marie, noting the black expression, bit her lip. The muscular woman continued to glower at her hostess. She seemed to be impervious to the demands of etiquette, or to the dominance of her hostess.

'Olga,' snapped Sebastian, incensed by the latest diversion, 'enough. You may have been an excellent bodyguard, but there's no need to be rude to your hostess.' His voice rose. 'It seems it's not possible that you might become imbued with manners. This is too much.' His face flushed. 'Marie is my fiancée. You must be civil to her. I cannot enjoy your company if you sit there pulling a face like a spoilt brat. Do you wish to be excused?'

Sebastian's outburst unsettled his guests. Everyone, except for the Admiral and the Dean, who hesitated marginally, looked embarrassed. Conversation died as an extraordinary change came over their host. Before their eyes Sebastian was mutating into a Mr Hyde. He had become disconcertingly suffused with rage and struggled to regain his composure. Clearly, noted Ben, Sebastian's sophistication is a veneer. He's living on edge. Something's bothering him.

Meanwhile Olga, undaunted by Sebastian's reproach, replied with a snarl. Her lips thinned into narrow, parallel lines as they stretched across her teeth. She looked decidedly frightening. Furiously gathering her bag and her considerable bosom, she sailed out, grunting and quivering with indignation. She slammed the door behind her with a resounding crash.

'Please do not distress yourselves,' said Sebastian smoothly, cooling off. 'Olga and I understand each other. Unlikely as it may seem she's devoted to me, but has a ridiculous temper. I suspect she's a trifle jealous of Marie.

'Let me explain about her,' he added. 'When I came across her, years ago, she was a teenage, homeless orphan. I have,' he smiled, deprecatingly, 'a penchant for helping the young. I took her in. She was physically remarkably power-ful. I decided that, with instruction in karate, she might become a useful bodyguard. No enemy would be on the look out for a woman . . . er, as a shield. I thought that was rather clever.'

Marie frowned and raised an elaborate eyebrow.

'She's been a faithful servant . . . but is getting on. She no longer acts as a bodyguard. There's no need for one here as you can see. Every door is posted with an armed guard.

'Actually, Olga's quite bright, but hates almost all of humanity, male and female alike, including herself. Don't worry, she'll simmer down. I'm used to that sort of display.'

Sebastian's exposition was received in incredulous silence. Marie continued to stare stonily at him.

'Sebastian,' she said, after a while, 'I wish you'd let her eat in her own room. One cannot teach her manners. We don't really need to hear about your past relationships . . . do we? Bodyguard, indeed.' Marie was frankly aggravated.

Ben stared curiously at his ex-wife. He could not, recalling Marie's penchant for bickering, for the life of him imagine how Sebastian had survived intact. Either he did not care for her, or he really loved her. Sebastian was more of an enigma than ever. As for Olga, a female bodyguard? Ben felt he was in some sort of looney household from whence there was no escaping to reality.

Maeve turned to George.

'You must have been brilliant to be a dean, I mean . . . so young?'

'Not at all,' he replied, with a modest smile, 'I was simply in the right place at the right time.'

'Surely that's not all?'

'Let me tell you about myself,' said the Dean. 'After reading economics at Cambridge, I became a junior partner . . .'

'I know, in a vast corporation where you rose to the top by your sheer outstanding brilliance.'

George grinned ruefully, 'You're pulling my leg, but that's about the gist of it.'

'We must get on with the next phase.' Sebastian had resumed his magisterial command, 'THE SURPRISE.' Raising a pretentious chin he announced, 'But wait, I think it would be better if we retired next door.'

At that moment, just as the diners were about to rise, the heretofore silent, lank haired woman with the pink, pointed nose, having been as quiet as a mouse at a cat's banquet, came abruptly to life.

'We've not been introduced,' she said in a clear, grating voice, 'my name is Deanna.'

Those nearest turned politely towards her, trying to locate her eyes and the source of the words. Hair fluttering over her lower face provided an approximate clue.

'Women are damn fools for letting you men get away with

shitty tricks,' announced Deanna to no-one in particular. Ben and Sambo sat back and beamed encouragement to her. It soon became apparent, however, that her agitation was genuine. In silence the guests resettled themselves, awaiting her next pronouncement. Sebastian, frowning, reluctantly resumed his seat, glaring a warning in her direction. His agenda was being delayed. Deanna's long slim fingers trembled.

'Why do we let ourselves be duped?' she persisted, staring at Sebastian.

Precisely at that moment Olga, grumbling to herself, regained her seat. Deanna swung her angry attention to her muscular colleague.

'I'll tell YOU why . . . '

Ben applauded, for, if as he had long suspected, he was in Wonderland, then Deanna's behaviour was appropriate. Nothing was predictable. Somewhat recklessly he decided to place a toe in the water.

'Diana,' he ventured, 'tell me . . . '

Deanna swung her head abruptly away from Olga, briefly revealing flushed, angry features.

'Don't interrupt,' she snapped.

'Sorry, I was about to ask for an explanation. Why do you believe all men are shits?'

'Listen you, first of all, get my bloody name right. It's Deanna, not Diana. Are you deaf? And don't try to distract me. Let me finish.'

'My apologies about the names,' said Ben, 'they're very similar. I didn't mean to interrupt. I thought you were challenging us for an answer.'

'Oh, no, you don't. You won't sidetrack me. It's an old male trick . . . not getting my name right.'

'But I've just,' insisted Ben, 'apologized.'

'You didn't mean it.'

'I'm sorry,' he said, biting his lip. The conversation had lost direction.

'I KNOW you're not sorry. I can see a smirk on your face. You're poking fun at me. Why do you do it?' bellowed Deanna. 'What are you grinning at?' Her disturbed hair parted again to reveal pinched features with tightly pursed lips set below a pink, glowing nose.

Why the hell did I start this? thought Ben, regretting his intervention. The rest of the guests, behaving like embarrassed diners in a smart restaurant witnessing an awkward scene, affected to ignore the altercation and continued to murmur barely audible inanities.

'I think there's a misunderstanding, Deanna,' Sebastian, anxious to get on with his announcement, intervened. 'Please settle down. We are getting away from my surprise. Ben,' turning to his brother, 'you are deliberately provoking Deanna. Please remember you are my guest. What's it matter if some men are vile?'

'There, you see, what did I tell you?' Deanna, instantly re-enraged, smashed a violently gesticulating hand onto the table, accidentally striking her plate, and sending its contents spinning across the table to land neatly on the Admiral's plate.

'You're dismissing a serious subject . . . and you, you give that back,' snapped Deanna at the Admiral, adding for good measure, 'you chauvinist-porker-whazzit. That's mine.'

'It wasn't his fault,' said Ben.

'Not his fault, not his fault . . . ,' she snarled. 'You see,' she turned to the cowed audience, 'you see, that's men for you. Always sticking up for each other.'

Deanna was by now distraught with rage. Her features had gone bright puce. She began to hyperventilate with alarmingly stridulous noises.

Ben decided it was time to recoup as gracefully as possible. To carry on in any fashion would be to court disaster. He was about to apologize again, although he knew this might be fruitless, when Maeve intervened. The ridiculous, undirected, row was disconcerting. It had been neither an entertaining nor an amusing exchange, and she was annoyed with all the participants.

'Look here, Deanna,' she said, 'pay no attention to Ben, he's a big tease.'

'I thought we were having an intellectual discussion,' objected Ben.

'Ben . . . stop it,' said Maeve, tartly, 'you're annoying Deanna and me. She's had enough. You're being silly. It's not funny.'

Ben shrugged and spread his hands apologetically.

Words like that from Maeve were sobering.

At this stage Sebastian interposed again.

'Deanna is known to be rigid in her beliefs. She gets upset and angry when they're questioned.'

'Hmmmph . . . ,' scoffed Deanna, not the least mollified, gratuitously adding by way of explanation, 'my father was a silly man. Perhaps not quite a shit. But he made me into what I am today. It's not my fault. I can't help myself,' she added grumpily. 'He had the knack of making me feel guilty by simply looking at me. I ALWAYS felt guilty. I couldn't please him. So I gave up. To hell with all you men. You make me feel like a fool.'

'Oh, well, that explains it,' said Ben, not unkindly, 'you're a victim of bad parenting.'

'Be a good boy and shut up.' Maeve gave him a stern look.

The Admiral nudged Ben and placed his fingers to his lips.

Sebastian rose to his feet. The audience fell silent. He was clearly now in no mood for further interruption.

'Have you finished?'

'Yes,' replied Deanna, and sank into surly silence.

'Since we haven't moved next door, I might as well tell it here. The surprise,' his South African accent, thicked by alcohol, was conspicuous, 'is a game I have devised for you. A contest with remarkable rewards . . . including freedom, if you win. I think it's very clever. When you hear the details you'll agree. But this ridiculous altercation has spoilt the atmosphere. I want you to be completely attentive. So, for the present we'll withdraw. Thank you for attending dinner.'

Taking her cue, Marie rose, walked around the table to join Sebastian, and together they sauntered out.

7

No-one spoke or moved for several seconds. The Admiral drew contemplatively on his cigar and exhaled slowly through puckered lips, carefully fashioning a series of near identical smoke rings. His bulging frog-like eyes were closed by lids veiled with minute rivulets of blue veins. His brown study was interrupted by the appearance of a servant.

'You are to follow me into the media room.'

'Follow here, follow there,' murmured the Admiral, and trailed after the lackey.

The chamber they found themselves in was as unusual as it was large. The walls to one side were covered with the ubiquitous abstract paintings. Maeve stood shoulder to shoulder with Ben.

'This is weird,' she said, looking around. The room was arranged as some sort of lecture hall but the furniture was unusual. In the centre of the chamber was an oblong sunken area, about ten by twenty feet, in which a long, low ebony cabinet formed a focal point. Facing the cabinet were several parallel, curved, sofa-like seats. Already installed in the back row were the two strange women.

Viewed from the side Ben formed an illusion of a dark island rising from a surrounding sea, an image which was enhanced by the deep, resilient carpet which affected their equilibrium, an effect encouraged by too much food and wine.

Sambo ambled over to the picture gallery wall. Their hosts' expansive taste in art was again demonstrated by a display of paintings by Chagall, Delacroix, Goya, Morton, Rothko, and again, several Dutch masters. All shared space, more or less equally, on the walls. Sambo, who fancied himself an art connoisseur, was entranced. The paintings were clearly the real McCoy, everyone a masterpiece and each worth a fortune.

Ben and Maeve found seats in the front row. Ben wondered if the Admiral knew what lay ahead. For someone so recently exposed as a double agent he seemed remarkably sanguine.

Forewarned by recent experience, the Admiral moved gingerly to a seat near Deanna. She muttered inaudibly to herself as he shuffled by. The others found seats more easily. Sambo dallied by the paintings.

'Sambo,' Ben motioned to his associate, 'come along, talk to me. We're not here to study art.'

Preoccupied with their remarkable, incongruous, surroundings, no one noticed Sebastian's surreptitious entry. He hesitated briefly, glanced at Sambo scrutinizing pictures, adjusted his cuffs, and walked in briskly to position himself by the central cabinet. The cabinet began to sink silently out of sight. The Admiral was reminded of a crippled ship slithering into the ocean. A small stage was revealed. Ben expected a theatre organ to rise reciprocally. Curtains descended with a whirr and closed off the sides of the stage. Sebastian gestured to Sambo to be seated.

Sebastian's face was now bathed in limelight. An overhead floodlight brightened, outlining his figure against the unlit, black backdrop.

Ben groaned; such amateur theatrics! Incautiously he let out a sigh. Sebastian, frowned, coughed, cleared his throat, smiled sardonically, and began.

'The second and perhaps the most significant part of the surprise package is the introduction of my partner, Ben's and my uncle, Randolf. Imported from Namibia, the principal architect of my success.'

'So he's here,' murmured Ben to Maeve, 'I wondered when the old buzzard would show up.'

'You may call him names, despise him,' snapped Sebastian, reading Ben's lips, 'just as the family ignored him – even when he had travelled to the side of his dying brother. Now, the tables are turned. Randolf is here, and you are there.'

Olga and Deanna fidgeting, like teenagers, sat back in their seats. Deanna decided that the show was sexist and muttered darkly to herself. Olga sneered at the staginess of the performance. Maeve and Amelia watched with anxious interest.

Ben was beginning to grasp the strange drive that propelled Sebastian. It was clear that Sebastian harboured an unrequited loathing for him, a fact of which he had been totally ignorant.

As the audience's eyes adapted to the dark, an amorphous shape began to materialize.

'Someone's there,' whispered Maeve, 'something's on the stage.'

'Yessss,' said Ben, calmly, 'it's going to be someone I ought to know, probably old Randolf.' Somewhere in the background a cello bgan to play a soulful melody which Ben recognized as Bruch's *Adagio for Cello*.

The overhead lights brightened to reveal a singular, skeletal figure, with inordinately shrivelled features. Slowly the skeleton raised a hand, an appendage covered in pale, atrophied skin. The music stopped.

Ben stared; he had little memory of Randolf as a young man. So, this grisly wreck on the stage was the embodiment of his Scrooge of days gone by, a ghost in his private Christmas Carol?

'Greetings one and all,' said the remains, with a pronounced South African accent, 'I hope you've enjoyed our little drama. Sebastian and I thought you would appreciate the lark.'

'No, we don't' said Ben.

'So there you are Ben,' said Randolf, swivelling his head, 'we meet again. It's been a long, long time. You won't remember me. So much has happened . . . since those days in South West.' He paused to lick thin, brittle lips.

'Here I am. Your poor relation. Have you any idea how condescendingly your family behaved towards me?'

'It's not so,' said Ben flatly, 'we did not treat you badly. None of us really knew you. I don't remember anything about you. How can you accuse me of something that never happened?'

'You took me to be a shiftless ne'er-do-well, not so?'

Ben withdrew in exasperation. Randolf was addled, Sebastian was mad, what was the use? Sensible discussion was out of the question.

'It's my duty to teach you the lesson of your life,' rumbled Randolf, his hoary mane trembling. 'You claim,' he said, sarcastically, 'you don't know me. You've conveniently forgotten, that's what. It's not good enough.'

Ben remained still and speechless. What had he forgotten? Distant memories of childhood began to swirl in his head. Dim images of parents, deserted houses, ghostly faces, black nannies . . . all drifted by. He saw himself, in his mind's eye, racing on a bicycle through the scrub-like desert with Ampies and Christiaan. But try as he might he could not revivify Randolf or for that matter, Sebastian.

The deep, hypnotic silence was fractured by a loud grunt from Olga. She rose to her feet and stumbled off amidst clattering noises in search of a washroom. Randolf having halted, awaiting a response from Ben, glared furiously at her retreating back. Nothing could interrupt the call of nature.

Ben decided, against his better judgement, to have one more try.

'Look here Randolf, I'm sorry you feel like this. But I had no part in it. I, like Sebastian, was a child. It's really none of the family's fault. I cannot remember you.'

Randolf's bony face tightened.

'Perhaps it's just as well you can't remember . . . if that's your excuse,' he said, caustically. 'In any event I have news for you. I don't believe Sebastian's enlightened you?' He chuckled, without a hint of friendliness.

'Let me tell you something about us. I nurtured Sebastian, the only decent relative I had. He's like a son, he IS my son. For years he and I, alone and ignored by the family, established a business empire. The time's come to settle debts. But,' Randolf scowled at Ben, 'we'll do it fairly, in a way that'll give you a sporting chance . . . something you never allowed us.'

'Sporting chance? Never allowed you?' exclaimed Ben, his voice rising. 'What can you mean? Seb and I are BROTHERS. And, whatever else you may be, God help me, you are my father's brother. Have you any idea the anguish you caused us by kidnapping Seb? It was a looney, criminal act. We moved heaven and earth to find him . . . Do you remember Sergeant Brenner, Dad's best friend? He tried his best to find you and Sebastian. If only he knew what you were up to.'

The malignant old man in the wheelchair grinned mockingly.

'Well he's not here, is he?'

They sat thus in tense silence, one scornful and derisive, the other furious and indignant, until Olga, returning from a satisfactory expedition, once again shattered the atmosphere. Groping her way clumsily to her seat, totally oblivious of the strain in the room, she settled her muscular bulk and completed her toilet by blowing her nose loudly into a tiny handkerchief. The bass reverberations were enough to put matters into perspective. Ben relaxed and glanced at the Admiral. The latter was sitting totally still, like a chameleon stalking its prey, staring into the distance under hooded eyes.

'The main purpose of this gathering,' continued Randolf, his grating accent more obvious, and glaring at Ben, 'is to outline the final event. This is to be the contest that Sebastian mentioned. A contest between him and Ben, to settle old scores, once and for all.'

8

'Naturally,' intoned Randolf, having regained his composure when Olga's trumpeting subsided, 'you're anxious to know what we have in mind for you?'

The Dean raised a tentative finger and was immediately silenced by a steely look from Randolf.

'I'll outline the contest and its rules. You would do well to pay attention.' Sebastian, sitting to one side, looked on with a small cynical smile.

'Now that you've been fed, and are accustomed to your surroundings, you must concentrate,' Randolf seemed to find it necessary to swing his head from side to side like a decrepit dinosaur, 'on the coming contest.' He fixed each member of the audience in turn with a beady eye.

'I have designed an exciting contest which will embrace all of you. The game entails skill and risk. Any one of you might win a fortune and freedom, or, you might lose a great deal . . . 'The principal contestants will be Sebastian and Ben. The rest of you will depend on their skills.'

Sambo, not especially interested in contests or games, began to visualize in his mind's eye the pictures on the walls. Now those were prizes worth a gamble.

'What we've devised,' repeated Randolf, slowly, 'is a chess match. A classical chess match. That is, several games. What's so special about that? It's special because . . . ' he paused for effect, 'each and every one of you will have a stake in the outcome. Each of you will be attached to an individual chess piece. The fate of that piece will be yours. The idea is that you won't be allowed to be passive spectators. And that's where the fun, for you, comes in.' Randolf cackled happily.

'Now for the rules. Winner will take all, and conversely loser will forfeit all . . . his life, in fact.'

Randolf was pleased to see his audience distinctly shaken.

'So that's it,' said Ben, 'so that's the game.' He sat bolt upright and looked for signs of reaction in the arcane Admiral. But there was no response.

'Each spectator,' Randolf was talking, 'will draw from a hat a token with the name of a chess piece inscribed. From that moment on he or she will be associated with that piece, and its fate.'

'But, what about . . . ,' began Deanna.

'In brief,' said Randolf, quashing her, 'the main idea is that if your piece is lost, so you will be, if the piece survives . . . well and good. The great prizes are for pieces with attached persons, surviving on the winning side. But, of course, it's a little more involved. If your piece survives on the losing side, you will survive, but without a reward. If your piece is lost on the losing side, ahh, well . . . then you're lost.

'The supreme prize is freedom, and one million dollars' cash in a Swiss bank account. How's that?' Randolf gazed triumphantly at his audience. No-one spoke. They were prisoners lost in a mad, dangerous, fantasy land.

Randolf tarried, expecting protest. None came. The audience continued to stare at him. The Admiral's expression remained inscrutable.

This is absolute, bloody, nonsense, thought Ben, deadly nonsense. A madman's notion of a game. I've got to get us away from my rotten family.

'I've prepared a little book of rules,' said Randolf, assuming a matter-of-fact pedantic air, 'I'll pass them along.' He signalled to a waiter. Several small, neat, blue bound, books were handed around.

'What are these?' asked Ben, his mood changing, 'The collected ramblings of Randolf and Sebastian? A dictator's guide to annihilation?'

He was rewarded by a frosty glance from Randolf that boded little good.

Sambo wished fervently that he was back in Washington, if only to cart files about at CIA headquarters. At least it was a sane world. His present dilemma was bizarre. Did his Control know anything? Was he being sacrificed? He realized with a start that Randolf was expounding.

'I trust what I've said so far is clear? Since there've been no questions, I'll hand you back to Sebastian.'

Ben glanced at his companions. The Admiral was his usual bafflingly placid self. He sat, an immobile mass, dispassionately appraising the scene through half closed eyes.

Olga and Deanna, by contrast, were wildly excited. The little blue rule books were being minutely scrutinized. The idea of riches beyond their dreams had temporarily pre-empted other thoughts. The consequences of losing had not yet registered. Olga's permanent scowl had eased a frac-tion. Somehow the effect was paradoxical and only made her look more forbidding. Ben decided she was one of those unfortunate individuals who looked better when angry.

'Thank you, Randolf,' said Sebastian, taking over smoothly, for all the world like a chairman at a business meeting, 'the match cannot end in a draw. If that should happen we will go to extra games. Now about the general rules. The match will be best of three. The time of the first game will be announced shortly. In the meantime make yourselves comfortable but do not, I repeat, do not even think of escaping.'

'I've never heard of anything quite so idiotic,' said Ben, 'you can't force us to play your game. You've no right to trifle with our lives.' But even while he was protesting the hair at the nape of his neck was commencing a familiar, rising tingle.

'My dear brother,' said Sebastian, with heavy emphasis, 'you're not in South West. Here we are absolute; you are prisoners; you are literally . . . our pawns. Think of this as a gigantic chess board.' He smirked, pleased with his simile.

'I say you're mad,' said Ben flatly, controlling his anger, 'and you won't get away with this. I can't think of a suitable expression . . . I am . . . staggered . . . by your lunacy. How in heaven's name do you think you'll get away with it? What sort of world do you live in? Don't be a bloody idiot. The CIA, MI5 . . . the Government of Madagascar, somebody, will find you out. This IS the twentieth century; pirates and buccaneers are extinct. This isn't Iraq. No one gets away with murder . . . on this scale.'

While he was holding forth Ben hung onto a faint glimmer of hope that this might be an elaborate, if horribly cruel, charade. But he saw no sign of humour, nor the slightest hint of a twinkle in Sebastian's vindictive eyes. This was, without doubt, a deadly game. Well, he thought, if that's how it is, we'll have to wait. Two can play this game. The stakes are enormous. I've won before, and I will again.

'What's to prevent the survivors,' asked Ben, speaking up, 'when they're out of your clutches, spilling the beans?'

'We thought about that. Knowing human nature as we do, we reckoned that greed, simple greed, would keep your mouths shut. If one of you decided to go to the police, you'd have to explain where and how you got your money. You would have to give it up. You might be regarded as accessories. Life is not quite so simple when you have a great deal of cash. We're confident none of you would risk exposure once you got your hands on a cool million. That's why we made the stakes so high. Besides, what's it matter? We're inviolate here. And should we have to venture out, we've safe houses round the world. If necessary I could disappear and blend into the background anywhere. I could go to any one of a dozen countries.

'As for you Ben, should you win, you have a slim chance of survival. I can't guarantee that. You will have to play for your life. You have no choice. Play you must.'

The Dean, who had been observing and listening with apparent, increasing apprehension, raised a finger, cleared his throat, and produced a nervous cough.

'I take it you're excluding those in your employ? You know, people like myself, the Admiral, the servants, and the guards? After all we were here long before the new arrivals. We have no part to play in your er, feud.'

He smiled ingratiatingly as he bobbed his magnificent shock of hair, 'Can we be assured that we are to be excluded? I don't wish to sound unenthusiastic about the match, but I'd much rather be a neutral observer. There was nothing about this in my contract.'

'Sit down,' snapped Olga, shutting her little blue book.

'I'm ashamed of you. Call yourself a man. We're all in this together. I always thought you were a little weasel. You're not on your silly campus now, handing out crap to a captive audience.'

The Dean, momentarily taken aback by the attack from this quarter, but seldom at a loss for words, replied soothingly, 'Look here Olga, what I'm saying applies equally to you and Deanna. We're not the primary targets. We're ordinary guests, and I'm an ordinary employee. There is a difference. I have your interests, as well as mine, in mind, don't you see?'

'Oh, piss off,' she said.

'Olga . . . ' said Sebastian irritably, 'I can see the Dean's point. However, it doesn't matter. I speak for Randolf and myself,' he eyed his mentor, 'we have absolutely decided that all of you will be part of the contest.'

The Dean sank back, his worst fears realized. For once his head remained still. His eyes glazed as he stared into the distance. His temples began to throb. He looked up in mute appeal to Randolf.

But Randolf, avoiding his eyes, remained cold and remote. He was a firm believer in his superior approach to life's problems. He was invicibly conscious of his role as a strong man guiding his inferiors. A master planner without peer. For most of his life he had assiduously cultivated condescension and manipulation, an attitude which served to discomfort friend and foe alike. His attitudes were preconditioned by rigidly adopted principles, and thus it was impossible for him to see any other point of view. He was always right. To compromise was a sign of weakness. He cared little for finesse, despizing charm as a necessary form of hypocrisy.

Randolf uttered a dismissive grunt and snapped his fingers. A pair of guards appeared. He had had enough. All the explaining had been taxing. He was no longer a young man. Sebastian and Marie made to follow. On the point of leaving the room, Sebastian stopped and turned to say,

'We're allowing you a respite. You may wish to discuss matters amongst yourselves. Help yourselves to drinks. Order anything you may want.'

Ben considered applauding as their misanthropic hosts

made their exit, but wisely decided against further provocation. He was faced with implacable enemies. The lights on the stage went out. The audience left their seats and walked over to a bar where hovered an anonymous servant.

Sambo strolled over to Ben, seemingly lost in thought.

I suppose you do play chess?'

'I used to play. I was school champion, but that's not saying much. At least I was able to beat my cousins. We played in the summer holidays. I usually won. As for Sebastian, you know I've no idea how good he is. We were very young when Randolf abducted him. It's odd, but I begin to have memories of him.'

Hands in pockets Ben leaned against the bar.

'We weren't so different. We were, I believe, I think, as good friends as twins could be. And now he hates me. I can't begin to tell you how astounding I find that. Sebastian is the last person I imagined would turn on me. Perhaps it's all the money he's accumulated, or radiation from . . . garbage, that's cross-connected his brains?' He reached for a drink.

'But there's no getting away from it, Sebastian and I are brothers. I wonder if he isn't really unhinged. He must be. I might be able to outguess him. Can it all be for revenge?'

'Uhuh,' agreed Sambo, 'revenge is a powerful force.'

'But it's a bizarre revenge.'

'I guess so.'

'Well, no matter. We're in a bloody mess. It seems we're stuck, for the time being, with this bunch of loonies . . . my family. It's my fault. I'll have to figure a way out and time's not on our side. I'll,' he looked directly at Sambo, 'have to play bloody well. I don't suppose any of us wish to end our days here.'

'We'd better start something.' Sambo glanced warily over his shoulder. 'I have some ideas. We need background about the fortress. What about talking to those women over there? They're involved, like it or not.'

The men strolled over to their objectives, Deanna and Olga.

'We'd like to have word with you,' began Ben with what he hoped was an irresistible smile.

'What about? You've got us into enough trouble,'

snapped Olga.

'It's entirely possible I might lose the match and, if you happen to own the wrong piece . . . you're history. We have to consider alternatives.'

'Such as?' asked Deanna, tossing her head, producing a ripple in her curtain of hair.

'There really is only one viable plan. We MUST escape. And to outline that we need info.'

'Such as?'

'What do you know about this place and its surroundings? We thought that as you were sort of friends of the hosts you might know something about the layout . . . the topography?'

'We know little,' barked Deanna, 'let me tell you that we don't like you or your crappy ideas at all. Everything was quite okay until you pitched up. You men are all alike,' she added gratis, and turned her back. 'Bloody males, nothing but trouble. Too much damn testosterone.'

'I say,' said Ben, addressing two hostile backs, 'perhaps you've forgotten that you're in this predicament by design of our hosts. And you might recall that they brought us here against our will. We didn't ask to be locked up. If I were you I'd try to be helpful. You never know, we might all end by pushing daisies up in the jungle.'

Ben regretted his outburst, but he need not have been concerned. His angry remarks made not the slightest impression. Deanna and Olga turned, looked him up and down and flounced off, dripping contempt. Ben shrugged and walked back with Sambo to the company of more agreeable women.

'Not much help there, I guess?' ventured Amelia. 'Incidentally, Ben, I wonder how the Admiral is involved? IS he really a double agent? You must have some idea.'

'Why don't you ask him?' replied Ben with a grunt.

'We'll find out soon enough,' said Sambo, as the object of their discussion, the Admiral, hands clasped behind his back, hove into sight. He had been walking slowly in their direction, reviewing the abstract paintings along the walls.

'A mystery to me, all this abstract stuff. Never understood it, or liked it. What's it all mean?'

'Admiral,' said Ben urgently, 'since I'm in your service, I

must have instructions. And information . . . what exactly is your role in this insane business? You owe me an explanation.'

'My dear chap,' said the Admiral, frankly, 'at present I'm as much in the dark as you. I can't give you sensible advice . . . not yet. But I will. I'll explain all when the time is ripe. For now . . . put up with me, others have. I'm thinking.'

Ben suspected there was a clue in the statement. If there was it was well hidden. He stood silent, thinking.

A door at the far end of the room opened. An unpleasant, whirring noise heralded the reappearance of Randolf in his electric chair. With him were Sebastian, Marie, and two guards.

'My apologies for keeping you waiting,' began Sebastian, 'we've ironed out details. I'll ask our mutual friend the Dean to come forward. He likes to natter, so we'll let him announce the terms of the contest.'

Before the Dean could utter a sound Sebastian tossed him a sheaf of notes. The Dean responded with an automatic head bob, catching the offering with nerveless hands.

'Sir,' began the brave academic, 'I am at your service. This sensitive matter will be treated with respect.' He walked over to Sebastian's side, scanned the notes, coughed nervously, and read out, 'One, there will be a supervized draw to decide whose name is attached to which chess piece. Two, no-one can be a pawn. Only major pieces will be considered. Three, prizes will be announced at the end of the match.' The Dean folded the notes and handed them back to Sebastian.

'I think that covers it,' said Sebastian, 'simple is it not?'

'How long do we have for each game?' asked Ben.

'My dear fellow, standard rules.'

'If you lose, do you also, er, become extinct?'

'Silly boy. The answer is not available.' Sebastian wagged a finger at Ben. 'I'm pitting myself against you. I'm in charge. I like winning. If you win that'll be humiliation enough. It's time for the draw.'

A guard to his left moved forward, carrying a silver tray on which rested a large crystal bowl filled with oblong metal tokens.

93

'Let's see . . . how shall we proceed?' mused Sebastian, 'Who goes first? What's fair? I think we'll arrange the names in reverse alphabetical order.' Sebastian gazed at the ceiling, his lips mouthing the alphabet. He looked around, obviously pleased with himself. 'That should suit everybody?'

'All right,' he said, after further seconds of mental effort. 'I think I've got it. This is the order. We start with Sambo, then Olga, Maeve, Deanna, the Dean, Amelia and lastly, our old friend, the Admiral.'

The Dean opened his mouth to object, thought the better of it, and shut up. Further debate was pointless. Here was trouble.

'We must start. The sooner the better,' grumbled Randolf, fast tiring, 'Sambo, you're first. Sambo hesitated for what seemed an age, made up his mind, walked to the proffered silver bowl, drew out and opened a small envelope.

'White bishop,' he said.

Olga, without prompting, lurched forward, exuding scorn from every pore, snatched an envelope from the bowl, and tore it open. Her first attempt to decipher the token was foiled as it was upside down. With a muttered curse she righted it.

'Black knight,' she said and, turning on her heels, lumbered back to her place by Deanna. The latter chewed nervously on a few hairs straying near her mouth.

'Come on, Maeve, you're next,' urged Sebastian.

Maeve walked up without hesitation and reached for a token. She opened the envelope and said quietly,

'White knight.'

'How appropriate,' sneered Deanna, adding more audibly, 'Oh, piss on this lot.' The guard flinched as she made straight for the bowl.

'I want to put it on record that I object to taking part in ridiculous masculine games,' protested Deanna as she reached into the bowl, 'It's all so childish . . . I do this under duress . . . you bloody men. It's all because of testosterone.'

Ben found himself developing a sneaking respect for feisty old Deanna. She was not easily intimidated. Sweeping aside her lank hair, Deanna announced sourly, 'White

94

rook,' and dropped the token onto the carpet.

'My friend,' said the Admiral looking at the Dean, 'it seems it's your turn. Proceed.'

The Dean, his head bob conspicuously absent, skittered up to the guard, and extended a limp hand to search inside the crystal bowl.

'I say, I'm a black Queen,' he murmured and retreated to ponder his fate.

Amelia smiled and walked up to the bowl with quiet dignity and withdrew her token in one smooth unbroken movement.

'Black knight,' she said, smiling at Sambo.

'So it's me. Here goes.' The Admiral reached in and withdrew the last token in its envelope.

'White Queen,' he said.

'So that's it.'

All eyes swivelled to Randolf. He waved an ancient hand in a contemptuous gesture of dismissal.

'Enough. We've established the rules and the players' tokens. We'll let you go for tonight. Come on,' addressing Sebastian and Marie, 'let's get out of here.'

'Good night, dear family, sleep well,' called Ben derisively.

'You'd better take them seriously,' warned Deanna, 'I assure you that Sebastian meant what he said. I've seen the way he deals with opponents, and it isn't nice. One or two servants aren't around any more, and I mean on earth. I hope you realize our lives depend on you?' Her voice had developed a slight quaver.

'I thought you didn't give a damn?' said Ben.

The party began to break up. One by one the beleaguered guests wandered off to their rooms. Olga and Deanna walking silently, left together, performing as they did their customary backward glance. Maeve, Amelia, and Sambo went off as a group.

'Come along', whispered the Admiral in the Dean's ear, 'best to get some sleep. Come along, George.' The Dean did not reply but allowed the Admiral to lead the way.

Ben found himself alone. After a while he walked, hands deep in pockets, along the corridor leading to his room. He undressed rapidly and was soon fast asleep.

9

Despite the hectic events of the day and all his forebodings, Ben slept soundly. Awaking refreshed he wondered how Maeve and Sambo had fared. He squinted at the dim liquid crystal dial of the bedside clock. It was seven in the morning. He retrieved the book on chess which lay casually open on the floor. He had no recall of anything he might have read the night before. Was there any point in further study? Time was not on his side.

Never a diligent student at best, he had squandered considerable energy and ingenuity devising methods to postpone study, preferring to cram at the last possible minute. In days gone by he had usually managed, with a caffeine-supercharged brain, to retain enough facts for a period limited to examinations, thereafter to be lost forever in the mists of his memory.

The events of the previous evening, together with Sebastian's notion of a fair contest with lethal conse-quences, seemed remote and unreal. He scanned the book, noting its pompous title; *The World's Greatest Chess Games, edited by Vassily Ostrakov*, and groaned. Ben had never bothered to study chess strategy other than to accept a modicum of tutoring from his maternal grandfather.

Ben's concentration wavered. His eyes scanned the furnishings and came to rest on a keyboard in a sliding panel under a desk. He was surprised he had not paid it much attention. He went over to the desk and opened the roll top where he was astonished to discover a monitor. Perhaps, he thought, I didn't notice it because computers are so ubiquitous? The type was familiar, a workstation, usually connected to a larger one elsewhere.

Mildly curious he sat himself before a screen. A promising looking switch by the side attracted his notice. Ben turned it on and the screen came to life. A simple menu appeared.

Ben chose an item labelled 'Games' and pressed the 'Enter' key.

'Please wait,' appeared on the screen. Ben complied. The screen flickered, steadied, and in its centre a set of instructions appeared in a small box.

'Enter area of interest.'

'Chass,' misspelt Ben.

'Re-enter area of interest.'

Ben frowned, studied the screen, and corrected his spelling.

'Chess,' he typed, carefully.

The computer responded in a split second with a set of instructions that seemed straightforward.

'Answer the following questions, by typing "Yes" or "No".'

Then followed a series of simple questions clearly designed to check his experience. He could see that the computer was not going to waste time with ninnies. It wanted to know exactly where to begin. Despite his scepticism Ben became interested. He was engaged in reading a set of instructions about setting up a demonstration game, when he was interrupted by a warbling note from the telephone.

'Hello.' It was Sambo. 'How did you sleep?'

'Well enough.' Ben wanted to get on with the demonstration.

'D'you feel like breakfast? I'll get hold of the girls. We can eat together.'

'Oh sure. I was just, er, beginning to do some work for the match, but I suppose I should eat.'

'How about meeting in half an hour in a breakfast room, wherever that might be?'

'I'll find it. I've only just got up.'

'No rush,' said Sambo, 'see you at breakfast.' And hung up.

'Oh, bloody hell,' groaned Ben and raised his arms over his head in one prolonged stretch. He fell back onto the bed and stared at the ceiling, then sat up to glance at the chess manual. He skimmed through the introduction, and moved to the first chapter. Two paragraphs later he realized with a sinking feeling that it was impossible to digest the convoluted instructions, let alone remember them. After a short break he returned to the terminal and turned it off. Better to go for breakfast. He was already late.

He walked over to the bathroom and turned on the lights. After a desultory exploration of the night's crop of blemishes he began to shave.

☆   ☆   ☆

Sambo, Maeve and Amelia, were already seated in a small foyer leading to a breakfast room, when Ben arrived.

'Can't say I've much appetite.'

'Come on, Ben,' urged Maeve, 'you must eat. You'll get a headache if you don't.' Ben smiled; he enjoyed her concern. 'Too bad,' he said.

'Don't be silly, eat.' Maeve was right, he was hungry.

Ben stood aside and let the others precede him. A waiter intercepted and escorted them to a table set with fresh linen, newly cut flowers and white china. Their orders were politely noted. They might have been in a restaurant in any city. Ben's cheerful mood persisted.

Fresh orange juice and fragrant coffee helped to refresh him.

'We have to plan some sort of strategy,' Maeve looked directly at Ben as she spoke. 'I was wondering . . . Sebastian is your twin brother. There must be a lot of similarity in the way your minds work?

'Maybe.' Ben looked curiously at her. 'But I know so little about him. He's different, not like me . . . I hope. Still, it's an idea.'

While he was speaking Ben took fresh note of Maeve. Her face radiated a fresh, intelligent beauty. Her hair was loose and shrouded her temples, with bangs over her forehead. There were many sides to her, many layers. Today she was a far cry from the silent woman who had driven them all those miles in the Range Rover. Today she was a warm, caring, young woman. For a few seconds Maeve met his gaze; then she dropped her eyes and switched her attention to Sambo.

'What WAS your training in the CIA about?'

'Not much about chess.'

'They must have taught you something about psychology. How to guess intelligently about your opponents' moves? Anything about communication?'

'Not exactly . . . '

'Well,' she said, trying again, 'what about this? How about transmitting information from, say, a book on chess, to Ben, during the match?'

'What d'you mean?'

'You know . . . signal to him . . . by radio, or whatever.'

'Chess is too complex,' interjected Ben, 'for that. You have to counter any one of a thousand possible moves. There wouldn't be time to look them up. One would have to think many, hundreds perhaps, moves ahead and then weigh up all possible counter moves. No, it ain't feasible. And secondly,' he added, 'where are we going to find the apparatus to get the information across to me?'

'I'm only trying to help.'

Despite himself Ben beamed at her. 'Why don't you think of something? It's your line isn't it?'

'I was thinking aloud. I can't see anything useful here. Maybe if I could get to a workshop? No, it was just an idea.'

'Wait a minute.' Sambo held up a hand. 'You're onto something. You've given me an idea. Computers, that's it. They're great for weighing possibilities at lightning speed. You can feed in thousands of alternatives and get answers in a split second. Why don't we use one of those in the rooms? It's obvious . . . maybe too obvious?' His voice tailed off as his audience looked attentively at him.

Encouraged, he continued,

'Suppose you fed Sebastian's moves into the computer? It could come up with a counter in a flash.'

'It's possible,' said Ben thoughtfully, 'but it brings us back to the same problem. How are we going to get the answers to me during the game?'

'We can work on that,' replied Sambo airily. 'We have to see if the first part's feasible. Anyone here know about them? There's one in every room. And, in case you've not noticed there are manuals with them. It's as if Randolf and

Sebastian meant us to use them.'

'Well, boys, for once we're in luck.' Amelia nudged Maeve. 'Maeve, here is the answer to our prayers, she's an expert. Go ahead, tell them.'

'I took a Master's degree,' explained Maeve, 'in Systems Analysis and Design at the LSE.' Both men stopped to stare at her.

'LSE?'

'London School of Economics.'

'Why didn't you tell us?'

'You didn't ask.'

'Maybe Sambo's idea has merit. But we still have that stumbling block,' said Ben, observing Maeve.

'Let's suppose she'd be able to help,' said Sambo, adopting the role of devil's advocate, 'and that we could transmit the information to you. What good's that if she knows nothing about chess? We would've been better off if she'd been a chess expert.'

'She doesn't have to know much . . . leave that to the computer.' Ben, now enthusiastic, turned on them impatiently. 'We can go on about this all day, talking back and forth.' The prospect of positive action was exhilarating. He was ready to start.

'Let's get on with it. Time's slipping by. Maeve and Amelia can look at the manuals. We'll meet again in about, say, two hours?' Ben beckoned peremptorily to Sambo and without further ado, the two walked off.

☆　　☆　　☆

'How are we going to do it?' Ben sat opposite the screen and reached for the power switch. He looked up the index in the manual, found a code, and pressed a set of keys. The computer blinked for a few seconds and then, unerringly, found the previous chess programme.

'Surely they must suspect we'd fiddle with the terminals? Am I being paranoid? It can't be an oversight,' asked Ben, gazing at the screen.

'If you want to know the truth,' replied Sambo, 'I wonder if it's a plant, to spy on us. On the other hand what have we to lose? Go ahead. The fellows who designed this place probably had carte blanche. They may have set it up without regard to cost. They may have assumed that Sebastian and company wanted all the latest high-tech stuff. For them it's like driving a car. As long as everything ran they wouldn't have to know about the works.'

Sambo stood looking over Ben's shoulder at the manual. He reached over and pressed the 'Return' key. A chess board filled the screen. Below the picture on the screen appeared a small oblong framed window with a question.

'Do you wish to resume play, or watch a demonstration? Type "P" or "D".' Ben typed 'P'. The screen replied with another question.

'What level do you wish to play? Your profile suggests level 4.'

'Cheeky thing,' said Ben, 'it remembers me.' He keyed in a 4, and pressed the key marked 'Return'. Instantly chess pieces began appearing one by one, moving uncannily into their preset positions. The screen politely offered white. Ben accepted and began with a standard opening gambit. It was immediately clear that he was rusty. Fortunately the familiar chessboard jogged his memory. He decided to try for a quick fool's mate. The screen countered with insolent ease. As Ben took longer and longer to move, the computer followed suit. Before long both men began to regard it with grudging admiration.

'To hell with this,' grunted Ben, as the computer relentlessly pursued his chess men, sacrificing major pieces in its quest for mastery. It was programmed to win . . . nothing else would do . . . a cold, heartless, efficient machine. Much to Ben's chagrin it swapped queens quite early in the game.

'I've the last word,' said Ben as he pressed the 'Reset game' key. The screen flickered, and in seconds the scattered chess men were back in their set places.

'It's no use. I can't become expert overnight,' complained Ben.

'I've been thinking,' coaxed Sambo. 'Let's see if we can persuade Sebastian and his gang to change the rules. Let's try for best out of five, that'll also give us more time to work on our escape.'

'Okay, but it's a holding plan. Escape is our main

strategy . . . not chess matches.'

'You got it.'

A thought occurred to Ben. 'How are we ging to find them . . . Sebastian *et al*, to talk to them? We don't know where they are.'

'The phone's over there.'

'You phone . . . '

'Me . . . phone bloody Sebastian?'

'Yes. I don't want to cringe . . . you speak to him.' Sambo, looking doubtful, agreed. It had been his idea.

He reached for the phone and dialled the operator.

'Hello.' A brisk female voice answered. Sambo hesitated, took a deep breath, and spoke firmly. 'I'd like to speak to your boss . . . Mr er, Sebastian.'

'Who's calling?'

'Sambo, on behalf of brother Ben.' Soft clicks and buzzes followed. Sebastian came on line.

'Yes? What do you want?'

'Something we have to settle.'

Sambo went silent and remained so for several seconds while Ben signalled in mime to him.

'Yes?' Sebastian enquired impatiently, his tone acerbic. 'Sambo, what is it? I must say your name's ridiculous. Why aren't you protesting about racism?' Sebastian's baritone vibrated in the earpiece.

'I've always been called Sambo. I like it. I got an uncle called Tom. But I'm not here to talk about me. I want to talk to you about the rules of the game you've cooked up. The odds are against us and we want fair play. If you want fun, you must even things up.'

'Oh yes,' said Sebastian, faintly interested.

'How about best out of five?'

'Anything else?'

'Yes, no-one gets bumped off until the overall winner is declared, and the match is over . . . finished. This way would make it more exciting for everyone, including yourself . . . keeping up the suspense to the very end.' Another silence. 'Well how about it?'

'All right, I agree. I'll clear it with Randolf, but it'll be okay.' Sebastian snickered, 'I like your nerve black boy, perhaps if you survive you might come and work for me?

102

Very good pay; lots of travel; no shortage of amusement.'

'I'll think it over,' said Sambo, gritting his teeth. Sebastian sounded so blasé. Turncoats were acceptable in his world. 'Right now Ben and the match are our main concern.'

'I take it he agreed?' Sambo recounted his conversation with Sebastian.

'I heard you say you'd think it over?'

'He . . . offered me a job. Bloody nerve. I meant to tell him to stuff himself. He IS balmy, but cunning. He'd like nothing better than to get under my skin.'

'You're American . . . he can't touch you.'

'I'm not so sure.'

'Turn on the terminal. I want to see a demonstration game. We might learn something.'

They watched with increasing fascination as the computer played brilliantly against itself. Time and again Ben stopped the game and retraced a move. It was a dazzling display of logic and it was difficult not to be impressed.

'I'm beginning to feel inspired,' said Ben, 'what's the expression? On a roll? Let's have another go. I'll play it by my rules and force it to move. Let's see if it gets reckless.'

The computer rearranged the board. Ben, following the instruction manual, set the level of play to 'Rapid solution', and made an opening move. Despite his instructions to accelerate, the computer seemed to have a mind of its own and took longer and longer.

'The bloody thing's thinking.' Ben poked the 'Speed up' hotkey. The computer responded with perceptibly faster moves.

Twenty minutes later Ben was in charge and hounded the opposing king without mercy. Still the computer would not give in. It was not programmed to surrender. Finally, when it was beaten, it signalled a grudging 'Checkmate' by flickering the king icon on and off.

'Teach you, you rotten, smart machine,' Ben said and switched off quickly in case it remembered. For a few brief moments he had forgotten his predicament. He had learned something. Confidence was partially restored.

'What you must do now is to memorize a few good opening moves. Fix them in your old grey cells.' Sambo yawned mightily. He leaned back in the Eames chair, closed his eyes, and immediately dozed off.

By now Ben was more than keen to continue. He restarted and keyed in 'Scan chess games'. In a few seconds a long column of names appeared. One rang a bell.

'Of course,' he said, 'how could I forget?'

After a while, his eyes burning with fatigue, Ben walked over to a window overlooking the courtyard. It seemed as impossible as it was ridiculous that they should be prisoners. Outside the sun beat down with relentless energy. All windows in the fortress were sealed to exclude the stultifying heat, yet the unending, monotonous screech of insects basking in the sun managed to penetrate the heavy glass.

Ben could see uniformed armed guards lounging near jeeps parked in the courtyard. Some, with panting Dobermann Pinshers straining on leashes, patrolled a heavy, chain link fence, M16 rifles slung casually across sweat-soaked backs. In the room Sambo, snoring mellifluously, slept soundly.

A soft knock on the door drew Ben's attention. He walked over, hesitating briefly before reaching for the lock. Maeve and Amelia, in skin-tight, revealing playsuits, were poised on the threshold.

'May we come in?' Without waiting for an invitation they brushed past Ben, trailing light, pleasant perfume. Ben's aching eyes recovered miraculously, his fatigue dissipated.

'Hey . . . Sambo.' Amelia nudged the sleeping form in the chair. 'Back on the old Mississippi? Sleeping on the job?' Sambo woke, and pulled a face.

'Listen, boys,' said Amelia, 'we've discovered something surprising AND interesting. Maeve was working with the terminal in our room . . . you knew she's an expert?'

'Yes, you've told us,' grunted Ben.

'You tell them Maeve, and perhaps they'll stop being so superior,' said Amelia patiently, as if to small maddening boys.

'I'll make it brief,' said Maeve, 'I checked the terminal. It's a straightforward work station. I can access their mainframe. They've left it open. No passwords. It's on all the time, of course, I don't know if they have techs to look after it. Must have. Clearly don't know much about it beyond some simple programmes. It's used to control communications, electrical supply, keep accounts, and maybe a few other odd jobs.'

'What about it?' Both men spoke, more or less simultaneously.

'A lot. The point is we can dig into their activities and find out what they're doing here.'

'So,' said Sambo, 'what's so great about that? We already have an idea about what's going on.'

'Okay . . . that's not all. I'm certain the mainframe controls all electrical activities.' While she was speaking, Maeve turned on the television.

'Standard procedure,' she whispered with a smile, 'walls have ears,' and she sat on the bed, and with a smooth, graceful movement of her arms, brushed the blonde hair back from her temples. Ben wondered again how so much of her had escaped his attention.

'I can change almost anything . . . communication parameters . . . anything . . . doors . . . lighting . . . I can do it. Better still, I believe I can mislead them. I'll have to be careful not to overdo it. So that's a good possibility.'

'And what's the other?' asked Ben.

'Well it leads on from what I've just said. If it works we'll be in charge of anything electrical, unless they figure out what's gone wrong.'

Her audience listened in silence.

'How will you do it?'

'I said, alter the computer programming. I can rearrange all sorts of activities that are under electrical control.'

'It sounds great,' said Ben, 'we're onto something here. You must do it. While you're at it, I must get on with my part. Who was it who said, 'So much to do, so little time'?'

'I think it was Cecil Rhodes,' said Sambo, 'he probably stole it.'

10

'Well, a bit of news,' announced Sambo, 'Sebastian's agreed to allow the contest to go to best out of five.'

'Why?' asked Maeve, dubiously, 'there must be a catch.'

'We asked. It gives us more time.'

'To get away?'

'Of course.'

The women rose, planted a soft, parting kiss on each man, and left. Ben returned to the screen. Sambo sat by trying to make notes. The next game went on for an hour during which Sambo filled several pages. Ben glanced at his wrist watch. The computer had so engrossed them that they had not noticed the rapid passage of time.

'If I try any more I'll be completely addled,' said Ben, wearily, 'but I am getting the hang of it.'

'Let's take a break,' suggested Sambo. 'I'll call the girls. See what they've managed. Do we dress for dinner?'

'I suppose so.'

'Ben, I know you're tired, but the point is that even if we use the chess match as a diversion, you'll have to play convincingly. You must play as if all depended on it, or Sebastian's sure to smell a rat. And,' he added, as a happy thought crossed his mind, 'if you should trounce Sebastian, Randolf will be greatly pissed off, and that can only be to our benefit.'

'I know, you're right. But when I'm tired I get depressed.'

Punctually at seven, Sambo and the women, having collected a refreshed Ben, arrived at the entrance to the drawing room. Everything, as usual, seemed uncannily civilized.

Maeve wore a tightfitting gown of light green chiffon, the

narrow waist of which emphasized her slim figure. The line of her thigh was clearly outlined by the clinging material Ben experienced a renewed surge of pleasure as she approached. She was becoming a fixed part of his existence. His unease dissipated.

'Maeve,' he said, 'when this is over, would you wear that dress again . . . to please me? You look gorgeous in it.'

'Of course,' she smiled, 'if you wish. Ask me to dinner. You know it's not mine? Amelia and I found these creations in our rooms, probably courtesy of Sebastian's minions. When we get away, I'll smuggle it out.'

It occurred to Ben that he had not dined in the company of a beautiful, intelligent and articulate woman for almost as long as he could remember. Dinner with Maeve, he thought, in the right setting, was certainly the most romantic thought that had crossed his mind in ages.

In his final year of marriage to Marie, dining out had become an excruciatingly boring, if not downright painful, experience. Partly because either she ate her food in stony, obstinate, silence or, if he was really unlucky, she contrived an altercation with the staff, himself, or anyone handy. More than once she had flounced out of a restaurant in the midst of a trivial, or more usually, a calculated quarrel, leaving him to deal with embarrassment and the bill.

Dismal, repeating, ruminations about wasted years with Marie were interrupted by the sight of Amelia snugly fitted inside a gown of silver tulle. The contrast with her light maghogany skin was striking. It appeared to Ben that Sambo, if he was lucky, might become as fortunate as he.

Sambo did his best to avoid gaping. But try as he might his eyes refused to obey and reverted like mesmerized rabbits to rest on Amelia's outline. He managed eventually, to drop his gaze only to catch sight of her legs, revealed by a slit in the front of her evening dress. When he shifted his focal point he found Maeve watching him with an amused smile. Amelia affected not to notice Sambo. She signalled to a waiter for a drink.

The amiable cocktail party atmosphere was abruptly enhanced by the appearance of another spectacular apparition. The Admiral, in full quasi-naval regalia, sailed into view. He was, on this occasion, staggeringly resplendent in a uniform of deepest blue with, not one but two crossed sashes over his ample chest. An array of service ribbons covered his left breast. A military-type belt supported a gold sword and scabbard.

Ben winced and pulled a face. The Admiral seemed to set on keeping up a comical charade and he was drawing – or was it diverting – a great deal of attention.

"Good evening,' said the Admiral with a formal bow. 'I see we, all of us, enjoy formal occasions.'

Ben, moving away from Maeve, approached the Admiral from astern and tapped him on an upholstered shoulder.

'Admiral, what IS this all about? What is this? What are you? What are we to believe?' said Ben, exasperated now.

The Admiral's normally cheery, rotund physiognomy froze in pained surprise.

'You are extremely visible. Is it deliberate?' persisted Ben, frowning.

'There's no need to be rude. These,' indicating the ribbons with a thumb, 'were given me by General Smuts himself.' The Admiral looked crestfallen. Ben regretted his attack.

'I'm sorry, forgive me. It's simply that you tell us nothing. We know so little about your role, your plans. You tell us nothing of importance.'

The Admiral spread his hands in a deprecating gesture, 'I dislike repeating myself, but you MUST be patient,' responded the Admiral, 'you must trust me.' He straightened sagging shoulders and waved a naval hand in the direction of the bar as a waiter came forward to offer him a glass of rum.

The Admiral was in the process of swigging his drink when a strange, ghostly apparition appeared. George the Dean, dressed from head to foot in a tropical outfit, entered. Everything he wore was, more or less, white; shoes, socks, suit, shirt and tie. The effect was blinding.

George beamed and bobbed his head with a curiously angled motion, like a man with a movement disorder, while he shook hands with anyone. He was partway through a series of undulations and unctuous, 'Good, good evenings', when Olga and Deanna made their somewhat less colourful, but no less impressive, entrance.

'Jesus . . . its Mr Clean,' said Deanna.

Next to arrive were Sebastian and Marie. The former, in his usual elegant evening clothes, took command. A slight gesture and champagne in crystal glass flutes, together with caviar, materialized.

Sebastian, Marie a pace to one side, faced his guests, a glass held on high.

'Ben,' he announced in baritone tones, 'before Randolf arrives, I'd like to give you a toast, for the sake of old times: To the lost days of our childhood. It's my wish that the events of the next few days will put to rest our rivalry, for all time; will wipe clean the slate. And may the best man win.'

So saying he drank deeply and then walked over to join Marie who was now sitting by the table, an enigmatic, smug smile on her face.

Neither raising his glass nor replying to the toast, Ben looked ironically at Sebastian, but was unable to discern any sign of brotherly affection. Sebastian was unconcerned and indifferent.

Ben shifted his gaze to Marie, standing by and possessively holding Sebastian's coated arm. Sebastian, he thought, must be in love with a conception. Sebastian would always see Marie as an image of what she had once been, a charming, elegant, and highly attractive, young woman.

Sebastian's almost frivolous reference to lost days of youth distressed Ben. Was it possible, he wondered, that Sebastian could have smouldered all these years with an improbable, implacable desire for revenge, only to refer to his motives in sentimental terms?

Ben's mind became a vortex within a vortex of images and ideas. He dismissed possibilities of reviving brotherhood as idle speculation, and turned his attention to someone nearer to his heart. Maeve, her usual peaceful, pleasant smile evident, was gazing fondly at him. She IS interested in me, he thought, it's not my imagination. In spite of his present quandary, life was, all things considered, becoming more and more worthwhile as well as engrossing.

At that moment heavy, double doors at the far end of the drawing room began to swing apart.

Poised on the threshold was the Great Panjandrum himself. Randolf, like Sebastian, was dressed in evening dress, inclining his head to acknowledge imaginary greetings as he entered. None of the guests moved. Randolf motioned to the guards to retreat. Once seated he coughed delicately, covering his mouth with an atrophied hand.

'Ladies and gentlemen,' he said, 'it is with the greatest pleasure that I welcome you again to dinner. Normally on this night we dine alone. Fortunately, for this occasion, you may join us. Although my physician has forbidden a reasonable diet, I'll enjoy myself with light fare. For you . . . there will be gourmet cuisine. Then,' he paused for breath, 'when we've finished, the main event will commence.' He rubbed his parchment-encased hands together in a rustling gesture of anticipation.

11

The meal was over. Overflowing ash trays, half empty glasses, cutlery, and crumpled napkins remained . . . mute evidence of the recent banquet. Servants began to clear the table except for a few remnants – a glass of cognac – a partially eaten serving of crêpe suzette.

During the meal Ben had been preoccupied. He had drunk only a small amount of wine and declined the excellent brandy. Sebastian, on the other hand, had eaten and imbibed his fill; devouring his food with every indication of gluttonous enjoyment. Neither his lack of table manners, (which contrasted curiously with his general air of sophistication), nor the coming contest with its dire consequences, seemed to be of much concern to him. Nor need it be, thought Ben. He found his brother's egocentric behaviour repugnant. Sebastian oozed domineering self-assurance.

Randolf, cast in the role of elder statesman, presided at the head of the table with equal *savoir-faire.* When satisfied his guests had eaten their fill, he held up a hand, palm outwards, until conversation died away. He rose creakily from velvet cushions, supporting his frail frame by leaning on the table, delaying until he had the diners' full attention.

'May I say,' he began, with familiar, sickening humour, 'with all due modesty, that you've just enjoyed an epic, a magnificent meal. Perhaps surpassing anything you may have enjoyed for some time? Hopefully, it'll not be your last.'

The remainder of the guests found themselves seats on the sofas facing the cabinet which, like a giant Moray eel, retracted silently into its burrow, exposing an uninterrupted view of the silver screen.

Ben fixed his gaze on a point two inches above Randolf's elderly cranium.

Randolf, secure in the knowledge that he was in complete control, and oblivious of the waves of disapproval emanating from Ben, announced, 'This, tremendously exciting match, the match of this century, is about to commence. We must not keep the contestants waiting. I'm sure they're anxious to get at each other.'

Sebastian strolled over to a console on the left of the screen. Ben made his way to a similar set on the right. Both men sat quietly, awaiting the master of ceremony's pleasure. Although finding it difficult to empty his busy mind, Ben acknowledged that it was time to discard his indignation, and to focus on the match at hand.

'Gentlemen,' intoned Randolf, 'you will find before you a board set up with chessmen. When a piece is moved that move will be duplicated electronically on your opponent's board, and on the screen. We will be able to follow your moves without intrusion.'

So saying he reached into a box, extricated a couple of chess pieces, one white, one black, which he held high for all to see. Tumbling them back and forth he raised clenched fists.

'Which hand?' he called to Ben.

Ben shrugged and indicated Randolf's left, adding for good measure in a clear voice, 'Your left hand.' Randolf opened his hand and produced a white pawn.

'Here we go,' muttered Maeve.

For several seconds Ben remained poised like a musician in a concert about to strike an opening chord. Abruptly coming to life, he moved his king's knight in a classic opening gambit.

The contest having begun, the audience relaxed perceptibly. Sebastian, frowning in deliberation, stared at the board. Ben's opening move was hackneyed. The youngest of chess tyros was familiar with it. Despite his confident exterior Sebastian was on high alert for ambushes. Long experience in business dealings had taught him caution. But in the end he made a standard response. Ben surveyed the board calmly for several minutes, and then deliberately moved his queen's knight. Each move was reproduced, magnified, on the screen. Each member of the audience, knowledgeable about chess or not, stared with fascination at the movements of their 'personal' chess piece.

Deanna and Olga began intermittently to glare at each other. It had lately dawned on them that, for the first time since their arrival in the fortress, they were on opposing sides. They had perforce during their prolonged stay developed a grudging tolerance of each other's idiosyncrasies. A sort of perverse closeness had developed. Suddenly all was changed. Deanna focused a bleak gaze in Ben's direction and willed him to fight on her behalf. He had to win; he had to save her. Her hair stirred uneasily. She breathed deeply in order to relieve the growing tension in her chest.

Maeve and Amelia, sitting like statues, clenched intertwined fingers, until they grew numb.

The Dean, searching for some sort of salient highlight, stole surreptitious glances at the other congregants. He tried smiling at Olga; she seemed so massive and so strong; but she ignored his overtures and stared stonily ahead. The disconsolate Dean concluded he was abandoned, without a congregation of his own. He was simply an anonymous constituent of a captive audience. No-one in the room seemed the least interested in him.

For the next hour the competitors played with intense, silent, concentration. Breaks between moves became longer. After two hours of cautious manoeuvring Sebastian, with the faintest of sneers on his elegant face, sat back, confident of success. Ben checked his sibling foe's features for clues. It was clear that Sebastian anticipated a victorious conclusion; he was satisfied with his performance. Success was within his grasp.

Ben abandoned his script and began to make unexpected, oblique, moves. His only hope was to unsettle his antagonist. And so it was.

Ben's sudden departure from a predictable course flustered and annoyed Sebastian. Unwilling to reorganize his strategy he decided, against his better judgement, to confront the ridiculous challenge by retaliating in kind. He offered, arrogantly, a sacrificial pawn. To his intense

113

chagrin he recognized too late that he had walked into a trap. Ben could not believe his luck. The initiative had, in one move, passed into his hands. Unable to restrain a grin, Ben began to use his queen to great effect, teasing Sebastian with adroit moves. It was obvious to both players where the game was headed.

While the moves were being relayed on the screen, the Admiral, not quite as sanguine as usual, bit his lips, and placed his hands with fingers interlocked behind his head in a slow gesture of resignation.

Sebastian, desperately seeking an amnesty, accepted another sacrifice and managed to capture Ben's queen with his rook. For a few minutes he began to regain some composure. But there was no escape.

The Admiral seemed to be in anguish. By contrast Olga, glowing happily, stared triumphantly at her fellow guests. Her satisfaction was short lived.

Sebastian strove desperately to regain his lost initiative. In his blind desire to capture Ben's queen, he had allowed a bishop into a position where it was able to lock onto his vulnerable king. Sebastian's breathing became irregular. Another idiotic, reckless, greedy move had brought him disaster. Oh, God, he thought, it's my childhood in South West all over again. Not for the first time had he underestimated his hateful brother. Only a grand master could have tricked him into such an impossible position. Mouthing a silent curse, he slumped back in his chair, defeated.

The audience, like concertgoers awaiting the conclusion of an unfamiliar piece, remained poised to applaud.

Abruptly Sebastian raised a hand in a gesture of surrender, and looking away from Randolf, said in a low, grating voice, 'I resign.'

For a second there was no reaction from the audience. Sambo was the first to come to life.

'Oooooooh,' he breathed, softly, 'fantastic.'

Maeve and Amelia hugged each other and then the nearest male, who happened to be Sambo. For good measure Olga stuck out her tongue at her old crony. Deanna's sneering reply was lost in the tumult. She remained seated sullenly alone.

His face a study in wrinkled granite, Randolf made no comment. His cadaveric features tightened. He studiously ignored the Dean who, once again all smiles, bobbed his head in hopeful salute towards him.

'Marvellous,' gushed the Dean, glowing with delight, 'Randolf, we live to fight on, thanks to our champion.'

Randolf gestured to the guards. Marie and Sebastian gathered disconsolately at the rear of the procession, and like a dark, passing cloud, the sinister group moved off. At the door Randolf made a visible effort to compose himself. Straightening his bent frame, he coughed, wheeled about, and in a perfectly reasonable voice said, 'It was a good game. I congratulate Ben. Tomorrow night our gladiators will meet again. The battle's lost but the war will continue.' he managed a smile. 'We never give up. We'll meet again, as usual, tomorrow in the dining room, at eight. Until then you may do almost as you wish. For the present . . . I bid you *adieu.*'

12

'Ben, Ben you did it.' Maeve cradled him in her arms almost before the door shut behind Randolf and Sebastian's departing entourage. Making no attempt to mask her tender regard for him, she added, 'Darling, you thrashed them on their home ground. I knew you could, and you did. Cheers.' She embraced him even more vigorously.

Despite crushing fatigue, Ben responded instantly to the warmth of her caress and raised her high in his arms.

'Thanks for the vote of confidence,' he said, 'but you know it was largely luck, plus Sebastian's overconfidence. It may not happen again and,' he added calmly, letting her slide slowly to the floor, 'maybe we're not better off. We may have bought time but it might have been smarter to let Sebastian win.'

Maeve, still on tiptoe, faced Ben with her arms encircling him. He became acutely aware of her firmly contoured body. For delicious seconds his aching exhaustion was replaced by a most pleasurable sensation which seemed to emanate from the soles of his feet and which worked its way around his body, continuing upward until it came to rest at the top of his tingling scalp . . . whence it vanished. Maeve assumed her presence had not gone unnoticed.

'Never mind, you were very, very good,' she said, smiling gently. The object of her admiration, returning her gaze, experienced a brief resurgence of the erotic warmth which had recently permeated his being. With an almost superhuman effort he restrained his natural reaction to respond. They were not alone.

'It was nothing much, it's been my lucky day,' he repeated, and before Maeve could contradict him, added, 'and it's off to bed. If you're like me you must be pooped. Tomorrow is another day.'

All, except Deanna, were impressed by Ben's modesty. The Admiral, pleased with his perspicacity in selecting Ben as a delegate, silently congratulated himself. All agents were performing beyond expectation.

'You're sure you want to go straight to bed?' asked Maeve, walking beside Ben towards their sleeping quarters.

'Well yes, I should . . . ' Ben hesitated marginally, then smiled, 'what else is there?'

'We could go for a stroll.'

'Here? Wrong time . . . wrong place,' he sighed.

'Why, what's wrong?'

'The whole shebang, guards everywhere, and this bloody place . . . the prison atmosphere. We couldn't do justice to the occasion.'

'You're putting me on ice?'

'I can't imagine anything nicer than not to have to . . . but it's . . . well you know . . . ,' he finished lamely. He was exhausted.

Maeve, fluttering her eyelids theatrically, leaned her body against him. The little play of affection was not lost on Olga and Deanna following close behind.

'Humph,' they sniffed in unison and turned off towards their quarters, noses raised, exuding waves of disapproval. Olga delayed her progress to remind them, 'Don't forget tomorrow's meeting. We may have something of interest for you.'

Sambo, following a few paces behind, alongside Amelia and the Admiral, eyed Olga's oscillating gluteal muscles as she propelled herself forward, with something approaching awe.

'That's all muscle,' he murmured, 'I think. We've found a powerful ally.'

'I wouldn't bet on it.' The Admiral twirled a finger in his sash. 'She was, and still may be, in Sebastian's pocket. Better be careful. I don't see any loyalty in those two. I may be wrong, but I don't like the smell of this. Least said soonest mended.' Having divested himself of his aphorisms, he broke off, bowed courteously, and sailed towards his room. Somehow, despite the comic, bulky outfit, he managed to convey an aura of controlled authority.

As soon as he was sure he was out of sight the Admiral's behaviour underwent a change. He scanned briskly up and down the corridor and moved off at a fast pace in the direction of his chambers. The relaxed, slothlike, demeanour had vanished.

'I wonder about that so-called Admiral. Which side's he on?' mused Sambo.

'Oh . . .' said Aemlia, 'how can we tell? We can go on and on about it. But he is sweet. I'm sure he's on the level, a bit mysterious, maybe. He's definitely cuddly,' she added with finality.

'Well then, that's the last word then about his credibility?' replied Sambo, 'If you sense he's okay, then we've no worries?'

'Come on, Sambo,' laughed Amelia, digging a finger into his ribs, 'no need for sarcasm. Haven't you heard of woman's intuition?'

☆　　　☆　　　☆

Ben, fully clothed, lay relaxing on his bed with head resting on his hands. What had he achieved? He tried to focus his thoughts on his childhood, but memory was clouded. Sebastian, a shadowy figure, a confused image, poised tantalizingly on the fringes of recollection. Was he recalling his brother or himself as a child? As for Randolf . . . there was nothing, a blank. Ben returned to consider the present. How to manage tomorrow's game? The last thing he wanted to meddle with was a computer.

He turned off the reading lamp and switched on the bedside radio. Vivaldi's *Il Sospetto* violin concerto wafted from the loudspeaker. The effect was magical. A soothing, relaxing calm engulfed his mind, displacing anxiety. How was it, he wondered vaguely, that there was so much good music around? He continued to listen with somnolent pleasure until his lids closed. In a few minutes he was fast asleep.

☆　　　☆　　　☆

Maeve and Amelia occupied adjoining suites. For this night they decided to sleep in the same room and donned flimsy nightdresses that always materialized on freshly turned beds.

'Someone is looking after us. I have a really creepy feeling that when I put on these clothes, someone is watching. They fit so perfectly. It's as if we're all under constant scrutiny.'

'We were probably sized up when we arrived. I don't see any peep holes, do you? Anyway, I hope they enjoy the view.'

'D'you want to see if there's anything on the telly?'

'Okay.'

'Get the remote control. I'm too excited to sleep. Find a blue movie,' she added, hopefully.

In the space of minutes Amelia managed to scan thirty channels, passing from one to another just when the screen showed signs of becoming interesting.

'Stop it,' protested Maeve, 'I can't stand it. Stop somewhere, or turn it off. It's maddening when you do that. How on earth can we get all those channels?'

'A dish,' said Amelia, tersely, and doggedly persisted with a search for a better programme.

Ten minutes later, the disjointed cacophony from the televison notwithstanding, Maeve became sleepy. Her chin sank onto her quietly moving chest. Amelia glanced at her companion but continued her remorseless channel switching until she was satisfied she had not missed anything. Finally, all possibilities exhausted, she dropped the offending instrument and turned off all the lights.

☆ ☆ ☆

Deanna glared at Olga's rotund shape.

'What exactly did you mean, you may have something to tell them? You're not really going to have anything to do with those invaders, are you?'

'Listen you,' snapped Olga, 'can't you, for once in your life, see we're in real trouble? That slimy charmer Sebastian has no use for us. He'd just as easily sacrifice us as he would the rest. And I know Sebastian better than any, except

119

possibly you. We go back a long way. You must know he's cold and ruthless, and weak. It's all a game for him. Anyone in his way will be squished. Stop being, for once, so damn pigheaded.'

'Ah, I see ... what did I tell you? You're becoming soft. They're getting to you. Men are all the same. Use you, use your body,' Deanna ran bony hands down the sides of her overly slim outline, 'and go off somewhere, with another woman, without so much as a second thought about their responsibilities. What do you think they'll do to us?'

She parted her straight, unappetizing locks and continued to survey with manifest distaste Olga's muscular outline. Olga refused to be drawn.

'Tell me Deanna, you talk so much, have you ever actually had it off with a man?'

'Don't be daft. I'm normal. I've had several ... men,' replied Deanna loftily, 'it's just that it's hard to find a suitable mate. Good men are a scarce commodity.'

'So I've heard. But be honest, have you done ... IT? I mean when you were actually in love? Done it for love? Lots of people screw, that's not what I mean.'

'For Christ's sake, Olga, don't be so naive. I suppose you think that sort of comment passes for sophistication?'

'Anyway,' said Olga, dismissively, 'I read about sex and all that in *The Advanced Feminist.*'

'And what's that supposed to mean?'

'It's a magazine written by experts, women in the know. Published by researchers in New York. They did lots of surveys. Psychologists ... social workers ... nurses ... and so on. I was impressed.'

'What in hell do a bunch of psychologists, or disaffected cows like yourself, know about anything? We're not rats. You know as well as I that most of what's written's a lot of shit. Men CAN be a bloody pain ... but there ARE a few nice ones. I'll never forget Arthur.' Deanna's eyes had gone all misty. 'All those years ... wasted. Bit of a miserable creep he was, though ... ,' she managed to convey a dreamy look, 'anyway, enough of this twaddle, getting back to us. What's going to happen? Maybe those newcomers are our only hope? I guess we'd better help. I don't want to be executed by some looney, and miles from home.'

120

'Well, if that's the case we've no problem,' said Olga, 'For once we're on the same track. What do we know that can be useful? How do you know we're not being watched? I'm sure Randolf has hidden microphones everywhere. I had a friend once whose husband bugged their house. She called the cops. Serves him right.'

Deanna sighed and tried to ignore Olga's prattling.

'We'll talk to them in the morning. We can give them some idea about the layout of this building . . . and so on. But watch your step.'

'I'm not as stupid as you seem to think.'

By now Deanna had undressed and sunk her tousled head with its greasy locks beneath the covers. Olga, somewhat slower, lumbered into her bed and turned off the lights. Almost immediately she was fast asleep and snoring rhythmically.

'Christ,' groaned Deanna, and sank her head deeper under the covers.

☆　　☆　　☆

George the Dean carefully closed the curtains over the window in his room. He stooped to extract a locked suitcase from under his bed and placed it on the cover. He turned off all room lights except for the bedside reading lamp, unlocked the case, and withdrew a well-used, leather wallet. Opening the wallet he selected two faded, tattered photographs. For a long while he sat and stared at the young couple in the snapshots.

He was looking at a portrait of a pretty, young woman with long, braided fair hair in a floral blouse and dirndl skirt. She was sitting by the side of a man in army uniform. His aristocratic bearing was unmistakeable despite the faded nature of the old photograph. On the collar of his tunic was the double lightning flash insignia of the SS. On his left upper arm was a broad white band emblazoned with a jagged swastika. There was no mistaking the uniform of Hitler's finest thugs.

The Dean gazed intently at the photograph. For most of his life he had carried within him a private shame. Whenever he turned his thoughts to his dead parents it was with a confused mixture of love and disgust. Tears welled in his eyes. Gritting his teeth he clenched his fists until his nails dug deeply into his palms. Although his dimly remembered parents had died in an accident at the end of the war, he remained forever terrified his origins would be uncovered.

Why me? he thought, blinking away tears. The concept of a posthumous revelation of his secret made him shudder. Although he believed he was devoted to the memory of his parents, the time had come to deny his own flesh and blood. He felt dreadful. He was a coward . . . a traitor to parents he had hardly known.

The Dean made up his mind. There was no choice. He had to destroy all evidence of awkward forebears. George tore the pictures into tiny, unrecognizable, shreds and flushed them down the toilet. No more fear of disgrace. With a long, forlorn sigh he walked back to his bed and slid, fully clothed, weeping copiously, under the covers.

☆　　☆　　☆

'Come on Fritz, you stoopid bloody animal,' cursed the guard, tugging roughly on the leash of the uncooperative Dobermann, 'stop liftin' yer fuckin' bloody leg every five fuckin' seconds.'

The two continued their reluctant patrol along the perimeter of the fence. The air was oppressive and stifling. Bass thunder rumbled far out over the jungle. Brilliant bursts of lightning lit the night sky, revealing for a flickering instant a multitude of silent lifeforms. Intermittently, and lightly at first, drops of rain pattered onto the dry earth. Soon the patter became a steady stream; the stream became a frank downpour.

A myriad rivulets merged to become torrents which, in turn, merged into the swelling river as it coiled its way through the jungle and swept by the fortress on its journey to the sea. The guard and his dog sheltered in a sentry box. The dog sat silently staring out while his master cursed the rain.

☆　　☆　　☆

The next morning, when Ben and company entered the breakfast room, a pure, brilliant sun was shining. The sky was clear; the air was fresh. Revitalized birds sang songs as beautiful and varied as their plumage.

Deanna and Olga were presently seated at a table by a large picture window overlooking the gently steaming jungle. An attentive waiter escorted the latest arrivals to a nearby setting. From here they too had a magnificent view high over the rejuvenated forest. Looking up briefly as Ben and company entered the room, the two women continued eating. After a few moments Deanna raised her head, murmured briefly to Olga, and walked over to the newly arrived quartet. Without waiting for an invitation she drew up a chair.

'Olga and I have been here almost a year,' began Deanna, abruptly. 'We have been bored stiff. Now we're, to be frank, scared stiff. We thought, in the beginning, that we'd found a peaceful haven. And so it seemed we had, until you lot barged in.

'But we were wrong in the first place. It's clear that we were simply part of a larger plot to get a group of people together as captive witnesses to Randolf's and Sebastian's game. Their objective seems to be to do away with your buddy here, Ben, though God knows why, he looks harmless.'

Ben acknowledged the backhanded compliment with a rueful smile.

'We've decided therefore,' continued Deanna, 'to throw in our lot with you. If we have to leave, and it's high time we did, we'd rather leave on our feet. We're ready to cooperate. What is it you want?'

A brief silence followed as the group digested her offer. Ben turned to Deanna. 'And what, may I ask, did YOU have in mind?'

'Well,' began Deanna, 'at first we believed your beating Sebastian at chess was a great idea. But then we thought it over. It's obvious that even if Sebastian were to win it would be no guarantee for our safety. There's too much to report. We'd be witnesses. We can't see Sebastian letting any of us off the hook. He's not trustworthy; he's a man, isn't he? We're certain now about his real intentions and we can see he's a raving lunatic . . . toying with us. Eventually he'll kill us all, he will.'

Olga sitting alone, finally put down her cup, rose from the table by the window, and walked over to join Deanna. Ben waited patiently for Deanna to continue.

'We must cooperate, that's it, isn't it?'

Tightening powerful shoulder muscles, Olga decided to enter the discussion.

'We can't fight Randolf,' said Olga, 'we've no weapons. We must help you find an escape route. The river's a possibility . . . Have you considered that? The problem is,' she shrugged, 'that it's too obvious and too heavily guarded. And after storms like the last, it can be dangerous.'

A soft noise drew their attention to the entrance. The Admiral had arrived and was waiting to be escorted to a table.

'I wonder what he heard?'

'I doubt much. Anyway, we have decided to go along with him. I knew him. I, er, met him in England. I'm pretty certain he's on the level,' said Ben, still troubled by the confusion surrounding the Admiral's role in the escapade.

'Okay,' said Deanna rising, 'he'd better be. We'll finish this later. I'm sorry but I don't trust him. Maybe we can talk it over in your room . . . later?'

As she made her way back to her table she passed the Admiral. He paused and with old-fashioned ceremony brought his heels together and bowed slightly. Deanna sniffed contemptuously and walked on. A waiter seated the Admiral at a table near the window.

'Good morning,' he announced cheerily, 'what a storm last night! It's nice and sunny now. A good omen.' The patient waiter was rewarded with a generous order. The Admiral's appetite had survived.

'Nothing like a good English breakfast,' he explained in slightly accented speech.

'So it seems,' agreed Maeve. The Admiral beamed at her. 'Incidentally, I couldn't help overhearing part of your conversation. I am not sure about those two. I know little, nothing, about them. They are most peculiar.'

'And what about you, Admiral dear?' asked Maeve, 'what

124

are we to believe? Who are you? You don't sound English. You appear to be working for Intelligence . . . but which? And, you recruit Ben . . . you once employed me . . . you send me here without telling me you'll be here. I ask you, WHAT are we to believe?' By now there was no stopping her. 'You send us off to Madagascar, and what do we find? I repeat . . . you are here. You said nothing about this to me in London.'

'I think you mentioned that,' murmured the Admiral.

'Now Randolf would have us believe you're in his pay. The whole business is VERY mysterious. It's time you laid your cards on the table.'

Maeve completing her speech, sat back. She had no great hopes for a reasonable explanation. She was not to be disappointed. The Admiral, serene and imperturbable, continued with his precise dissection of the grapefruit.

'Too many questions, Maeve,' he said, waving his spoon in the air, 'I'll expose my position later. There is much to tell. But not now, not now. We must be,' he gestured to the ceiling, 'circumspect.'

'That's a lot of help,' said Maeve, turning to stare at him, 'I had hoped for more this time.' The Admiral avoided her eyes.

'Well, what did you expect?' said Amelia, distinctly enough for the Admiral to hear. 'He's in Sebastian's pay. Playing a double game and filing this conversation in his mind. Reporting everything.'

The Admiral stiffening perceptibly, looked reproachfully at Amelia, but continued to concentrate on his grapefruit.

Ben drained his coffee, and shoved his chair back. He was, more than ever, unsure of the Admiral's position.

'I'd better get back to my room.'

'I think we should all go with Maeve and Amelia to the library,' said Sambo, 'and follow on there. Not here.'

All rose, nodded to the Admiral, and departed. The Admiral heaved himself up a polite inch as they passed by, then sank back in his seat and continued his disrupted breakfast.

125

The library was a large, pleasant room, with a long translucent ceiling. A large, oblong picture window overlooked the river. Bookcases lined walls from floor to ceiling. Berber carpet of light brown wool covered the floor. Comfortable, adjustable chairs were set at intervals around the circumference of the chamber. In the centre were several antique reading desks and chairs arranged in a star shaped fashion, producing a pleasing symmetrical pattern. Ben chose the set of chairs furthest from the window.

'Here,' he motioned, 'this'll do,' and gestured towards the chairs. He sank immediately into one facing the window.

'What do you think we can expect from Deanna?' asked Maeve.

'It's hard to say,' replied Ben. 'One can only really trust people who are in danger themselves. They must have a powerful motive to escape.'

'Those two, what a couple. I'd hate to rely entirely on them.'

'We have little choice . . . do we?'

'That female weightlifter, Olga, looks as if she'd like to eat us alive.'

'We'd better hear them out. They're not stupid and have a plausible reason for escape. We can't afford to pass up any help.'

Amelia walked out to find a phone. She dialled 'O'.

'Yes,' a voice answered.

'May I speak to Deanna?'

'I'll connect you.'

How obliging thought Maeve, and how easy to listen in.

The telephone hissed and then clicked.

'What?' There was no mistaking Olga's rasp.

'Is Deanna there?' The phone clattered. Maeve heard distant voices.

'What do you want?'

'We want to continue our, er, conversation,' Maeve spoke cautiously, mindful of eavesdroppers, but could think of no subtle way to convey her message, 'over a game of bridge.'

'Bridge?'

'Yes, in the library.' The penny dropped.

'Of course.' Maeve wondered if they were fooling anyone

with their clumsy subterfuge.

Half an hour later all were seated by one of the antique tables in library. Amelia, Maeve, Olga and Deanna held playing cards. Sambo, in the fifth chair, sat between Maeve and Deanna, ostensibly to observe.

☆   ☆   ☆

Ben swung open the door to his room. The monitor was blank, idle, awaiting instructions. He re-set the chess programme. The computer was its usual implacable self and beat him time after time with insolent ease. Frustrated with his inadequate performance, Ben realized ruefully that frustration had become a way of life. He struck harder and harder at the keyboard, but that did little good. He continued to play erratically, hoping, like all amateurs, that at the right time under the right circumstances, he'd pull something out of the bag. After all, despite predictions to the contrary by knowing friends, had he not reached the top in the world of business? He was a paid-up engineer and he'd won the first game. In the end Ben switched off the computer and headed for the toilet. Air-conditioned rooms increased the filtration efficiency of his kidneys.

☆   ☆   ☆

'Two no trumps,' said Deanna, not bothering to look at her cards.

'What?' barked Olga, 'your bid's nonsense.'

'I want,' whispered Deanna, glaring at her friend, 'I want things to look normal, you dope. Now shut up and don't interrupt.'

Olga lapsed into sullen silence. Irritated almost beyond endurance, she tightened her pectoral girdle muscle until the straps of her dress cut deeply into her flesh. Deanna, continuing with her pretence at bridge, leaned forward, glanced around, and spoke softly.

'Olga and I have come up with two alternative plans. We want you to consider them carefully, and meet us after the next game.'

127

13

The sun seemed to expand and change colour as it sank towards the horizon, leaving in its wake a smoky blue sky turning amber. A flight of birds winged across convoluted clouds and disappeared into the approaching night.

Outside the stronghold, off duty guards strolled about in leisurely fashion, smoking, and swapping endless grouches. Security dogs lay basking in the balmy evening air. Snatches of desultory conversation drifted upwards. All was peaceful.

Inside, formally clad guests had once more congregated in the drawing room. A casual observer would have seen a sophisticated assembly of smartly dressed men and women gathered in small groups, conversing amiably.

'So Ben, may we expect a repeat performance?' asked the Admiral, breezily. Ben, distracted by conflicting thoughts, stared absent-mindedly at his chief. He did not immediately respond.

'I'll give it a try,' he replied, 'while we're at it ... anything, anything at all, to report?'

'My dear boy, we MUST play our parts,' answered the inscrutable Admiral, with a trace of impatience, 'just carry on, and leave the rest to me.'

How was it possible to take the Admiral seriously? The uniforms, the cryptic comments, were they camouflage or the opposite, distracting plumage?

Ben's reply was cut short by a metallic click as a door opened. Sebastian and company entered. The attendants withdrew.

'Observe,' murmured Ben, 'our overlord and his pack. Take a look at the attendants. They're mercenaries, that's what. We'll have to reckon with them, a bunch of psychopaths and yobs. One thing they've in common is a love of guns, and they'll use them, given the slightest excuse.'

Sebastian approached and indicated with a pointing finger the direction of the dining room.

'Well,' exclaimed Sebastian when they were seated, 'how nice. Randolf,' he hailed the saturnine figure, 'why don't you order the wine.' Sebastian leaned forward, placing elegant elbows on the table with precision, so as not to disturb the cutlery.

'Marie my dear, see to it that our guests are comfortable.'

Marie smiled and turned to the uncomfortably reluctant guests.

'Good evening all,' she cooed, 'welcome . . . welcome again.'

Ben studied his former spouse with academic detachment. His attention was drawn to flashes of light emanating from her fingers. She was wearing on her right forefinger a large, elaborate ring encrusted with diamonds and rubies. With a slight shock he recognized the stones; they were his late mother's jewels. Marie had had them ostentatiously reset, an action which seemed, somehow, disloyal to his mother's memory. Marie is a scheming, mercenary woman, he thought, Sebastian deserves her. How did I ever get involved? I can't understand it.

'Ben,' said Marie coyly (she might have been reading his thoughts), 'I can't help thinking about the old days. You know . . . we were happy once. We could've carried on, if only . . . ,'

'If only I'd been a boring, socialite millionaire?'

'Don't be silly, dear boy. It wasn't money. You were rich enough, and I had more than enough of filthy lucre. It's that you worked so . . . laboriously. You left no time for me or for fun. You were so boringly conscientious and, well, old fogeyish. You never did anything spontaneously. And you hated my friends.'

'They were a bunch of brainless nincompoops,' replied Ben, defensively. To his consternation he observed an expression, which he identified as a salacious leer, crossing her face. He recognized her awakening passion. Hastily he

129

began to head her off.

'Marie, that was long ago,' he said, coldly. 'You and I are total strangers. It was bad enough when it ended, but it's over. You're better off without me, and vice versa. We had too little, nothing, in common. It was a mistake.' he finished, hoping his suppressed quiver of revulsion would not be misinterpreted.

Marie was not one to be easily deflected.

'Come on Ben, certain,' she grinned wickedly, 'parts of you are, well, remembered. Just like Sebastian's. In a way, we've not lost touch.'

Despite himself Ben shuddered. Marie predictably mistook his tremors for spasms of passion, and responded with an inviting grin.

Maeve, who had been observing Ben's discomfiture, decided it was time to intervene.

'Marie,' she said, in a voice clear enough to divert Marie's attention from the object of her desire. Marie removed her gaze from Ben.

'Yes?' she said, irritably.

'What's on the menu for tonight?'

Marie, displeased by the diversion, directed her attention briefly to Maeve.

'I never know in advance,' she snapped, 'Sebastian and Randolf concoct it. We've three chefs. Anyway I don't cook, I find it boring. I'm not really interested in food.'

☆   ☆   ☆

An ashen-faced Dean sat utterly still, lost amongst the guests, oblivious of his surroundings. An artery pulsated in his left temple. He was in the throes of a familiar, pounding headache; his sight was steadily becoming obscured by shapeless blotches; he believed himself to be dying. Waves of nausea swept through his body; sweat dripped from his forehead as he compressed his temples with his forefingers.

His antecedents had left him one additional, disagreeable legacy. From his mother's side he had inherited the curse of migraine. Many an occasion had been sabotaged by his unpredictable affliction. He sat now, isolated from events and fellow guests, concentrating only on suppressing waves of queasiness. He was managing reasonably well until his efforts were sabotaged by the arrival of strongly aromatic food. A final, powerful, wave of nausea engulfed him. He rose to his feet, lips compressed, and began to stagger on buckling knees towards the door.

'What is it?' exclaimed Sebastian as the Dean made off, 'What's wrong? Is it the food? You look like death. Sit down man, we'll get you an Alka Seltzer.'

'I must get out,' muttered the Dean, 'I must leave, don't try to stop me. I'm . . . ill.' He walked, sweating and haggard, towards the door. The rest of the diners contemplated his retreating back curiously. His exit was so sudden no-one offered assistance.

A loud moan from Randolf distracted their attention.

'Boiled fish, cabbage, broccoli, yegggghh,' Randolf clasped his aquiline old nose and pulled a face. 'I should be ill, not the Dean.'

Marie leaned over and patted his forearm.

'There, there, Randolf. It's not so bad. Try it.'

'It's all very well for you to talk. You've the insides of a tank,' growled Randolf disdainfully.

'Come on, be a good boy,' she cajoled, 'take the rough with the smooth.' And struck by her originality, she added helpfully. 'Every cloud has a silver lining . . . you won't get fat. And look at this occasion. Isn't it worth all the excitement? If it wasn't for Ben and Sebastian, life here would be er, boring. Why fuss about a little bland food?'

Randolf glowered at her. A brief flicker of disgust passed over his countenance. Regaining a measure of composure he began to pick at his food. After a few mouthfuls he turned to his favourite nephew.

'Sebastian,' he said, confidentially, lapsing into Afrikaans, 'look here . . . while this isn't the time or place to reveal my plans, I feel compelled to tell you something most important, something I've had on my mind for some time. You know I'm unconventional, so I'll proceed, anyway.' He glanced around the table. 'They can't understand us.'

'We are blood relatives, not so? Members of our own brotherhood. I can trust you with my life. When the events of the next few days have been played out, I want to show you my will which is entirely in your favour. You are my sole heir. After we've,' his voice dropped to a whisper, 'disposed of all the er, evidence.'

'Really Randolf, you're too generous,' responded Sebastian in halting Afrikaans, glancing at Marie and those guests who might be within earshot, 'No need to say more . . . I cannot thank you enough. I will try to live up to your expectations. You've done so much already.'

'I'm glad it's all working out,' replied Randolf, complacently.

Sebastian smiled at his brittle, old benefactor. The idea of untold wealth was certainly more than appealing. No doubt it would be marvellous to have as much as one could possibly spend . . . so many places to visit . . . so many things to do . . . so many women. He glanced at Marie who was watching with rapt interest. Not understanding the language she stared at Sebastian, her eyes huge and round. Something was happening. In her usual imperceptive fashion she misread Sebastian's expression. Casting aside all thoughts of Ben, she switched her attention to Sebastian, the cool, the all-powerful; surely she had chosen well? Unquestionably he was hers.

More than ever, Ben, who had heard nearly every word, felt betrayed, estranged – an intruder. These, his blood relatives had ostracized him, totally. Was this what Sebastian meant? For a few moments he reverted to the fatherless boy in South West Africa. This dreadful bunch of madmen, once part of his family, were excluding him. In their eyes he did not exist. Why did this trouble him, he wondered, surely he was better off without them?

A glance from Maeve's warm brown eyes dissipated his melancholy reverie. Well, I'm NOT alone, he thought, she's all I want, all I need. I'm the lucky one. They have nothing like her. He gazed fondly at Maeve. It's a bloody mess with Sebastian. I'll never understand this nonsense with Randolf.

The Dean, his complexion normal, apparently refreshed, re-entered the room, and regained his seat.

'Black coffee, please,' he asked quietly.

Dinner was over and once more Ben and Sebastian found themselves by their consoles. Ben to the right and Sebastian to the left. Ben could not stay the slight tremor in his hands. He refused coffee because he had no wish to alarm his supporters by the nervous rattling of the cup in its saucer.

Sebastian, on the other hand, was his old self, casual and cool. Exhilarated by the information from Randolf, he sat back and elaborately stifled an invented yawn. His recent defeat seemed to have been forgotten. Once again Randolf reached for the chess pieces and raised his bony old fists.

'Which hand?' To Sebastian.

'Right.'

Randolf held up a white chess piece. After a brief, confident pause, Sebastian made his opening gambit.

Twelve moves on, an hour later, the guests were beginning to show signs of strain. Ben stared fixedly at the flickering black and white squares. He rubbed his eyes in an attempt to ease their burning discomfort. His moves had been for naught. Sebastian, uncannily revitalized, had him on the run. Many pieces had been lost. Try as he might, Ben was unable to gain the initiative. For a brief period he had managed to mount a counter attack, only to be beaten back. Those in the audience who had been 'sacrificed', sat glumly waiting for the end of the game.

There seemed to be no chance that Sebastian might make an unforced error. The skill and ease with which he played was unnerving. But Ben would not yield. Maeve and the Admiral, side by side, displayed faces etched in tension.

'Check,' said Sebastian finally, as he took Ben's remaining rook.

Ben squinted bleakly at the board. It seemed to him that he could divine Sebastian's moves and intentions more readily than his own. Fatigue and frustration combined to disrupt his play. Oh, hell, he thought, I might as well go for broke, and moved his remaining knight to threaten the opposing queen. For a few minutes there was no response.

Overblown with confidence, Sebastian ignored the impudent knight. Moving a pawn towards Ben's king, he repeated the warning more emphatically, 'Check.'

It was hopeless. Sebastian gave no quarter. The opportunity never came.

'Checkmate,' said Sebastian finally, grinning through tightly twisted lips.

Randolf stirred and leaned forward, 'Well done, a magnificent game. I enjoyed every minute. Marie, my dear I wonder, now that the excitement is over, if you would like to entertain our friends with some music?'

'Did you know,' he addressed Ben, 'that Marie had become an accomplished pianist?'

Ben was too despondent to care. Nothing about his ex-spouse was of the slightest interest. For all he cared she might have been a musical astronaut. But he had gained time.

'I wonder if you'd think it very rude of me,' he said. 'I must get some sleep. Perhaps another time.'

Without waiting for a reply he left the console and walked out of the room. Maeve, Amelia, and Sambo taking their cue, followed. Randolf, not the least put out by the sudden exodus, raised his chin and indicated to the Admiral and the Dean to remain.

Two servants rolled in a Steinway grand. Marie adjusted the seat and began an imitation of a Chopin étude. Randolf, eyes blissfully closed, sighed with pleasure.

'A singular predicament,' murmured George the Dean, nudging the Admiral.

'What is?' asked the drowsing Admiral.

'Our position,' whispered the Dean, 'I don't want to hear this racket. I happen to like music.'

'We must listen.'

The Dean groaned.

'You and I, my friend,' said the Admiral, 'are in a BIND. We must listen and be natural. But, don't despair, I may have a surprise or two of my own.'

The Dean began to experience twinges of recurring migraine as he struggled to decode Marie's music. The Dean wondered if he should declare his hand. Lifelong caution prevailed. He was unsure of the Admiral's identity. Yet his credentials seemed impeccable. Timing was everything, disclose too much too soon, and all might be lost.

Maeve lay fully clothed on her bed, her head propped up by pillows, staring at the television. Amelia turned on her side and faced the wall.

'Goodnight, I'm going to sleep.'

Ben undressed and walked naked to the bathroom. He ran a hot bath. A melancholy string quartet was playing on the radio. The music seemed appropriate. Blissfully he lowered himself into the scaldingly hot water. Finally, with a grunt of sheer pleasure he submerged beneath the soothing liquid. He held his breath for several seconds and then surfaced ike a breeching whale. As his head emerged he thought he heard a soft knock on the outer door. He groaned and re-submerged, but when he came up he heard the knock distinctly. A great reluctance to leave his warm haven overcame him. Again the gentle knock. He thought he heard a voice calling. He rose from the bath dripping water, drew on a towelling gown and walked, grumbling to the door.

Maeve stood poised on his threshold. Before he could utter a sound she moved in and shut the door behind her. She came swiftly towards him, held him in her ams, and drew his face down.

'What are you doing?' protested Ben, rolling over, 'What time is it?'

'It's three am darling. Time I got back to my room. You need some rest.'

'I've had a lovely sleep, come on, come back . . . please.'

'I think I'd better go. We'll do this again, when we're out of this mess.'

'We may never get out. Please stay, I'll behave.'

'That's just it, I don't want you to. For your sake and mine, you must get some sleep.'

Ben reached over and drew her down. Her kisses, with softly parted lips, were delicious . . . alive. With a light laugh Maeve pulled free and walked to the door. She turned, blew him a kiss, and was gone. Ben, happily relaxed, curled up under the sheets and immediately fell into a deep stupor.

It seemed that he had only just gone to sleep when he was awakened by persistent knocking. He threw back the covers and slipped into his dressing gown. He walked, barefoot, swiftly and hopefully towards the door.

'Oh, it's you. I thought . . . come in. What time is it?' The disappointment in his voice surprised his visitor.

'Sorry about this.' Sambo sauntered in, located the luxurious Eames chair, and lowered himself into it, carefully positioning his feet on the matching footstool.

'It's seven.' Sambo looked about the room, glanced at Ben. He seemed to make up his mind.

'I've been doing a bit of thinking. You don't know much about me, do you? I'd better declare my hand. You've probably guessed anyway. I've dropped enough hints.'

'The CIA?'

'Right on. I was sent to follow you and to assist in this operation.'

'What exactly is the operation?'

'You really don't know?' Sambo paused, looking directly into Ben's eyes.

'I've a decent idea,' replied Ben cautiously.

'Let me explain. Your brother Sebastian isn't just after your blood. He's killing two birds with one stone. He's getting you and, at the same time, protecting his interests in Madagascar.'

'But he's drawing attention to himself . . . capturing us, you especially. It doesn't make sense.'

'It was inevitable. We, all of us, were already on his trail. What could he do? He improvized and waylaid us before we could locate him and report back.'

Ben sat looking out of the window at the distant jungle. The morning mist was settling like a shimmering, twisting veil in a breeze over the crowded tree tops.

'Sebastian's refining nuclear material. No-one believed a private individual could do it. But they hadn't reckoned with his drive or his greed. He hired East German technicians, and managed to set up a nuclear refining plant. His 'servants' are mostly technicians.'

'Who buys the stuff? How is it distributed? You needn't answer. I guess there are plenty of customers. Iraq?'

'Everything was going well, until he and Randolf began to get overconfident and made it known to a larger Middle Eastern block where they could buy the stuff.

'And, on the back burner of his mind, he retained the idea of revenge.'

'I rather gathered that.'

'I see now you had no idea Sebastian was here. That's incredible.' Sambo shook his head. 'I could see you were staggered by the amazing coincidence when you found Sebastian, the Admiral, and the Dean here. It was no coincidence. Your journey here was in part arranged by Randolf and Sebastian, with the help of the CIA and the Admiral, who incidentally, is definitely working for the Brits.

'Sebastian believes he's bought his way into the right places. But what has taken place has been with the full knowledge and connivance of both our intelligence services. THEY LET IT HAPPEN.'

'And you knew this all along?' Ben was not quite as indignant as he sounded. 'And Maeve? How does she fit in? Is she paid to 'cooperate' with me?'

'Maeve is a loyal agent and she's on the level with you. She's a terrific woman, and you're a lucky sod.'

'I agree.'

'The Dean, odd though he may seem, is an agent. He set you on the road to the Admiral. Remember the reunion dinner at Magdalene? I heard all about that from my Control. Your joining the Admiral's outfit was the result of the Dean's and the Admiral's cooperation.'

'Your Control told you this?'

'Well, of course.'

'All along I've believed the Admiral had to be genuine. So far he's not been much help. Just drops hints. It WAS a shock to find him here, dolled up like a Christmas tree.'

'He's certainly not what Sebastian thinks he is.' Sambo shut his eyes and paused for a long time. Ben wondered if he was drifting off.

'There's one more thing. I've not been able to contact my control. I don't know if they can do anything for us.'

The telephone chirped as if clearing it's throat, and then gave out a familiar warble.

'Hullo,' said Ben into the microphone.

'It's me, Maeve. Amelia and I are off to breakfast. Will you join us?'

When they arrived in the breakfast room they found the Dean and the Admiral sipping coffee. The Dean had completely recovered from his recent torment and had regained much of his lost unctuousness.

14

'What is it?' snapped Randolf. No-one, not even a favourite nephew, disturbed his siesta without incurring immense displeasure. Age had transformed sleep into a blissful escape from reality to which he returned with reluctance.

Sebastian shifted his weight from one foot to the other like a schoolboy with a full bladder. Dreading the interview, he had decided on an oblique approach. This seldom worked with Randolf, who liked to get to the point.

'May I have a seat?' Randolf replied with a grudging, imperceptible, nod.

'We've been getting worrisome intelligence.'

'What do'you mean?'

'Just what I said. The time has come for me to clear up some troubling business.'

Randolf leaned back in his bed, his face impassive, unfriendly. Sebastian recognized danger signs, but continued with his prepared brief.

'Randolf . . . let's see, how shall I begin? I've always had unbounded affection and admiration for you. I've always sought your approval before embarking on any new venture. I've tried my best to emulate your example. No project has been undertaken without consulting you. Our lives have been inexorably interlaced . . . ever since my childhood in South West. Everything I am, I owe to you.'

Randolf flicked his tongue in and out. Sebastian found the mannerism disgusting, but persisted.

'We have,' he said, 'a problem, more than one. This is it. You are in the habit of paying scant attention to my advice and opinions. If we are to continue on together I must ask you to modify your attitude. We should define ground rules.'

139

Randolf continued his accurate imitation of a basilisk stare.

'For instance, when I mention danger signals, you're hardly interested. Do you think I'd disturb you if I did not consider the matter important, serious? What really aggravates me is that you expect me to do exactly as you wish, but without any reciprocity on your part. You don't even bother to pretend to pay any heed to my opinions. You treat me as if I were a child. Nearly all decisions which also concern me and my future are made by you and you alone, without any consultation, whatever.'

'I think you've made your point,' said Randolf, dryly, licking his parched old lips.

Sebastian ignored the sarcasm. Anger begot courage. He continued, bolstered by his self-feeding indignation.

'You may be convinced that you know what's best, and that because you act for our common good, you need not discuss anything with me; you believe only you are competent.' Sebastian was by now in full stride and gathering momentum. 'Sometimes, when you feel so inclined, you might, casually, mention your intentions, sort of in passing. But in the end all important matters are decided by you . . . and only then, when it's a fait accompli, do you tell me. I'm tired of your condescending attitude.'

'Finished?' asked Randolf with slight smile.

Fuming with resentment Sebastian shoved his chair back, and made to leave.

'Hold on, hold on, hold on,' said Randolf, 'just a minute. Let's look at things a little more calmly and rationally. To begin with, have I made any mistakes?'

'That's not the point,' Sebastian, vacillating, sank back into the chair.

'Well, what DO you want? What do you expect? I can't run this operation like a committee.'

'I knew you'd say that.'

Randolf, momentarily silenced, stared thoughtfully at his disgruntled nephew.

'Anyway,' he said after a while, 'what did you mean by 'worrisome intelligence'?'

Wrapped in a cocoon of irritation, Sebatian made an effort to speak calmly. He began again in a more measured tone.

'Lately, because you're so obsessed with getting even with Ben, you've not been paying attention to the faxes I've been leaving on your desk.'

'I see . . . which ones, specifically, do you mean?'

'The ones from our South African connections. Certain people in other countries are making enquiries about nuclear waste disposal. Need I say more?'

'Aha, who? Anyone we know? The CIA, MI5, the KGB? Or is it the same bunch of nervous twits in the South African cabinet? The 'verligtes', the moderates, those idiots who worry about world opinion? You know as well as I that there's always trouble brewing in that country. We get daily alarm signals from someone over there. I've learned to ignore false alarms.

'Look at us, where would we be if we let that sort of nonsense interfere? As for the faxes, I HAVE been reading them,' explained Randolf, with mild protest. 'Anyway, our association with South African interests has limits. Nothing political, just plain business. They can't afford to, er, deal with us openly, and we accept that. So, who are they?'

'I've no idea who's behind this,' said Sebastian, his anger suppressed, 'but you must realize that sooner or later something will surface. No matter how well we've covered our tracks, some nosy official will start sniffing along the right trail. Some political body will get wind of it. If you have a contingency plan, for God's sake let me know.'

'Look here my boy,' said Randolf, 'if by chance we had to close up shop I wouldn't worry. We've more than enough money in safe banks around the world. We can, at a moment's notice shut down, pack up, and be on our way. You could resume your life in almost any country.

'And, furthermore, if you believe I pay no attention to your advice, you're wrong my dear fellow. I may not SEEM to listen, but I do. When I make decisions, I do take into account your counsel. It's just that I'm not, er, a demonstrative person.

'I have explained that all my hopes and aspirations are pinned on you, you, my only true, blood relative. We have our bonds, as I said. Why do you think I've been so ruthless with your brother? He's not, and never was, one of us. He's like the rest of the family. I've told you you are to be my only heir. The rest is of no consequence.'

Randolf's evident sincerity began to allay Sebastian's doubts and thus he turned his attention to the second matter which had been bothering him, namely Ben. This now seemed unexpectedly difficult. He had, so far, blotted from his mind any trace of conscience concerning his brother's fate. Lately memories of a brief boyhood shared had begun to occupy his mind. The past was not as easily obliterated as he had thought. Blood, in the end, counted for something. Somehow, he had to strike a more sympathetic chord in his chilling uncle.

For all his worldliness Randolf was curiously vulnerable to flattery. Sebastian had long recognized this aspect of his uncle's pernicious personality. There had been times when he had manipulated Randolf shamelessly, and successfully. At this point his emerging conscience dictated he use any method, including cajolery, to achieve his purpose. For a brief, transient period, he became a different, altruistic being.

'Randolf,' he began, 'I know you are, beneath that stern exterior, a kind man. I've only to recall all you've done for Marie and myself. But . . . '

'But what?' frowned Randolf, alerted.

'About Ben . . . '

'What about Ben?'

'Well, to tell the truth, I'm not at ease with your plans for him. I am . . . I WAS . . . I am his brother. Like it or not, I can't accept doing away with him as readily as you do. Look here,' Sebastian, entangled by the emotion attached to his role as Ben's advocate, allowed his eyes to glisten, 'we've achieved what we set out to do. We've had our revenge with Ben. Surely we can call it quits? You've been brilliantly successful, and in full control of our fates. As you said, we're all millionaires many times over, all thanks to you. Now's the time to be magnanimous . . . to reach out, to become, a great man.'

'Sebastian, my dear chap,' objected Randolf, wearily, 'let me enlighten you about my philosophy and please, don't start accusing me of being condescending. Money is not everything. Power is. We lack power, real power. We've been underdogs far too long. In this age, as in every one for the past thousand years, money has brought power. I tell you money IS power. We haven't reached that pinnacle yet. To do so we need plausible credentials. If we leave any evidence lying about, anything that might be misconstrued, we'd be risking everything we've gained. Nothing must stand in our way.'

Sebastian listened with one ear. How to save his wretched brother? Randolf had woven Ben into a grandiose stratagem.

'What has all this to do with Ben?'

Randolf leaned back, arms folded across his chest, and continued, disregarding Sebastian's concern.

'Let me give you some insight.' Randolf wrinkled his beak of a nose as he marshalled his thoughts. Sebastian, detecting signs of incipient reminiscing, let his mind go blank.

'In my younger days, while toadying up to the men of the business world, as well as to self-seeking polticians, I used to wonder at their arrogance . . . how did they get there? I realized that it was money, money, and money. Influence? Oh, yes, but also, credibility, all of which were factors. But my boy, money is the surest, quickest, way to achieve substantial power. Show me a successful politician and I'll show you a large bank balance.

'But, to get back to my development. I thought, if those men could achieve success, so could I, who, and I say this without false modesty, had twice their intelligence and drive.

'Sebastian, the next chapter will be our inescapable climb to power. I repeat . . . we cannot afford to leave hostile witnesses behind. Ben and his lot have crossed my path. If it means his death . . . so be it.'

Sebastian, to his credit, persisted. For the sake of lingering scruples he had to save Ben, or at the very least, try. Ironically it had become his distasteful duty to rescue a hated brother, no matter how much his endeavours annoyed his mentor.

'That's all very well; why can't we carry on, without doing away with Ben?' He spoke evenly, trying to sound conciliatory, 'I would like to enjoy the fruits of your labours with a clear conscience. I ask you, for the last time, stop this deadly game before it's too late. Come on Randolf, show mercy . . . .' His impassioned advocacy was rewarded by a cold, indifferent stare.

'And, by the way,' asked Sebastian, paling at the thought, 'have you ever actually killed anyone?'

'What do you think?' replied Randolf, amused, 'Of course not.'

'Why start now? It's a bit gruesome even to think of killing anyone in cold blood, let alone a close relative.'

'My dear Sebastian, life is short and mostly excruciatingly dull. As for me, I accept that money won't buy longevity. So why not play, while I'm still around, for genuine thrills? The ultimate thrill must be to be able to order the execution of one's enemy.'

'Ben's a human being. Forget the past.'

Randolf, ignoring Sebastian's protest, continued with his life's theme.

'Why work hard, only to find there's no time left for enjoyment? Don't you see that this game as you call it, is in fact the exercise of absolute power?'

'Randolf,' said Sebastian recklessly, frustrated by the old man's intransigence, 'I thought it was money and power you were after, in a more normal sense. Revenge is for lesser mortals. This game isn't worthy of you. It's cruel to no purpose. You've scared Ben and his lot shitless. Isn't that enough?'

Randolf sat, his mouth working, staring angrily at Sebastian until the latter lowered his eyes.

'Quite a speech. I had no idea you harboured such humane feelings.'

Sebastian, surprised by his own outburst, shrugged and turned away. Randolf was implacable.

'Before you go,' said Randolf, coldly, 'I'm expecting visitors shortly, in air transports, to remove their bodies.'

'Bodies?' Sebastian, although fully aware of Randolf's intentions, was nevertheless, horrified.

'Don't be so surprised. We CAN NOT go soft. We'll have to get rid of the evidence. This is the most efficient way.'

'So you will go ahead?' asked Sebastian, soberly.

'Yes, no more discussion. My mind is made up.'

Sebastian realized that being his brother's advocate was a

dangerous waste of time. Bloody, bloody Ben, if only he knew the trouble he had caused.

An hour later Sebastian, having set aside the battle of his conscience, was seated in an armchair in his study. He reached over to lift the telephone receiver.

Maeve and Amelia were dozing before the television screen where a plastic hostess chattered on about the lives of cocainized rock stars. The inane commentary had lulled them into somnolence. The phone by Maeve's side rang.

'Hello,' she said, surfacing.

'Amelia?'

'No, it's Maeve.'

'Good. This's Sebastian. Come right away, don't be seen.'

'I'll try.'

Maeve rose carefully, and glanced at her sleeping companion. Satisfied, she donned a pink, towelled robe, and left the room. A quick peek around and she strode swiftly in the direction of Sebastian's quarters.

'Sebastian watched her approach across the deep carpet and motioned her to sit. Maeve slid into a seat opposite. Outwardly calm and poised, she crossed her legs with a tidy gesture, and smoothed out some invisible wrinkles from her bath robe. Only the rhythmical swaying of her foot betrayed her unease.

'It's time to have a talk.' Sebastian, unconsciously aping Randolf, sat back, opposing his fingertips, and shut his eyes.

Rounding a corner into the library, the Admiral came upon a curious scene. He had stumbled onto an assembly of furtive plotters. Deanna was holding forth.

Olga, a few seats away, sniffed grumpily, unhappy with her secondary role. It had been her lifelong conviction that her powerful bulk was sufficient evidence of a 'presence'. She was not accustomed to being ignored.

As the Admiral approached, Deanna looked up, compressed her lips, and ceased her exposition.

'Look here,' began the Admiral, without preamble, 'there's no time for finesse. I have to interrupt your meeting.' He waved a silencing forefinger at Deanna who was about to protest.

'My contention,' he said, as he seated himself on the nearest chair, 'is that you have no option but to pool resources with me. I must emphasize, time is not on our side.' His audience looked afresh at him. He was impressively decisive. Olga suspended her sniffing.

'Whatever Deanna and Olga have to say must be considered,' he said, 'but only in conjunction with other alternatives. The very fact that I'm talking to you, conspiring with you, exposes you and myself, to danger. I decided,' he said, 'a while ago, that I had to take action. I've been lying doggo, gathering information. You have to believe me. Ben knows me . . . from London. And I have knowledge about him and his family. I'm on your side, absolutely.'

All the while he was speaking, Deanna and Olga continued to stare at him. When he finished they exchanged knowing looks.

'You HAVE changed,' grunted Olga, 'what's happened to you? All action, why? Are you playing games? Your manner, your attitude is, different. Who are we to believe?'

'You have no choice,' replied the Admiral, coolly, 'you have to trust me. My manner as you call it, was assumed for a purpose. It was for the benefit of Randolf and company. They know me in my intelligence role. It's their belief that I'd been bought.'

'Marvellous,' muttered Deanna.

'My position's been complicated, to put it mildly,' said the Admiral, 'but I will, when the time is ripe, tell you everything. I repeat, you'll have to trust me, and I'll have to trust you. Anyway, I'd hardly be showing you a part of my real self, if I didn't wish to escape.

'My main purpose is to put paid to Sebastian and Randolf's enterprises. But I cannot do it on my own. Don't be fooled by promises of wealth. Sebastian's playing cat and mouse with you. I assure you he has not the slightest intention of letting anyone get away.'

'What do you want of us?' demanded Deanna.

'We must work together as a team.'

'I think, Admiral, that that is our consensus,' said Ben, dryly.

'Well, will you follow me?' The Admiral looked around.

'I don't know.' Deanna spoke slowly, echoing everyone's reservations. 'I find it hard to accept that he could do us all in, and then carry on as if nothing had happened.'

'Look here,' interjected Olga, 'you could just as easily be trying to trap us for Randolf. How do we know you're not their . . . agent provocateur?'

'Oh dear,' sighed the Admiral, 'how to convince you? You have NO choice. What else can you do? Sit tight until the end? Think about it.'

Maeve had made up her mind. She turned to face the Admiral.

'Okay,' she said, decisively, 'you're on. I worked with you in England. I'll vouch for you. He is okay.' She turned to Ben who signalled agreement with a brief nod.

Deanna and Olga shrugged and reluctantly concurred. But they continued to regard the Admiral with ill disguised suspicion. Deanna sat in surly silence, deferring to the others. Olga remained bolt upright. She opened her mouth several times, thought the better of it, and remained silent.

'All right . . . it's settled then? Let's begin with a review of your plans,' said the Admiral, assuming command. Maeve hesitated for a fraction of a second.

'One of our ideas,' she explained, 'was to find out if Sebastian was actively using the central computer. You know, not simply relying on it to run the works. Was he using it as it could be used?

'The other idea was to tap into it, to get useful information, and manipulate it ourselves.'

'Not bad,' said the Admiral, in control and ignoring the latent hostility surrounding him, 'it's a bit complex. Too many variables. What else had you considered?' He faced Ben.

Ben began slowly,

'I thought because Sebastian and Randolf are preoccupied with plans for revenge, we'd gain time by continuing with the match. More time to design an escape.'

'That's better. Let's go over what we know,' said the

Admiral, 'what are the facts?' He leaned forward. 'Sebastian, Randolf, and Marie are our identifiable enemy. Which one's the real boss . . . the brains? Does it matter? Everyone seems to defer to Randolf. He gives orders, and as far as I can tell, they're obeyed. As for the mercenaries we must reckon that they're loyal.

'As for you two ladies,' he faced Olga and Deanna, 'we know little about you. Are you really two wandering misfits? What do we know about you?'

Deanna bridled but refused to speak.

The Admiral seemed to come to a decision and continued, 'I agree we carry on with the match. It's our turn to play games. We plan while we play. Any other suggestions?'

'Sambo,' Ben turned to his normally cheery companion, 'how about taking a closer look at the exterior? Talk to the guards. With a bit of luck you might get useful information. If they're like most mercenaries they're bound to be nitwits, dangerous and stupid. Do a dumb 'nigger' act. D'you think you could manage?'

'Sure . . . ' replied Sambo, almost confidently, 'why not? Maybe you ought to rough me up a bit outside the courtyard? Convince them I'm your lackey?' Sambo, warming to his theme, smiled with down-turned lips.

'Don't,' cautioned Amelia, 'get too cocky. Better to be scared than dead. If I know you, you'll get carried away and start singing Ole Man Ribber.'

'No need to worry . . . I am scared all right,' said Sambo, 'but I'll manage.'

The Admiral gazed contemplatively at Maeve.

'Maeve,' he asked quietly, 'why did you visit Sebastian shortly after you arrived?'

Ben's jaw dropped. He stared first at the Admiral and then at Maeve. She seemed unruffled. How did the Admiral know that? The muscles in his cheeks rippled. He became, in an instant, a lovesick, jealous swain, unreasoning and unreasonable.

'Perhaps you'd better,' said Ben, very quietly, 'explain.' He felt suddenly more uncomfortable than he could remember. He was not sure he wanted to hear her revelation.

Maeve's smile faded. She felt drained. It seemed an

eternity to Ben before she spoke.

'Like the Admiral I had a role to play. But it's over. You,' she faced the Admiral, 'know about me. You set it up.' She turned to Ben, 'It's all in my dossier.' Maeve took a deep breath, 'I came here specifically to gather information for British Intelligence.'

Ben began to experience a slight feeling of relief. But he remained perplexed and stared unblinkingly at Maeve.

'Go on,' he said, his mouth dry, 'let's hear it.'

'It's quite a long story. When I was a student in London, I had scads of friends. One in particular interested me. He wasn't a student. At first I was put off by his self-assurance. But in a few months we became good friends. I knew he had girlfriends in other countries. I believed that I was 'safe'. I wasn't ready for any form of commitment at that stage of my career. Well, it didn't quite work out like that. In a while we became closer and closer. We spent much time in each other's company. I took him to meet my family. He went overboard over me and began to press me for a more lasting relationship. Something about him worried me. I couldn't place it. I didn't know a great deal about him, or his job.

'I tried to move away, but he became quite persistent, demanding, and sent me presents, flowers, poetry. In the end he hinted strongly that without me his life was not worth living. I began to weaken; was I really in love? Looking back now it's clear I was not. My parents couldn't abide him. Naturally that made me rebellious.

'Despite great misgivings we married. In a very short time unpleasant aspects of his character that I had noticed but submerged, began to surface. He started to flirt at parties, began to talk down to me, ignored my opinions, you know, the usual, unkind behaviour of insecure men. I kept hoping that things would improve.

'It became obvious that our tastes were quite, quite, different. In the beginning, before we were married, he pretended he enjoyed classical music, plays, walks in the country . . . the usual romantic stuff. But it was fake. What he wanted was to control me, to dominate me. When he couldn't, he became abusive. I lost all confidence in myself. Still, I hoped things would improve. I hadn't entered marriage with the idea that it was a short term experiment.'

149

Ben sat in silence. He felt intensely distressed for Maeve, but at the same time, absolutely wretched. Why am I being so unreasonable? He thought, I have no right to sit in judgement. She's talking about the past. What's it matter? She's still my Maeve.

'To cut a long story short,' said Maeve, her hands folded on her lap, her eyes unseeing, 'I tried to save the marriage by having a child. We had a boy. When he was three he was killed in a motorway accident with my husband driving. He had been drinking. I,' Maeve paused, 'never got over that. When I felt strong enough I told him that it was over. There was nothing left. He made no answer, just walked out of my life, forever, I thought.

'When I surfaced from my depression I decided to make a life for myself, alone. I was recommended by friends to the Admiral.' Maeve looked to the burly figure. 'The Admiral gave me a job, partly to train recruits, and partly to act as a sort of administrative assistant. I myself underwent the usual agent's training.

'One day, the Admiral asked me to do a special assignment. It was then that I learned that my ex-husband was in Madagascar. Then the Admiral told me about Ben, a new recruit who was being sent to Madagascar, and why. When I saw Ben I was staggered.' Tiny, pearly, tears trickled down her cheeks. Maeve made no effort to stem them. She turned to look at Ben, her eyes red and wet.

'You see, it's not just your life that's complicated. I'm sorry but I can't undo my mistakes.'

'It was Sebastian, wasn't it?' Ben had never felt so devastated nor so miserable in all his existence. 'I don't know what to say. I would like to be alone for a while.'

And he walked away.

'Go on,' said the Admiral, gently, disregarding Ben's departure, 'tell us the rest.'

'I had a tremendous struggle making up my mind about coming along on this trip. I knew it would be incredibly tangled and dangerous, and that was before Ben. Now, it's . . . I don't know how to put it.

'When we arrived I could see that Sebastian was flabbergasted. He was amazed that I was in Ben's group. He didn't know what to make of it. I had had no contact with him for five years. I could sense that he was frantic with curiosity.

'So, when Sebastian sent a message to visit him, I simply had to comply. He wanted to know what my business was, and I was determined, somehow, to find out if I had made a mistake when I left him. Now it seems my worst fears have come true. All you have seen and heard about Sebastian is true. He must have thought I'd go to any lengths to get him back. He's incredibly conceited. He had thought that I had come along to re-join him.

'I had to pretend to be interested. All I've succeeded in doing is to ruin the best thing that's ever happened to me.'

'What are you going to do?' asked Amelia.

'I must wait and see what Ben decides. In any case we must get on with our plans. Sebastian is bad news. We're none of us safe. Not for a minute.'

The Admiral shook his shaggy head and, smiling encouragingly, encircled Maeve's shoulders in a bear hug.

'I knew I had chosen well.'

Maeve's shoulders sagged and, for the first time, she burst into tears. She sobbed, helplessly, and copiously. 'Oh, Ben, oh, Ben. What am I to do?'

15

A giant television glowed with brilliant colours before Sebastian and Marie, reclining hedonistically on an art deco, king sized bed. A video recorder hummed in the background. On the screen a detailed and exruciatingly boring pornographic film struggled to find a plot amongst the explicitly depicted genitalia. Sebastian averted his gaze with reluctance.

'I wish you'd watch, Marie,' he said, 'I ordered this specially for you.'

'Oh, come on, you know I prefer the real thing. Nothing on that silly screen is the least bit erotic. It's unreal and bloody boring. And,' she added, 'we've done it all. I mean look at their silly expressions and all those giant, ridiculous, props . . . I can't see why you bother. I suppose it's different for men, hairtrigger responses and all that.'

Marie, peering through half-moon glasses as she lay propped up on satin pillows, resumed her reading. Sebastian returned to his scrutiny of the events on the screen. Suddenly, in the twinkling of an eye, whips were flailing about. All characters somehow changed into outfits of narrow, glistening, black plastic straps. The screen seemed to be occupied by a group of agitated black beetles in search of a gang bang. Sebastian, believing he might have missed a subtle change in the script, watched intently.

'I think it's time Randolf got on with it,' said Marie, not looking up, 'he's holding up our plans.'

'Umm, I suppose it IS getting tedious,' murmured Sebastian, eyeing the television, 'my problem is that I don't know exactly what he's got in mind . . . even for us. The chess match is a bore. He's making an awful fuss about it.

Who cares if Ben or I wins? One thing, I know is he's got other, far ranging, ambitions. (And so have I, he thought.) Sometimes I'm convinced he's bonkers, and wouldn't mind if we all got killed.'

'Don't be ungrateful. He wouldn't harm us, we're his relatives.'

'So's Ben,' said Sebastian. Diverted by her remarks he swung his attention away from the screen. 'In case you've forgotten, he is my brother. I wonder if we aren't a bit too ready to blame others, like Ben, for our misfortunes?'

'Perhaps, but no matter.' A new thought struck Marie. 'What if they escape?'

'It's not possible. This place is a fortress. There's jungle all around. They'd never get away.'

Sebastian, exasperated by Marie's distracting chatter, switched off the recorder just as a giant male member in tight close up appeared, waggling rhythmically like a conductor's baton.

'It's fortunate,' he said, grimly, 'that I do dislike Ben or I'd have a problem dealing with Randolf's philosophy. By the way,' Sebastian digressed, 'what was it like being married to my brother? There are times when it irks me to think of you two at it. I'm not the least jealous of your other lovers. But for some reason I can't abide the thought of you and my brother in bed. Maybe it's too near to home? I've never really asked you about your marriage to Ben.'

'What, exactly, d'you mean?'

'You know . . . everything. How did you get together? Was he good in bed?' Sebastian grimaced. 'I don't like thinking about it, but I'm morbidly curious. It's a bit like incest.'

'Oh, grow up. He was a husband, who by chance was your sibling. Darling, he was nowhere near as good as you. Is that what you wanted to hear?'

'Tell me something about how you met?' Marie peered at him over her glasses, sighed, and dropped her book.

'When I met Ben I was young,' she said, 'and sexy. So I was told. I had lots of mooning young men. The more they adored me the more they bored me. And I wasn't happy at home. My parents were divorced, my father several times. My mother had gone off to America. I never saw her again. I

153

was sick of the girlfriends and stepmothers who were either my age, or younger.

'But, I enjoyed living with father. It was a life of luxury. We had a large mansion in the country, and apartments all over ... New York, Monte Carlo, I forget where. We travelled a lot but I became more and more bored. I let one or two witless young men into my pants, mostly because I was curious. I became steadily more dejected.' Marie let out a long sigh. 'Nothing seemed to last.'

'Then one day everything changed. I found Ben, and I knew I'd discovered my man. It happened at a party on a country estate given by some Egyptian friend, Fakry something or other, I can't remember. He was lecturer in Arabic. From that day on my life changed.'

Sebastian rolled over and fixed Marie with an unwinking stare.

'Tell me.'

'Well,' continued Marie, 'at that party, crammed with the usual brainless guards officers, debutantes, and poofy ballet dancers, Ben stood out like a beacon. He was aloof, and didn't notice me. Worst of all he snubbed me when I tried to strike up a conversation with him. That did it. I did my level best to get him to dance. I was absolutely infuriated when, after practically dragging him into the floor, he seemed only interested in getting away. I remember it was a rumba. I danced and pranced around him, making a right idiot of myself – I'm a very good dancer – ,' added Marie, 'but he just stood there, embarrassed. I damn well hurt my back swinging my hips. He made a ridiculous excuse about having to go off and deliver a message. And the bugger stalked off. I was livid. What's more, an hour later I saw him stuffing himself with food, a simpering deb on each arm. I decided then that I was going to get him.'

Sebastian reached for the popcorn. Marie pushed on with her tale of unrequited love. 'A friend told me who he was and where he lived. I heard he loved cars. So I drove back and forth, ever so slowly, past his apartment in the Ferrari, until it began to overheat. I borrowed the Rolls and cruised up and down his street, until the police began to take down my licence number. Finally, in desperation, I parked the Rolls, walked up to his block, and rang the bell. No reply. I tried phoning, but his number was unlisted. I was going mad with frustration. Shall I go on?'

'You'd better.'

'I screwed up all my courage,' giggled Marie, 'and drove up to his apartment again and again. Finally I found him in.

'"Oh", I said, when he came to the door, "I just happened to be in the neighbourhood and wondered how you were? Aren't you going to ask me in?" I knew immediately he had no idea who the hell I was.

'But he stood aside and let me in. I wore a sable coat and nothing underneath. God, it was hot. I seated myself on the lowest chair in the room. I let him glimpse my boobs as I leaned forward. I gave him a brief view of my thighs, as high as possible, without actually being starkers. I knew that'd work. It did . . . he told me later . . . it blew his mind.'

A perverse mixture of desire and jealousy suffused Sebastian. He lay back with eyes shut. Marie, reliving her story enthusiastically, continued with her narrative.

'Well, one thing led to another and we ended up screwing all night, and most of the next day. When I'd finished with him I'd made him my slave. He became besotted with me. For a while I pretended that it was the other way around, that he was doing it to me . . . that I was his chattel. For the next few weeks we were inseparable. I introduced him to my parents and many friends.

'When he was properly hooked I began to make myself scarce. I made all sorts of excuses when he phoned. I skipped dates. When he asked for an explanation, I said casually that I was 'not motivated'.

'Once, during that time, we went off for a holiday. He thought it would be like old times. But I played hard to get; flirted with other men; told him not to fuss; to be patient and he'd get his share. He didn't like that phrase one little bit.

'All this made him jealous and more determined to have me. I simply used the tricks every tease uses to get the whip hand.'

'Why then did you marry him?' Sebastian broke his silence. 'It doesn't make sense.'

'I suppose because I realized I was getting on. I didn't want to be left on the shelf. Most of my friends were married and settling down. Houses, children, nannies . . . you know,' she grimaced, 'he was the best available. At least he had interested me for a while, and Daddy didn't mind him.'

'Why did you break up?'

'Well, that's another story. It was a mixture . . . lots of reasons . . . they all added up. In the beginning we were happy. But he had to work too hard and that became tiresome. No doubt a lot of it was my fault . . . who knows? Why do people go off each other? It's not always black and white. I know he withdrew, and so did I. We squabbled too much. Mostly because I was pigheaded. He didn't like my friends, and vice versa. Maybe we were simply incompatible, that's a fashionable phrase, isn't it?

'Then, when I met you, my darling, I was ripe for romance. I fell for you. At first you seemed so warm and understanding, so attentive. I realize now,' Marie paused to give Sebastian a nudge, 'that you're a cool, tough cookie and not exactly madly in love with me. You're different; you don't really have deep feelings. Maybe that's why we don't quarrel? You never try to correct or change me.'

A familiar tingle began to course through Sebastian's loins. Without ceremony he rolled over to Marie and began drawing her into his arms. He struggled to raise her skirt. Marie lay back, an anticipatory smile on her lips. There were times when a quickie was much preferable to endless foreplay.

That night yet another elaborate scene in the fortress confronted the involuntary guests. The room they found themselves in was, as usual, lavishly furnished. The centre piece was a long dining table covered with snow white linen, set with delicate china, glittering crystal, and gold candelabra and cutlery. Elegant vases filled with flowers graced the table at measured intervals. Golden bowls of fresh fruit had been placed before each guest.

It was a scene to rival any nineteenth century feast. Only the extraordinary dinner affairs of England's Prince Regent, held in the Brighton Pavilion, could have been more gross than the display in Sebastian and Randolf's jungle fortress.

Randolf's presence, as usual, dominated the gathering. For this occasion he was dressed in white tails. It seemed to Ben there was an alternating black and white chess motif in his environment. A white carnation resided in Randolf's button hole; he was weirdly elegant; a Clevelander's idea of a creature of surpassing sartorial elegance.

Marie was resplendent in an evening gown of white lace. On her head sparkled a diamond tiara. Her fingers were encircled with numerous rings encrusted with glittering precious stones which Ben took to be real.

'They're pulling out all the stops,' said Maeve to Ben sitting on her right, 'every dinner gets more, sort of, crass.'

'Yes, you're right. We have to play on with their charades. This is all gold night.' Ben twisted sideways to look at Maeve. 'Anyway, you look terrific. You make me feel good. Just the sight of you. I'm so glad I found you. Wish it had been in the real world.'

'Oh, so am I.' Maeve gripped his upper arm and squeezed hard, 'I do love you Ben.'

Randolf, in high good humour, smiles gruesomely at all and sundry.

'Please begin,' he said, and without waiting for his guests began to stuff his mouth with specially prepared hors d'oeuvres, hand over hand, like a sailor in a hornpipe.

I'm looking forward to the next game, Ben,' said Randolf between mouthfuls, 'it's clear that you and Sebastian are well matched. It should be good.'

Sebastian, his recent conference with Randolf in mind, studied his brother in exasperation. For once it was Ben's expression that was fanatically inscrutable.

Deanna and Olga, personal troubles shelved for the present, were eating urgently, almost outdoing Randolf's determined onslaught on the food.

The Dean's head, balanced and still while he fed, began to bob again as he made an effort to engage the Admiral in conversation. The tics of a life time were hard to discard.

While his guests were eating, Randolf, having demolished his special diet in record time, in a quietly menacing voice (for which Vincent Price would have given his whole fortune) announced,

'A brief news item . . . '

'Here we go,' said Ben, *sotto voce*.

'I've agreed,' continued Randolf in a harsher tone, 'to extend the match to five games.'

'How,' interrupted Ben, choking with a paroxysm of coughing, 'good of you.' Maeve passed him a glass of water and patted him on the back. Ben regained his voice.

'Have you decided about Sebastian? What if he loses?'

Randolf scowled at his bothersome nephew, and began to reply, only to be cut off.

Sambo, across the table, felt he was doing quite well considering the ominous ambience. Although he generally presented a jovial and relaxed exterior, it was not easy for Sambo to forget his origins in a small town in the western United States. His had been a black middle class environment which had sheltered him from much of what was unpleasant for a black boy in a predominantly white city. Constant taunting by his, not always unfriendly, fellow students had left him with subliminal feelings of inferiority. Thus his defiant adoption of a nickname which served to cock a snoot at his detractors.

'I think it's time,' said Sambo, as Randolf lapsed into silence, 'that I declared my hand, that I told you about myself.'

'Go ahead,' Randolf resumed eating.

'I'm not what I seem.'

'Who is?' smirked the host, 'Before you go on I must warn you . . . what you may say may not be news. Don't be disappointed if I don't fall over with amazement.' Randolf had reverted to his default, sardonic state and let out a cackle.

'The fact is,' persisted Sambo, 'that I'm an agent of the United States Government.'

'Oh, really?' Randolf was elaborately interested.

'Okay, so you knew. What you don't know is that my presence here is known in Washington. And unless my Control receives coded signals from me, he will automatically begin a retrieving operation . . . and may already have done so.'

While he was uttering these words Sambo realized he had made an error. He was a poor liar, always a disadvantage in his profession. Randolf must have guessed he was bluffing.

By issuing impotent threats he was worsening his predicament. Better to have kept quiet.

'How very interesting,' said Sebastian, exchanging smirks with Randolf, 'no doubt you won't mind filling in a few details about the proposed rescue mission? I mean we would like to make them welcome.' Sebastian's sarcasm served to confirm Sambo's worst fears. Torture, anyone? Sambo, lost, fiddled with the bread on his side plate.

The meal proceeded with diminished animation. Food was now being consumed with finicky appetites. Very little wine was drunk. Maeve and Amelia pecked away slowly, and finally gave up.

'Shall we adjourn, and go directly to the games room?' Randolf, who had eaten his fill, rose and was wheeled out. The rest followed gloomily.

Once more Ben found himself by a chess console. The score in games was even. The third game was about to commence.

☆ ☆ ☆

Ben, playing badly, had opened with a well known Bulgarian gambit. Sebastian countered. Unable fully to concentrate, Ben switched to a defensive position and amateurishly piled every piece solidly around his king. His defences seemed to be impenetrable.

Sebastian began offering major pieces in a determined effort to break through. Ben resisted as long as possible, but finally when a knight came within range, he took it.

Sebastian, suppressing a smile, moved his queen, and sat back. His position was solid.

'I think we could all do with a break.' Randolf broke the silence, 'Coffee will be served.'

Ben stretched his aching back, rose, slightly dizzy, and walked slowly towards his supporters. Sambo had disappeared in the direction of the toilets. Maeve whispered in Ben's ear before going over to Deanna and Olga.

'The plans . . . of the building. Do you have them?'

'Not yet,' said Olga, less gruff than usual, 'we're trying. What exactly do you need?'

'A rough sketch will do. You must have some idea about

159

the layout. What's in the basement? Where are the doors, store rooms, guardhouses, you know . . . anything at all? We must start somewhere. The match is keeping Randolf occupied. We must be getting on with a plan.'

Deanna tugged at Olga's arm, dismissed Maeve, and made off to re-enter the games room. There they sat isolated on chairs at the rear of the room, heads together. The board displayed on the screen was ignored.

'She's right you know,' said Deanna, 'we'd better shape up. We'll have to sketch from memory. What do we know about this place?'

'You're keen to help,' whispered Olga, nervously, 'why can't we sit tight? And furthermore,' she continued with increasing ire, 'don't think I don't know you've been screwing Sebastian, or used to. You must have some idea what's going on in his mind? Look . . . I mean when you're really intimate . . . you must have had SOME idea about his intentions?'

'Olga, watch your tongue. You've no right,' said Deanna irascibly, staring ahead, 'to say things like that.'

'No one can hear us. Come on Deanna, what's up? What about Sebastian?'

'If you want to know the truth, he's a cold-blooded fish,' said Deanna, 'and a lousy lover. He never ever said anything to me that was the least bit romantic or erotic. It was all mechanical. Just gave orders. I don't know why I did it. I thought I was being liberated and doing my own thing.' She laughed. 'Why am I telling you this? When I think back . . . it was all disgusting. We might as well have been in a zoo for all he cared. As for sharing his thoughts, I don't think he had any.'

'Why can't you try again?'

'Not a chance. I couldn't. What about Marie, ey? And, anyway, he hasn't been near me since 'they' arrived. Probably got his beady eyes on the new women. I told you all men were shits.'

'Yes, yes, we know that. You've mentioned it once or twice. But we have to use them,' said Olga, 'it's clear to me that you and I are worth nothing around here. We don't count. We'd better get out while we can. There's no other way.'

☆   ☆   ☆

'Your move,' said Sebastian, tersely. Ben leaned forward and stared bleakly at his pieces. He was tired but continued as if playing for his life which, of course, he was.

'Admiral,' Maeve spoke quietly to the semirecumbent body on he left, 'I've been thinking. I've got an idea. Listen. Everything here depends on an adequate electrical supply. You know, lights, the communication setup, the doors, especially the fence, even Randolf's chair's batteries have to be recharged.' The Admiral evinced mild interest.

'There must be a central power supply. I hear engine noises at night. If there is a central power supply, it's likely to be run by automatic controls. Are you listening? This is my idea. The computers . . . can be the answer after all.'

'How, what do you mean?' asked the Admiral.

'It's highly probable that all electrical apparatus in this place is computerized.'

'So?' The Admiral responded slowly, not taking his eyes off the screen.

'It might be feasible, using the terminals in the rooms to, you know, manipulate the power supply.'

The Admiral's head dipped perceptibly. Maeve, getting little feedback felt discouraged, but persisted. She knew the Admiral was listening.

'Well, I'm trained in programming. You know that. I think I can hook up a workstation terminal, via the local network, to the switchboard in the power room. If that works, we're in business.'

The Admiral continued to stare stolidly at the screen.

'If that can be done then we can control the power supply and, in turn, the whole place. Think of the possibilities. We could set up a series of 'events', like a stage manager. We could write our own script.'

'Suppose it can be done, how do you propose to go about it?' The Admiral spoke through barely moving lips.

'I tell you it's possible.'

'Have you discussed this with Ben?'

'In a way.'

His concentration failing, Ben moved his queen to stave off Sebastian's unrelenting assault. Yet even as he moved Ben realized that his action was unwise. Sebastian contemplated the lax tactic for a long time. If nothing else Ben's departures from the obvious always put him on guard. He searched for a trap. By now he had planned several moves ahead. He could see no pitfalls. His game was becoming more and more confident. Victory was in sight.

Ben began to play angrily, recklessly. In so doing he became paradoxically exhilarated. Exhaustion and frustration conspired to make him bold, a combination which might have made him a dangerous player, had his position not been so hopeless. Sebastian experienced a complaisant twinge of sympathy for his brother. Randolf's pernicious personage overshadowed even his enjoyment. No-one could play a sensible, calculated game with that presence around. Tonight he was winning by default.

'It's too late,' said Ben suddenly, and shoved his chair back, 'I can't go on. I resign.' He rose, and without another word rejoined his stunned companions. Yet, in his mind, he was not particularly despairing. After all, the main idea had been to gain time, and he had.

'Well, that's that,' said Randolf. 'A magnificent effort by Sebastian, don't you agree? Note the positions of the pieces. We must record this game. And,' he swung round to face the loser, 'Ben, not to worry,' he said, 'all is not lost, yet.'

The guards, together with Sebastian and Marie, surrounded Randolf like worker bees around the queen, and the triumphant procession made off.

16

The Admiral rose from the comfortable queen sized bed and stubbed out his cigar in the ashtray by the telephone. He started to dial, changed his mind and replaced the receiver. For a while he sat by the telephone, lost in thought. After a long pause he walked over to a wardrobe where he recovered an old, red hooded dressing gown, and from the floor a pair of well worn slippers. After many years of usage the slippers displayed their decrepit age. They had accompanied him on many of his adventurous journeys. He had never left home without them.

Passing by the bedside clock radio, he bent down and switched it on. Living constantly in a covert world resulted in small automatic precautionary actions. He delved into a scuffed brief case by the bed and retrieved a small leather tool case which he stuffed into a pocket. Noiselessly closing the door behind him, he glanced in both directions along the corridor and ambled off, insulated in his comfortable slippers. He made only the faintest of rustling noses as he padded along the silent passage.

A knock on the door alerted Ben. He had been dozing in an armchair, a book open on his lap.

'Who is it?'

'It's me . . . the Admiral.'

'It's not locked.'

The door opened slowly. Ben looked up and beckoned to the heavy set, red clad figure.

'Come in . . . find a seat . . . like a drink?'

'Thank you, yes, whiskey, water, no ice. Incidentally,' he gestured towards the ceiling, 'I'm fond of music, you know, classical, Bach or Mozart. Get a station on the radio.' Ben complied. In elaborate pantomime he mouthed, 'Why?'

The Admiral frowned,

'I don't want them to know I'm here. So,' he gestured, 'keep the radio playing.'

Ben slouched in a favourite position, feet on the bed and spine sunk deep, so that he was curved like a strung bow. The Admiral settled in an incongruously small love seat.

'Ben,' began the Admiral, holding a glass in a fleshy hand, 'although you may have guessed part of what I am about to tell you, it's time I told you the whole, strange tale.

'I am a divisional head in a branch of MI5. In this capacity I recruited you. I had you trained. You may wonder why I chose you, and why I didn't tell you I would becoming along on this operation?'

Ben made no comment.

'Let me explain why I chose you.' The Admiral paused to sip his whisky. 'You are about to hear something exceedingly interesting. I have known you . . . much longer than you could possibly guess.'

'Yes?'

'It goes back a long, long way. To a small boy and his father in South West Africa, now the independent state, Namibia.'

Ben swung his legs over the side of the bed and stared at the Admiral.

'Your father and I,' the skin around the Admiral's eyes crinkled as he smiled, 'were once close friends. Ben's stare became an incredulous gape.

'I am, obviously, not English, I am an Afrikaaner.'

'That explains the accent. I thought I recognized it. But it's not quite South African anymore is it? Living in England?'

'I suppose so. Now, about myself. I was the sergeant in charge of police in Kalkfontein when you were a child. My real name was, is, Gert Brenner. When your father lay dying in that hotel in Port Nolloth, I felt a tremendous, an overpowering, guilt, for it was I who persuaded him to come prospecting. Your mother was against it but I prevailed. I believe it was largely my fault that you lost your father . . . and your twin, Sebastian.'

Ben was stunned. The Admiral had to be telling the

164

truth. No one else could have concocted such a story. The facts rung true.

'There's the matter of Randolf, your uncle, and Sebastian. Neither has the faintest idea who I am. If they knew I was Brenner, I'd be a dead man. They believe I am with British Intelligence, but in their pay. A double agent.' The Admiral took another sip of whiskey, 'I'm here to make amends, and at the same time rid the world of a growing menace. My motivation is bilateral, personal as well as official.'

Ben remained silent. So this was THE Sergeant Brenner. It was all too astounding, too incredible. Ben's mind overflowed with questions. He did not know where to begin. Eventually he spoke.

'What about all this? You knew then that Sebastian and Randolf were here?'

'Of course. I've been biding my time . . . waiting for an opportunity to get at them while following your career. Things are working out, but not strictly according to plan. By the way, I'm sorry about your marriage and the divorce. It seems to me that you may have found someone . . . worthwhile?'

'That's true. But why did you not tell me that Sebastian was here? What's really going on with him and Randolf?'

'I'll try and explain, it's complicated. Both the CIA and MI5 wanted to know what Randolf and Sebastian were up to. I became involved because I was for a while, liaison officer between the two agencies. I was ordered to investigate, especially because fissionable material was beginning to turn up in Iraq.

'In any case, I knew where to find the right man, you. I could not, I was not allowed, to tell you the whole truth. I'm very sorry about that. I didn't plan that. By a strange coincidence, your relatives had been putting out feelers for you. So, after we had recruited and trained you, I set off to Madagascar myself, alone. You were to be joined by Sambo and Maeve who, incidentally, is a super person. I fixed it so that you'd all be on the same plane and to meet the Potentate, our only ally in this part of the world.'

'You did all that?' said Ben, 'Very . . . good.'

'Bear with me. A game was going on. Their side didn't

165

know what the other was up to. But we knew. Sebastian thought he was manipulating us. We let him believe that.'

'Another drink?'

'So arrangements ... thank you ... were allowed to proceed,' said the Admiral, his fist encircling a refreshed glass.

Ben stretched and uncrossed legs, numbed with pins and needles. For a while he looked long and searchingly into the Admiral's face.

'It's certainly complicated. I'd look very silly if you were actually Sebastian's man, wouldn't I?'

'I cannot be. You met me in London. I am Sergeant Brenner, your father's best friend. I know you. It must be obvious to you that I'm not a fake?'

'I suppose not. It's just that the situation is so incredible ... Sergeant Brenner? You amaze me. The whole set up is so far out.'

Ben swirled the drink in the glass, drank the last of the liquid, and made up his mind. He would have to accept.

'Admiral, Sergeant Brenner, you're on. We go ahead.'

The Admiral heaved a long sigh of relief.

'I have a plan,' he said, 'put down your drink and we'll be off. I'll explain on the way. We're about to set the stage.'

☆   ☆   ☆

The two men, the Admiral leading, left the room with the radio playing. They walked silently along the corridor, past the row of guest bedrooms, until they were out of sight. A few yards on they came upon a solid, white painted door marked 'Linen', and below this, in incongruously large, red lettering,

ABSOLUTELY NO UNAUTHORIZED ENTRY

'In here,' whispered the Admiral. A bunch of keys appeared in his hard. He unlocked the door.

'Inside, quick. Shut the door after you.'

The interior was dark, forcing them to grope. When their eyes adjusted to the faint light, they made out row upon row of shelves loaded with linen, towels, unmarked boxes, and

166

sundry items of clothing. Several large laundry baskets were lined up near the door.

'Aladdin's cave,' breathed Ben.

The Admiral began to feel his way along the wall immediately to the left. Like a giant crab he shuffled sideways, fingers sliding along the wainscoting. A few feet along he came across a small projection on the underside, midway along the wall.

'Here goes,' he whispered, and pressed the protruding microswitch. For several seconds nothing happened. Then a hidden panel began to swing noiselessly upwards.

'How did you know that?' Ben's suspicions were aroused. 'I didn't hear you say 'Open Sesame'.'

'Deanna told me,' replied the Admiral, tersely.

'Deanna? She's fallen in with us?'

'Yes. She told me about this little trick. She used this passage to visit Sebastian in his rooms before we arrived. He didn't want Randolf or, especially, Marie, to know.'

A flight of concrete steps led down from the opening. The Admiral produced a tiny flashlight.

'This'll last hours, selenium batteries.'

Ben counted at least a hundred steps. It seemed they would never end.

'We must be in Australia by now.'

'Just keep going,' urged the Admiral. They reached a cold cement floor and walked along in silence. Thirty feet on and they came across an apex in the long, narrow passage from which two lateral passages led off.

'Which one?'

'Deanna said bear left all the way. The right fork leads into the mercenaries' quarters. This's the way they get upstairs in emergencies. Normally they don't use this route.'

The walls of the passages were damp and chilly. The air had a distinctly oily reek. A low pitched vibration could be felt rather than heard in the ground beneath their feet.

'Diesels . . . we're on the right track.'

They walked on soundlessly, passing several plain, slatted, wooden doors fitted with simple latches. Ben sniffed.

'That pong . . . latrines. The smell's universal.'

A few yards on and the passage opened into a chamber

167

with several doors set at intervals in the far walls. To the left, protruding several feet into the hall-like space, was a glass walled office, the interior of which was brilliantly lit. Every detail was clearly visible in the glare of the lights.

A guard lounged in a secretary's chair before a semicircular console bearing six flickering monitors. From their oblique vantage point Ben and the Admiral could make out views of doors, the hangar, as well as different exterior areas of the complex. The guard seemed largely oblivious of the screens. Occasionally he spared them a cursory glance. He was engrossed in a tattered magazine. His booted feet rested on the desktop next to a thermos flask, a mug, and a dried out, partly devoured sandwich. An M16 rifle was propped against the side of the console. More magazines lay in a heap by one of the screens.

The two intruders retreated until they were well out of sight.

'So there's only one,' whispered the Admiral, 'that's better than I'd hoped. We'll have to immobilize him.'

'How are we going to manage that? He'll see us coming a mile away.'

'My dear chap, there are METHODS. You've forgotten Mother Nature.'

'Mother Nature?'

'Remember the latrines? I was hoping we'd find some here. Sooner or later our friend's going to have to relieve himself.'

The Admiral reached once more into his dressing gown and produced a small plastic bottle filled with pink capsules.

'What're those? How are pills going to help? Are you going to shoot them at him?' muttered Ben. 'Where's your peashooter?' He was beginning to feel like an actor in a farce directed by a nutty naval person.

'Very droll. These are a modern miracle. I knew they'd come in hand.' Ben gazed, baffled, at the Admiral. Miracle pills?

'Are you going to poison him? Ask him to swallow them?' Ben was becoming aggravated, but decided to wait for clarification.

'Look, for years I've been taking these for my blood

168

pressure. They make me pee like mad. So, here's the plan. If we disabled that guard physically, we'd put the cat among the pigeons. They'd know for sure we'd been here, and that we'd tampered with the works. So, I had a flash of inspiration. In my line you have to improvize.'

Ben began to grin.

'They do work, believe me. When that guard gets up for his usual leak, and sooner or later he'll have to, one of us will slip into his office and drop a few of these little beauties into that thermos.' Ben's grin widened. The old boy was brilliant. But who, he wondered, was going to be the hero? He decided that it was his duty. He was younger and more agile.

'How did you know he'd have a thermos?'

'They ALWAYS do. Either that, or pop, or a water jug. Now we wait. Don't worry, when he makes his move, I'll do the pill dropping. Don't argue. You have to cover me. The pills are fast acting. You start to pee in minutes after you've swallowed one.'

Ben started to protest, but was interrupted.

'Look,' said the Admiral, firmly, 'leave this to me. Maeve's given me a list of instructions. Your part will be crucial. When I've loaded his thermos I'll beat a retreat. Eventually he'll take a drink and before long he'll be off for the next pee, and the next, and the next. Each leak will take him longer. He won't think there's anything wrong, after all, peeing's a natural function. He'll blame it on the coffee. Then,' said the Admiral, as the pee-breaks get longer and longer, I'll have time to make my move. I have to get to the power room with the control panel while he's busy emptying his bladder.

'I'll depend on you to give me warning. You'll have to listen for the sound of rushing waters. As soon as they stop you must signal immediately so that I'll have time to hide, or get back here. We'll have to play it by ear, or,' he added, mirthlessly, 'by bladder.'

Both men fell back, well past the offensive latrines. Squatting on his haunches. Ben prepared for a long wait. The Admiral touched a cautionary finger to his lips and inched forward until he was as close as he dared to the illuminated cubicle. Before long Ben began to feel a cramping urge to relieve himself. All the talk about diuretics, the nervous tension, and the cool dampness in the underground passage were beginning to have an effect on his bladder. Gritting his teeth he tried to think of Maeve.

Another half hour passed. Ben and the Admiral were becoming stiff from inactivity and the frigid atmosphere. Ben, in lighter clothes, was chilled to the bone. At long last the guard yawned, probed a finger into an itching ear, dropped his magazine, and simultaneously farted so loudly that the sound penetrated the glass walls and echoed down the passage. The breaking of wind seemed to energize him. He rose to leave his enclave.

'Good,' grunted the Admiral.

The guard stumbled through the door of the cubicle, letting it slam shut with a clatter. Busily occupied with scratching almost every accessible part of his body, he made for the door of the lavatory and disappeared inside amidst another thunderously loud, prolonged, explosion.

The moment the door shut the Admiral rose to his feet and walked forward, moving lightly on slippered feet, into the office recently vacated by the gaseous guard. The air inside was rank. The Admiral dropped six pills into the flask.

A dim shape approached Ben.

'Okay, we're set,' the Admiral rubbed his hands gleefully, 'now we wait, and wait.'

'It's done? Great.'

'Yes. As soon as he makes his next and, hopefully longer visit, I'll head for the engine room. When the sound of his water works slows you must warn me.'

'How?'

'Oh, yes I'll explain. I'll pay out this nylon line. As soon as you think he's about to finish, tug the string once. If it's too late, tug twice and I'll stay. I hope he doesn't notice the string, it's a fine fishing line.'

'Christ, I hope it works.'

Ten minutes later the guard strolled back to the lavatory, beginning the first of many journeys.

The door to the engine room slid open on well oiled runners. Dominating the room were three enormous diesel generators. To one side, about six feet away, was a large

170

electrical control panel and beyond that, a smaller diesel starter motor. Two of the diesels were rumbling. The third was silent. The place was spotlessly clean. The strong odour of diesel fuel and the deep bass noise of the engines reminded the Admiral that he was at the very heart of Randolf's fortress.

So far so good. But this was not the room he was after. He scanned the walls for clues. Where were the master controls? The place was run by computers, but where were they? Where were the monitors and keyboards? If they were not here . . . he dared not think. He was now at the far side of the pounding engines and looked warily behind a door near the fuel tanks. Nothing. He opened another door, and another.

To his immense relief the third door opened into a large room literally crammed with banks of electronic equipment. This was it. Across the room he saw a keyboard, and above, three screens. Nearby was a large gently humming metal cabinet with winking red, green, and amber lights. He recognized the mainframe computer. The air here was fresh and cool. Two of the screens were active with rows of numbers and diagrams. A cursor blinked.

A single tug on his belt alerted him. The Admiral spun round and scurried out of the room past the empty glass cubicle towards Ben.

'Ben,' said the Admiral in a hoarse whisier, 'I believe we can do it.'

'You cut it fine. He must have a small capacity. You won't have enough time. You were almost too late.'

'Don't worry, we'll make it. We have to.'

Ben's admiration for the Admiral was growing. Once more they settled down at their post by the stinking latrines and waited for mother nature's next intervention.

Before long the guard, scraping his crotch, unzipping his fly, returned to the lavatory.

'Hold on Admiral,' said Ben, 'let's time him.'

'Okay.'

Ben counted forty-five seconds on his watch before the guard emerged. Regaining his seat the latter reached for his coffee flask, poured a full cup, and drained it. He was very thirsty.

171

'Good boy, that's it. Take your medicine. Won't be long I guess,' whispered Ben, his heart pounding.

Ten minutes later the guard, grunting irritably, rose once more, glanced briefly at the screens, and walked out of his office to head for the latrines. By now he was hurrying perceptibly. He disappeared into what was fast becoming a second home.

'Okay let's go,' urged Ben, nudging the Admiral. An ominous thought struck Ben. The monitors, they could have repeaters. But the Admiral, crouching low, moved nimbly – for such a large body – forward and made straight for the console room. As soon as he returned Ben pulled him down and said, 'The monitors . . . Admiral. If he has them in that room, there may be others upstairs.'

'You're right.' The Admiral had had the same thought. How stupid to forget. The monitors were undoubtedly connected to cameras in the engine room. Somewhere, in each room, there had to be a surveillance camera. They would have to blind them. He searched the ceiling, and sure enough spotted a lens. The Admiral walked out to look cautiously at the camera from the side. It did not move. He paced silently back to Ben.

'Ben,' hissed the Admiral, 'a slight problem. But I think I've got it figured out. Next time I'll blank off the TV camera. I'm not too worried about that camera. But there's no point in ignoring it.'

The guard returned to his station, drank a full cup of coffee and had barely settled when, with a muttered oath, he swung his legs down from the desk, and literally trotted back to his urinal.

The door had barely closed when the Admiral set off for the control room, trailing his nylon umbilicus. Once inside he located the small TV camera. This time he was prepared. He reached into the voluminous red dressing gown, extracted his leather case, and withdraw a small camera of the instant variety. It had been part of a toolkit, thoughtfully adapted for him by his service.

From the blind side of the video camera, he photographed the room. The picture was ready in seconds. Next he produced a tiny, folding unipod with adjustable jaws, attached the photograph, and strapped the contraption to

172

the front of the camera lens.

I hope this works, he thought. Now for the job. Pray to heaven that no one's paying much attention to the monitors. We'll know soon enough.

The Admiral paused to compose his thoughts for what seemed like an eternity, then sat himself before the keyboard. From his pocket he drew a sheet of notepaper filled with Maeve's instructions.

At first there was no response. Nothing seemed to be happening. A blinking cursor waited patiently. The Admiral consulted the sheet of instructions, laboriously keyed in a set of numbers and directions. This time, almost instantly the screen responded. The Admiral studied the rows of numbers and diagrams displayed, consulted his notes, and grunted with satisfaction.

At this point, Ben, sensing an abrupt change in the guard's activities, tugged twice on the string. The Admiral hastily gathered his notes and ducked behind the console.

The guard, grumbling and grunting irritably, stalked out of the latrines. He did not notice that the monitor screen viewing the engine room had altered slightly. The Admiral lingered, awaiting the guard's reaction. Before long, the latter, freely cursing his over active waterworks, skittered back to the latrines, undoing his fly on the run as he approached the door. Ben tugged the thread. The Admiral returned to the keyboard and completed Maeve's instructions.

It was done. The Admiral dripped sweat. His chunky hands trembled slightly as he fled the room and rejoined Ben.

In the toilet the guard scowled at his reflection in the mirror and squeezed the last drop from his highly energetic bladder. By then the Admiral and Ben had made their way back to the guest rooms.

Sambo applauded their efforts by clapping his hands silently. His pessimistic scepticism had vanished in the heady excitement that now enveloped them.

'Terrific. We have, at least you have, done something

173

positive. Our first step in the right direction.'

'This is great,' added Maeve, 'you boys have done your bit superbly. Now I have to figure exactly when to reset the control system. Just tell me when. Ben, please help.' Maeve invited him to sit by her before the screen.

'What's amazing,' said Ben, 'is that this place is such a mixture of sophisticated technology and incredible sloppiness. I mean, supplying us with terminals. It's almost as if they wanted us to use them.'

'Probably decoration, to impress visitors.' Maeve began to key in commands as she studied her notes.

'It's hard to understand. I don't know what to think. All I know is we'll do our best to get out, alive.' said the Admiral.

'Let us get on with it then,' said Maeve, impatiently, 'give me an outline, Admiral, you too Ben. What you think? Tell me what you want and when. I'll set it up.' Ben, obligingly sat as close as possible.

'We want lights to go on and off at random times, doors to open and close, and so on. Let's look at the electrical blueprints.'

Ben and the Admiral drew up a list of suggestions. Maeve scribbled a series of numbers on paper, looked thoughtfully at them, then tore up the sheet and began all over.

17

An hour later Maeve was still busy with the keyboard. Settling himself into an armchair the Admiral decided to make enquiries.

'Is it working?' He squinted at her, gesturing in the direction of the clock radio. 'Turn it on,' he mimed. Then, in a normal voice, when it came on, added, 'Let's see, where've you got? Our timing's crucial. We must get it right.'

'I've worked it out. I need your input now. Once that's fed in I can make a dummy run.'

The Dean shifted his bottom on Randolf's elaborate, silk sofa.

'Randolf, er, sir,' he began, stuttering slightly, 'you're not really, actually planning to, er, really, er, . . . dddestroy the losers, or anybody else, for that matter, are you? Er, it's a joke? Yes?'

'Tell me,' countered Randolf, 'wouldn't you like a million dollars deposited to your name in Switzerland?' Randolf had positioned himself stiffly upright behind an enormous, depressingly bare, rosewood desk.

'Who wouldn't?' sighed the Dean with an emphatic bob of his head, 'but not if someone has to be sacrificed.' The nervous stutter vanished. 'I couldn't countenance that. It reminds me of another country . . . somewhere in Europe . . . something that happened, long ago.'

He seemed to come to a resolution and his obsequious manner, along with the stammer, evaporated. 'Look here

175

Randolf,' he said, firmly, 'I agreed to help you set up your business and to advise about investments. You have to admit I've been singularly successful. You did pretty well with mergers and take-over bids. You walked away with huge profits. I've given you your money's worth. But, murder? No sir, it's not . . . civilized.'

The Dean's head no longer bobbed. He paused to stare directly into the eyes of his cranky, old, employer. Randolf was somewhat taken aback by the Dean's new disposition.

'Murder . . . my dear Dean, why call it that? What's in a name? I'm exercising my legal rights. I AM the law, here. Think of it as a judicial execution.'

'You're joking?'

'If you think so. Wait and see.'

The Dean sat motionless with eyes fixed unwaveringly on Randolf's ancient, crazed, but still handsome face. This man IS mad, he thought, I've got to warn them.

'Don't get any heroic ideas about helping our guests,' said Randolf softly, accurately divining the Dean's intentions.

'It's not my business. I'll not interfere.'

'Good. Then we can all get on with the day's business. See what the stock markets are doing. What's happening with gold? With the South African boycott, gold may become genuinely scarce. I don't think the Americans will want to buy Russian gold. My informants tell me an investor in the Middle East's speculating in gold stocks. Look into it.'

He inclined his head dismissively towards the door. The Dean stood, a faint smile on his face. Without further ado he made for the exit.

The Dean shut the door to Randolf's suite and walked swiftly to the set of rooms that served as his office. He unlocked the door to his private chamber and began a rapid search amongst a series of mobile filing cabinets. In a few minutes he had located the files he needed. He walked over to a bright red copying machine, and set it to 'COPY and REDUCE'. When he was satisfied that the machine was operating correctly he copied several pages, folded the reduced prints, and placed them in an inner jacket pocket.

While he was thus busily occupied in the office illuminated by fluorescent lighting, he became aware of a fluctuating, spreading, scintillating, conflagration, sparkling in his right visual fields. A familiar and unmistakeable, throbbing pain began to pulsate in his left temple. Oh, shitting hell, he thought, not now. With a groan he walked to an adjoining washroom, opened a cupboard, searched frantically, and found two small plastic containers. He selected one labelled, 'Take as directed', and swallowed two buff coloured tablets. God . . . I hope I can abort this attack. I must have a clear head. I must be able to think.

It was not so much the pain which distressed him as the thought of the approaching, prostrating nausea, vomiting, and disorientation that invariably accompanied his seizures.

☆   ☆   ☆

A tentative tap on the door to Sambo's room stifled conversation. The Admiral raised a cautionary finger.

'Who can it be?' whispered Ben, rising to answer the door. 'I'd better open it,' he said, knowing it would not be possible to ingore the knock.

'You'd better,' said the Admiral, softly.

A pale, agitated figure stood irresolutely on the threshold. The Dean stepped inside.

'I . . . I hope you'll forgive this intrusion.' It was a statement not an apologiy. His head was pounding fiercely, 'I've something of immeasurable importance to share with you.' Despite the growing fuzziness in his mind he forced himself to think and speak with precision.

'Something . . . life-saving . . . vital.' He stopped. A swirl of vertigo engulfed him and he became deathly pale. He was sweating profusely.

'My dear fellow, have a seat,' suggested the Admiral in a concerned, kindly voice. He had dropped all pretence of impassivity. The Dean, now in enormous distress, obeyed. He sank onto the nearest seat.

'Care for a drink?'

The Dean waved a hand in a feeble gesture of dismissal. 'No thanks. What I have to tell you requires all my concentration. I have to make my information clear to you in a short a time as possible.'

Ben was impressed by the Admiral's gentle tone. Sambo stared steadfastly at his glass, swirling the fluid around and around.

'Go on then,' said the Admiral, encouragingly.

'I have with me,' the Dean produced a bundle of documents, 'a detailed set of plans . . . engineering and architectural drawings of this place and its surroundings. You will find everything here, all electrical, mechanical, and structural diagrams. There are also circuits of the central computer, its connections, and the local area network.' He paused. 'Could I have a glass of water?'

The Admiral, trying to take the measure of the fantastic windfall, did not immediately react to the request. But Maeve, sitting in the background, came forward and offered him a glass of water. The merry tinkling of ice in the glass caused the Dean to wince with sonic pain. He breathed deeply, steadied himself, and drank. The room spun giddily.

'I've come to warn you that you must escape. You must not question why. I assure you I'm not exaggerating. You must act on my advice, and use my information. But, be VERY careful. Do not act in haste. Oh, God.'

The Dean replaced his glass with meticulous care. Wave after wave of increasing queasiness attacked him. He felt utterly wretched. His ghastly pallor increased. Sweat poured copiously from his ashen, grey, forehead and flooded his eyes, further obscuring his vision.

'I have to leave immediately. I must not be missed. They must not know I've been anywhere near you.' His nausea was overpowering and he began to gag. On the verge of vomiting he rose and staggered on shaky legs towards the door.

His exit was barred by Maeve.

'You look absolutely awful. Lie down for a minute. We'll look after you.'

'No, no, I must get away. Please, move out of my way or I'll be sick over you.' Maeve stepped aside and let him go.

The Dean walked as rapidly as possible along the corridor, swaying as he misjudged his passage between the parallel walls. He barely made it to the nearest toilet when he began violently to retch.

18

The Admiral spread the Dean's extraordinary gift of folded documents on the table, and smoothed them carefully.

'What a break,' he said, 'we'll dovetail all this information with the computer program. It's more than we could have dreamed of.'

'I say, Admiral,' said Ben, after a futile attempt, standing on tiptoe, to overlook the Admiral's broad shoulders, 'we can't see through you. How about splitting the plans? That way we can look at different sections. Divide them into categories . . . you know, electrical, structural, and so on.'

'Good idea.' The Admiral passed over several sheets and returned immediately to the page he had been scanning. 'I'll stay with the structural bits . . . let's see . . . .' The Admiral contemplated the diagrams. 'Where are the lighting circuits?'

Maeve stood by Ben as they scanned a portion of the Dean's donation. 'Are there automatic emergency lights? I don't see any,' Ben traced the blueprints with the tip of a ball point pen.

'Aha,' he became elated, 'Admiral . . . here . . . I see the lighting wiring. We can establish connecting circuits at all levels. I can trace them to the power station. See, this section must be for the outside lighting, and this is the electrified fence . . . the guards' quarters, the hangar . . . it's all there.' He leaned back, pleased with his expertise in unravelling the complex blueprint.

'Good, well done,' said the Admiral, not looking up.

'And this is Randolf's suite.' By now Ben was engrossed. 'Side by side with Sebastian's. This place was designed by a team. The plans are professional. There are signatures and logos everywhere. Everything's nicely labelled. Even the occupant's names are in designated areas. How convenient. 'Perhaps,' he turned to face Maeve, 'with this knowledge the easiest thing to do would be to cause a total blackout? They've no back up power. On second thoughts,' he paused, reflecting, 'a better plan might be to create confusion by disabling different systems in random fashion? Only we would know which, where, and when. Of course, that's it. It's much easier to localize a total breakdown. Intermittent faults are always a problem, I should know.'

'So, it's a predictable, apparently random system you want?' asked Maeve. 'Like fractals?'

'Sort of.'

'I'll work on it, may take longer. It'll be systematic, not chaotic . . . for us. Show me which circuits and which areas you wish me to work on.'

'Sambo, I've been thinking,' said the Admiral, frowning thoughtfully. 'Sorry to interrupt, Maeve. Sambo, it's time to make use of your undoubted talents. I think it's up to you to make contact with the guards, as Ben suggested. Survey the exterior. We need every scrap of information we can get.'

Sambo received the suggestion in what could only be described as profound silence. Amelia gave him a long searching look.

'Maybe,' he said, after a long pause.

'Sambo, it's essential that we know the outside layout,' added Ben, 'you're the best man for the job. You can fool them if anyone can. But don't provoke them, no smart, ambiguous jokes. We want information, not to score points.'

'Hold on,' said Sambo, 'I'll think about it, work it out.'

'If it's too much, we could try one of the women?'

'Sure, why not?' said Amelia, coming forward.

'All right, don't push,' said Sambo, gently restraining Amelia, 'I had considered that, and it's dotty. The men out there must be curious about us, especially about you women, and a black woman at that. No, it'd better be me. We need a stereotype, black and dumb. Not a threat, and not er, alluring.'

'You'll do,' grinned Ben. Sambo wrinkled an upper lip.

181

'I'd better get moving.'

He walked over to a cupboard and drew on a crumpled bush shirt, a relic of their journey from the Potentate's capital.

'Hope they're not queer. Some of the mercenaries we used in the company were muscle bound poofs.'

'I'd have thought it might be the idea of the Ku Klux Klan outside that'd bother you, not this lot.'

'What's the difference,' said Sambo, 'you whiteys all look alike.'

'I hope you'll be all right,' Amelia was edgy, 'I suppose you can look after yourself?'

'Of course,' replied Sambo, pleased by her concern.

As soon as Sambo left, the Admiral resumed his study of the Dean's plans.

'Well,' he announced, with evident satisfaction, 'I've finished a quick, preliminary survey. We'd better get on with the final plan, a flow sheet. One we can fix in our memories. Let's get on with the outline.' The Admiral beamed. 'Things're looking up.'

Sambo made his way to the foyer and paused before a large, sealed, plate glass window overlooking the courtyard. He peered through the vertical slats of the Venetian blind. Below he could see a desultory group of armed men lolling about, smoking and talking. Those without side arms had M16 automatic rifles slung across their backs. A few stood, more or less at attention, by fence gates and by ports to the main building.

The heavy door yielded a tentative inch. Two guards, attracted by the slight creak of hinges, turned to peer in Sambo's direction. One, a veritable giant in all dimensions, the other, a contrasting scarecrow of a man. The remaining guards, dwarfed by the sheer bulk of their leader, stared curiously at Sambo. Intimidated despite his resolve, Sambo shoved the door open and strolled out into the brilliant light. He began to descend the steps. No-one intercepted him. At the bottom he halted before the two nearest guards.

'And, who de hell are you?' demanded the giant guard, sauntering over.

'Sambo, one of the guests. Out for a breath of air.'

'Sambo? Youse kidding? A guest? Got permission?' asked the skinny guard.

'I just thought I'd get some fresh air.'

'Oh, I'd just like some fresh airr,' mimicked the skinny guard.

'You de black fella?' asked the giant guard with fine rhetoric. Sambo, thinking of his school days, was disappointed. He had been expecting the more usual epithets. The door behind him shut with a firm click. He was now completely vulnerable. He stared blankly at his interrogators, and saw only an insolently inquisitive, motley group of men.

'Hey guys, it's him all right. Whattcha make of this? Any of youse got some hominny grits?' A chorus of guffaws rewarded the guard's sally. Carry on, boy, you're doing just fine, thought Sambo, still blinking in the unaccustomed light. He grinned ingratiatingly at his tormentor.

'Back to de good old jungle, ey, Sambo? Wanna swing through de trees?' The quality of the banter left Sambo in no doubt as to the guard's intellectual gifts. I can handle this lot, thought Sambo, and continued to smile blandly.

Sambo wondered why he had imagined the guards to be fighting fit. Close up they were not only sloppy and unwashed, but wildly out of condition. Sweat soaked uniforms were stained with food and oil. Unlaced, holed, scuffed, boots completed the outfits.

A particularly rotten stench wafted from the direction of the giant guard's boots and mingled with a pungent odour emanating from his short sleeved shirt. The combined effect was to produce an aroma so powerfully rancid that Sambo was forced to shut off the air supply to his nostrils, and to breathe through his mouth.

'Look, er, sir,' said Sambo in a nasal voice, 'I'm already out, so how about a walk? I won't go far.'

'You sure won't, Sambo me boy. Walk about to your little heart's content. Youse among friends.' The guard, overcome by his sense of humour, leaned back, snortling helplessly, while at the same time managing a quick glance around. Recognizing their cue, his colleagues responded with contrived laughter. They began to crowd Sambo, forcing him backwards.

'Hey . . . enough of dat youse bums, let him alone. He's mine.' The large guard, coming to the rescue, scowled ferociously at his colleagues, 'I'se in charge heah.'

Sambo grinned sheepishly. Vaguely grateful, he tipped a forelock to his protector and ventured a few hesitant steps towards the fence, seemingly fascinated by the thick underbrush beyond.

'Watch out Sambo, or youse'll be fried chicken. Stay away from de electericity.'

'Okay, okay, I'll watch my step. What about over that way?' The huge guard snickered, bowed low, and motioned with a wide sweep of his grubby hand for Sambo to proceed.

'Hey Doug, take ovah, watch that dere port. Me, ahm gonna accompany mah young Sambo here on his inspection of de premises.'

More chuckles. He hadn't had so much fun in weeks. Who'd have thought he'd be an escort for a tame nig? Something to tell the good old boys back home when he got back with his tax-free salary. Anyway there wasn't much going on. He needed a break.

'See dat dere Sambo?' The guard gestured expansively, 'Dat dere's de hangar where de bosses keeps deir poisonal helicopter. Dat dere,' he indicated a squat white building adjacent to the hangar, 'is where we keep de ammo, jeeps, machine guns, an' two-way radios. Wid all dat equipment we could take on any of dem goons around in dese parts and lick 'em wid one hand tied down.'

He winked owlishly, clearly relishing his role as a tour guide. Sambo grinned back, nodding energetically. He was beginning to understand why the Dean had so many headaches.

'There must be a lot of you . . . ?'

'Nah, don't ya believe it fella. We'se only a dozen . . . hand-picked though,' he added, 'we'se all experts. We cin hold our own, against ennythin' in dese Godforsaken parts. Dere are also three or four helite guards. But we done mix

184

with dem. Dey're officers.'

'I guess you're Yanks?'

'Nah,' said the guard, 'ah myself's from the USA . . . in de South. We got South Africans, some Brits, a few Irish, and a coupla terririst Ayrabs.'

'Really? Are they good?'

'Yeah, pretty good wid time bombs. Not much sense of humour. Keep pretty much to themselves. Always prayin'. We only take de best for the job. You see,' explained the guard, 'we've got specialists for ennything. Some of us wuz trained in Southern Rhodesia, in ole Ian Smith's time, and some wuz in de Palestine police. Taught those Yids a thing or two. A few've worked wid Mad Mike Woodroffe . . . you recall 'im? De greatest, he was.'

'Was? Where's he now?'

'Pushing up daisies somewhere, I guess.'

'Too bad,' said Sambo, 'I guess he's a loss.'

'Where you from Sambo?'

'The US.'

'No kidding?' The guard softened, 'De National Guard . . . tried to join 'em, but I guess my feet or sumpin', stood in de way. Dey take nuddin' but de best. We ain't got nobody here from dat outfit.'

While the guard was busy expounding they had reached the far side of Randolf's headquarters and were now directly opposite the hangar. Beyond flowed the broad river. A few yards further to the right Sambo saw a jetty with several moored craft rocking rhythmically in the oily green water as it swept silently past.

Sambo turned back towards the fortress. Viewed from any angle it was an exceedingly ugly and depressing piece of architecture. A low, seemingly impregnable, squat building of dark grey concrete. He made a mental note of the positions of the heavily guarded doors.

Directly opposite the hangar was a steel door of the type that swung over and upwards. For some reason it was unguarded. Somewhat further to the left, as he faced the building, he noted a sloping driveway leading downwards to a door set lower in the wall of the basement.

'What sort of helicopter did you say it was?'

'Ah didn't say, boy. But ah believe it's a big 'un. Can

carry six or seven passengers as well as de pilot. Dey're murder to fly, ah hears. Not much range either. De bosses uses it to get to de airfield twenty miles up river, by de factory. Dey's got two fast execitif jets stashed away dere. Dey ain't used dem for months. Not much action here lately. But what do we care. De pay's great.'

'Factory?'

'Hey boy. Not so many questions.'

The guard was beginning to tire of his unaccustomed bonhomie. Being a gracious chaperone had its limits. Without an audience to appreciate his performance he was becoming bored.

'Back we go. Walkies is ovah.'

Sambo had seen enough. More questions would have raised suspicions.

'I needed that fresh air. It was great. Thanks.'

The guard escorted Sambo to the door of the fortress and unlocked it with a flourish. Sambo restrained an impulse to tip him. It would have been a small satisfaction, but he wisely thought the better of it. It had been more difficult than he had anticipated to play a subservient role to a trained baboon.

☆   ☆   ☆

Night in the jungle fell like a broken blind. Blazing floodlights came on automatically and bathed the courtyard and perimeter in brilliant, blue light.

Formally dressed guests had once again assembled in the drawing room with the private bar. Ben wondered if life abroad a cruise ship could be quite as boringly routine as their present enforced ritual existence. The usual punctilious servants filled their orders. Drinks in hand, they wandered over to the dining room.

'With any luck this could be the last game.' Maeve stood as close as possible to Ben, her warm body pressed firmly against his side, an affectionate hand resting lightly on his forearm. 'How're you doing my friend?'

Ben rewarded his companion with a confident smile and restrained a powerful impulse to take her into his arms.

Amelia and the Admiral were seated at the table, talking

quietly. The atmosphere was calm.

Olga and Denna, late arrivals, approached the Admiral.

'Any luck?' asked Olga, pausing by his chair. A glimmer of her customary glower lingered, but her manner was friendly.

'Yes, as a matter of fact we have,' he said, cautiously, 'thanks to Sambo. What have you to say?'

'We're drawing sketches. Deanna says she can't talk to Sebastian at all. And even if she could, what could she ask him? No, really, not much to add.' Olga looked almost apologetic.

'Well, we've had another bit of luck. I'll fill you in later,' said the Admiral, turning back to the table.

Ben escorted Maeve to her seat, guiding her with a firm hand lingering on the small of her back.

'Maeve,' he murmured, 'let 'em do their worst. We're together, we will cope. You're my inspiration, something to live for. This worm is turning.'

Maeve's eyes glistened, but she did not reply.

'The match will be over tonight,' murmured the Admiral, his head angled towards Amelia and Olga on his right. 'We will be going, win or lose. Randolf would like to drag this out. He's procrastinating, wants to go on toying with us. I won't let him.' His voice faded as a door at the far side began to swing open, heralding the entry of the Randolf gang.

Randolf was promptly transferred to his seat at the head of the table.

'It's my pleasure to welcome you to our table,' announced Randolf without overture. 'Tonight we've arranged a banquet which should surpass the last. And then, of course,' he smiled fiendishly, 'THE most exciting game, possibly a grand finale? I hope some of you are prepared to become instant millionaires?' The announcement was greeted in silence. Undeterred he continued, 'I'm right, aren't I, when I say that the prospect of good food and enormous wealth are enough to brighten anyone's future? Let's enjoy ourselves.'

And the losers? thought Ben as he stared at Randolf's hateful features. Don't give a single damn, do you?

Sebastian walked around the table to approach Ben.

'Ben,' he said, with every indication of sincerity, 'no hard feelings? *C'est la vie*, you know. There's not much time left, but one of us has to win. There's no going back. I've done what I can for you,' he added, lowering his voice, conscious all the while of Randolf's glacial bleak eyes focused on him. Sebastian walked, casually, back to his seat.

Ben was now certain he detected a change in his brother. But, across the table, Sebastian's face remained expressionless. A professional poker player could have done no better. Randolf continued to gaze intently at his favourite nephew.

'Come on, all of you, you may soon be rich enough to buy anything your hearts might desire.' Marie, sensing bad vibrations on her side, attempted to defuse the atmosphere. 'Let's see what the cooks have come up with?'

She ignored, or did not notice, the disdainful expressions around her and continued, apparently untroubled by the dismal fate which awaited her guests, to beam at one and all.

Ben eyed his former spouse with undisguised distaste. He was immensely thankful she was out of his life, a stranger. The pain was gone. What was it that had attracted in the first instance? Sex . . . had that been all there was? Or, was it possible that she had changed out of all recognition? The Marie of his memory had been warm, charming, attractive and, above all, compassionate. He saw no trace of those qualities. Before him sat a smug, vacuous woman, a shell of her former self. While he was contemplating his past, Marie rose and walked to Randolf's side to place an affectionate arm across his bony shoulders. She hugged the bag of bones with manifest pleasure. Ben decided that, apart from being an accomplished actress, Marie was in truth, totally shallow, and utterly self-centred.

As promised, the dinner was exceptional. Randolf behaved impeccably, unloading buckets of gracious effervescence. Marie oozed charm and perfume in equal quantities.

In spite of forebodings about their foreseeable future Ben managed to maintain a flow of animated conversation. In reality his mind was filed with apprehension. He had long decided that when he escaped he would spend a year away from human contact. The idea of sailing single handed around the world had been inordinately appealing. But no longer. His gaze strayed to Maeve, sitting calmly, speaking to her neighbour. His heart filled with pleasure. His gloomy fantasies vanished, totally.

Seated next to the Admiral, George the Dean bobbed his head vigorously and conversed with apparent enthusiasm that disguised a growing unease. He fancied he could detect subtle signs that his employers had knowledge of his recent actions. If so, they gave no sign. Eventually he shrugged, restrained his bobbing head, and decided he would have to go ahead. There was no alternative.

His mind filled with misgivings, George inspected his dinner companions. The Admiral, it seemed, was genuine. How did he know that? The CIA, his omnipotent employer would, surely have vetted the Admiral? He knew that the Admiral had made certain his part in recruiting Ben had been acknowledged. Yet, doubt clouded his mind. Was it possible that the Admiral was . . . a double agent?

The Admiral twitched as if George's thoughts, travelling through the ether, had bounced off his brain. Twisting his powerful neck around to face George, the Admiral enquired, affably, 'What is the matter my friend?'

George the Dean stared blankly, a slight frown on his face. The Admiral continued.

'I can see you're worried. We have to thank you for your, er, interesting contribution. That took some doing.' He spoke softly through lips barely parted. A professional ventriloquist could have done no better.

Only ceaseless crumbling of bread crumbs betrayed George's inner tension. He prayed fervently that no one at the head of the table could overhear.

'Ah, yes,' he said suddenly, in a voice rising as Randolf's gaze fell upon him, 'business must be stimulated. Randolf has made a valid point. His business here cannot go on supporting the economy indefinitely. Along these lines,' he raised his voice a few more decibels, 'Randolf and Sebastian have, I believe, been contemplating upgrading our friend the Potentate's domestic industries.'

Amelia put down her fork abruptly.

'What about the Potentate?'

'The other day,' explained George, 'Sebastian, Randolf and I were discussing the depressed economy of this area, where, as we all know, there are no decent industries, and precious little commerce. This is a desperately poor land, mostly jungle, with one big river, and ruled by a benevolent dictator. We know the old Potentate. What we have to do is to help him upgrade his economy, not hand out charity. He doesn't seem to be doing much on his own. What,' he shrugged, 'can one expect?'

Sebastian, overhearing, decided to enlighten the Dean.

'George, you're talking about Amelia's father.'

Amelia directed an unblinking stare at Sebastian. Was he changing? He was unpredictable.

George's features rearranged themselves into a caricature of surprise. For a few seconds he was silent. His head bobbing had ceased.

'Amelia . . . your father, how embarrassing,' he floundered helplessly. 'What can I say?' He raised a glass of wine to his lips, swallowed, and plunged ahead. 'Well, then, we simply must include you in our discussions. Randolf,' he twisted around to appeal to his overlord, 'what say you we go over the plans for industrial development again, and that we include this young lady?'

Randolf, who had been dozing, and whose meagre supply of energy was fading, awoke to gaze vitriolically at his economic guru. Struggling to control his irritation he growled. 'Of course WE knew about Amelia. Of course, WE intended including her in our discussions. What d'you take us for? You've not been keeping up to date. We'll talk about this, later.'

George grimaced and fixed his eyes on his empty plate. He was sure now that Randolf was not aware of his actions.

'As a matter of fact, Amelia told us about what went on before, the whole story,' said Sambo quietly, 'she filled us in a while back.'

'Did she now?' said Sebastian in a portentously interested voice, 'It's possible, you know, to say too much.'

'Well, then we have no secrets,' interposed Randolf, silencing Sebastian, 'let's not worry about details. These things have a way of settling themselves.'

'Coffee and liqueurs will be served in the drawing room,' cooed Marie.

Randolf drew back creakily from the table and made off

in his wheelchair. The remaining guests rose, and one by one followed him into the drawing room. Sebastian had gone ahead and was busy with liqueurs on an elegant Chippendale-style sideboard.

'What'll you have?' he enquired genially. 'Amelia,' singling her out, What'll it be?' Amelia walked over, her eyes on the bottles.

'A glass of freedom?'

Sebastian, unsmiling, poured a glass of Cointreau.

'Now that we are gathered,' announced Randolf in a nauseatingly amicable manner, 'we must have a chat. Before the final game. We might not have an opportunity to do so again.

'I thought it might be amusing to imagine a journey through fantasyland. What might you have in mind to do with a million dollars? There's no doubt some of you will be much richer before this night is over.

'You cannot complain about being bored, whatever else you might say.'

Randolf at ease, was every inch the civilized host. Not a hint of threat persisted in his benign expression. He spoke in a convincingly open manner. Maeve looked away, fearful her thoughts might be transparent.

Randolf's probing produced no response.

'Oh, come now,' he expostulated, 'you must have a notion . . . a flat in Monte Carlo; a villa in Spain; a new romance . . . you must have SOME fantasies? Are you all lifeless?' He swung round to inspect Olga and Deanna. The latter, moody and irascible as usual, shifted disdainfully and took a deep breath. A powerful urge to speak overcame her.

'Uhm,' she coughed, clearing her throat, her lank hair forming a horn-like tunnel from which sound issued. 'Well,' she began, 'I, for one, would found a club for single women. An exclusive club, with every convenience.'

'Oh, come on,' groaned Maeve, 'be original. Save us the woman's libber stuff. Not here.'

'I was only going to say,' snapped Deanna, turning her favourite shade of purple, 'that I would put my money to good use. I never said anything about bloody liberation . . . or men.'

'We know the codes,' Maeve dismissed her. 'Randolf,' she said, 'save your money. We don't want it. Let us go.'

Sebastian answered with his finest sardonic smile.

'Not until we've settled scores.'

Randolf nodded approvingly to Deanna.

'Carry on.'

'I'll run the club by committee. It'll be democratic. We'll allow some men to join.'

'For God's sake,' said Maeve impatiently, 'do shut up.'

Deanna, choking with burgeoning anger, unable to continue, began to turn deep purple. Ben offered her a glass of water. She snatched it from him without a word, gulping the contents.

The Admiral, timing his intervention well, cleared his throat and said,

'It's my ambition, my intention, to retire to the English countryside. Cornwall's the place. A manor house with ample grounds. Friends to stay.'

'Let us hope your ambitions will be fulfulled,' said Sebastian, frostily. 'Which friends? Do you have any?'

'Ah, well,' said the Admiral, smoothly, 'I have made many new ones in your house. Would you care to be invited?'

'Very clever.' Sebastian glared at the bulky figure. Smart Alec. What had possessed them to employ such a man?

'Time to resume the match,' announced Randolf. 'The next game may be the decider. Let's get on with it.'

19

The screen at the rear of the stage came to life. Chess pieces, black at the top, white at the bottom, slid eeriely into place. But now there was a difference. For the first time in the series, the members of the audience saw their names, in clear, gold lettering, arranged vertically in oblong boxes to the right of the chess board. Each box also held an icon representing a major chess piece.

'You will observe,' Randolf spoke calmly, as if addressing a convention of business associates, 'that we've at last prepared for your intimate participation in this game. As this could be the final, concluding play, you'll not want to forget which piece is yours. We don't want complaints when the final tally is taken. We've set out your names as decided by the draw. Kindly check your designated piece.'

Olga peered at the board and saw her box with the black queen's knight; George the Dean, was perturbed to see his name, as a title, in the box with the white king's rook; Amelia's name was by the black king's bishop; Deanna shared a box with the white queen's rook; Maeve's had the white queen's knight; Sambo's was with the white queen's bishop; the Admiral's box held the white queen.

'All set?' Randolf looked expectantly towards Ben and Sebastian. 'As this may be the penultimate or, possibly, the final round, we will allow more than fifteen minutes per move. It's Sebastian's turn to begin. He's white.'

His mind preoccupied with Maeve and the impending flight plan, Ben hardly noticed his surroundings. Something in his memory was stirring. What was it he was trying to recall? He became more and more frustrated as he scoured a faulty memory. What on earth was it? He shook his head and began to focus on the game.

Sebastian, by contrast, was eager to kick off. After a brief, opening pause, he moved his queen's knight into position before Ben's bishop's pawn.

Ben responded automatically by moving his queen's knight, duplicating Sebastian's move. The audience, intensely immersed in the game, reacted as their hosts had hoped. Olga looked pained, and glanced over to Maeve with a rare, wry, gesture of sympathy. Maeve, spotting her icon's move, winced. How ironic she thought, my piece is in action, but with the wrong knight. She felt ridiculously vulnerable; the chess piece had become an extension of her body.

Randolf watched with a complacent smile on his face. Everything was going smoothly, according to plan. He was delighted with himself, his cleverness, his management of the stage setting. The grand design was coming to fruition. It had been worth the long wait.

Ben, still racking his brains, looked blankly at the board. It seemed to him that he was surrounded by motionless mannikins; part of a silent, frozen tournament. Only Sebastian and he had the power of movement. Randolf was their puppeteer.

An hour and a half later the players had managed to manoeuvre their pieces into compact defensive positions. Setting aside his memory search and all thoughts of Maeve and escape, Ben commenced to play earnestly. He became acutely aware that their lives depended on him. He started to cherish each piece as a shepherd might his sheep. To complicate matters, he found it impossible to risk the lives of his friends, albeit in effigy. The strain was immense.

Sebastian, for quite different motives, played with extraordinary intensity. A successful outcome could solve his latest tribulations. He had, at all costs, to mend his fences with his irascible patron. Randolf's manner had, in the last few days, developed a distinct coolness which Sebastian attributed to two recent events: his ignominoous defeat and his attempted defence of his brother. A spectacular win could reinstate him in the eyes of the old bastard.

But it was Ben who drew first blood. The maddeningly elusive recesses of his memory had yielded. Everything came flooding back. He could not imagine why he had forgotten that episode in his life.

During a nostalgic visit to the country of his birth, South West Africa, Ben had heard rumours about a young Bushman who played phenomenal chess. He had listened, with scepticism, to a description of a chess match between the Bushman and the then reigning world chess master. The game had ended, incredibly, in a draw. The story was intriguing.

Ben was able to persuade a friend, a widely travelled district surgeon, to arrange a meeting with Shongalollo, as the inhabitant of the desert was known.

The doctor organized a safari into the depths of the Namib, to an area where he had come across the tribe of Shongololla. Fortunately the Bushmen had not moved. The expedition managed to locate Shongalolla. And so, after exchanging gifts of sugar, tobacco, and clothing, they were introduced to the chess player.

One evening, under the stars and the wary eyes of the elders of the tribe, Ben and Shongalollo played a series of games of chess, late into the night. It was soon evident to Ben that the reports had not been exaggerated. He was astonished by the brilliance of the ingenuous, diminutive, aboriginal. It transpired that while at a mission school in a desert outpost, Shongalollo had demonstrated a remarkable mind and had been tutored in chess by one of the teachers, a Catholic priest.

In due course Ben persuaded Shongalollo to allow his moves to be recorded. Ben filed the remarkably ingenious moves in his diary, and then forgot all about them.

Fortunately for Ben, Shongolollo's unorthodox strategies surfaced . . . and not a moment too soon.

Desperately anxious to reinstate himself, Sebastian shed his elegant posturing. He became increasingly harassed and infuriated by Ben's switches in strategy.

Sebastian, imitating Ben, moved a sacrificial pawn into a provocative position, then thought the better of it. Too late, he reflected, I should have known better. Although it seemed at first to have been a relatively minor sacrifice, there had been no good purpose to the move, a move that handed Ben the initiative.

'Well, Shongalollo,' muttered Ben, 'let's see what he makes of your tactics.' Ben experienced a lightening of his burden. He was in control, and perhaps, perhaps, of their destinies.

Inwardly strung like a bow, Sebastian remained impassive, his features cool, his dark eyes searching for an opening.

At long last Sebastian made his move. Ben deliberately stayed his response.

The Admiral rose, shook out hands numb with pins and needles and whispering an apology, pushed past Sambo to walk tiptoe towards a door leading to the toilets. Passing the solitary guard he inclined his head in salutation. The guard remained stolidly inert. A few minutes later the Admiral returned and quietly regained his seat. Nothing on the board had changed. Ben had not yet moved.

☆　　☆　　☆

For the past hour George the Dean had been unusually quiet. He sat, pale faced, leaning forward, elbows on knees, knuckles compressing temples. There was no doubt about his distress. As soon as the Admiral returned, the Dean rose groggily, muttered something incomprehensible to those nearest, and indicated by gesture that he too was off to relieve himself.

Walking unsteadily towards the door he passed the impassive guard and, making no effort to seek permission, let himself out. No one spared him a second glance. The icon indicator board and the game riveted their attention.

As soon as he had left the room the Dean's balance stabilized remarkably. He spun on his heel and headed smartly in a direction away from the toilets. His pace quickened as he walked towards Sebastian's office complex. Upon entering he made straight for the inner office. The door was unlocked, as he had anticipated. He opened a filing cabinet, and selected several files from a folder labelled, '**CONFIDENTIAL: Future Proposals**'. Flicking rapidly through the files he selected three, and stuffed the rest back into the cabinet, and shut the drawer.

Hurriedly quitting the room, he crossed the secretarial space, and entered an adjoining, larger, office. Here he searched rapidly for and found a small safe nestling at the rear of the room hidden amongst an array of filing cabinets. The combination lock presented no problem. Opening the safe, he withdrew a set of keys, a small metal box, and a wad of paper currency which he stuffed into his trouser pockets.

The Dean now headed directly for Sebastian and Randolf's private quarters. The dial of his wrist watch indicated an elapsed time of five minutes. He would have to rush. He did not want to be missed, yet.

The corridor to the private suite was empty, the usual guard on duty being presently with Randolf. He hoped the rest of the guards were enjoying the cool night air.

A heavy, ornate, wooden door sealed the entrance. The Dean produced the keys and, after some frantic fumbling, succeeded in unlocking the door. He found himself inside a foyer furnished in extravagantly bad taste, the predominant colour theme being red and black. Red carpets, red wallpaper, and red velvet curtains surrounded him. By contrast every piece of furniture, except the seat bottoms (which were of red plush), was finished in gleaming black lacquer. Everything was either red, black, or both.

The Dean spared his lush environment a cursory glance. He was on full alert for hidden alarms, cameras, microphones. None were visible. His racing pulse was audible in his ears. He paused and willed his heart to slow its fast, pounding pace. Sinking to his knees at the rear of a red chaise longue, he searched and found an almost invisible join in the carpet. he separated the heavy material and, after further hectic scrabbling under the pile, located a hidden partition in the floor. A trapdoor was revealed.

Gripping the latch tightly, holding his breath, he heaved with all his might. It moved. Below lay a sloping staircase. He stepped in and, with infinite care, arranged the carpet so that it rested on the open flaps of the trapdoor. He lowered himself, step by step, into the maw of the stairwell, allowing the trapdoor to close over his head. The carpet folded into place, neatly sealing the gap.

As soon as his feet contacted the cold cement of the passage, he switched on a flashlight. Using its pencil beam to light his way, he moved cautiously forward. In the distance he could hear a low pitched rumble of engines. He was far below the surface of the fortress. Ahead lay a tunnel which led to the main power plant. A few steps on he swung right to enter an adjoining passage leading away from the power plant. This was the passage which led towards the guards' quarters. A short distance on, to his right, just before the main entrance to the guards' quarters, he located a heavily bolted metal door. Once again he produced his assortment of keys and began to work on the first of several locks.

Randolf stirred and began to shift restlessly in his chair. He motioned to his guard; the game was proceeding too slowly.

'Get me a brandy.'

The guard complied with alacrity and, returning to his post, continued to survey the scene before him with soulless eyes. He readjusted a small earpiece connected to a two way radio, but it was silent. The guard began to wonder why the Dean was taking so long, but decided to remain at his post. No-one seemed to notice.

Ben had resumed and was playing superbly. Sebastian's eyes were bloodshot. Not for the first time since his brother's arrival was he filled with a sense of impending disaster. He squinted, stretched, massaged his orbits, and filled his lungs with long, slow breaths. Marie, who had been sitting placidly by Randolf, bent her head to murmur quietly into the latter's ear. As she did so she toyed with the straggly, white, hair at the nape of Randolf's neck. Maeve, noting the intimate gesture, averted her gaze. What was Marie's game? Which was her man?

If the strain is unbearable for us, thought Maeve, turning back to the screen, what can it be like for my poor Ben? She had an aching impulse to enfold him in her arms. An aura of pleasure surged through her as she recalled the memory of his body. I love him, she thought, I KNOW he loves me.

Sebastian, despairing rapidly, began to play recklessly. He had, at all costs, to break through Ben's defences. He would have to go for broke, there was no other course. When he scented an opening he moved to take advantage.

'Queen,' he called, tersely.

Ben flashed the faintest of smiles. The game was going exactly according to Shongololla's strategy. Ignoring Sebastian's threat, he paused briefly, and mounted a counter challenge to Sebastian's queen with his knight.

'Queen,' he responded, not looking up.

How would Sebastian react? It did not matter. Either way Sebastian was beaten. A rational move would have been to exchange queens, but this would only have prolonged the game for a few moves. The conclusion was inevitable. Both knew it. Their roles were reversed. The mouse was toying with the cat.

Sebastian, loathe to admit defeat, scowled, and retreated. It was useless. Ben had dominated the game from start to finish.

Deanna stirred and recrossed her legs, accidentally kicking her muscular neighbour in the calf. Olga, who had been dozing, awoke irritably. She opened her mouth to curse, recognized where she was, and sank back into her seat.

'What's happening?' she asked in penetrating whisper. Then, more softly, as she gazed around, 'Where's that little twit, the Dean?'

'Who?' asked Deanna, her eyes concentrating on the screen.

'That little, wet creep . . . the Dean.'

'How should I know?'

'Probably gone for a crap. Constipated, no doubt. Never eats the right food. Who's winning?'

'Ben, I think . . . do shut up,' muttered Deanna. Olga miffed, sniffed, and lapsed once more into a sulky state.

'Where is the Dean?' she repeated.

'Gone off with another silly headache,' snapped Deanna, after a pause, 'can't take it. Useless male.'

☆   ☆   ☆

199

George the Dean, continued his cautious journey along the dimly lit tunnel. He paused every few feet to listen. He shuffled on, passing several low passages intercepting the main corridor. The rumbling diesel noises grew fainter. Ten yards on his flashlight outlined a metal door. It was massively constructed of shiny steel and securely bolted, but not locked. A push-bar worked a latching mechanism. The door was impregnable from the outside, but designed to allow easy egress.

He slid the oiled bolts open and tried a light, exploratory shove on the push-bar. Thank you Lord for good maintenance, thought the Dean, and opened the door a fraction of an inch.

Cautiously applying pressure he forced the door a further inch. He switched off his light, remained absolutely motionless, and listened. Artificial light seeped in through the long vertical slit formed by the opening. A few more inches, and he could see out into the courtyard.

Blazing halogen lights flooded the perimeter of the building. Trillions of night insects singing in unison produced a high pitched, shrieking sound which invaded the silence in the corridor. It was music to his ears. He was almost there.

Hot, humid air flooded his nostrils. The door opened further. His angle of view increased until he could see ten degrees in each direction. He was now able to make out the outline of the boat house. Beyond he could see the infamous electrified fence. There were no dogs or guards. His luck was holding.

The door opened a few more degrees. The Dean's hands dripped sweat. His legs trembled uncontrollably with knees at the point of buckling. The random fluttering in his chest tormented him. He began to wonder if his heart might not get out of hand and self destruct in a paroxysm of uncontrolled activity. All was still in the courtyard. He looked at his watch. It was fifteen minutes since he had left the game.

The gap in the doorway had opened to a narrow bodywidth. The Dean slithered through. Now exquisitely exposed in brilliant light, he cowered, frozen, against the wall of the fortress. The Dean gathered the last vestiges of his strength and courage and set his shaking limbs for action. Stooping until his nose was inches off the ground, he started to scramble rapidly, like an agitated insect, towards the nearest wall of the boat house.

The river, a rippling, rustling body of water surging past the boat house, came into view. Inching along towards the door in the side of the boathouse he fumbled for and nearly dropped the set of keys. With manic frenzy he worked on the lock and let himself in. At the far end faint beams shimmered irregularly; floodlights reflecting off the water. Moist, warm air enveloped him as it swept in on a breeze, drawing with it palpable vapour from the river.

He continued forward, still bent double, his face hovering mere inches from the floor, and made for the jetty which he judged to be directly ahead. The fluttering in his chest had subsided.

A gently rocking motorboat came into view. Like a foraying snake he eased his body over the gunwale, and crawled painfully along the bottom of the boat to the seat by the controls. The aroma of oil and fuel was strong but not unpleasant. Faint heat from the motor wafted up and surrounded him. He was almost away.

Inch by inch he eased the rope from the moorings. With infinite care, using a rag wrapped oar, he pushed the boat away from the jetty. An obstinate dead weight it was, maddeningly inert. Almost imperceptibly the boat gained momentum and began to glide away. It seemed to take an age to move a few millimetres. A few more thrusts with the oar and it began a steady swing out from the jetty as the current took hold with exasperating tardiness. And then, at last, it floated free into the main stream of the river.

'A good time for a coffee break,' rasped Randolf, shattering the spell which had fused the motionless spectators. The guard was instantly by his side. Randolf's bony body was expertly manhandled into his chair. Sebastian had been, temporarily, reprieved. The pieces on the board and their icons, remained locked in position.

The audience rose, yawned, and squinted. One by one

they made their way to the drawing room.

'Amelia,' said Sambo, casually taking her by the arm and drawing her aside, 'have you seen the Dean?'

'He's not here?' She looked around. 'He must've gone off to bed. Another migraine probably? He looked ill.'

'I guess so.' Sambo shrugged and sipped his coffee.

☆　　☆　　☆

Five minutes into the resumed game and Ben, wasting no time, moved in for a finish. Shongalollo's unprecedented moves were working to perfection. Sebastian, defeat inevitable, threw caution to the proverbial wind, and played wildly. It was abundantly clear that he was about to go down. Frustration gave way to anger.

So bloody what? he thought, I don't have to do this. Piss on Randolf's stupid, asinine games.

There was no possible escape, yet he could NOT resign. He had no illusions about Randolf's reaction should he surrender. I don't know who I dislike most at this moment, Randolf, or my wretched brother.

Ben brought the bishop assigned to Amelia forward and said, with exultant finality, 'Checkmate.'

Sebastian glared impotently at the board. Black despair coursed through his mind. He exhaled in a long, grunting sigh. He dared not meet Randolf's gaze.

Maeve shivered with delight and hung onto Amelia's arm.

Randolf raised a bony hand, gestured at the ceiling, and with short vicious stabbing movements, exclaimed, 'Well, well, well. Ben wins again. We'd not expected a repeat performance. I must say I was not prepared for Sebastian to fail so easily.'

Sebastian scowled at the floor. Bloody old bastard, he thought, furious with his loss of prestige.

'I . . . I will have to retire,' continued Randolf. 'I will decide what course of action to take. Tomorrow is another day and, by the way, this does not change the rules. Don't think about rewards, yet. I'm a man of my word. Right now I'm naturally upset. Ben, with some help from Sebastian, has caused me, not for the first time, to postpone my plans.

But, not to worry, I won't welsh on my deal. There will be a final game. No-one's in a hurry, I presume?' He let out an hyena-like cackle.

The guard swung the chair and wheeled Randolf out. Marie, followed by a sombre, sullen Sebastian, walked out. The door closed behind them.

☆　　☆　　☆

The Dean lay adamantly on the bottom of the boat for minutes that seemed like hours. The boat swayed and rocked as the current swept it into the middle waters where the river flowed more swiftly. When he sensed the boat to be moving steadily on course, he sat up cautiously. No lights were visible. He was surrounded by total, inky blackness. He guessed he was about half a mile down stream.

Moving forward, the Dean groped for the boat's controls on the instrument panel. He found a switch, turned on a light, and began to fiddle with wires behind the dash panel. Boat electrics were usually straightforward, as well as accessible. In a few seconds he had located the starter button. From there he traced wires to the ignition circuit.

He reached into his trousers for the Swiss multi-purpose pocket knife. Although he had never, so far, found a use for it, he had always kept it available for emergencies. And now, at long last, the purchase was justified. Congratulating himself on his foresight, he sliced through the twin wires leading from the ignition switch. Stripping their insulation he touched the ends together. A fat spark, and a short, stuttering whine from an exhaust fan in the engine compartment rewarded his efforts.

Success. THIS WAS IT. He twisted the bared ends together and hoisted himself onto the seat by the wheel. Priming the choke, he pushed hard on the starter button. The engine groaned, fired, and sputtered out. He primed the choke again, and peered, in the dim light of the instruments, at the fuel gauge. The tank was half full.

The Dean jabbed frantically at the starter button. The motor responded instantly, coughed, caught, turned over a few times, only to die away. Christ, must've flooded it, he thought. Beside himself with anxiety, he peered into the black gloom bebind him. He was on the right track, but also well on the way to a heart attack. Something . . . had to work . . . just had to work. His heart resumed a fluttering dance. He paused, counted slowly to ten, gritted his teeth, and prayed. What he did not need was a flat battery.

Fragments of childhood nightmares, in which he always fled in terror from unknown pursuers, came flooding into his mind. Shit, shit. Why wouldn't the bloody motor start? In a near panic he opened the throttle wide and jabbed again and again at the starter button. The motor coughed, and then settled into a most wonderful, throbbing roar. He sped on for another mile, switched off the motor, and turned to the small electric outboard.

20

Ben brushed his teeth in desultory fashion, abstractedly searching his reflection in the bathroom mirror for blemishes. He was too tired to sleep, much less, able to evaluate the events of the day. His had been a pyrrhic victory, a temporary thrill. He hoped, maliciously, that Sebastian was having a disturbed night explaining his ignominious defeat to Randolf.

At first Ben did not heed the soft tap on his door. The tap repeated as a firm, insistent knock. Muttering fretfully, he dropped the toothbrush into a mug. He was in no mood for company and hesitated, tempted to ignore the summons. Eventually, spitting toothpaste, he walked, reluctantly, to the door.

It was Maeve, standing still, a small smile on her lips, who awaited him. Without ceremony she came in close, and wrapped him in her arms.

Dawn was breaking when Ben awoke. Around the bed beams of light glistened through a haze of dust. In the background, interwoven with a chorus of cheerful bird songs, was the inescapable, pulsating screech of the jungle.

Ben rolled over and propped himself on an elbow to study Maeve's peacefully sleeping form. Her back was turned. One side of her face was half burried in a halo of thick, blonde, hair spread out on the pillow. He traced the line of her cheek where it blended into the curve of her neck. A small regular pulse stirred the skin beneath her jaw.

The light in the room began to change from soft yellow to

white. Gently Ben shook her shoulder. Maeve, mumbling incoherently, stirred, and turned onto her stomach. He shook her more vigorously. Suddenly she was awake, struggling upright.

'What? Where am I? Oh, . . . ,' she smiled sleepily, 'hello there.'

'Good morning. Did you sleep well?'

'Oh, yes . . . marvellous. I had such a beautiful dream. Oh, Ben, this is lovely. Can I tell you about it?'

'Sorry darling, but it's time to get moving. We've to meet the others. This's the day we get going.'

'Oh, God, yes,' she was now fully alert, 'today's the day. I'm scared Ben.' Maeve rose from the bed and headed for the bathroom. She paused and turned back, giving Ben a bonus, full frontal view.

'Ben, I'm terrified something will come between us. Something awful . . . might happen to one of us. I can't bear the thought of a life alone. Oh, Ben, we must succeed.'

Ben rose and wrapped his arms around her, 'Nothing will come between us. Nothing.'

☆   ☆   ☆

'Tonight's THE last game.' Ben paced up and down, 'the one which Randolf hopes will be the decider.'

'He'll have to go on anticipating that we believe in his game plan, won't he?'

'He's going to be chewing carpets, when all his elaborate arrangements . . . our capture, the witnesses, the icons, all that . . . come to naught when we skedaddle.'

'I only wish we could stay to see his expression.'

'By the way, I may have to revise the programme,' said Maeve. 'I keep two copies with me. I didn't want to leave any lying around, just in case I mislaid them.'

'Timing is everything,' Ben looked at his watch, 'when we get going everthing must flow along from that point.'

'I think we agreed to start just after dark. We haven't set the exact time, but I can arrange it easily.' Maeve handed Ben a copy of her notes. Ben studied the tidy lettering and diagrams. Names, times, and circuits were neatly set out. He paid special attention to those areas in the fortress and its environs that Maeve had highlighted.

'Explain,' ordered Ben, impressed by her handiwork.

'I will, as soon as we get the Admiral and Sambo over here.'

'We'd better include the Dean---I hope he's recovered----and collect the terrible duo. We've a breakfast meeting arranged.'

Surrounding Maeve with a protective arm, Ben was about to usher her out of the room when a sharp rap on the door halted them. He motioned to Maeve to step aside and released the latch.

'Good morning, Admiral. No need to batter the door down. We were just setting out to find you.'

The Admiral, no longer unflappable, was ominously solemn. Something was amiss. He stepped inside.

'What's up?' asked Ben, amiably.

'There are guards swarming all over the place.'

'Oh, oh, . . . shit . . . why? For us?'

'They're looking for the Dean.'

'The Dean?'

'He's missing and, what's more, so's a motorboat.'

'Christ . . . he's taken off. Bloody hell . . . that'll bugger up everything. I KNEW he couldn't be trusted. The little weasel.'

'No wonder he wanted those plans,' said Maeve, 'but why bother to share them with us? To throw us off the scent?'

'Well, the fat's in the fire,' said the Admiral, adding to the flurry of metaphors, 'they'll check through all his papers and so on, and find a lot missing. Then they'll descend on us. Security will tighten. It's anybody's guess how Randolf or Sebastian will react.'

'We'd better get to breakfast. Do the others know?'

As usual Deanna and Olga were firmly entrenched at the breakfast table. The two eccentric women, engrossed in their meal, at first paid scant attention to the approaching group. But as they came nearer Olga put down her tools and turned to face them.

'Morning,' she said, shortly.

'Hello Olga,' said Maeve briskly, 'we've some news. Bad

news.'

Olga shrugged and turned away. Maeve responded with a downturned grimace. She took a seat at the next table with the Admiral and Ben, and proceeded to scan the menu. Deanna and Olga munched on steadily.

It was at this stage that Sambo, with Amelia by his side, strolled in. The Admiral decided to wait until all were seated.

'The news for today,' he announced, heavily, 'is that our friend, the Dean's, disappeared.'

'What did you say?' Amelia, Sambo, and Olga spoke in unison. Deanna froze, a fork halfway to her mouth.

'Just that. Gone . . . escaped . . . went away. Probably last night while the game was on. Obviously planned it all carefully. Fooled all of us, including his rotten employers.' Having delivered the announcement, the Admiral reached for a pot of coffee.

'That migraine, oh, the crafty old bugger,' said Ben, softly, 'How clever. Well, that's going to wreck our chances.' He looked curiously at his chief. 'Now what do we do?'

'For a start,' said the Admiral, 'we'll keep a low profile. Wait and see. Continue with our present plans.'

'What's the point? We won't make it. They'll be twice as vigilant. Randolf won't make the same mistake twice. He'll never let us slip through his fingers.'

'Maybe, maybe not. But we're not dealing with a rational mind,' said the Admiral calmly. 'We can count on his being so enraged by the Dean's vanishing act---that, and Sebastian's public humiliation---that he'll throw all his energy and all his men into getting the Dean back, dead or alive. He'll ignore us until he's accomplished his task. He's got to save face. I know his mind.

'In the meantime we're still here . . . captives . . . safe . . . very much under his eye. Whereas the Dean's successful escape would severely deflate his ego.'

'What's more,' interjected Ben, 'he, they, know that the Dean's bound to come back with help. He's nothing to lose . . . no winnings to account for. You're right, Sebastian and Randolf will go all out to recapture him. It's my opinion, for what it's worth, that if we act now, while there's much confusion, we may still have a chance. But, it will be more dangerous.'

208

'Agreed?' The Admiral looked around, 'The action will begin tonight as planned.' He caught sight of Deanna glaring, speechless with indignation, and faltered.

'How could it be,' she demanded, 'that you had no idea, not the slightest suspicion, about your pal's plans?' The Admiral struggling to keep an even keel, started to explain, but was cut off.

'See . . . ' sneered Deanna, looking around, 'what've I been saying? True to form, just like a man. Thinks we're all idiots.' She wrinkled her nose in disgust. Her rock bottom opinion of the perfidious male gender was clearly justified.

'And I'd hoped he might be different,' said Olga with a wistful sigh, and proceeded, with contempt borrowed from Deanna, to obstruct the Admiral by ignoring him and returning to her breakfast. Deanna was, bloody hell, right.

The Admiral had faced tougher opposition,

'Look here, I had no idea . . . '

'Why don't you shut up and do your scheming elsewhere?' demanded Deanna, jabbing her egg with a vicious fork.

'As I was trying to explain,' persisted the Admiral, 'we, certainly I, had nothing to do with the Dean's escape. Believe what you like. We're still going to go ahead with our plans. And anyway,' he added, addressing the two disaffected women, 'you agreed to join.' He felt obliged to clarify the position. If there was to be any hope of an escape they had to work as a team.

While the Admiral was attempting to convince his flock, the original officer-guard who had captured them in the jungle, entered the room and walked directly to their table.

'What, do YOU want?' snapped Olga, her peevish personality intact.

'I'm sorry to interrupt,' apologized the officer, 'but my employer conveys his compliments and wishes you to join him in the library . . . right away.' He inclined his neck a fraction, straightened, and retreated.

'Well, that was coming.' Ben was prepared for a tirade. He was however, puzzled by the Admiral's apparent lack of knowledge of the Dean's intentions. Weren't they linked, by their respective intelligence services?

The Admiral seemed unperturbed by the imminent summons. He appeared to have accepted that it was inevitable and summoned a waiter to place an order. But when the food arrived neither he, nor anyone else, had much appetite. It was clear that there were, for today, stressful events ahead.

☆　　☆　　☆

The library they found themselves in was pleasantly furnished, belying the threatening ambience surrounding the presence of Sebastian and Randolf. The latter basked in baleful silence at the head of an oval conference table flanked by Marie and Sebastian. A step behind, arms aggressively folded, stood armed guards. Sebastian gestured perfunctorily and the prisoners found seats around the conference table.

'This is my reward,' sputtered Randolf, barely controlling his fury, 'for being a good host. Did you know that for the past several months I had employed the Dean, at an inflated rate, as my financial counsel? I treated him with respect AND consideration. I sheltered him in my own home. Gave him free run of the place.

'Imagine my astonishment when I heard he'd taken leave, run from my house . . . my hospitality, without the slightest warning. No goodbyes. Stole money and important papers. A slap in the face. And, and,' he quivered with rage, 'adding insult to injury, ran off in one of my motorboats. Words . . . fail me.' He glared, temporarily speechless, at his awed captives.

After a long pause, he recouped and resumed, 'Did any of you know about this?'

Randolf, not expecting a response, tore on. 'What IS the world coming to? It's all TYPICAL . . . typical of declining morals. The result of rotten educational standards . . . overpaid teachers . . . immorality, all that . . . and more to the point, undisciplined upbringing. It wasn't like that in my day.

'What's happening to the universities?' he bellowed, going off at a tangent, staring through the audience with glazed eyes. 'How could a man like that have become a dean? Certainly not at my university. But it seems any fool of a wimp can succeed these days.

'Let me tell you I could see he was nothing but a second-rater.' Randolf's gaze wandered off into the distance; he

210

seemed incapable of coherent thought.

'Bloody administrators . . . politicians . . . ' he grumbled, lapsing into morose silence. His audience remained uncomfortably silent.

Ben was relieved by the direction of Randolf's random ravings. The heat was off him, for the present. As far he was concerned Randolf, in full stride and dripping fury (as long as it was directed elsewhere) was simply an aberration.

The silence in the room was abruptly shattered by the sound of an engine starting up in the courtyard. The throbbing racket of whirling rotor blades, combined with the rising scream of jet engines, made any attempts at further speech impossible. After a few minutes the commotion began to fade.

They're off, thought Ben, in search of the Dean.

'Hear that?' screamed Randolf, springing to life, 'At this very moment my troops are in hot pursuit of that . . . that . . . that criminal academic. And that brings me to another matter,' he added, glancing at Ben, 'I've decided to stay all proceedings against you, until we've recaptured your devious colleague. The last game will have to be postponed. When that bastard is recovered I'll want all of you to be present. I pride myself in dealing fairly with everyone. I want you to be here.'

Ben needed no further evidence that his uncle was a raving lunatic.

Randolf turned, signalled to Sebastian to take over, and lapsed into a withdrawn, catatonic state.

Ben was cheered to see that Sebastian was as ill at ease as any in the room. It was clear now where the power lay. He had lately been experiencing a resurgence of hope. He was not quite sure why? Perhaps because he sensed a change in Sebastian, that his brother was having second thoughts? Recollections of shared childhood adventures stirred in his mind as he pondered his twin's demeanour.

'You may return to your quarters,' said Sebastian, 'but do not, under any circumstances, attempt to leave his building, or you'll be shot on sight. The guards are on high alert and have orders to shoot to kill. Apart from that, you may do as you wish within the confines of the fortress. Randolf and I are drawing up new plans for your . . . er . . . future. We'll discuss details at dinner tonight.'

So saying Sebastian sauntered over to Marie and, with every indication of affection, encircled her waist with an arm, and escorted her to the door. Randolf was ushered out by the guards, leaving Ben and company seated.

'What did you expect,' asked Deanna, 'congratulations?'

'Well, Ben, what do you think? Is there any reason why we should stay around and await his lordship's pleasure?' Maeve came up to him.

'We'll discuss this elsewhere.'

Deanna nudged Olga. 'Okay?'

'Yes,' replied Olga, curtly. 'that creepy little Dean . . . ' She shook her head in disappointment, and walked out.

☆   ☆   ☆

Preparations for the retrieval of the delinquent dean were proceeding at full tilt. The courtyard was in a state of constant turmoil. Heavily armed guards trotted back and forth, guns flapping at their sides. Jeeps with engines running seemed to be everywhere; some were armed with machine guns; others had been assigned as troop carriers. At a given command three jeeps hurtled out through the gates down the road leading to the jungle. Two peeled off and headed for the river bank, leaving one to head inland.

At the jetty the remaining motor boats rocked precariously as men tumbled in. With throttles wide open they roared off, leaving behind billowing furrows of foaming water which washed up the river bank, disturbing birds and submerged crocodiles. Practically all the guards had been sent off on the man hunt.

'You bloody idjit, look what youse got us into. How did that little shiite get by youse? Asleep were you, you stupid fucker?' The chief guard, hastily dressed and beside himself with vexation, paused to vent his considerable spleen on his skinny and equally dishevelled colleague. 'Stupid useless pricks, all of youse.'

'Look Fred, no one could've guessed it. He had a key to

the boat house. I didn't give it him. It aint my fuckin' fault. I was watching' the fence on the other side. Anyway, whose fault is it he got out? Where were you?' The skinny guard explored the interior of his nose and spat on the ground in disgust.

'Well, anyways,' allowed the chief guard, 'de boss is shitting hisself. And iffen we done get him back what he wants, we're in de crappin' soup. Who cin blame him? He pays us to do a job, and den dis fuck-up happens. You'd better get on back to bloody South Africa, you useless lump of dung. You sure as hell won't get another fancy job like dis . . . , wid such good pay. You'd better pray dem helicopter guys gets him alive.'

Two straining, cursing, guards, hauled along by eager Doberman Pinschers, slithered by on their way to a belated patrol outside the fence. The chief guard made a great show of checking its integrity. In order to do so he donned heavy rubber goves and boots. Stepping back, he flung a small green branch at the fence. With a sharp hissing crack the stick began to steam and exploded as high voltage coursed through it. The guard, satisfied with the demonstration of his expertise, stalked off.

'Well dat's workin'. No one can get by dat little baby. If dat done get 'em, the crocs sure will. Maybe you'd like to try it . . . ey?' The skinny guard glared at his tormentor.

'The more occupied they are the better. All those guards falling over each other can only suit us,' said Ben, surveying the chaos in the courtyard from a window, 'we keep out of the way.' He wagged a mildly reproving finger at Deanna and Olga sitting sulkily by themselves while they continued to glower at him.

'Our best chance will be after dark,' announced the Admiral, 'with a bit of luck, by the time it's pitch black, we'll be well on our way. We'll have to watch out for returning guards.'

'Don't you think,' said Ben, 'that they'll leave some guards posted outside, near exits?'

'I'm banking on that,' replied the Admiral, 'we want them

213

to be there, to be confused. We want bodies in the way, their bodies. Ready , Maeve?'

'Yes,' said Maeve, 'Ben and I arranged the programme's timing. It gets dark quickly. We must wait until the lights are supposed to come on.'

'They'll be expecting every light to come on, simultaneously, as usual,' explained Ben, 'anything different would confuse them. Everything must appear to be normal, at first.'

'Well, let's hope it works. If it doesn't . . . ' Maeve shrugged.

'Confusion's our best ally,' reiterated Ben, 'and judging by what's going on, there's no shortage of that.'

'Once the main lights are on, the programme will start. I've varied the areas as we discussed,' said Maeve, 'we're counting on them chasing about after shadows.'

'I like that. They can't be guarding everywhere at the same time,' said Ben, 'Well, anyway, that's the general idea.'

'We absolutely must keep cool heads. Let's pray there are no surprises.' The Admiral raised a hand to cover his eyes.

'Sambo, you've not said a word,' said Ben, turning to the black CIA agent, sitting quietly by himself.

Sambo took his time to reply. Ben wondered if he had heard and repeated the question.

'Did you hear . . . Sambo?'

'I heard . . . I'm thinking. Trigger happy guards will be a problem. I can't think of anything sensible to say. It's all been said.'

'Well try and look enthusiastic. Okay then, we lie low. Let them fall over each other,' said Ben, adding incredulously, 'Who'd have thought that the Dean would abscond before us? There's no turning back for us now.'

☆　　☆　　☆

Sebastian, seated in the library, stared morosely at the brandy swirling in his glass. He was surrounded by books; books everywhere, on shelves, in glass cases, on desks. Every inch of wall space was decorated with books. Despite his avowed dislike of intellectuals, Randolf liked to affect an image of literary worldliness.

214

'While we're waiting,' asked Marie, dropping her copy of *Vogue*, 'what about Ben . . . and the others?'

'I have NOT changed my mind,' snapped Randolf, with more than a hint of irritation, 'it amuses me to toy with Ben. He must think us a bunch of blockheads. As if we had no idea what he and his bunch're up to. Let them stew, all of them. I've plans for them . . . killing several birds with one stone, ey?' His body shook as he chortled mirthlessly, displacing angular elbows resting on the desk.

'Randolf,' said Sebastian, frowning, 'I wish you'd reconsider your position. I repeat, this business . . . you're not really going ahead, are you? After all we're both, like it or not, related to Ben. I told you I'm NOT happy about killing him. Murder is not my bag. It's all very well to talk about judicial 'executions' but, let's face it, it's really murder. There must be another way. Why not leave him here in the jungle? He'd never get out.'

A black cloud passed over Randolf's face. He was in no mood to consider any form of clemency. His heir, his nephew, was showing distressing signs of weakness; not behaving as he was expected to. Randolf would not, could not, under any circumstances, countenance a change in plans. Never.

'Look here, Sebastian, I thought we'd had this all out a while ago.' Randolf was as cold as ice. 'My ego simply won't allow me to make any concessions. I never compromise. And don't try my patience. The subject is closed.'

'Yes, but . . . '

'No 'yes buts'. We're going through with it. And that's final.'

☆   ☆   ☆

The power boats had been travelling at high speed for over two hours. The chase had been fruitless. They had slowed to a crawl and were drifting limply in a sheltered bend of water. The river at this point broadened into a wide sweep several hundred yards across. There was no sign of the fugitive dean.

'We're running low on fuel,' warned a guard, 'can't understand it, he must've had about the same as we have on board. Where can the bugger be? Where's that stupid boat?'

An officer scanned the banks of the river with powerful infra-red binoculars.

'All I can see are crocodiles sleeping. No choice now,' he said to the guard at the wheel, 'we've got to turn back.'

He raised a microphone to his lips.

'Search team Alpha calling base. Do you read?' A hissing crackle answered. He repeated the call twice, and then turned to the others.

'Nothing works out here. Come on, let's get back. It's upstream, so go slow . . . save fuel. I don't want to swim for shore.'

The boats moved off in a circle, engines throttled back, making a wide sweep and headed for home. The officer continued to scan the banks of the river.

21

'Sambo,' said Amelia, pensively, 'Father's probably beside himself with worry. I should've left some sort of note, an explanation.'

'Yeah, well,' said Sambo, resting his feet on the desk, 'he must know what you're like. It's a bit late to worry about your old man. Look at me, I should have made better arrangements with my control in Washington. But,' he shrugged, 'nobody's perfect.'

Resuming his role as coordinator the Admiral focused his attention on the black man from the CIA.

'Sambo,' he asked, 'are you all right?'

Sambo's hearing seemed to have malfunctioned.

'Sambo . . . did you hear, are you okay?' repeated the Admiral, tapping the table. Sambo removed his feet from the table.

'Sorry,' he said sheepishly, 'I was thinking about my control. As far as I'm concerned everything is fine.'

The Admiral swivelled to face Maeve, 'that includes you and the programme?'

'Everything's ready,' answered Maeve, 'What route have you finally decided?'

'Yes, that brings us,' said the Admiral, soberly, resting his chin on a hand, 'to the $64,000 question. Ben and I've worked out a route. See if you agree. Let me tell you what we think is best.

'The river way is out, for obvious reasons. Firstly, as our friend here, Deanna, pointed out, it's been used. Secondly, it's crocodile infested. And thirdly, they'll have disabled the motorboats, and be guarding them.

'The jungle? Everyone's thought of that. But it's very, very chancy. Much too difficult to make it through from here. They'll hunt us down. Even if we made it through the fence, with the power off, and got away, we wouldn't survive in the jungle without a competent guide.

'That leaves the helicopter. And that's what it has to be. By the way, I should've asked. I read in your dossier Ben, that you had flown helicopters. I hope that information was correct?'

'It was, is. I thought you knew,' said Ben, 'but I'm rusty. Haven't flown one for ages. My company had one.' He smiled apologetically.

'Won't they be guarding it?' asked Sambo.

'They will, but if we arrange it, we'll draw them away. It's in the plan. We'll have to take a chance. If necessary I'll disable the guards. I've got a weapon. The random lighting should help. But it will have to be the helicopter. I had it in mind all along.' The Admiral spoke forcefully. 'Sambo's reconnoitred the outside of the hanger; Ben's timed the run from the fortress. I think, I hope, I've worked out all the details. With Maeve's programme to confuse them, we should just have enough time to board. Success will depend on two vital factors, their confusion, and our ability to get to the helicopter rapidly. I believe we can do it.'

Deanna, who had been sitting solemnly silent, glanced at her companion, Olga, and leaned forward.

'All right, we're coming along,' she announced, 'if you'll have us. We will simply have to trust your judgement. Can you give us any idea exactly when we . . . er . . . are going to get moving? Olga and I want to be prepared. We'd like to get a few things ready.'

'Get things ready?' The Admiral's voice rose an octave with astonishment. His accent became pronounced. 'I'm afraid not. You can't take anything along and,' he added, reinforcing his rasping admonition, 'to show any sign of preparation, would be the height of folly. Do you want to advertise our escape?'

Deanna's visage began to turn a familiar, suffused pink.

'There's no need to be sarcastic,' she mutterted, 'you're

all into your superior act again.'

'Hold on Deanna.' Ben held up a placating hand. 'We're all on edge. The Admiral didn't mean it that way. He was, surprised . . . by your request. Look,' he went on, 'when we get out of here we'll make it up to you. Accept us for what we are . . . worried and very nervous.'

'The programme then,' resumed the Admiral, when Deanna settled, 'is to meet after dinner. We'll find an excuse to withdraw early, in a way that won't arouse suspicion. That's the part I cannot plan, the only part where things could go astray. You will have to take your cues from me. You have to trust me implicitly, and follow my instructions . . . to the letter. Things will be happening all around us.'

No one spoke for several seconds.

'Have we set the time?' asked Ben.

'I was coming to that. It'll depend on what happens at dinner.'

'Maeve, the programme's to start just after dark? You may have to change that.'

'No problem,' replied Maeve, 'I can reset it to any time you choose.'

'We're go then, at last,' said Sambo, heaving a long, tense sigh.

☆   ☆   ☆

Randolf looked up from the spreadsheet.

'Marie, in spite of recent, unsettling events, tonight must be a super gala experience for us. We'll show them we're civilized.' He put aside for the moment the portfolio of columns and numbers. 'I feel I owe our guests a decent last supper. And,' he grinned wolfishly, 'since we have nothing to fear, I'm going, finally, to enlighten them.'

'Yes, of course Randolf. I'll make sure Sebastian has it all arranged. He'll want Ben to have a proper farewell.'

A vaguely troublesome thought entered her mind. 'I suppose you are right, you usually are. We should let Ben have all the facts. Do you really intend . . . ' her eyes were large and round, 'to do away with him? You're not just trying to frighten him? He is your brother's son. It'll be a bit

219

awkward later, don't you think?'

'God,' groaned Randolf, 'you too. It's all arranged, don't concern yourself with details.'

☆   ☆   ☆

'Hurry up Olga, stop gaping at yourself,' hissed Deanna, 'be on time, for once. We can't be late ... it's going to be absolutely crucial tonight. We can rely on those men to be early.'

'Look here, you, stop giving me orders,' snapped Olga, 'I'm sick of your bossiness. I'll take as long as I damn well please. If you're in such a bloody hurry, go on ahead.'

'Oh, shit, you must have the curse. Come on, COME ON, will you?'

Olga moved, if anything, more deliberately, puttered around, and then coolly donned a silk stole, pausing to admire the effect in a mirror. Infuriatingly, for Deanna, she hesitated and retraced her steps to search for a different evening bag. Finally, when the right one for the occasion was discovered, she walked out.

☆   ☆   ☆

Sebastian brushed an imaginary hair from the sleeve of his midnight blue tuxedo. He glanced at Marie seated before a large oval mirror by her dressing table, and sighed. Only a few more weeks. In his mind he reviewed his agenda, his face expressionless.

'Sebastian darling, do I look all right?'

'Exquisite, gorgeous.'

'Thank you,' she smiled, gratefully, 'sometimes you say such nice things. I know I'm no longer gorgeous. Still, love overcomes all, doesn't it, darling?'

'My dear love, in you I see everything I've always wanted in a woman,' replied Sebastian, in a low, sincere voice, 'to me you are, and will always be, beautiful. Besides which, you are beautiful. I carry in my mind a picture of you as you were when first we met. I have to leave now. See you shortly.' He stopped abruptly and walked out.

Marie continued to fuss with her toilet, smiling com-

220

placently at her image in the mirror. Mirror, mirror, on the wall, now tell me who's the fairest of them all? The words of the fairy tale echoed in her mind. Not me alas, she sighed, not any more.

☆　　☆　　☆

Dinner was in full swing. An unobtrusive corps of waiters circulated, assiduously attending to the diners. Sebastian had ordered that nothing, absolutely nothing (as long as their whims were of a culinary nature) was to be regarded as impossible. Sartorially elegant in white tie and tails, he seemed to have overcome his recent aggravations, and oozed charm in overpowering quantities. He interlaced witty comments with flattering compliments. Suddenly, a fixed smile on his lips, Sebastian swung round, and faced Ben.

'Ladies and gentlemen,' he began smoothly, not taking his eyes off his brother, 'may I have your attention? The time has arrived for me to announce an item of news. What I have to tell you will, I suggest, more than surprise you. Ben, you especially ... I venture to suggest that you especially will be rocked by what I have to relate.'

'Another awful family secret, I daresay,' murmured Ben to Maeve on his left.

'Under the present circumstances,' Sebastian paused marginally and then continued, 'it matters little if the information becomes public knowledge.'

Ben had a distinct notion he was in for another dose of disagreeable news.

'Our futures are shaped and directed by the past,' said Sebastian, portentously.

In spite of himself Ben, experienced a familiar, cold finger tracing a line down his spine. The nape of his neck began to tingle. Maeve found and held his hand under the table.

'Ben,' Sebastian, annunciating carefully, went on, 'you will be surprised, I am sure, when you learn that Randolf had every intention of marrying our widowed mother. If that had come to pass, you and I might be sitting here as partners, not as opponents.' Sebastian paused, clearly savouring the sensation he believed his words were causing. Seconds passed before the words permeated Ben's mind. His first reaction was disgust. Was this some sort of tasteless, grotesque, joke?

'After Father died, we heard that Mother had gone into mourning for ages. We heard also that later she got over it, and came back to enjoy life. You know she had quite a few proposals? Well, one was from Randolf. I know all this because he confided in me. He wrote to her. But . . . she rejected him, outright, without meeting him.

'We have reason to believe it was because of you, yes, you, dear brother. What happened was that she wrote to Randolf that, although she was relieved to hear that he and I were alive, so much time had passed that she wouldn't let anything, anyone, interfere with your precious little interests. All she wanted was me back.'

Ben was nonplussed, but not with dismay. He resisted an overwhelming impulse to burst out laughing. Randolf . . . and his mother. So that's what was going on in their feverish minds. His mother had never mentioned the proposal. He had been expecting something unpleasant, not preposterous. Randolf had been a great lurker. Always in the background. No-one really knew him.

And here he, Ben, was being blamed for something which was not of his doing.

22

'Enough, Sebastian, it's time to withdraw. I am not amused,' said Randolf, grimly. Ben's struggle to suppress his mirth had not escaped his eagle eye. Sebastian, Marie, and Randolf rose from the table and left the room in icy silence. Randolf's long quest for revenge was drawing to a close.

Ben, both diverted and baffled by the disclosures, twisted around to face Maeve, 'is there anyone in the world with such weird relatives? They're . . . nonsense, as well as mad. Where do they get their ideas? One thing is clear, if we don't get away soon, they will kill us. I think Randolf saw my reaction. I couldn't help it.'

No sooner had Sebastian and company departed then the Admiral came to life.

'Couldn't be better. This is it. This is the break we've been waiting for. We move.' He dumped a scrunched up napkin on the table and strode out, not bothering to look back. Deanna and Olga gathered their incongruously tiny evening bags and trailed after the Admiral's retreating bulk. Maeve, pulse racing, followed suit. It seemed that they were forever following the Admiral.

The hour was dark. Servants were abed. Sounds of life in the fortress had died away. Outside, discordant, chattering, screeching jungle noises had decreased to a muted murmur. A restless dog in the courtyard barked defiantly in response to a mocking challenge from the depths of the jungle – a distant animal testing the night air. Guttural sounds drifted upwards from the courtyard. A few guards were whiling away hours of boring duty with aimless gossip. Nothing appeared to be about to disturb their easy lifestyle.

☆　　☆　　☆

Marie dropped the glossy magazine which had been riveting her attention, and switched off the bedside lamp. She turned her attention to the slumbering form beside her and began to explore its spine. She reached around Sebastian's waist in a fumbling search for the cord of his pyjamas. She had lately adopted the habit of sleeping nude, whereas Sebastian, more or less in self-defence, since he was not bashful, slept in pyjamas.

'What is it?' he grumbled.

'Darling . . . ,' Marie blew erotically in his ear with superhearted breath, 'I feel like IT. I feel like making love.'

'I was fast asleep,' he protested, 'I must get some sleep. Tomorrow'll be hectic.'

'Come on, darling, where's your spirit?'

'Spirit? What spirit?'

☆　　☆　　☆

Sambo lay fully clothed on his bed. He glanced for the tenth time in ten minutes at the dim, luminous hands of his wrist watch. Almost an hour had passed since he had entered his room. It was now nearly ten, and pitch black outdoors. He sat up, swung his legs over the side of the bed, and extended his arms above his head. Oh, Christ, he thought, it'll be better when we get moving. The others must be ready.

A knock on his door caused his heart to leap. Ben let himself in.

'All set?'

'More or less. Must have a leak. The thought of danger gives me spasms.'

'So I heard,' said Ben, stoically ignoring his own churning gut.

'Here,' said Sambo, emerging from the bathroom, 'blacken your face with shoe polish. Be a soul brother for tonight.'

Face smeared with black wax, Ben, swathed in dark slacks and sweater, padded softly down the corridor, followed closely by Sambo. The ebony twins were barely visible in the dim light. Within minutes they had collected three more bodies, Deanna, Olga and Amelia. All were smeared with shoe polish. The stealthy quintet made its way to Maeve's room. Ben knocked cautiously and opened the door.

'Maeve?' he whispered into the dark.

'I'm ready.'

'It's time. Start the programme. We're set. Smear this stuff on your face.' He handed her the tin of shoe polish. Maeve walked to the computer terminal, rapidly keyed in instructions, and with a single final keystroke set in motion the sequences that were to set them free.

'That's it. Let's move.' Ben gestured to the expectant group. He was reminded of a picture he had once seen of a clutch of wetly clinging monkeys, somewhere in a Japanese sea.

A few yards on he stopped.

'We're aiming for the entrance to the main underground passage; it starts behind the screen in the games room. We checked it a few nights ago. There is another, easier entrance to the same passage through Sebastian's suite, but that's not for us.'

He squinted at the strained faces around him. Satisfied they had understood, he led off. The human train lined up behind him sprang to life. Shuffling along in Indian file, they reached their destination. The games room was in total darkness. Ben gestured soundlessly for a halt and went ahead to explore the wall to his left. He located a panel of switches, counted four in a row, and pressed the fifth.

A single spotlight above the fireplace blazed. Although only a narrow focused beam, it seemed to the frenetic fugitives that it had illuminated the whole world in a cruel, unmasking light.

Their passage was blocked by the familiar, long, low cabinet. The screen at the rear of the stage was retracted.

'In a second I'm going to douse that light,' whispered Ben, 'I want you to grab hold of the one in front, and follow me in the dark.'

He reached over and switched off the light. The room vanished. Bodies moved on jerkily, their motion smoothing as they gathered momentum. Maeve suppressed a nervous giggle and an impulse to sway her hips in time to a conga beat.

Ben edged forward, hands outstretched. He had the distinct impression of walking into a black abyss and steeled himself for a drop, but he continued, more slowly, with wary steps. Just when he had begun to doubt his sense of direction, his hand located the edge of the cabinet. By now his eyes had adapted to the dark. Faintly, in the glimmering light shining through a window, he could make out a line of crouching bodies trailing him. When he moved they moved, until all had congregated by the far side of the cabinet. Ben paused again to search over the smooth surface of the desk until he located another, smaller metal knob.

'Okay,' he whispered, 'I'm going to open the entrance to the passage. Move slowly . . . and duck low. We're at the top of a set of stairs that lead down into the underground passage. the door's low . . . bend double. Feel your way forward. Once inside I want the door shut. As soon as that's done I'll switch on my flashlight. Careful . . . for God's sake don't jostle. Gently . . . quiet.'

☆   ☆   ☆

'Sebastian.' Marie jabbed frantically at the slumbering form beside her.

'What IS it now?'

'The lights are out.'

'For God's sake, Marie, get back to sleep.'

'Sebastian, I tell you something's wrong. The clocks have stopped . . . the dials are out. I can't switch on the reading light. I'm scared . . . '

'Hell, it's probably a fuse.'

'What's that noise?' Marie's body was trembling violently.

Sebastian, finally fully awake, rubbed his eyes, rolled over reluctantly and listened. He lay thus for several seconds, then quietly reached into a drawer by the bedside,

226

and drew out a pistol. Holding the butt of the weapon in his left hand, he drew back the firing mechanism with his right hand, inserting a round into the chamber.

Someone was knocking furiously on the door to their suite. A muffled voice, impeded by the thick wood, was barely audible. The message was incomprehensible.

'Sir, sir . . . ' – muffled noises – more knocking.

'What the HELL d'you want?'

'Sir,wake up.'

'I AM awake, you blithering idiot.'

The chief guard outside the suite was drenched in sweat. He had reached Sebastian's quarters at breakneck speed. The fail-safe alarm rigged to Sebastian's quarters had never to date uttered the slightest warning squeak. But tonight it had gone off with a deafening shriek. The effect had been electrifying. The chief guard, like his most of his mates, had been groggy with booze, sleep and boredom. The shattering clamour of the alarm had practically deranged his small parcel of brains.

Sebastian slipped into a dressing gown, walked quietly to the door, pistol at the ready. Aware of Marie's terrified gaze fixed on him as she sat shaking in the bed, petrified with fear, he felt vaguely ludicrous as he aimed the pistol at the door. Marie sat glued to the mattress, tremors of fright coursing through her body as she clutched a bedsheet to her bosom. Sebastian levelled the pistol at the centre of the door.

'WHO IS IT?' he demanded into the intercom. There was no reply. No sounds issued from the loudspeaker. The mechanism was mute.

'You're right . . . there is no power.'

This observation caused a renewed outburst of gibbering from Marie.

'Who's there?' barked Sebastian hoarsely, attempting to transmit his voice through the door.

A muffled voice replied, slightly more intelligibly, 'Its de night patrol, sir. Your alarm's gone off . . . we'se followin' orders to invistigate, no matter what.'

Sebastian groaned as he peered through the eyepiece in the door. Sure enough, the chief guard and two colleagues, outlined by their flashlights, were tottering about outside, rifles unslung and, he was alarmed to note, aiming them at the door. Sebastian unbolted the door and stepped swiftly aside.

'What the bloody hell's going on? Put those guns down. What alarm? Have any others gone off?'

'No sir, just yours. You sure you're okay?'

'Yes, of course I am,' snarled Sebastian, 'check around, make sure it's not a false alarm, and search, search everywhere. Start with the boss's suite. Come to think of it,' Sebastian scowled, 'check all the guest rooms . . . and report back to me right away. And keep all servants in their rooms. I don't want them shot.'

Sebastian walked back into the bedroom, reached for the phone, hesitated, and then replaced the receiver.

'I'd better not wake Randolf. I can't trust the bloody guards. They're much too jumpy. They're so stupid anything could be happening.' He changed his mind. 'Maybe I'd better. If my precious brother's tried to imitate the Dean, he's a dead duck.'

He dialled Randolf's number.

☆　　☆　　☆

'Open up, come on, you stupid bastards . . . open up.' The chief guard hammered on the bolted door. 'Break it down.'

He stepped back and signalled to his more agile junior partner.

'Go ahead open it. No, no. Don't shoot, you bloody idiot.'

The younger guard reluctantly lowered his M16 rifle.

'You're not fuckin' Rambo, just kick it open. It ain't strong . . . kick in the stoopid door.'

The door splintered easily. The guards poured into the guest room, rifles levelled, but there was no sign of life.

Look everywhere . . . in de shit house . . . under de bed.' He stood back prudently covering his reluctant mate. They searched in vain.

'No-one here Fred . . . the horses've bolted.'

'Aw bloody sheet, what a fuckup. Dere'll be hell to pay. Come on, we'd better look through all de rooms.'

After a brief, thorough, search through obviously vacant quarters, the two found their way back into the courtyard.

Here they were joined by a motley group of partially dressed men, fumbling and stumbling over each other, rifles flailing dangerously in all directions. All this to the accompaniment of incomprehensibly jumbled orders and counter-orders. Any semblance of military discipline had evaporated. The élite guards, led by their senior officer, came pounding up to report the fortress empty.

'Bloody wonderful . . . we knew that.'

Sebastian, now clothed, ran over to assume command. The guards' futile, aimless, brownian-type movements served only to confirm his worst fears.

'Well,' he bellowed, in a good imitation of a parade sergeant's voice, 'get on with it, don't stand about farting, you pathetic bastards . . . search. They must be somewhere. The fence's not broken. Keep on looking. And I mean you lot too.'

The commander of the élite guards saluted and took off with his men at as fast trot.

While he was issuing orders, Sebastian realized that all the interior lights had come on. The helicopter hanger blazed with light. In almost the same instant he was plunged into total darkness as the perimeter lights went out. Sebastian peered around in the pitch black, momentarily nonplussed.

☆　　☆　　☆

'Get to de fence, get to de boathouse . . . dey's sure heading dat way.' The chief guard, belatedly attempting to salvage his tattered authority, let loose a string of invectives at his hapless, bemused men. 'Come on you turds . . . brainless bunch of pricks . . . git movin'.'

The guard lumbered off to the side entrance of the boathouse. A short heated altercation ensued. A moderately sober guard posted inside obstinately refused to unlock the door. He had his orders. The door was to remain locked. Orders were orders.

'It's me, you bloody stoopid fuckin' idjit . . . can't you see me? Unlock it or I'll cut your stoopid balls off.'

'What's the password?' asked the guard, playing for time.

'What bloody password? You know me. We didn't fix no

229

password. Just open de fuckin' door. The prisoners've gone
. . . can't you understand you stoopid,' he searched for a
suitable invective, 'bloody, hopeless, little ape.'

Reluctantly the guard slid the bolts open and stood aside.
The enraged chief guard and his team stormed past,
swarming everywhere, totally disorganized. Their wild,
misdirected excitement stimulated the dogs to snarl and
bark menacingly. The confused hounds began to stalk their
handlers in a comic reversal of roles.

'The battery's flat.'

'Jesuss Keerist. What're you doing? Get a fuckin' light
here right now. Use matches.'

Finally a beam of light came on, wavering to and fro,
blinding the assembled guards.

'Not on us . . . you dumb fucker . . . shine de light
outside on de river and de fence. Here . . . give it me.'

The guard snatched the flashlight from its owner hand
and swung the beam around the boathouse and on to the
boats swaying by the jetty. Everything was intact; no sign of
life.

'Come on, look in dem bushes, deeper . . . deeper,' swore
the chief guard, rushing outside. The rest of the guards,
surging out through an open gate, disappeared into the
underbush.

☆   ☆   ☆

Ben and company were at this time bunched tightly in a
small, damp, oily room leading off the main underground
passage. They had settled inside a fuel storage compartment deep below the fortress. Large sealed drums of diesel
fuel were stacked along the walls. On the far side were
several dark blue containers of aviation fuel. The odour was
strong but not overpowering. Overhead the ceiling vibrated
and rumbled as boots pounded erraticaly back and forth.
Dogs barked incessantly. Occasionally a loud yelp interrupted as a frustrated guard dealt with man's best friend.
Shouted orders, curses, bangs and clatters, waxed and
waned, and eventually slowly ebbed.

In spite of their predicament, Ben found the pandemonium outside exhilarating, and grinned encouragement to

230

Maeve. If anything the guards seemed more panic stricken than he had hoped. It was no fun working for a mad dictator. The price of failure was high.

Gradually the irregular racket subsided, to be replaced by a more orderly beat of boots overhead. Once a pair of guards marched past the inconspicuous entrance to the fuel storage room, pausing only to check the door bolts. It seemed a miracle that the dogs had not been brought along. Fortunately for the escapees Randolf had an extreme aversion for all things animal. Dogs and their parasites were not allowed inside. Regardless of the current emergency his orders were being obeyed.

Right on time, according to Maeve's schedule, lights in the courtyard blazed. Brilliant, blue tinted, floodlights dazzled the groping guards and dogs. All stood transfixed, starkly outlined against the dense black backdrop of the jungle. Nothing beyond the fence, outside the perimeter, was visible.

'What's going on?' demanded Sebastian, wearily, of the chief guard. There was to be little respite for him this night.

'Dunno boss, I ain't no electrician. I just dunno. Get dem technical boys into de act.'

'I have, you fool . . . they're checking the power plant. Can't locate any faults. That's the trouble with all this fancy electrical stuff.'

☆   ☆   ☆

Ben became aware of Deanna's bony frame trembling uncontrollably as she leaned against his thigh. Olga, by contrast seemed remarkably resigned. She sat cross-legged, moodily quiet on the oily floor. Maeve, head inclined, ear cupped towards the door, listened for sounds relaying the progress of her programme. So far, amazingly, it was going well.

'It's only a matter of time before they find us. We can't stay here much longer,' the Admiral spoke softly to the huddled group, 'I'm going for a quick look.'

He began to unlock the bolts. The storage room door opened a fraction of an inch. He paused, listening intently. Remote noises from search parties in the courtyard, and

231

beyond the fence, filtered down. Stealthily easing his bulk into the passage he disappeared. In a few moments he re-entered, 'It's clear. I'm going on to the end of this tunnel. If the coast's clear, I'll whistle twice, like this.' He produced a soft two tone note. 'Then follow, immediately. Remember, don't move unless I whistle.'

The Admiral slithered off like a large chuckawalla lizard. Maeve bit her lip. She could feel her heart pounding remorselessly in her chest. She gripped Ben's hand tighter. They had spoken very little since the plan had gone into action. Ben replied with a reassuring squeeze. Her mouth was dry and her legs were ridiculously wobbly. She had never in all her years experienced such agonizing excitement. There was real doubt in her mind as to her ability to stand upright, let alone walk. Everyone and everything around her seemed petrified. The fuel room was their haven; a refuge from perils awaiting outside. She was terrified to leave. Not even Ben's reassuring presence provided relief.

Amelia, distinctly tense, leaned against Sambo. The latter's irreverent attitude was comforting. He was becoming an important fixture in her life. He seemed to be that unlikely of male species, capable as well as humorous. Sambo, she thought, if only you knew your worth. You and Ben are scarce commodities.

Amelia's reverie was cut short by a warbling whistle. The Admiral was signalling.

'We move,' whispered Ben, tugging Maeve's hand, and forced open the door. Maeve had no time to think about her terrifying paralysis. One by one they slithered into the dark passage and stumbled after Ben. Sambo trailed last, checking their rear.

A few yards on the fugitives came into the guards' quarters and found a chaotic mess. During their hasty, scrambling exit much equipment had been discarded and left scattered about. The Admiral, searching, opened door after door, passed from room to room, until he found an exit. The gateway to freedom was a large, steel door that swung upwards, with an inside latching system. Once through this, a marvellous sight greeted them. The helicopter hanger was exquisitely visible in the floodlights and,

THERE WERE NO GUARDS.

The far side of the fortress was in total darkness. In the distance flashlights glinted and glimmered like so many glow worms. Invisible men could be heard floundering about. The mercury vapour lamps in the yard began a stuttering, tantalising, on and off sequence.

'We're in time.' said Maeve studying her watch, 'in two minutes the lights in the hanger will go off.'

'Get ready . . . we have to sprint like mad for the hanger . . . flatout.' The Admiral spoke urgently, 'Darkness on the other side will hold the guards a few seconds. Ben, you ready?' Ben nodded.

'See that door, dead ahead,' said Ben, 'just to the left of the overhead one? It's electrically controlled; in fifteen seconds it'll unlock for only thirty seconds, and then it'll relock. Memorize the exact line to the door.'

'Go, we'll follow,' muttered Sambo.

'We've got to be inside,' said the Admiral, 'when the interior lights come on, and keep down. If they see nothing they won't come pounding up to investigate, God willing.'

The overhead floodlights began to flicker intermittently and went out. Darkness was sudden and total.

'Come on . . . run,' hissed Ben, and raced for the spot he had memorized. More by good fortune than anything else his aim was dead accurate. The rest of the team followed closely on his heels. Sambo, moving swiftly, bounced off Olga's buttocks as he overtook her in the dark. She grunted but did not falter.

Their short, panicky journey was completed with seconds to spare. They had barely hurled themselves into the hanger when floodlights began to flicker, steadied, and came full on. The guards, as if rehearsed, noted the brief lighting changes, reversed direction away from the hanger, and headed for the darkened courtyard.

'Awh, shit . . . sh-iite . . . all dis galloping about. It's like a stoopid French farce.' The chief guard, congested lungs heaving for air leaned, panting painfully, against the fortress wall. 'Ah's gonna throw up.'

'They MUST be inside the fortress,' shouted Sebastian from the courtyard, 'get back and search everywhere inside again.'

The helicopter was exposed in light as bright as the noonday sun. A twisted umbilical cord dangled from its belly and trailed to a control panel festooned with dials and multiple coloured lights. Several electrical cables connected the control panel to a battery pack stacked at the far side of the hanger.

A large part of the rear wall of the hanger consisted of an enormous door ranging from ceiling to floor. A squat towing tractor was parked by the tail of the helicopter. It seemed as if everything had been thoughtfully set up for a quick start.

The Admiral looked around, seemed satisfied, and beckoned vigorously, 'Now we move REALLY fast. We've only seconds left. All power will fail, except to this hanger.' The Admiral turned to Maeve. 'Right?'

'Right.'

'As soon as that happens,' said the Admiral, 'Sambo will start the tractor, and you'll all pile into the helicopter by that door over there . . . and stay down . . . in the rear compartment. I'll get to the panel, turn on the power and start the motors. Ben will be in the pilot's seat. Sambo, get into the tractor, and get set to back us out . . . . '

☆　　☆　　☆

A deafening crash . . . . The walls of the hanger imploded amidst showers of dust and debris and cut off the Admiral's words. Simultaneously doors at the sides of the hanger burst inwards. Elite guards led by an officer, M16 rifles levelled and ready, poured in to surround the paralysed refugees.

The Admiral, eyes wide, froze, his mouth agape. His face had turned an ashen white. Dense, choking smoke swirled and eveloped them.

Gradually the fumes began to clear. Sebastian walked in and coolly surveyed the shambles in the hanger.

'I'll have your gun . . . if you please.' The Admiral, slowly regaining his senses, reached into his waistband and produced a small automatic pistol. Holding it by the barrel he proffered it numbly to Sebastian.

'Drop it, don't worry about dirt, you won't be needing it.'

Sebastian motioned to a guard to retrieve the weapon.

'Well that's that, isn't it?' smirked Sebastian, 'I must congratulate you. You nearly made it. But, you underestimated us, you forgot the surveillance cameras. You thought in all the commotion that they wouldn't be working. You miscalculated. Tut tut. Each time power and lights came on the monitors worked. And it was Randolf, sitting alone in his bedroom, who spotted you.'

Olga, who all along had been cynical about their chances for escape, recovered from the upheaval. Not one to mince words, she took up her cudgels.

'Well, fuck you Sebastian, you're a bloody, smarmy shit. You, and your stupid uncle, all of you . . . go to hell. What d'you think you're going to do to us now? Hang us all?'

Sebastian turned to stare at his furious adversary and grinned appreciatively. A stoat-like expression, hovering between a smile and a sneer, spread over his dust-covered features.

'Olga you were a good bodyguard, but no orator. Your language and your manners . . . dear, dear.'

Olga, unfazed, summoning the remains of her irritable courage, walked towards Sebastian, ignoring the rifle barrels pointing at her, and spat on the floor. For good measure she held up two fingers in a universal sign.

While this was unfolding Ben stood stock still, his arms, with painfully clenched fists, hung loosely by his sides. He had an overpowering impulse to hurl himself at Sebastian. But a glance at the women forced him to desist. He trembled as the urge subsided. He was drenched in sweat. It was all over.

23

The squad of mercenary guards, reputations salvaged, brusquely herded each of the escapees into newly designated quarters. Doors to the solitary rooms were double bolted. A sentry was posted outside.

Completely dejected, Ben and company found themselves closeted in quarters that resembled a jail in a Middle Eastern country. The entire area was set deep in the cellars of the citadel. Each sunken room had only a small, barred window opening at ground level, through which filtered faint noises from the jungle. Furnishings were so sparse as to be almost nonexistent. A narrow bed, with a crude, coir mattress and a coarse blanket, occupied most of the cell. The floors were of bare, filthy cement. Toilet facilities consisted of tiny washbasins with matching – in filth – open toilets. The prisoners' gloom was so overwhelming that their dismal environment was of little consequence.

Total isolation, by order of the rulers of the fortress, was strictly enforced. Reinforced doors were opened only for transmitting food and essential supplies. Communication between prisoners was not possible.

Ben lay supine on the uneven bed, arms folded behind his head. After a while he rolled over and buried his head under the brick-like pillow in an attempt to blot out his misery. A persistent hissing in his ears from the explosions remained. He had decided that it would never be possible to describe, nor ever recapture, the black melancholia which engulfed him after the débacle of their attempted escape. His feeling of hopelessness was accentuated by total lack of contact with the woman he had come to love. He wondered whether Maeve, if she was alive, was suffering similar miseries.

For the next two weeks the prisoners remained completely sequestered, drifting deeper and deeper into black depression.

It was evident to the Admiral that their captors knew their business. A fatalist, he had decided to cope with the situation in the worst possible light. He was aware that total isolation was highly regarded as an effective form of torment by those organizations and individuals engaged in the age old practice of torture. Insanity was around the corner.

As an antidote to madness he let his imagination roam and conjured up visions of a country estate, but memories of life in South West Africa intruded. For a while he was able to replace sad remembrances with agreeable fantasies. He saw himself riding in an English meadow; pottering in the garden; sitting in a study surrounded by books, and sipping a glass of sherry. In the distance he fancied he could hear his wife calling to their grandchildren.

On the fifteenth day, Ben could stand it no longer and sent a message via a guard to Sebastian. He had almost given up all hope of being acknowledged when late in the afternoon his door opened and two guards beckoned to him to follow. When he set foot outside his cell he realized that maximum security was still in effect. He was forced to walk in single file with one guard following, and one preceding, so that he was sandwiched fore and aft. There was no chance of escape.

Ben made up his mind that his, and his companions', only hope for survival was for him to lay bare his soul, to plead, to beg, anything, for a reprieve. He was prepared for every form of human degradation in order to save Maeve, and their companions; Ben was ready to confess to sins he had not committed.

He was ushered into an office of square shape, furnished with secretarial chairs, a long, rosewood desk littered with bric-à-brac, dossiers, two multiline telephones, and a microphone. Three computer monitors were in wall units beside a rack of communication equipment. On the wall opposite clocks and maps displayed different time zones. Numerous filing cabinets were in evidence. He was in the central nervous system, the brain, of the complex. One very large window opened onto the courtyard. This was where Randolf and Sebastian planned their activities.

One armed guard posted himself by the door through which they had entered. The other motioned peremptorily to Ben to be seated by the desk, and walked over to the opposite side in order to keep a close watch on his prisoner. All three settled down to wait. Neither guard uttered a sound.

While he was sitting thus, wondering how to begin his plea, Ben had occasion to reflect on his life. He cast about in his mind for memories of happier times. There seemed to be few pleasurable encounters in his past; all he could recollect were unhappy events.

It's this place, he thought, our miserable lot. It can't have been so bad. But try as he might he could not recall when last he had been a happy man. He squirmed with guilt when he thought about his boyhood desertion of Ampies. He thought sadly of his mother sobbing and holding him close. I'm doing a good job in the self-pity department, he thought.

Finding no solace in the past, he switched to the present and immediately experienced a most pleasant glow as Maeve entered his thoughts. But his pleasure was tempered by fear for her safety.

Ben's gaze wandered out through the window overlooking the courtyard. In the distance he could make out the endless green canopy of the jungle leading off into the vast, free, world.

A door behind the desk began to open. His captors had finally arrived. The guard stood deferentially aside as Randolf, in a purple, velvet smoking jacket, entered. He was trailed by Sebastian and Marie who, like waiters in a busy restaurant, studiously avoided Ben's eyes.

The long wait had done little for Ben's confidence. For the benefit of his performance he simulated a calm, almost beseeching, expression.

Brandishing a cigarette holder à la Noel Coward, Randolf waved a languid hand to ward off a stray wisp of smoke. He spent some time adjusting his seat as a finicky driver might before setting off.

Randolf continued to tinker with the locks in his desk; stubbed out his cigarette; lit another and drew deeply on the weed. He proceeded to rifle through file after file. Throughout this performance the attendants, standing at attention, waited in silence.

Ben, becoming more frustrated by the minute began, uninvited, to speak. In an even, measured voice he said, 'Randolf it is clear that I've been an aggravation, to put it mildly, to you and to Sebastian. I understand that in the past I, somehow, ignored you. My only explanation can be that it was childish thoughtlessness. After all, I was very young. What was I to do?

'When Sebastian disappeared, after Father's death, we mourned, but I recovered fast. I don't think Mother ever did. It is possible that I was cruel, but no more than any thoughtless child. I ask for your understanding and forgiveness. I'm extremely sorry for any humiliation I may have caused. It was inadvertent.'

Randolf's hearing seemed to have deteriorated. Ben, despising himself, turned to his brother.

'Sebastian, we loved you, we did. But you disappeared.' Oh, God, what am I saying, he thought, but went on. 'If only Randolf had told us about his troubles . . . we would have done . . . something.

'Look, all that time when I was growing up in Namibia, or later when I was at Cambridge, I often wondered what had happened to you.'

Ben paused and coughed to clear his throat. 'It was a dreadful shock to find you both here. You knew I existed, but I didn't have the faintest idea you did. I thought you were dead. Come on Randolf, please, stop.'

Ben realizing that he was beginning to whine, began a different tack.

'Why involve others? They're innocent of malice against you.' He raised his hands in a gesture of supplication. 'They're only doing a job. Do what you want with me, but don't involve them in our feud.'

It was hopeless. Ben recognized his pleas were falling on deaf ears. He was dealing with the supremo of cold fish, a marauding shark, a madman, his uncle. It was inconceivable that they had genes in common. Yet, he saw no alternative but to persevere. He switched to a different tack again.

'You must be aware that the prisoners you hold are agents of world powers? You can't take on whole governments; you can't hope to get away with murder.'

Randolf glanced up, coldly, a faint sneer on his lips. Ben took a deep breath and doggedly plunged on.

'If anything should happen to them you'd never be safe, anywhere. No-one's above the law. You're behaving like a terrorist. Look here, Randolf, you can still salvage your empire. Release us, before it's too late.'

In the midst of Ben's fervent speech, a distant, rumbling noise growing steadily louder, could be heard. After a few moments it faded. Randolf pored over papers on his desk. Throughout Ben's discourse he had been mute, seemingly unmoved.

A sudden, startling, hissing, crackling noise, spilled from a loudspeaker, breaking the silence. All eyes swivelled to the grill. A harsh, barely intelligible, voice issued.

'Delta one calling HQ. Delta one factory calling HQ . . . HQ . . . do you read? Aircraft approaching. Correct codes transmitted. Requesting permission to land airfield. Over.'

Sebastian came to life, reached for the desk microphone, flicked a switch, and spoke into the mouthpiece.

'Receiving you, delta one. We read you. This is control HQ. How many aircraft? What markings? Which codes? I repeat, which codes? Over.' The scratchy voice replied.

'Three heavy transports. Correct codes received. Message indicates Hercules aircraft, numbers 1681, 1687, 6542. Arriving ahead of schedule. Pilot states material on board for processing. Ready to take on manufactured goods. Commander of flight recorded in our log as Christiaan Oberholzer. Does that read? Clearance to land requested. Over.'

'HQ to delta one. Affirmative. Repeat . . . affirmative. Out.' Sebastian switched off. 'So Ben,' he said, breaking his silence, 'you see even Petrus Oberholzer's brother is on our books. Oh, yes,' he smiled, 'business goes on as usual, despite your efforts. You must understand that after your misguided efforts to investigate and then to escape, we cannot possibly let you go?

'Incidently, you may find this hard to believe, but I've been your advocate. I had almost persuaded Randolf to grant you a reprieve when you tried to escape. But that's all past, now.'

Randolf stirred and leaned forward.

'I might as well tell you, Ben, since it no longer matters, that a vital part of my planning involved the arrival of those transports.' He shrugged. 'Those arrangements will have to proceed. You and your companions will be transported on the planes.'

'What do you mean?' Ben stared at him. 'Where to?' He sensed the answer. 'As prisoners?'

'More or less,' replied Randolf, grimly.

'More or less?'

'You, and your friends, will be humanely dealt with. You will be set free from the bonds of this world. Your remains will be removed to another place.'

'You mean you're going to kill us, and then dispose of the bodies as cargo?'

Ben felt his throat contract. His pulse skipped several beats. Despite all indications, all warnings, he had not really come to grips with idea of being executed. He glanced at Marie. She sat, pale faced, her lips tightly compressed.

'Ben,' said Randolf, from what seemed a great distance, 'I've no wish to prolong this discussion.'

Ben shook his head in disbelief.

For several seconds the room was quiet. Ben tried to rise, but his limbs refused to obey. He was a prisoner in his body.

In the courtyard the helicopter began its start-up routine. Rotors began to throb as they gathered momentum, until a pulsating roar filled the air. Sebastian made ready to leave.

'I'm going to follow the usual routine.' he shouted, above the noise. 'I'll take the helicopter to the airfield. I'll meet Chris. I find,' he was becoming hoarse, 'it's getting too depressing here. I'll see to the loading.'

He turned to Marie. 'Want to come along?'

She shook her head. The noise outside began to fade as

the helicopter moved to the take-off area.

Ben sat grimly silent, his fingers intertwined. He could not plan. Nothing came to mind. Was there anyone on earth as helpless as he?

A tremendous burst of light accompanied a shattering explosion that rocked the foundations of the fortress. Sebastian and Randolf froze as if captured by a gigantic electronic flash. In exaggerated slow motion the microphone on the desk toppled over. The loudspeaker squawked once and fizzled out.

'My God,' blurted Sebastian, already half way across the room, 'the helicopter's exploded.' He ran to the window overlooking the courtyard and stood there transfixed. Too late, he ducked aside. Almost immediately a second, stunning detonation blasted inside the room. Window glass shattered into whirling splinters. Sebastian was hurled across the room. He settled in a heap by the wall, blood trickling from nose and ears. His immaculate clothes were in tatters. The explosion and the following blow to his head had knocked him senseless.

A third, colossal blast shuddered the interior of the room. A stun grenade, lobbed in through the open window, went off with a thunderous crash right under the desk. Randolf was blown clear of the leather chair. The élite guards doubled over clutching their ears, instantly rendered impotent. Choking, acrid, impenetrable, black smoke filled the room.

Staccato bursts of gunfire rattled outside. A spent bullet bounced off the rear of the office and fell, still hot, by Sebastian's sprawled body. Frantic curses and screams echoed throughout the courtyard. Fragments of shattered metal ricocheted and reverberated against the walls of the fortress.

The blast had knocked everyone to the floor. It seemed to Ben that a crazy orchestra, complete with giant cymbals and berserk conductor, had started up in the courtyard. In the midst of the bedlam Ben was immensely relieved to discover that he had not been seriously injured. But he had gone stone deaf.

It was abundantly obvious that this turn of events was not part of Randolf's arrangements. In the space of seconds a miraculous change in their circumstances had come about.

'My God,' muttered Ben, as he raised his head, 'there must be a God.'

Ben brushed the dust from his eyes. His ears were ringing; his face was covered in grime but he was grinning, hugely; he had survived. He was alive.

Ben had received the least of the blast and recovered his wits rapidly. He moved decisively. Kneeling over a gibbering guard he wrenched the Uzzi machine pistol from his nerveless grasp. Coughing and spluttering in the smoke, Ben stumbled over Marie's immobile body, lying like a beached whale on the carpet. He found his way to the shattered window and turned to face his captors, covering them with the machine pistol. But it was not necessary. His erstwhile foes lay moaning and groaning like so many discarded rag dolls. Ben turned to peer cautiously through the window.

The scene outside was indescribable. The courtyard had been devastated. Uniformed bodies, oozing blood, lay grotesquely twisted on the pockmarked floor. Death was everywhere. Gradually, as the corrosive smoke cleared, windows of visibility emerged. Ben surveyed the aftermath of the short, fierce, battle. The hanger sported an enormous, ragged cavity in its side through which poured thick, oily smoke. The helicopter had been blown in half and was burning with a fierce glare. The electrified fence had been breached.

Green clad, steel helmeted, troops were pouring in through gaps in that once impregnable barrier. A tank clawed its way through a rift to join three already in position in the courtyard. Their guns rotated and ranged around the shattered battleground. All resistance had ceased.

A highly professional, precisely coordinated, attack had been carried out with exceptional efficiency. All objectives had been attained, apparently without loss to the invaders. The only bodies Ben could see were those of Sebastian's and Randolf's mercenaries.

Ben waved the remains of his jacket from the window. Nothing happened. He peered out once more.

The hatch on top of the leading tank began to swing open. A vaguely familiar figure emerged and dropped to the ground. The figure was immediately encircled by troops arranging themselves in a defensive formation, guns facing outwards, like spokes of a wheel.

A shattered, steel door leading into the fortress swung to and fro, creaking mournfully in the slight breeze. The mercenary army had vanished.

The smoke in the study cleared. Sebastian, a pathetic scarecrow of a figure, squatted amidst rubble on the floor, head in hands. He sat with dazed, blank eyes, mopping a dripping nose with a blood stained handkerchief. Marie had managed to roll over onto her back, thus continuing her convincing imitation of a whale out of water.

The stupefied guards had automatically assumed a position of surrender, and were sitting by the wall, hands folded on their heads. Their extensive training programme in mercenary school had included a section on surrender protocol.

'Help me . . . somebody . . . I can't move,' cried Randolf, piteously, from his position on the floor. 'Help me, Sebastian . . . Ben, my body . . . I'm hurt, please . . . for pity's sake, help an old man.'

'Get the old buzzard up.'

Ben gestured with the Uzzi. He restrained an impulse to reinforce his command, and kept his voice level. Sebastian heaved himself painfully to his feet, and staggered to his supine mentor. Sebastian's once handsome features had been slashed by shards of flying glass. His clothes were in shreds. Streaks of blood ran down his jowls. One blackened eye was swollen shut. A pathetic wretch had supplanted the dandy.

'Ben,' said Sebastian, in a voice choking with smoke and emotion, 'whatever happens, and I'm not pleading,' he added, with a semblance of dignity, 'it wasn't my idea to kill you.'

'It doesn't matter,' snapped Ben.

'I tried to help . . . '

'I believe you. But it's too late. I don't know who's behind this rescue. Certainly not anyone friendly to you.'

'You must help Marie.'

'We'll see.' The irony of his position was not lost on Ben.

'I, most of all, deserve what's coming.' Sebastian sank down onto his haunches and once more buried his head in his hands.

Ben swung round to the cowering guards.

'Tie them up . . . the lot. Sebastian, Randolf, Marie . . . all together. And yourselves, make yourselves into a daisy chain. I don't want anyone loose.'

The guards, hoping to be regarded as ordinary soldiers obeying orders, made haste to comply. Although only a few minutes had elapsed since the first explosion, Ben's first impulse, as soon as he had secured his tormentors, was to locate Maeve and the rest of the prisoners. He ran out of the office and collided with a large, palpitating mercenary. Ben glared into the pig-like eyes of the chief guard, lately of the fence patrol.

'WHERE are the prisoners held?'

Ben aimed the Uzzi at the guard's paunch, his finger on the trigger.

Fred, the chief guard, swallowing, replied hastily,

'Dey's all in de basement. You cin git to dem if you go down into de passage . . . de one dat goes right by de power plant. De keys is wid a special guard. It ain't my responsibility, but I can get dem and lead you dere. Iffin you want it?'

'Come on,' Ben gestured with the gun, 'come on, show me the way. We don't need any keys. And you'd better pray no one's harmed, or I'll shoot you on the spot, myself.'

The quaking guard headed hastily for the foyer, scrambling over smashed furniture and plants with frantic agility. He staggered on, glancing frequently over his shoulder as would an obedient dog checking the progress of its master. Ben followed closely. The foyer was a mess.

A green clad soldier barred their passage.

'Halt, right there. Who are you?'

Ben raised his hands and approached,

'I'm an escaped prisoner. Name's Ben Brookhouse. This fellow here was my guard. I must speak to your commanding officer.'

'Hold it ... right there.' The soldier indicated with his gun. 'He's on his way. We'll sort this out when he gets here. Stay put.'

He released the safety on his carbine to emphasize his intentions. Ben, by now more than accustomed to weapons, complied and raised his arms. No point in being shot in error. The former chief guard tactfully assumed a similar posture.

A camouflaged jeep, complete with fluttering flags and soldiers, bearing a middle-aged, uniformed man by the driver, drew up. The soldiers dismounted, saluted, and trotted round the vehicle to station themselves by the entrance. Two remained by the distinguished, grey haired, black man. He was clearly in charge. His uniform was distinguished by three gold emblems on the lapels.

The commanding figure saluted his men with a swagger stick, walked briskly into the remains of the foyer, and squinted into the gloom. He did not immediately notice Ben.

Ben could see him clearly. Not for the first time that day his heart began to skip. He recognized him as the man who had popped out of the tank. But there was something more familiar about him . . . . Then it all came back.

The commander stared bleakly at the havoc. He seemed to be searching for something and did not like what he saw. When his eyes adapted to the gloom he discovered Ben standing before him.

'It is you, the agent from the Admiral. Where's my daughter, Amelia?' He came forward and greeted Ben with a ferocious hug.

'Tell me she's unhurt ... she's well ... she is all right?'

Ben regained his breath,

'I hope she's safe. We'll find her. You arrived just in time. How did you find us ... how did you do it?'

The Potentate-General, for that is who he was, waved away the questions.

'Later. Where is Amelia?'

'We've all been in solitary confinement,' said Ben, 'the

246

explosions, the mess, it's all so sudden . . . God knows you're a welcome sight. How did you trace us?'

'All in good time. First Amelia . . . my daughter. Let's find her.'

The commander waved his baton at Ben.

'Lead on, you know the way.'

'This turd'll lead us. He works here. Come on, get going.'

The fat, chief guard rushed off.

The door to Sebastian's suite had been smashed open and hung by a single, twisted hinge. A brief search in the rubble uncovered the trapdoor. Before them stretched the flight of steps. A dozen flashlights illuminated their way as troops came pounding along the corridor to the cells.

Amelia, hearing a sudden commotion outside her cell, broke down and began to tremble uncontrollably. She had been expecting something awful and lay curled on her bed, face to the wall. Her tormentors would find no satisfaction in seeing her terror. She was certain her friends had been executed and that it was now her turn.

The pandemonium ceased. Amelia heard a familiar voice calling her name. The door to her cell crashed open. Two soldiers burst in. With a low moan Amelia fainted. When she came to, she felt dreamy and relaxed. Her father was kneeling by her side, dabbing her forehead with a damp cloth. Overcome, she burst into tears.

As soon as Ben saw that Amelia was in good hands, he rushed down the corridor calling to the Potentate-General's soldiers to follow.

'Amelia's okay. Leave her with her father. Help me with the others. In here . . . Maeve . . . where are you?'

The soldiers began to smash down door after door in the passage. In the third cell they found Maeve.

'Ben, I KNEW you'd come for me. Are we free?'

☆   ☆   ☆

An hour later the rescued prisoners gathered in the ragged remains of Sebastian's office. Sambo had commandeered the president's chair where he sat with feet resting on the scarred desk. The Admiral stood, hands clasped behind his back, staring at the devastation in the courtyard.

'The Potentate has some incredible news,' announced the Admiral, turning away from the window, 'it's frankly . . . unbelievable.'

The survivors were too relieved and dazed to care. What more could there be in store? Their experience had left them numb.

The Potentate-General forced open a broken door and entered the office. He was followed by an extraordinary apparition . . . a filthy tramp, a tattered, scraggly bearded, middle-aged, hippy stood before them.

'Now what? Who's this?' grumbled Olga. Her perpetually angry face was lined, yet oddly softened. Remnants of her normal personality lingered.

'My friends,' began the Potentate, 'allow me to introduce you to your bona fide saviour.' Baffled silence greeted this proclamation.

'It's him . . . it's George . . . it's him . . . it's the Dean,' exclaimed Olga, her face opening with an astonished smile.

The battered figure grinned sheepishly in reply, and extended his arms in a papal gesture of blessing.

'Yes,' said the figure, 'I'm afraid it's me.'

'How . . . how . . . did you get here? Where have you been?' Ben, mouth agape, was as perplexed and lost as the rest.

'Perhaps you'll let him have his say.'

The Potentate motioned to George.

24

The grand dining room had been miraculously refurbished.
Bewildered servants, obedient to new masters, had managed to retrieve sundry items from the once extravagantly
stocked sideboards. Two gold candelabra, slightly dented,
together with clean linen, undamaged cutlery and china
adorned the table. The end result was, all things considered, impressive.

After the fracas the reluctant senior chef had been coaxed
into reviving his expertise. (He had been located under his
bed in the servant's quarters). With the assistance of aides
recruited from the ranks of the mercenaries, he provided an
adequate meal. Randolf's wine cellar had escaped damage
and a selection of the best wines was provided to accompany this, the most memorable – for it was to be their last –
meal in the fortress.

Randolf's waiters were conspicuously absent. Cheerful
soldiers in battle fatigues served instead. By all accounts
the meal was an unqualified success. Excellent spirits
abounded on the table and in the guests.

The Dean, his body replenished with food and wine, his
conscience at ease, basked in the candid admiration of his
companions. He had become an authentic celebrity. And
so, with very little prompting, he proceeded with his
interrupted tale in a deprecating, engagingly modest, style.

'Well, there I was, drifting in that boat down the
unfriendly river, terrified the crocs and the guards were in
collusion and out to get me. But let me go back to the
beginning . . .

'I had been planning the escape for months, long before
you arrived. To cover my tracks, I spread a smoke screen. I

made certain everyone knew about my migraine. I do have it. It runs in my family. Anyway, it was easy to play it up.

'My opportunity came during the chess game. When I left the gathering that night, everyone assumed I'd gone to my room to suffer my usual miseries. Instead, I put into effect my escape plan. In my mind I had rehearsed it at least a thousand times . . . all possible aspects.

'I'll cut this short,' the Dean, misinterpreting Olga's fascinated, glazed, expression for boredom, hastened his delivery. 'I can see you're tired, I'll skip the bit about getting out into courtyard and into a motorboat. That part went without a hitch. The rest was not so, er, easy,' he added, with wry smile.

'I let the boat drift for what seemed ages, but probably was only thirty minutes or so. Luckily I had selected an ideal boat. Not only did it have sufficient fuel and a good engine, but I was delighted to discover, it had one of those tiny outboard motors used for trolling, dangling from the stern. You know . . . the sort that works off batteries. I could hardly believe my luck.'

The Dean drank from his glass and continued.

'My intention was to slip away by drifting downstream and then to double back. I was certain the guards, alerted by my escape, would rush down to the boathouse, find a boat missing, and not hearing anything, would assume I was miles away. Instead I would be hiding nearby. The idea was that they would overshoot me. Which is exactly what happened.

'I waited until they had passed, started the trolling motor, and headed for the far bank. I was hidden by the overhanging branches of the mangroves, and not far from the fortress. No one thought of searching under trees near the fortress.

'Blind luck? Incompetence? No matter. Boats, full with guards, continued to shoot past me at full speed; waves tossed me about but they didn't spot me in all that commotion. After a while . . . '

Olga, fascinated by his tale of derring-do, sat gazing with unabashed admiration at her new hero.

'When things quietened down,' continued the Dean, 'I looked around, saw the coast was clear. I heard no more

250

boats, and quietly cruised upstream, still hidden by the overhanging branches.

'I slipped past the fortress. All the lights were blazing in the courtyard so that they couldn't see me in the dark outside. I continued upstream where I ditched the boat. My luck had held.

'I walked away from the river for about a quarter of a mile in pitch blackness, and then waited for daybreak. The next morning, I tried using my watch and the sun to guide me, but it was difficult in the jungle with all those trees. Anyway, I headed for the nearest town. I had with me one of Randolf's maps of the surroundings, but, by and large, I had to guess where I was. Randolf's fortress was not on the map. After two days without water, millions of insect bites, and no food – I must confess that there are parts of my journey I can't recall clearly, I was faint with hunger and a bit feverish – I was beginning to get very weak. I became more and more scared, and became sort of static. I had not planned that part properly. In my haste to get away I had forgotten about provisions. I was about to give up hope when . . . well, you know the rest.'

Olga's lips opened a fraction wider. She continued to goggle at the wonderful, daring Dean.

'Come on, I can see you've left out lots. That jungle . . . it's horrible to think of it.' Olga shuddered. 'You are amazing. You know you really are marvellous.'

Deanna observed the metamorphosis in her pal with dismay. With a great effort she was able to contain her disgust, and to disguise any overtly disagreeable facial reactions. She paid lip service to their saviour's presence with a wan smile, and suppressed her internal disquiet by concentrating on the food before her. In the end the effort was more than she could stand. Half way through a tiny helping of salad she mumbled an unintelligible apology and rose to leave, muttering, 'Toilets'.

On reaching the lavatories she slammed the door shut and let off a few unlady-like curses, as well as other sundry noises, in the general direction of her erstwhile bosom

251

friend. For good measure she stuck her tongue out at her image in the mirror. Slowly she regained her equanimity.

'That's life,' she muttered to the mirror.

☆   ☆   ☆

Olga, leaning forward, deposited her generous bosom on the table, causing her plate to tilt several degrees. She continued, with insatiable interest, to press her modest champion for details,

'Why did you come back? What made you do it?'

George the Dean, confident in his role as a fearless adventurer, decided to allow himself the luxury of a public confessional. It was time to unburden himself, to lay to rest the spectres in his life.

'For most of my life,' he said, quietly, 'I've behaved like a coward. I had a secret shame. By helping you I thought I could make amends. Let me explain.

'I've always been ashamed of my family background . . . terrified of being 'found out'. And for something not of my doing. Talk about guilt! The fact is, that my parents, not German – they were Romanian – were Nazis.

'My father was an officer in the Waffen SS. No doubt he helped quite a few Jews and others, including Romanians, to their death. I won't bore you with details of the lengths I went to hide this, but that awful knowledge dogged me all my life. I lived in constant dread that someone, somewhere, would find out. All the more agonizing because I felt it my duty to be loyal to my parents. I wanted to, had to, love them.

'But it was impossible to reconcile my abhorrence for their political activities with love for them. It seems ridiculous now, but because of the conflict in my mind I never married. I was too mortified to share my intimate secrets.'

His audience, having long grasped that they had completley misjudged the Dean's character, remained silent.

'When I discovered what Randolf was planning I made up my mind that I was honour bound to thwart him. To me he was the incarnation of the Nazi evil that once almost ruled the world. In a dim, unformed way I hoped to make

252

amends for the sins of my ancestors.'

'But, my dear man,' protested Olga, 'how could you be responsible for the acts of you antecedents? Anyone with a grain of sense could see that as a child you had no hand in the activities of the Nazis.'

'Ah, yes, yes, that my be so, but people are funny . . . logic fades, even with the most reasonable of people, when emotions are involved.'

The Admiral nodded slowly.

'To get back to my story,' continued the Dean, 'a plan began to take shape in my mind. I realized I had more than one problem. Not only had I to play the part of a migraineur, (which wasn't acting at all for me), I had also to alert you about the possibility of a rescue, without revealing my own intentions. I didn't want you to give up hope, antagonize Sebastian and Randolf or, on the other hand, to jump the gun and try to escape prematurely.

'A major advantage was that I had access to their inner workings. I had gained their confidence. They regarded me as a harmless economist. I was allowed to come and go at odd times as their dedicated financial adviser. I knew exactly where everything of importance was filed. I knew all the routines. When the opportunity came I stole the blueprints and gave you a copy. Perhaps that wasn't wise? It's hard to say,' he shrugged. 'I thought I should encourage you, to give you hope. I was in a quandary. It was very difficult to walk that tightrope . . . to keep my mouth shut. I didn't want you to get into trouble. I was sure you couldn't have managed an escape without outside help. In the end I decided to go ahead with my plans, to escape alone.'

He paused to sip his port. The audience watched. Every move, every gesture, was scrutinized in case it might have some special significance. This was not an academic dealing in abstractions, but a true-to-life adventurer.

Olga had completely lost her muscular heart and made no bones about it. She was convinced she had found her knight. At this point Deanna re-entered and returned to her seat where she remained loftily poised over her food, pecking away ungraciously at the chef's creations. She was inordinately miffed when no-one noticed her ill humour.

'Unfortunately,' said the Dean, 'as I feared, you tried an

escape, and brave and clever though it was, it was bound to fail. Of course, Randolf and Sebastian were expecting you to try. It's amazing that you got as far as you did. From what I've heard you certainly surprised them.'

'Go on,' prompted Olga.

'I think you've heard enough.'

'No, please don't be modest. Go on ; . . '

The Dean complied cheerfully,

'At one stage I thought I was going to die. I didn't care. I was weak. I was sick, frightened, and helpless. I considered lighting a fire to attract attention. But I had no lighter . . . nothing. I ate tubers, lizards . . . but it wasn't enough. Ughhh. I was terrified at night. There were some very odd noises in that jungle. As I said, I had almost given up hope. I remained, alone, weak, waiting for the end.

'Suddenly everything changed . . . a miracle . . . I was sure I was dreaming. Out of the bush appeared soldiers, friendly soldiers. Amelia's father's men had been reconnoitring and stumbled on me lying delirious and groaning, under a tree.

'They revived me; took me to his place. After a rest and medical attention, I had a session with the Potentate-General, Amelia's father. He had been out on a patrol with a commando unit. I told him everything, including the inside layout of the fortress, you know, everything.

'I told him about the airfield, about it's radar system. I told him about the identifying codes for visiting aircraft. I told him about you . . . about Amelia, whom I believed safe, for a while at any rate.

'Your rescue was carried out by Amelia's father and his men, not by me. He had his planes painted to hoodwink Sebastian and Randolf. That's how we came in so easily, we used an acceptable route. It was a total surprise. The fact is,' he added meekly, 'I was only a courier and,' he added even more humbly, 'anyone could have done it.'

Ben rose from his chair, glass in hand.

'Look here, had it not been for you we'd probably not be alive. Your escape was brilliantly, bravely, done. You may not remember this, but I once told you that I thought you were brilliant. I wasn't exaggerating, was I? There's no doubt whatever, in MY mind, that we are forever in your debt. We will never be able to thank you enough.

'Ladies and gentlemen,' Ben raised his glass high, 'I give you a toast . . . to a genuine hero, the Dean.'

All stood and drained their glasses. Deanna brought her glass to her lips, but did not drink. Like a hermit crab, she had withdrawn into her shell of hair. Not even her pointed nose and teeth protruded. She had made herself invisible, in their midst.

'Have you ever,' asked the Admiral, settled in his seat, 'considered a full-time career in MI5? I mean as an instructor?'

The Dean swallowed his port and smiled at Olga.

'No, I think not.'

'What about our late hosts?' asked Ben, thinking in particular of Sebastian. 'What lies ahead?'

'Kill the bastards,' interjected Deanna, coming out of her pout briefly, 'hang the fuckin' lot from the nearest tree.' Her hair fluttered vigorously as the words hissed between her lips.

Ben looked to the Potentate-General. 'But what are we going to do with them?'

'They'll be transported to the capital in Madagascar and charged. They'll have the benefit of a trial. Our courts,' added the Potentate-General with a slight smile, 'are modelled on the British system which, I'm reliably informed, is not quite like the law of the jungle. You'll never see them again.'

Despite their harrowing adventures of the past few days, Ben felt a twinge of pity for Marie, and perhaps, for Sebastian. None for Randolf. He managed however, with no great effort, to banish them from his conscience.

Ben turned to Maeve. 'What about our postponed moonlight stroll? Apart from the exercise, I need an excuse to be alone with you, and I'd like to take a last look at this place.'

'I hate it. It gives me the creeps. But how can I resist your gallant invitation, so charmingly phrased?' replied Maeve, with a mischievous grin, 'You don't need an excuse to be with me.'

'Let's go, then.'

Ben walked around, tapped her lightly on her shoulder,

and inclined his head in the direction of the exit. Maeve took his arm and walked alongside him through the now permanently open French window.

A pale moon cast monochrome shadows over the shimmering foliage. The air was filled with hordes of tiny insects, pursued by gyrating, hunting, bats.

Maeve and Ben walked slowly down the road that had brought them to the fortress. The great river, rippling and glimmering with reflected moonlight, flowed by, in rustling silence.

Ben turned to move closer. He brushed Maeve's cheek lightly with parted lips. Her response was instantaneous. She turned into his arms and held him in a powerful embrace. Ben could feel the pulse of her fast beating heart.

'Ben, I've got to speak to you.'

'This is the time, darling.'

'Yes, I think this is the time. If I don't speak now, I may never get a chance again.' Ben saw her face was serious and a little anxious.

'Please, go on, Maeve.'

'You must let me have my say without interruption.'

Maeve sat by him on a bench. 'It's very hard for me to say this, because we haven't known each other for long. But we have been through so much that I feel I know you better than I have known anybody.

'Ben, I love you. I enjoyed sleeping with you very much, and I enjoy your company. But I find increasingly that my worries about the future intrude and detract from that enjoyment. I am afraid that it is affecting the way I might behave towards you and I am afraid it may get worse. I am sure I have found the right man. I'm terrified I may lose you and this fear makes me speak.

'I understand why you might be hesitant about making a commitment, having gone through a break-up of a marriage, that, and our very short relationship. This may shock you, but I would like us to have children. I think you feel that too. But there is a difference. I have a constant nagging reminder that for me, a woman, time is relentlessly passing. Where am I going? No, don't say anything yet.'

Ben opened and shut his mouth.

'What will happen when we get out of here? If am not

going to marry you and have children, then I have to think about my plans for the future. I know our future looks rosy now, but I have, and I know it's premature, fantasies about our life hereafter. I think like any normal woman. At the moment I am in no man's land. I want to have something to live for when we get out of here. There, I've said it.'

Maeve, rose from his side and began to walk back to the ruined fortress.

'Hold on,' Ben called out. 'Maeve, my dearest, sweetest of all women. Please listen to me. It's my turn.

'Right from the very first time I met you and spoke to you, I fell for you. If I had to conceive a requisition for the sort of wife I wanted, I can think of no one else but you. You have it all, intelligence, character, humour, looks . . . I only hope it works both ways. I think it does. I'm not making excuses but I thought that after our predicament I would not put pressure on you. That I love you more than anyone, goes without saying. I want you. I need you. I would be very happy, delighted, if you married me.'

A smile displaced Maeve's troubled expression, her eyes glistened with soft tears of pleasure. She stopped and waited for Ben to catch up.

'That's all I want to hear.'

A mist swirled and twisted over the jungle, and gradually evaporated. Morning broke through fresh and clear. One by one the inhabitants of the fortress stirred and woke. The sun was high by the time the soldiers of the Potentate-General had cleared signs of the struggle. Dead mercenaries had been buried. Three troop carriers, two salvaged jeeps, and a dark blue limousine were lined up by the entrance to the fortress. The tanks had been sent on ahead.

The reprieved chef, and the few remaining lackeys not incarcerated, had cleared the balcony of all debris, repaired some of the damaged furniture; and set up a meal on the balcony. The Dean and the Admiral were sitting quietly looking out over the river.

Olga appeared, a transformed woman. Her hair had been washed and tied back in a simple bun. She wore a cheerful floral dress which, together with the general change in her demeanour, made her surprisingly presentable.

'Good morning.' she bellowed, eyeing her quarry.

Maeve, Amelia, Sambo, and Ben were next to arrive. For a while they sat in stillness breathing moist, warm, air.

'Ah, yes, so beautiful and civilized, it's everywhere. What a morning.' Maeve seated by Ben, and reached for her coffee.

'Incidently,' said Amelia, 'my father's men discovered a sizeable cache of gold. This should do very nicely in place of Randolf's prize. You've no IDEA what Randolf had stashed away in the underground vaults. The old bugger could very easily have kept his promise about money in Swiss bank accounts.'

Intrigued by the idea of wealth and gold bars galore, the company did not at first notice Deanna's entrance. She stood, ominously quiet, in the background. A cigarette protruded from somewhere beneath her nose. Her hair was parted. Olga's discarded scowl had been adopted with success.

'Just, as I thought,' she sneered, 'hypocrites, the lot of you, counting your shekels. Rich aren't we? What about the rest of the world . . . battered women and children, the poor, the revolutionaries . . . ey . . . what about them?'

'For Christ's sake Deanna, shut up, sit down, and cool off,' said Olga, 'we've only just been rescued. No-one here has any right to that money, or wants it, except the people of this country. We weren't laying claim to anything. It's for Amelia's father to decide what's to be done. And do us a favour . . . get rid of that stinking weed.' Olga, having divorced herself from her former associate, turned her attention to the Dean on her left.

'I can't stand smoke. Gives me a headache.'

'Well she's got a point about distributing the money,' said George the Dean in a conciliatory tone, 'but you're right, it's up to Amelia's father to decide where it goes.'

He offered a seat to the disgruntled woman. 'Come along Deanna, plenty of time to take up our lives again. One can go back to doing good deeds later . . . where one left off.'

'Don't bloody patronize me. I know what to do with my life. I've had a bad time, little do you know. As a matter of fact I had a nervous breakdown brought on by some . . . shit of a man. I was ordered to rest. That's why I came out here, dragging that ingrate along. Just because you've helped me gives you no right to tell me how to behave . . . ,' Her voice tailed off.

Something in her angry mind was battling with the novel idea of gratitude. It was not something she could reconcile with her ingrained sense of chronic outrage. She detested the very idea of being under an obligation.

'Well, it WAS a lovely day,' sighed the Admiral, 'why don't we try and keep it that way? How about some peace and quiet? It's time for rest and recreation. Deanna, if you wish to continue hectoring us,' he sipped his drink, 'kindly do so after we've eaten.'

'Oh, bloody hell,' snapped Deanna, and snatching up a piece of bread, stalked off.

'To think I used to take her seriously,' said Olga, 'God, we were a miserable pair. How's it possible to be so unhappy at a time like this?'

At that point the Potentate-General stepped onto the balcony.

'Sir,' ventured Sambo, 'what's going to happen to the paintings in the fortress?'

'Would you like one?' countered the Potentate-General.

'I did rather take a fancy to the idea. Maybe a Chagall, or a Morton,' said Sambo, believing the Potentate to be jesting, 'are you suggesting I might have one? A memento?'

'I'd be delighted to offer each of you something from this place, as a token of gratitude. I owe you a great deal, more than I can say. Please, please,' said the Potentate earnestly, 'select something, anything.'

When the time for departure arrived, Ben and company were oddly reluctant to leave. Like newfound friends at a holiday resort, they assembled by the main entrance of the fortress to bid farewell to the place.

The waiting Mercedes started without fuss, moved forward, and paused to accept the women into it's incongruously lush interior. The men were loaded onto open jeeps. The rest of the commando troops clambered into military trucks, leaving behind two men to guard the entire remainder of the devastated fortress. And so the convoy set off for the outside world.

Ben glanced back as the jeep bounced down the road. It seemed an age since he and his diverse companions had staggered, exhausted, into the clutches of his dreadful family, into what was to become a most remarkable chapter of their lives. He stared unblinking, backwards, until a final bend in the road obscured his view. He shook his head and sank back. It was time to enjoy the cool fresh air of freedom. The flight to the capital was short, noisy and uneventful.

25

True, I talk of dreams,
Which are the children of an idle brain,
Begot of nothing but vain fantasy.
[Romeo and Juliet]

'Someone to see you sir.'

'Who is it?'

'A lady, sir. Madam X, incognito. Okay to come in?'

'Hold on a minute, must get myself decent.' The handsome, white haried, elderly man glanced critically at his image in the mirror, patted a few stray hairs into place, adjusted his purple velvet, smoking jacket, and wheeled his chair to the door. In a firm, clear voice he called out,

'Please, enter.'

The male nurse unlocked the door from the outside, checked around, seemed satisfied, and walked in. As he did so he indicated to the female figure behind, to follow. The nurse walked over to a large sealed window overlooking the rear of Kew Gardens, checked the view, drew the curtains, and switched on interior lights.

'How are you madam?' enquired the occupant, expansively. He gestured to the hesitating figure in the tailored suit with blonde, extravagantly coiffured hair. 'How good of you, dear lady, to visit me so soon after your challenge.'

'We have much to discuss, Sir Randolf,' said the woman in the wig. 'Firstly, thank you for your advice about my leadership. Secondly, Dennis and I've been going over your suggestions. My successor may implement your recommendations. Here are some of our thoughts. I'll be back when you've had a chance to go over them.'

261

'Do you have a moment? Please . . . find a seat. Make yourself comfortable.'

Marie dismissed the nurse, and seated herself. She was carrying, in addition to a fake Gucci handbag, a Harrod's foodstore paper bag, and some tattered paperback novels. The immaculately styled wig glistened and teetered on her head.

'I have a few delicacies for you, left over from a cabinet meeting at Number Ten. Caviar and smoked salmon.'

'You are too kind. I must express to you once more how proud I am to have served a premier who, despite fame and misfortune, still retains the common touch. I realize that these are trying times and I'm sorry about all this seclusion, but one must have peace and quiet in order to arrange one's thoughts. I'd not be much of a civil servant if I were beset with distractions, would I?

'Yes of course,' replied Marie, delving into the Harrods bag, 'I appreciate your opinion.'

'Quite so. On the other hand, although I accept that you reached your high office, with marginal help from myself, it's gratifying to know that you followed my advice about an appropriate time to resign.'

Marie nodded gracious acknowledgment and hitched up the skirt of the tight fitting suit she'd bought a week ago in the Portobello market. She walked over to the table, carefully laid out the small repast, and placed some novels on a roll top desk. Randolf Brookhouse wheeled himself over to the table and began immediately to eat.

'I think he's settling down nicely, don't you?' said Marie, as the male nurse unlocked the door and let her out.

Two hours later Marie was back in the underground, heading for the Gloucester Road tube station. She left the train and waited patiently for the ancient lift with its equally ancient pilot. As soon as she reached street level she dodged into the women's toilet, emerging ten minutes later, literally a changed woman. She looked old, careworn, and as tired as she felt. She wore a checkered head scarf, a long robe, and carried a brown paper wrapped parcel. The

262

fake Gucci bag had been inverted, and now displayed a fragmented plastic exterior. Marie turned into Gloucester Road and walked north, in the direction of Hyde Park. She stopped outside the entrance of a newly refurbished flat and rang the door bell. A television camera whirred and turned slowly towards her. A sepulchral voice enquired as to her identity.

'It's me, it's visiting day.'

The camera seemed to survey her for an interminable period. Finally the door lock buzzed. Marie pushed wearily against the door, and after a brief struggle, found herself inside. She had entered a pale grey chamber furnished as a reception area. She walked over to what appeared to be an armed secretary. The secretary looked up briefly from her newspaper, and pointed to a time sheet. Marie signed in, noting the time. She heaved a another long sigh, and walked over to the elevator.

The figure in the bed was barely visible. A duvet drawn up to the nose hid most of the face. The eyes stared blankly at the ceiling.

'Saddam . . . ' began Marie.

'For Allah's sake, sit down and don't talk so much. After all these years . . . don't you know your place? Wait until I speak.'

'Sorry,' replied Marie, wearily, 'it's time to get dressed. The Revolutionary Council will be meeting soon. You must dress in your field marshall's uniform. The one you designed. You have to make a good impression, or all will be lost. You don't want to be outvoted, do you?'

'What's the use? Any fool can see I've been betrayed. I trusted them like I trust you. We must accept our fate with dignity. They won't see me cringe. Did you bring the magazines? And the humus? I'm sick of reading about myself.'

Sebastian rolled over, turning his back on Marie. She sat down heavily and shook her head. There were times when she found all this too much. One looney was enough, but two? It was scarcely better than prison. She let out a soft moan.

What was it that they'd done to her men at that scientific institute in Mill Hill?

After the débacle in Madagascar Randolf and Sebastian had been returned covertly to England. An extradition treaty had been arranged with the Government of Madagascar, which had been only too pleased to rid themselves of Randolf's embarrassing presence and, at the same time, avoid an expensive trial.

Upon their arrival in England Randolf and Sebastian had been incarcerated – on the advice of both MI5 and the CIA – in one of Her Majesty's mental health facilities. Then followed considerable discussion between various scientific, psychiatric, and government organizations as to their disposal. Eventually it was decided to try something novel.

For some time psychiatrists had known, based on evidence from rat experiments, that it was possible to reorganize those parts of the brain which controlled behaviour and memory. It was possible to make a new personality out of a preexisting one by injecting extracts of emulsified brain into a recipient. No one knew whether the changes would be permanent.

The decision to go ahead led to a scientific experiment without precedent. Psychiatrists at the National Institute of Health in the United States, and from the Department of Experimental Psychology in Cambridge, came together to set up a joint venture. The moral and ethical implications were discussed but shelved. Randolf and Sebastian were considered appropriate subjects, the alternative being extensive electroshock treatment.

The experiment was designed to wipe out all preexisting memories, personalities, and emotions. The two men were to be totally amnesic for their past existence. Manufactured memory engrams were to be implanted. The final result would be to create completely new identities for Randolf and Sebastian. The 'new' personalities had been whimsically selected by a young psychiatric resident at a London hospital. The experiment was a complete success. But just in case matters went awry, and their memories returned, Randolf and Sebastian were to be kept under lock and key, for observation, for an indefinite period.

As for Marie, her part in the strange affair in Madagascar was condoned, on condition that she accept a major role in the experiment. As a result, for the past year she had been leading an extraordinary double life, attending at frequent intervals to the peculiar needs of the two 'new' men, neither of whom had any inkling of the other's existence. Each believed she was a fixture in their lives.

The dual role she had assumed was tremendously taxing. There were occasional times when she wondered if she was not herself losing her mind. She was obliged to play a consistent game of charades. Fortunately she found this relatively easy; not only because her hysterical personality lent itself to a life of fantasy, but also because she found living in the imaginary world of the two men not unlike her former existence with them in Madagascar.

☆   ☆   ☆

The silver Nissan 300ZX swung round a corner of the Bayswater Road, entered a side road, and parked in front of an immaculate, terraced house. The driver, a youngish, good-looking man, with thick, wavy, nut brown hair, wearing a tan raincoat over a business suit, let the engine idle for a few seconds, and switched off. He sat for a while with closed eyes, relaxing.

Ben reached backwards, withdrew a briefcase nestling behind the seat back, and exited. The door shut with a precise clunk. Pausing briefly to scan the interior of the letter box, he sprinted up a short flight of steps leading to the entrance of the elegant Victorian house, and unlocked the door.

'Hello, hello . . . anyone home?' The door closed. Ben dropped his briefcase on the hall table, and with one smooth, practised movement removed his raincoat, and slipped it neatly over a peg on the clothes rack.

'Darling, I'm here, in the study.'

The familiar voice never failed to lift his spirits. Smiling in anticipation Ben strode briskly across the black and white squares of marble floor in the hall. With theatrically exaggerated movements he flung open the door to the study.

'Hullo, again.'

Maeve was sitting by her desk. surrounded by a pile of bills, magazines, and cancelled cheques.

'Guess what?' she said.

Ben kissed the nape of her neck.

'What, my love?'

'We've a very interesting invitation.'

'Uhmm . . . who from?'

'You'll never guess. It's from the dear old Admiral. A reunion on his estate, in Cornwall. Here, read it.'

Ben reached over and helped himself to praline coated popcorn.

'Can't stop eating that junk. It's addicting.'

Maeve tossed him a small embossed envelope which he caught in mid air like a performing seal, while simultaneously extracting the card from the envelope a split second before his body landed full length on the divan. Ben was a firm believer in conserving energy.

'How about a drink? I'm exhausted. What's this?' He inspected the card and read,

Esteemed Members of the Far East Expedition:

Gert Francois Brenner, also known as the Admiral, late
S.A.P., (Rtd),
Sends greetings, and requests the pleasure
of your company, for June 20th to 28th,
at his Residence, 33 Bryanston Manor.
R.S.V.P. P.O. Box 3807: St Mayes, Cornwall.

'Ben, we have to go,' said Maeve, 'it'll be fun. It's only three months away. Besides which I want to find out . . . things. I must know what's been happening to everybody. After you told me the story about Sergeant Brenner and your family, I want to see him again. I can only think of him as the Admiral. I've a lot to catch up on. It's ages since we had news. I want to ask him a lot of questions.'

Maeve concentrated her considerable charm on Ben sprawled on the divan. He squinted lazily at the card.

'Gossip, you mean?'

'Well, of course. Can we go?'

'Sure, why not? With enough notice I can fiddle a few days off from the Foreign Office. I'm due for a break after all in the Middle East comings and goings. Colonel Khaddafy and Saddam Hussein can do without my undivided attention, for a while.'

'Good, oh, good. We've time to make arrangements. I'll leave the dog with Mummy. I'll phone after dinner.'

'It's a great idea,' said Ben, dreamily. He wondered how Sambo and the others had been faring. His curiosity grew.

'It is a good idea.'

'Of course it is, darling. What on earth shall I wear? It's for a whole week. And he's begining to show.' Maeve patted her belly.

'You look good in anything, and best in nothing. And, he or she'll enjoy the outing.' Ben gazed fondly at his wife's thickening profile.

'Silly twit,' said Maeve.

Identical invitations arrived at residences in Madagascar, Montreal, and New York. None arrived at two secluded mental institutions in London.

I'm sick of committees,' mumbled the Dean, disconsolately, his mouth half full with food, 'nothing is ever finished.'

'Don't complain, George dear. YOU had a choice. You accepted the job. Don't you have authority? Can't you delegate?' Olga, sitting opposite at the breakfast table, looked up briefly from the Montreal daily paper.

'You'd think they'd spare me this mindless infighting. I suppose academics are the same, everywhere. Children squabbling over a piece of territory.'

'I said, dear, delegate. That's what a dean's for. Let some bearded, hippy-type enthusiast in sandals do the work.'

'Olga, that's not nice. But, it is boring. Nothing gets done. We never make a decision without shelving it. One ad hoc committee after another.'

'Feeling better dear?'

'Sorry to moan so much.'

'Well, if it helps,' said Olga, with a fond grin, 'read your mail, it's on the table beside you. George, you're putting on weight.'

George the Dean sighed, patted his stomach, and protested.

'It's your good cooking. You look after me too well.' He reached for the mail.

'A letter from England.'

George slit open the envelope,

'It's from the Admiral,' he exlaimed, mildly surprised, 'an invitation to a reunion. How about that?'

'Let me see.' Olga leaned over and took the embossed invitation from his hand, 'well, how nice. George, we could go to Europe, see the Admiral and the others, and have a lovely, undisturbed holiday. I think it's a great idea. It's time we had a proper honeymoon.'

☆   ☆   ☆

The cabinet meeting had ended. The ministers had departed. A tired, exasperated potentate rose to leave the empty room. He looked pensively at Sambo.

'Those ministers gave me a rough passage. I don't deserve it. Democracy's gone to their heads. The world recession's not my fault. Sure, I promised to hold taxes. But no sooner said than I'm forced to go back on a promise, or two. A politician's life is a pain. I'd resign if there was anyone in line I could trust. What do you think?'

'The money invested,' said Sambo, 'from Randolf's enterprises is not enough to cover our national debt.' Sambo had acquired a serious mien, partly the result of a full, curly, black beard. 'It's a pity interest rates have plunged. As for the stock market crash, who could have foreseen that? It's made a hole in the treasury. Income doesn't match outgoings.'

'What're we to do? Declare bankruptcy? As Minister of Industrial Development, what do you advise?' Before Sambo could muster a reply, the potentate sighed.

'It's difficult. I could do with a break.'

'Well, there is some good news on the horizon. We're prospecting for minerals.' Sambo, hoping to cheer the despondent potentate, when on. 'As a matter of fact I heard, unofficially, that tantalum's been discovered. A surface mine. If that's accurate our troubles may be over.'

'Wouldn't that be lovely.'

They walked on under a long, pleasant pergola roofed with flowering bougainvillaea. A uniformed aide approached.

'Mail for Your Excellency. Your private secretary ordered it to be handed directly to you.'

'Thank you.' The potentate accepted the proffered post, selected an interesting envelope addressed to him, and passed the rest to Sambo. He squinted at the card he had withdrawn from the embossed wrapper.

'I say, look at this,' he exclaimed, 'I can just read it. Such tiny print.' Sambo peered over his shoulder, 'I see we've the same invitation.'

☆   ☆   ☆

The office block in Brooklyn had seen better days. On the third floor back, up a flight of rickety stairs, was situated the headquarters of a small publishing company. Faded, gilt lettering on the door panel proclaimed:

THE NEW LIFE QUARTERLY
Editor-in-chief and Publisher
Deanna van der Frohlich. B.Ed.

Inside, the reception area displayed more than a standard cluttered mess. Here was a special jumble, a defiant mess. A serious, ponderous and heavily bespectacled secretary was busy sorting the mail. In the process she spilled a cup of coffee into a cat food tin can which served as an ashtray. The resulting paste was dreadful.

'Oh fuck,' said the secretary, and went on with her task.

Rapidly discarding most of the assorted mail, she came across an interesting, small, obviously expensive, envelope addressed in script to 'The Editor'. The secretary heaved

269

herself upright, ambled along on lyle stockinged legs to knock on the editor's door. From within she could hear the intermittent clacking of a mechanical typewriter, interspersed with muttered curses.

'Yes, what IS it? Can't you see I'm busy? I lose my train of thought when you barge in like that.'

Deanna, cigarette drooping from lips recently revealed to the world by a severe, bobbed hair style, paused to glare at her unfortunate assistant. She accepted the bundle of letters without a second glance and discarded them onto her desk. However, one piece of mail caught her eye. The post mark and stamp were from the United Kingdom. Deanna transferred the smouldering stub of a cigarette from her lips to the edge of her desk where it joined a row of parallel burn scars. Holding the envelope up to the light she slit it expertly with the end of a broken finger nail, and drew out the Admiral's invitation.

'What on earth?' she exclaimed.

World Airways flight 911 from New York and Montreal, packed to capacity, landed on time at Heathrow. Passengers disembarked without incident.

George the Dean and his wife Olga collected their baggage and headed for one of the many car rental companies bunched together in the airport. A standard, rude, young Englishwoman assigned a car to them as a great favour. An hour later they were stuck in the traffic on one of Britain's famous motorways, heading in the wrong direction.

Ben and Maeve, having deposited the dog with Maeve's cheeful little mother, were enjoying a fast drive down the M4 Motorway to Cornwall. The weather was perfect. The 300ZX growled purposefully as it cruised along, Mozart's *Emperor Concerto* wafting from multiple speakers. Ben dozed fitfully in the reclining passenger seat. Maeve, who enjoyed fast driving, hummed softly to herself.

'It's another two hours to St Mawes, isn't it?'

'Yep, just carry on. When we get near we'll stop for lunch at a pub and look at the map. I know St Mawes is delightful. Cornwall's one of my favourite counties. This is a great life.' Ben snuggled back into the seat and gazed up at the cloudless sky peeping through the glass sunroof.

'I wonder what Mozart would've thought about his music being whizzed along at eighty plus?'

'Approved, no doubt.'

The Japan Airways jumbo landed with the firm precision of a karate chop and braked hard to a fast, efficient stop. Everyone seemed to be in good spirits. Sake and raw fish had entertained the passengers and miraculously, despite the excessive turbulence, had stayed down. Sambo had long given up worrying about parasites in the sushi. The sake should have put paid to them. An unexpected storm near London had not deterred the intrepid pilot from landing the big jet like a Zero fighter in the midst of gusts of windshear and blinding sheets of water. A few pieces of flying luggage had not distracted the permanently smiling, geisha-style stewardesses.

Not one, but two, of the charming air hostesses escorted the potentate and his companions to VIP Immigration at Heathrow. He had been upgraded from executive to first-class when it was discovered that he was indeed a potentate travelling incognito. The Japanese captain bowed low when the potentate deplaned.

Despite their anonymous mode of travel the British Foreign Office had got wind of the visit. A limousine, complete with television, bar, and two flagstaffs, awaited them at the exit of the VIP lounge. The driver was a slightly dazed, elderly, man with more than a passing resemblance to the late Edmund Gwen. He seemed unfamiliar with the car's controls, and groused that the automatic transmission was too complicated. After a few sudden surges and swerves, he settled down, and they began to enjoy a comfortable journey to Cornwall.

☆   ☆   ☆

271

The extensive estate, with its superb mansion, on the outskirts of St Mawes, had been carefully restored. Sergeant Brenner, lately the Admiral of MI5, in hacking jacket, riding breeches and polished boots, walked about, surveying his domain with undisguised pride. Inside the house he could hear his wife, Anna, speaking in Afrikaans-accented English, giving orders to a house maid.

The paddock had been hosed down, the horses groomed, the bedrooms aired, and the larder stocked with venison, wines, spirits, as well as every variety of fish and vegetables. Lawns had been freshly mown, and flower beds trimmed. the swimming pool had been filled with filtered, heated water, and the tennis courts restored to their pristine state. As far as could be judged the grounds were immaculate, and would have done credit to a stately home, which indeed it was. The proud, expectant Lord of the Manse had gone to endless lengths to ensure his guests were to be cossetted.

Two chefs, one salvaged from Randolf's empire, and the other a local cordon bleu graduate, had been briefed. The rest of the servants, apart from the butler and an au pair girl, were out-of-work actors hired from a London theatrical agency.

'Sam,' explained the Admiral, addressing his butler, 'please remember our guests are my special friends. I know I don't have to remind you, but you MUST make every effort to make them comfortable. Their least whim is to be satisfied, if you don't mind.'

'Quite so sir,' agreed the butler, and walked off in the direction of the kitchens.

The first to arrive was the potentate and his entourage. The chauffeured limousine squealed to a jerky stop by the main entrance. Sam was not impressed, and proved to be an unexpected obstacle. Politely but firmly the passengers were directed to wait in the car. The butler stalked off with an unhurried, dignified, tread to locate his master.

'A rather strange delegation from, I presume Africa, awaits outside. How shall I deal with them, sir?'

'Sam,' said the exasperated Admiral, 'That "delegation"

must be my guests. who else could they be? You MUST be civil.'

He rushed off and flung open his front door. For an instant he stood gazing with delight upon the passengers, his very first guests. The elderly chauffeur came to life and clambered out to open the limousine's doors. Amelia rushed up to embrace the ecstatic host. Her hands almost met behind his ample back. The rest stood to one side, beaming.

'Welcome, welcome,' repeated the Admiral, 'Anna, come out. It's all come true, they're here. Come in. Come in,' he said, beside himself with pleasure. 'I must say you're all looking very well indeed.'

The potentate moved forward into the hall.

'I am really delighted to be here, my friend. What an excellent place you have. It's what you wanted, is it not?' The potentate gazed around appreciatively. 'A lot better than the fortress.'

The Admiral smiled broadly. 'Yes,' he replied, 'thanks to you. In the end it was worth it. Sometimes I think it's too good to be true. But here we are. It's really quite wonderful . . . for us, my wife and I.'

'Well, it's mutual,' said Amelia.

'Pardon me, madam,' sniffed Sam, interrupting, 'may I relieve you of your baggage?'

'Now look here Sam . . . ,' protested the Admiral, and turning to his guests, explained, 'he comes with the place.' Sam busied himself with issuing orders.

'Sam's one of the last genuine snobs in this country. He knows his value. He doesn't approve of me, or my origins, but posts like his are scarce these days. We understand each other. He believes he's introducing me to some important aspects of civilization. Come in, I want to introduce you to my wife.'

Maeve and Ben, having completed a relaxed tea at the Two Bridges Hotel, set off to complete the remainder of their journey. An hour later they drew up late in the afternoon at the Admiral's residence. A joyful scenario was replayed on the steps of the mansion. Sam performed his role to perfection.

When greetings and sufficient small talk had been exchanged, the Admiral's guests proceeded upstairs to their respective rooms. Just before dinner everyone gathered for cocktails in the drawing room.

'What does this remind you of?' Ben looked at Maeve.

'Oh, yes, indeed,' said Maeve, 'only, here there is a tremendous difference. There's nothing phoney about the pleasure of this company. No menace, a total absence of Sebastian and Randolf; no Marie and her diamonds.'

'Does anyone know what's happened to them?' asked Anna, the Admiral's wife, 'Gert won't say anything. Says he doesn't know.'

The Admiral relented and provided a brief outline.

'They're safely put away. Marie looks after them. They're in institutions . . . brain drained.

'Brain drained?'

'They know nothing of their past. They have new identities.'

'How weird. Poor old Marie.' Maeve, spoke with genuine sympathy.

'When are you expecting?' asked Anna, the Admiral's wife, smiling at Maeve.

'In two months.'

The phone rang.

'For you sir,' sniffed Sam, walking in, bearing a cordless telephone.

'Hello,' said the Admiral into the mouthpiece, 'my goodness . . . you're near. Drive on to the first pub to your right and turn right. You'll see a sign. From then on it's easy. Follow the road, you can't miss us. Goodbye,' and he rang off. Sam walked off with the offending instrument.

'That was Olga and George.'

'Olga and George?'

'Yes, you didn't know? Olga married her hero, the Dean. They live in Canada.'

'Remarkable,' said Ben, 'such an unlikely pair.'

'And Deanna?'

'Well, one no show isn't too bad. Didn't expect her to come. But I had to ask her.' The Admiral shrugged

274

apologetically.

'It's possible she didn't get the invitation.'

'There's not much we do about it. Let's go in for dinner.'

The next morning broke radiantly with dazzling sunlight, highlighting the beginning of a flawless English summer day. Delicious warmth bathed the Admiral's guests.

Maeve and Ben had risen early and were enjoying a stroll in the lush green countryside accompanied by the Admiral's pleasant, retiring, wife.

'I'm so glad I've finally met you, Ben. Gert told me so much about you. You knew that he had sent me and the children to England, long ago?'

'Gert, er, the Admiral, told us very little, in fact nothing, about his private life,' said Ben, 'I think I remember him vaguely, as Sergeant Brenner, in South West, when he was my father's friend. But I'm not sure that I'm reconstructing my memory. I was a child. I knew he had gone abroad. We lost track.'

'Gert, when he decided he had to go after Randolf, resigned from the South West Police, and sent me and the children to England. He had already gone on ahead and found a place for us. It was all carefully planned. Now we're very happy here. We have grown up children, a son at Cambridge, and a married daughter in Canada. I've almost forgotten my roots.'

At the bottom of the mansion's garden a high, stone wall merged with the side of a small country church. Olga and George were seated in the shade of the church spire reading *The Times*. The potentate lay basking in the sun in a lounge chair, immersed in a novel. Sambo and Amelia, frolicked like happy children in the pool, and filled the air with earpiercing shrieks. It was hard to imagine a more complete domestic scene.

That evening the tranquil companions, once again formally attired, assembled in the sitting room. Everyone spoke simultaneously. A good deal of repetitious reminiscing took place. The supply of anecdotes seemed inexhaustible.

Sam served several rounds of cocktails and then made himself scarce.

A bell clanged in the front hall. It amused the Admiral to

retain the old-fashioned system which simultaneously rang a bell in the hall and in the servants quarters. Sam's dignified tread could be heard crossing the floor to the door. Faint, muffled, voices drifted into the sitting room.

'Who can it be?' murmured the Admiral to his wife sitting across the room. He was mildly curious. They had not invited anyone else.

Sam entered the room with an unhurried tread and headed calmly for the Admiral. Inclining his head a few degrees he addressed the Admiral's left ear, 'A Miss van der Frohlich is in the hall, sir. She says she's a friend and is here by invitation. But it's my understanding that all your guests are here. And it's late. Cook's not prepared for extras.'

'Miss van der Frohlich?' The Admiral was puzzled.

'Good Heavens,' exclaimed Olga, 'it's Deanna, she's come. That's her surname.'

'Bloody Hell, we're in for it,' grumbled Ben, 'just when we were having fun.'

The Admiral rose and followed Sam into the front hall. He reappeared, followed by a svelte, alluringly groomed, youngish blond.

The Admiral stood aside, gave a small formal bow, and began, with a smile, to introduce the woman with the flaxen hair.

'My GOODNESS, it IS Deanna.' Once again it was Olga who interrupted.

'Deanna, you look . . . fabulous. George,' she elbowed her husband, 'isn't she amazing? I can't believe it.'

Ben, and for that matter everyone else in the room, had been struck dumb and stared, like peasants in a circus, at the poised, elegantly sophisticated woman who stood smiling pleasantly before them.

'Hello, darlings,' said Deanna, in a low husky voice, 'how are you?' And accepted a chair from a remarkably deferential Sam.

'Deanna . . . what a difference. Tell us, how did you . . . how did it happen?' Olga spoke almost reverently, her eyes fixed on the cool, relaxed woman who, a few months ago, had been their most obnoxious companion.

'Oh, it's me all right. Not much to tell, darlings.'

'Stop being coy, tell us,' groaned Olga.

'It's not complicated. You might say I came to my senses. May I have some wine?' Deanna settled in her seat. Sam rushed over with a glass of champagne.

'After we escaped, I returned to New York. I went back to my wretched magazine. I published a few issues. I bought a few off a bookstall to encourage circulation, but it was evident that it was not breaking any records. To be frank, we sold hardly any, well, if you must know, none.'

Deanna sipped here drink. 'I took a good look at myself. I realized I had achieved practically nothing in my life. I was sick and tired of rationalizing that everything that had gone wrong was because I was a female; that all circumstances were beyond my control. It didn't take any genius to see the light. If I was to get anywhere I would have to be master of my own destiny, and bugger the rest.'

Deanna, despite her air of sophistication, or perhaps because of it, had lost none of her earthy idiom. She paused to accept a refill from Sam hovering in the background.

'I recognized that I had to stop moaning and get on with life. More than anything, I had to change direction. It seemed to me that although I had many women friends, most of them were boring; or dull as dishwater and, like me, blamed anyone or anything convenient, except themselves, for their misfortunes. To us everything was bleak or negative. We had closed minds.

'One fine day I took a good look at myself. I realized that I was not at all bad looking. I knew I wasn't stupid, only misdirected.' Deanna drank deeply. 'It took a lot to accept a change, but I did it. I went out, bought some really fine, extravagant clothes, got a new hairdo, sacked my lazy staff, sold the magazine, and found a nice enough apartment in New York. I began to go to parties, some were singles, where I found interesting men who were intelligent . . . and who found me . . . attractive. That did wonders for my ego, and other parts.

'Incidently, dear potentate, your 'care package' of money came in very handy indeed. Many, many thanks.'

The potentate smiled deprecatingly. 'Oh it was nothing. It was your share.'

'I'll try and keep this short. I want to hear your news, especially yours my dear Admiral.

277

'Okay ... what I did was to talk to one of my new friends, who happened to be a writer. I gave him an outline of our adventures in Madagascar. He was obviously interested and said, 'Why don't you put it down on paper and show it to me?' I rushed out bought a word processor, read the instructions, and started from scratch. I composed the first paragraph twenty times. Soon I couldn't stop. I engaged a young prof of English to coach me, and I finished the manuscript.'

'And?' prompted Olga.

'The writer, who started it all, suggested I contact his agent. The agent turned out to be an irritable woman who was more interested in correcting my punctuation that the story. She missed the point entirely, never mind the humour. In the end the prof suggested I contact a publisher directly. I was surprised and tickled pink when the second one I tried wrote back that draft showed promise, but to rewrite parts. They put me in touch with a more perceptive and helpful agent. So I now have an agent, the book is published, and I'm over here to meet my public.

'It's not a great work. You're all in it, disguised, of course. I'm in it too, looking silly. As for my agent, he's arranging screen rights AND, darlings, he's single, attentive, handsome and so on. Divorced of course, with a couple of grown up children. We get along very well.'

'I can't get over the change,' said Ben, 'how we misjudged you.'

'You didn't. I was a miserable pain. I hope you'll overlook the old Deanna and join the new me at my publisher's party?'

While Deanna was speaking the Admiral, sitting back and relaxed, surveyed his friends with great warmth. As soon as Deanna finished he rose to his feet.

'I'd like to make a toast ... ,' he began, beaming happily at his wife, sitting opposite, 'please join me Anna, I want to say something.'

Together they faced the diners.

'I wish to make a toast. Here's to each and everyone in this room; to my dearest wife and patient family; and to you, my best firends. May we remain friends for life; may we enjoy the pleasures and rewards we have earned; and

278

may I take this opportunity to extend to you an invitation to meet in this house, every year, from this day forward.'

Ben, ensnared by the sentiment of the occasion, smiled fondly at his wife, Maeve, reached for her hand, and said, 'I would like to second that. But bear in mind that this, all this,' he swept his hand around the room, 'is the direct result of Randolf's misguided machinations. When you think of it, it's fantastic that we, all of us, owe our good fortune to a bizarre family, my family. More than anything, we owe everything to a great, excellent, policeman, an Afrikaaner, Sergeant Gert Francois Brenner, also known as the Admiral, lately of MI5. Were it not for them our paths would never have crossed.' He raised his glass higher.

'Let us rise and drink one more toast . . . to the Admiral.'